The Whitechapel Girl

The *Whitechapel* Girl

Gilda O'NEILL

CANELO

First published in the United Kingdom in 1993 by Headline Book Publishing

This edition published in the United Kingdom in 2019 by

Canelo Digital Publishing Limited
57 Shepherds Lane
Beaconsfield, Bucks HP9 2DU
United Kingdom

A CIP catalogue record for this book is available from the British Library.

Print ISBN 978 1 78863 560 8
Ebook ISBN 978 1 78863 458 8

This book is a work of fiction. Names, characters, businesses, organizations, places and events are either the product of the author's imagination or are used fictitiously. Any resemblance to actual persons, living or dead, events or locales is entirely coincidental.

Look for more great books at www.canelo.co

Printed and bound in Great Britain by Clays Ltd, Elcograf S.p.A.

For Jem, Jel, Jeremy…

Three names for one much loved son

PART ONE

May 1887

'I'm telling yer, Maisie, I ain't going home no more and that's final. I ain't never going back to that bloody dump again.'

'Aw, Ett, yer always saying that,' Maisie dismissed her lightly.

'Well, I mean it this time,' said Ettie solemnly. 'Cos if that bastard touched me once more I'd have to stick a knife in his great fat belly. I swear to God I would.'

'Can't yer mum do nothing about him, Ett?'

'Like what?' Ettie Wilkins spoke to her friend, but she was staring, a hard challenging glare, at a mud-spattered, tanglehaired boy who was trying to edge his way nearer to the front of the queue. 'Oi you, just watch it,' she snapped at the boy. 'We nearly broke our necks getting here for the show, and we don't intend losing our place to no snot-nosed, raggy-arsed kid like you. See?'

The boy slunk back to his position further back in the crowd, his progress followed by jeers from his equally filthy mates who had dared him to sneak forward in the first place.

'I was saying,' said Maisie, casting a haughty, threatening look towards the now giggling boys, 'can't yer mum do nothing about him – throw him out, or something?'

Ettie braced her thin, bony arms, preparing to use her elbows against anyone else who dared try to move in front of them. 'Yer all right saying that, May,' she said, 'but yer know what it's like with her and her blokes.'

'Yeah, I know,' said Maisie, 'and I also know he'll be gone in a couple of days – like all the rest of them.'

I

'Right, and as soon as he's gone, she'll go down the docks and find some other "uncle" to come and live with us.' Ettie rearranged the rat-trimmed tippet which adorned her cape. 'She has to have someone to keep her in gin, don't she?'

'I know Sarah likes her drop of Jacky, but it can't be that bad.' Maisie stepped neatly in front of the boy who was making another attempt to take over their position in the line. 'Watch him, Ett, he's back again. We'll lose our place to the little sod if we ain't careful.'

Ettie shuffled forward with her friend, forming a solid wall against all comers. They had been waiting for over an hour already, and no one was going to get in front of them, not if she had anything to do with it.

'May, to be honest,' she went on, with a world-weary sigh far too knowing for her barely seventeen years, 'yer don't know the half of it. Mum's really got worse, soon as she's finished her half-bottle every night, she's out for the count. Sparko.'

'So what's new about that?'

'Well,' she began hesitantly, 'the last couple of blokes she's brought home – this one in particular...' Ettie nibbled her lip anxiously. 'Let's just say that nowadays she don't give a monkey's who's got his hand down me drawers.' She paused and turned her eyes from Maisie's searching gaze. 'It really *has* got worse lately,' she added quietly, her mind racing with the unspeakable memories of the night before. Even though it was a warm spring night, Ettie felt as though iced water was trickling down her spine. She closed her eyes and shuddered.

'Bugger off!' Maisie's sudden, raucous shout brought Ettie back to the blessed relief of the present. The unwilling object of Maisie's attention was a haughty, top-hatted man who had made the momentary mistake of oggling her, eyeing her lecherously as he walked past the queue outside the penny gaff in the direction of the London Hospital.

'Just who d'yer think yer looking at, yer ugly old goat?' May called out in her harsh cockney growl.

The infuriated, red-faced man tutted and walked along quickly towards the hospital steps, mumbling indignantly about how the young people of today could all do with some lessons in manners, and how the lower orders no longer knew their place.

'See, Ett. All blokes, they're all the bleed'n same. All they're interested in is a bit of how's-yer-father. Pig's face!' She yelled at the departing figure. Then May returned her attention to her friend, laughing loudly with an appealing, yet slightly alarming lack of inhibition which showed the remains of her cracked and broken teeth as she threw back her head. 'It's nothing new, yer know, Ettie Wilkins. Yer might be prettier than most, but that don't mean nothing. They don't care what yer look like. They're all at it. Even posh old geezers like him.' Maisie jerked her head in the direction of the hurrying man, making her tatty straw bonnet bob precariously on her tightly pinned hair.

'I dunno why yer laughing, May. It ain't funny,' said Ettie, still shuddering at the thought of the repulsive touch of her mother's lodger. 'I know Mum's brought home some right dirty bastards in her time, but this one's the worst. Honest.' She hesitated. 'He's different somehow.' She lowered her voice, aware that the other members of the queue were glad of her story as an entertaining distraction while they waited for the next show to begin. 'He wants me to do him all sorts of "little favours", as he calls them.' Ettie's voice began to crack. 'He's vile, May. Really vile. And he stinks terrible from working in the slaughterhouse. Makes me feel ill. No, I ain't having no more of it, and that really is final.'

'He wants a kick right up the jacksie by the sound of it,' said May indignantly.

'And I'd usually be the one to do it and all, yer know me,' said Ettie. Her face tightened into a worried frown. 'But I'm really scared of this one, May.'

'You, Ettie Wilkins? Scared? I don't believe yer.'

'It's the truth, May. He really is different to any of the others.' Maisie looked steadily into her friend's eyes; she couldn't find even the glimmer of a smile in the deep blue, which usually sparkled with laughter, or at least with the promise of a bit of mischief. 'Blimey. Yer serious, girl, ain't yer?'

'Too right I am. I've been thinking about it for days now, and I know there's no other way. I'm gonna have to get out of that hole for good.'

'It's all right you saying it, but how yer actually gonna do it?' Maisie, never one to concentrate for long on anything that either didn't make her laugh, or didn't involve something to eat or drink, let her attention be drawn by a pretty fair-haired young woman rushing up the hospital steps, calling out to the man who had earlier made the mistake of giving Maisie the glad eye. 'I know. Yer can get yourself all poshed up like her over there.' She nodded towards the expensively dressed young woman. 'Then you can get yourself one of them rich blokes and live in luxury up West.'

'Why shouldn't I have nice things?' murmured Ettie flatly, ignoring Maisie's sarcasm.

'Because you know the only way the likes of us'd get clobber like that. And you'd wind up getting stuck with a kid and a dose of the whatsit chucked in for free and all. That's why.'

'Going on the game can't be the only way out for girls like us,' said Ettie wretchedly.

Maisie desperately tried to lighten what was becoming an unfamiliarly serious conversation. 'You don't half go on,' she said, nudging Ettie in her usual heavy-handed yet affectionately meant way, hard in the ribs. 'Right bloody dreamer ain't yer, girl?'

'Why shouldn't I dream, eh? Tell me that.'

'Leave off, Ett. To hear you go on, yer'd think yer was the only one ever got touched up by a bloke.' Maisie was beginning to sound impatient. 'Anyway, he'll be long gone, like all the rest, before yer even know it.'

'I don't wanna talk about him no more, May, and anyway, it's time I was finding me own way in the world. I'm off, and that's the end of it.'

'Well, there are other ways.' Maisie laughed, surprisingly shyly for her. 'Why don't yer find yerself a husband, eh? And there's no need to roll yer eyes at me, Ettie Wilkins. There's one or two decent fellahs around, even in Whitechapel. Me mum keeps saying I should get married, yer know. She'd been married nearly two years by the time *she* was seventeen.'

'And she already had two nippers and all. No thanks, May. I've had enough of all that. That dirty swine pressing himself up against me every night has put me right off.' Ettie closed her eyes and flinched at the memory which had again invaded her mind. 'Makes me feel sick just thinking about it. Hands all over yer. Horrible.'

'What, even with someone like our Billy?' said May craftily. 'I thought yer fancied him rotten.'

Ettie opened her mouth but didn't get the chance to answer.

'Oi, oi, girls! Let us in then. Go on, May, shove up.' A boy, not unlike the rest of the dishevelled, ragged urchins in the queue, had appeared in front of them and was now bouncing up and down like an eager puppy hoping to have his ears tickled.

'Hello, Tommy, what you doing here?' Ettie asked, ruffling his dirty, straw-coloured hair, glad of the distraction from the subject of his older brother Billy.

'He's meant to be seeing what he can find behind the hospital,' said May threateningly. 'So why ain't yer, Tommy, eh? Answer me that.'

'There ain't nothing there, May,' he said, shrugging his rag-clad shoulders.

Maisie narrowed her eyes doubtfully at her little brother.

'Straight up,' said Tommy, all injured innocence. 'They ain't thrown the scraps or dripping out yet. I have looked, honest. There's nothing there.'

'Well, you'd better get back over there and wait, hadn't yer? Cos if them other kids get it all, Mum'll give yer a right larruping when yer go home empty-handed.'

'Aw, May, let's go in with yer. Please. I've heard all about this geezer from me mates. Bleed'n amazing they reckon. Let us in the queue. Go on.'

'Don't yer start whining, yer little bugger, or I'll give yer something to whine about.'

Tommy pulled himself up tall. 'You start on me, Maisie, and I'll run home and tell Mum yer going in the penny gaff.'

'You do, Tommy boy, and yer'll never talk again.'

Tommy's face puckered as though he were about to cry.

'Hold up, Tom, calm down. Look.' Ettie reached under her skirt into the pocket of her grey woollen petticoat. 'There's a farthing, go and get yerself some stickjaw off the Indian toffee man.'

'Cor, thanks, Ett,' he beamed, all sign of tears banished from his face and, just like he'd seen the stall holders do, he bit on the copper coin to check its authenticity. 'How about giving us a kiss and all then, eh?'

'Gerroff.' Ettie cuffed him playfully round the ear. 'Yer can take too many liberties yer know, Tommy Bury.'

'What, prefer fellahs yer own age do yer, Ett?' said Tommy, resuming his bouncing round the girls. 'Someone more like our Billy?'

Ettie went to speak, then changed her mind. Instead, she raised her hand to him again – less playfully this time.

With eyes widened and an expression as righteous as a cherub's, Tommy treated his sister and her friend to a sweet, gap-toothed smile, and skipped away to peruse the food stalls which night and day lined the Whitechapel Road, intent on spending his spoils wisely.

'Yer'll break our Billy's heart one day, Ettie Wilkins,' he called over his shoulder, 'yer just see if yer don't.'

'And don't forget them scraps,' bellowed Maisie after her rapidly retreating brother, 'or Mum'll have yer. She ain't soft like us. And no jumping on no wagons for no rides neither. Do you hear me? That's all I need, taking you home all squashed to bits.' She kept watching her brother's gleeful progress along the stalls and barrows, but she spoke to her friend. 'Yer didn't have to give him nothing, Ett. And, like yer say, he can be a right little liberty-taker that one.'

'Well, we didn't want him telling yer mum we was going in here, now did we?'

Maisie laughed at the thought of her mum finding out that she'd been in a penny gaff; her mother knew all about the dangers of such places. On the promise of a free cup of tea and an almost fresh bun, Myrtle Bury had once attended a meeting in the local mission hut. While she was there she had learned to call the shows put on in the penny qaffs "lewd and immoral displays of depravity". Everyone in the area already knew that the gaffs were the haunt of many of the most notorious young criminals in the neighbourhood, but the mission had confirmed for Mrs Bury that they were certainly no place for *her* youngsters. A little woman, who always kept herself astonishingly neat and clean, Myrtle governed her rowdy offspring with a ferociously maternal concern for their betterment in life. So, after the meeting, gaffs were put strictly out of bounds for the Bury family, as were the people who had anything to do with them. Maisie didn't dare say so, but she considered her mum's attitude a bit of a joke considering what her beloved boys got up to, especially their Alfie, the oldest of the Bury brood. And everyone knew that Tommy, the youngest, looked set to follow in his big brother's footsteps. He was already involved in the petty crime and other dodgy dealings that were a way of life for so many of the boys around Whitechapel. But Mrs Bury was a real one for turning a blind eye when it suited her. Even if they did have to survive on scavenging the left-overs and scraping out the dripping pans from behind the London Hospital, they could still be decent. And who could tell, one day they might just be destined for better things than their old mum had had to put up with? Although Myrtle Bury was no fool, like Ettie and a lot of others from round Whitechapel, she could still dream that life might get better.

'Yer still can't afford to treat Tommy like that,' said May to her friend. Her voice sounded harsh, but her expression was one of gratitude.

'Maybe it'll stop him diving into the Thames for ha'pennies,' said Ettie.

'Maybe.' Maisie didn't sound convinced. 'But I don't think so. Not when there's them silly enough to chuck the money in for him.' She tutted. 'I wish he was more like Billy and less like our Alfie.'

'Ne'mind, Maisie, yer only five once, aren't yer? Yer might as well let him take his chances when they come and live it to the full.'

'Yeah, yer right, I suppose,' she said gloomily, but then suddenly brightened. 'And talking about chances coming along,' Maisie winked broadly at Ettie, 'just look who's coming along now. Our Billy boy. Talk of the devil and he'll appear they say, but more like an angel in his case. Wotcha, Bill.'

Ettie's throat blushed a bright scarlet, the flush creeping uncontrollably towards her cheeks.

'Hallo, girls,' said Bill, acting very casually, aware of all the nosy-parkers in the queue. 'Gonna let me sit with yer in the gaff, then?'

'If yer like,' Ettie answered, swinging her shoulders from side to side as she did so, and studying the apparently fascinating toe of her scuffed brown boot.

'Yer looking nice, Ett,' said Billy. 'That green colour suits yer.'

'It's only a bit of old ribbon I got down the market,' said Ettie coyly, fiddling with the emerald velvet band she had fastened round her neck.

'Here, we ain't got time for all that soppy lark, Ett,' hissed Maisie, shoving her friend hard in the ribs. 'Go on, quick. Shift yerself. Here she comes.'

The appearance from behind the doorway's flapping canvas of Lou, a huge-bosomed woman dressed in a short spangled costume, was met by ribald yells of enthusiasm from the milling crowd. They had been waiting for almost an hour and a half to go in and see the delights of the penny gaff, and were more than ready for the show to begin. Their anticipation had been whipped up by the advertisements for the acts, which were gaudily painted on the canvas sheeting covering the disused shop front. They had been standing in their ragged line, not very patiently, since the first house had been admitted. But now their wait had been well rewarded: they gasped in appreciation as the startlingly costumed woman lifted her already saucily brief skirts and spanked her ample, stockinged thigh. They had not seen so much leg since, well, since the last time they had been to a gaff.

'Them what wants tickets, have yer penny ready!' bellowed Lou, flashing her thickly powdered dimples.

'So it's all right if I come in with you two girls then, is it?' said Billy eagerly.

Ettie turned round to look at him. She was taller than most girls of her age in the East End, but Maisie's brother Billy was even taller. He seemed to be looming over her. He was also older than Ettie, nearly nineteen, and had good prospects for a lad from the slums. Unlike his older brother Alfie, who earned his living doing what he called 'wheeling and dealing' and 'doing a bit of this and a bit of that', Billy was getting himself a trade, learning to be a cabinet maker with a firm in Shoreditch. Being in the furniture game had been his mum's idea, anything to get him away from the hard and unpredictable existence of being a casual down at the docks that had killed his old dad, or the life of crime that was getting hold of his big brother, Alf. And although he'd be the first to admit that, with his pale red hair and his open, plain face, he was no oil painting, he was definitely a grafter *and* he could make Ettie laugh.

'I told yer,' Ettie said calmly, as she nonchalantly brushed at the ingrained grime which covered her skirts. 'Yer can come in with us if yer like.'

They began to move forward. At first, the queue retained a semblance of order as the customers filed towards the entrance, but they were so keen to get their first glimpse of the attractions which lay behind the tantalisingly decorated canvas draped over the doorway, that they were soon pushing and shoving at those in front.

'Oi, watch it!' shouted one of the boys in reply to a sharp elbow.

'Give over, yer'll squash us bleed'n flat!' complained his pal.

Lou, the spangled lady, seemed oblivious to all the argy-bargy. She held the canvas sheet aloft with a delicacy which suggested that it might have been made from spun gold and, all the while, despite the ruckus, she acted like a true theatrical, not missing a single beat of the rhythm which she played faster and faster on the battered drum hanging from her fleshy neck. The increasingly disorderly line rapidly dissolved into a surging mass, as nearly two hundred impatient young cockneys vied for the premium places in front of the showcases along the corridor leading to the inside of the gaff.

With a final toot on the little tin trumpet which had been bouncing around her besparkled bosom, Lou held her grubby hand aloft in a dramatic, dancer-like gesture. 'That's all I can let in for this show,' she hollered in a voice that could have done useful service as a fog warning on the Thames. 'You lot still out here'll have to wait for the next performance.'

The collective moans of protest from those not fortunate enough to have been admitted into the wondrous delights of the gaff were quickly quelled by the well-practised show woman.

'But don't worry lads,' she said treating them to a saucy wink and a flick of her ample hips. 'I'll be back out in a minute to entertain yer's for a bit while yer waits.' She flapped her hand casually at the objectors. 'Don't fret yerselves, there's non-stop shows all night. Yes, darling, all night! Now, if yer'll excuse me.' She tossed her grubby net train to one side, spun round and talked coquettishly over her shoulder. 'I have to collect the tickets from that mob in there. But then I'll be right back to yers!' She made a little clicking noise with her tongue, rolled her eyes suggestively in response to the whistling and hooting crowd, and sashayed out of sight behind the canvas.

Inside, the gaff might well have been just like the hundreds of others which regularly sprang up overnight throughout the East End: a dirty, dusty corridor leading to a space that had been converted from a disused shop and its adjoining warehouse into a temporary, illicit theatre – but it was still a place of magic for the young audience. And this particular one had the added attraction of the *Famous Professor Protsky's Genuine Freak Show* lining the corridor: sights to be gawped upon and gasped at, "As Seen by the Crowned Heads of All Europe". And all for the all-inclusive entrance price of one penny.

The spangled lady pointed melodramatically to the exhibits as she led the pressing herd past the crude paintings of desert islands and mountain tops which decorated the passageway.

'And here,' she declaimed in her rasping, foghorn voice, gesturing at a dim figure behind a gauzy curtain, 'is the one and only Electric Lady.'

At that moment, sparks shot out from the hazy form, accompanied by gasps from the front of the crowd.

'All right, all right. There's no need to shove,' she bellowed, 'there's plenty of time for yer all to have a good butcher's.' She returned to the electrical wonder. 'An angel with the power of the devil,' she said portentously, then wiggled her way voluptuously along the corridor to the next wonder. 'Now, behold,' she croaked in a loud stage whisper. 'The skeleton of a mermaid, as was caught in the China Seas by fishermen, who hadn't expected to find *her* in their nets, I can tell yer.'

'Looks more like a bleeding pile of old haddock bones to me,' chimed up a lad from the crowd.

'Aw, we've got a cocky one here, have we?' said Lou, eyeing the unfortunate young man. She grabbed unceremoniously at the lapels of his shabby jacket and jerked him to the front of the crowd. 'Let's see how brave yer really are, sonny.' She pointed with a flourish of her chubby, bejewelled hand to the next booth, where a barely visible figure was sitting on an upturned crate. 'The Hooded Man,' she intoned. 'Too terrible for humans to look upon!'

A sneering whisper of disbelief quickly passed through the crowd, led by the lad who had been plucked from their midst in so cavalier a manner.

The spangled lady quickly regained their attention. 'There was a man who once was foolish enough to look upon him...' she began.

The murmuring started to build again. Billy sniggered loudly, hoping to impress Ettie with his bravado.

'Unfortunately, nobody knows what he saw,' she continued, unperturbed. 'Cos he's spending the rest of his natural days in the lock-up ward of the loony bin. Struck dumb and mad from the shock of it, he was.'

She shoved the now disgruntled-looking heckler back to his mates. 'Don't look so sad, darling,' she said, grinning at him. 'Worse things happen at sea. And I should know, I've been with enough sailors in me time!'

To the accompaniment of hoots of appreciative laughter and vulgar comments, she led them forward before dissent could swell again. Next they stopped by the Fantastic Fairy Family, who, from Ettie's place in the mob, looked like nothing more than the sort of stunted children to be seen in any one of the dingy streets of the slums outside. The only difference was that the Fairy Family were dressed in ill-fitting costumes, complete with paper wings, and one of them was curiously familiar.

'Here, don't that look like your Tommy? The one in the pink frock,' Ettie said, dragging Maisie in front of her so she could get a better look.

'Bloody hell. Get out of there yer little bugger,' hissed Maisie, much to the amusement of all those around her. 'Just you wait till you get home.'

Tommy answered his sister, but his words were lost on Maisie as she was swept along by the ever-vigilant Lou to the next exhibit. Clearly Lou knew the importance of keeping control: trouble could quickly get out of hand and spread through the whole audience.

'At least yer've got something on him now, May,' said Ettie, grinning at the thought of Tommy in his fairy's frock. 'He won't be able to tell tales to yer mum about you being at the gaff now, will he?'

'I'll give him tell tales,' said May, tight-lipped with anger. '*You* don't know anything about all this, I suppose, do yer?' she said, turning on Billy.

The look of complete innocence which appeared on her older brother's face would have done credit to any professional performer of the dramatic arts; Lou herself couldn't have done any better. 'Me, sis?' he asked.

Before Maisie could press him for a confession, Billy was saved by the next item of entertainment. 'Yer get yer money's worth here all right, don't yer, Ett?' he said, relieved.

Ettie didn't answer, she was too busy peering round the boy in front to get a closer look at what was crouching in the corner of the showcase behind a filmy curtain of dusty muslin. What she saw was something that looked for all the world like a poorly made model of an elderly, extremely hairy man.

'And here, ladies and gentlemen,' announced the show woman boldly, pointing to the apparition without even the merest hint of a smile on her lips, 'we have the Mysterious Maid of the Mountain, as was found wandering about in the wild and rugged mountains of the county of Cornwall. Found by Professor Protsky himself, no less.'

'But there ain't no mountains in Cornwall,' yelled an obviously much-travelled spectator from the back.

'And that, my good sir, is the Mystery!' proclaimed Lou, with an extravagant, two-fingered gesture at the heckler.

There was nothing a crowd liked so much as someone else being embarrassed by a quick-witted performer, and the mountain expert blushed a most gratifying shade of crimson. The uproarious mood was contagious, and Maisie, like the rest of the crowd, was now thoroughly enjoying herself. Everything would be all right, she was sure: Billy was shrewd enough to get their Tommy out of the show and back home without him getting into too much trouble; and the little sod would even have earned himself a few pennies, like as not. Tommy had the knack of coming out of most things smelling of roses.

Well, there was *almost* nothing a crowd liked as much as someone else's embarrassment. What they actually liked best of all was anything that smacked of the horrible or macabre, and the final display was that all right.

Flinging back a thick, dirty cloth to reveal a fly-blown glass case, Lou, the seasoned entertainer, spoke in a conspiratorial undertone to her rapt audience. 'The piece dee resistants!' she declared.

They stared intently, not sure what they were meant to be looking at, but keen to be appalled. All they could see was an array of vicious-looking, but extremely rusty weaponry.

'The most spine-tingling part of the exhibition,' she announced ominously. 'This here case contains the actual, the very actual blood-stained knives as was used in a series of horrible murders throughout the snow-driven wastes of Imperial Russia.'

Lou had worked the audience well, and the young men and women were now in fine form to be appalled. Some were reduced to a gawping, half-terrified silence, while others, raucous with a phoney boldness, were anxious to let everyone know that they'd seen it all, if not worse, many times before.

'Now, ladies and gentlemen, if I might have yer tickets,' said Lou, dropping the cover back over the gory collection of weaponry. 'Then yer can shift yerselves through into the show proper.'

The spangled lady snatched the tokens from the excited customers with calm, practised efficiency, and directed them into the main arena for the show. The seats were filling up quickly and Billy used his long legs to clamber across to lay claim to places in the front row, whilst Ettie edged carefully along between the benches, the grimy linsey of her frock catching on the seats' splintered surfaces.

'Hurry up, Ett,' shouted Maisie, pushing her friend, 'it'll be starting soon. I don't wanna miss nothing.'

Billy, with a quick sideways movement, pulled Ettie down beside him. 'Come on, girl, do as yer mate says.'

Ettie plonked down ungracefully, glad that her blushes couldn't be seen in the dim yellow light of the oil-lamps which lined the front of the makeshift stage.

Maisie parked her broad bottom next to her, squashing Ettie even closer to Billy's sinewy body.

'Gawd blimey, who's let one rip?' The pimply, pasty-faced youth who was complaining pointed accusingly at Maisie as the sulphurous stench of rotten eggs permeated the crowded auditorium. 'I have to live in the next court to her,' he said grimacing. 'She's always bleed'n farting. The stink wafts right over the wall. Worse than the sewer it is.'

All faces turned towards the accused.

'Don't yer blame me, Jimmy Tanner,' said Maisie, tight-lipped and indignant. 'I'm a lady, I am.'

The audience responded with a series of ribald, incredulous jeers, but they were quickly halted by the appearance of the first turn. It featured Lou, in a different hat and without her drum or trumpet, giving a high speed, obscene recitation on the subject of virginity. Her strangulated words were accompanied by the musical talents of a five-piece ensemble, who somehow couldn't manage to find a common note between them, but whose efforts were repaid with magnificent approval from the cheering crowd. Lou hastily took a bow and strode off in the direction of the restless youths still queuing outside. The last thing a penny gaff needed was a fight attracting the attention of the local constable.

Next on stage came a short but satisfyingly gory playlet entitled *Savages of the Colonies*. The story was enacted with considerable spirit by the cast who, even in the weak lighting, looked suspiciously like some of the exhibits in the *Famous Professor Protsky's Genuine Freak Show*. When the final family members were horribly murdered, most of the girls in the audience took the opportunity to scream loudly and move closer to their boyfriends. And Billy wasn't slow to slip his arm protectively round Ettie's shoulders. She only half protested, but hissed a whispered, 'Shut up, May,' as her friend treated her to a knowing wink.

'Yer well in there, girl,' Maisie whispered loudly. 'Yer might wind up as me sister-in-law yet.'

At that, Ettie pulled away from Billy's side and, deliberately not caring who she disturbed, clambered across Maisie's lap and sat herself at the end of the bench by the aisle.

Billy mouthed an angry reprimand at his sister, but it was wasted on her, she was too interested in the next part of the show.

'And now, the amazing Professor Jacob Protsky!'

As his introduction was shouted from the stage by a man of barely three feet in height – without doubt a close relation of the father of the Fairy Family – the oil-lights were dimmed even lower by the other members of the cast.

At the sound of someone entering from the back of the gaff, all heads in the audience turned as one.

'Look, Ett, look, Bill. Look, there he is,' said Maisie, pointing excitedly at the tall, slim man in his thirties, dressed entirely in black, who seemed to be gliding towards them along the aisle between the benches.

'Ssssh!' warned the little man from the stage. 'The Professor requires absolute quiet for his demonstration.'

As Professor Protsky moved past her, Ettie felt the soft wool of his long, flowing cape brush the side of her face. The cloth felt so soft and he smelt so sweet and fresh, better than anybody she had ever smelt before.

With one final, extended stride, the Professor leapt effortlessly on to the little stage, sending up a cloud of dust from the boards – puff! – into the front three rows.

He raised a pale, elegant hand, and the oil-lamps were immediately adjusted to lend once more their full illumination to the proceedings. He took off his high, silk hat with a sweep and gave a long, deep bow. As he stood upright, Ettie gasped at the sheer handsomeness of him. His black hair shone with pomade and his close-cropped beard and moustaches highlighted his almost sculpted bones, emphasising the olive gleam of his skin. His eyes burned black.

'Wouldn't mind taking you home for tea, darling,' called one of the more daring young women from the benches. 'Eat yer right up, I would.'

This brazenness was rapidly followed by a volley of increasingly bawdy remarks referring variously to his good looks, his elegant attire and his general all-round desirability. The female voices were quickly countered by a series of sneering doubts as to the Professor's masculinity coming from the rather peeved young men in the audience.

Just as the situation was looking to get out of hand, the Professor spoke.

'I call on you, oh spirits,' he intoned in his resonant, faintly foreign-sounding voice. 'Bring me some token, some thing from the beautiful girl…' He paused, a brief, heart-stopping moment. 'The beautiful girl there!' he commanded.

'Ett!' squealed Maisie. 'Look, he's only pointing at you, ain't he!'

'Bloody load of old toffee,' mumbled Billy sulkily.

'Bring me some token, something that she knows to be hers and hers alone. Oh spirits, come to me. Come to me now.'

'I'm coming, I'm coming,' promised a girl behind May.

'Shut yer gob, yer mouthy cow, he's talking lovely,' cooed Maisie, basking in the reflected glory of sitting next to Ettie, the object of all the attention.

Ettie herself never spoke, she was transfixed, her eyes held by his extraordinary stare.

With the slightest movement of his fingers, a sudden flash of bright light sparked, making everyone blink in its blue-yellow flare. Then, from nowhere, he produced a length of dull green velvet ribbon.

Ettie put her hand to her throat and let out a small gasp of wonder.

'Yours, I believe,' the Professor said, his head held slightly to one side as he surveyed Ettie. He then held out his hand to her. The movement was a silent order.

Without saying a word, Ettie stood up and moved towards the stage.

'Blimey, what's up with her, Billy boy? She's in a bloody trance.' The words, which came from two benches behind Billy and Ettie, echoed round the otherwise hushed room.

'Yer've been told once, Jimmy Tanner. I'd shut me noise if I was you,' Billy warned in a low monotone without turning to look at the owner of the teasing voice. 'If yer know what's good for yer, that is.'

Professor Protsky took Ettie's hand and helped her step up on to the stage.

'Your ribbon, I believe,' he said, looking at her fixedly.

Ettie nodded and allowed him to turn her round to face the audience, while he retied the velvet band around her throat.

The crowd loved it. They clapped and whooped and cheered. They had seen magic worked by the spirits, in front of their very own eyes. *And* it looked like Billy Bury was building up for a ruck with Jimmy Tanner. It was turning out to be a promising evening all right.

'Thank you, ladies and gentleman,' the Professor continued with a slight inclination of his handsome head. 'And now, if I might impose on the young lady a little longer.'

'That what they call it where you come from is it, mush?' called Jimmy Tanner, pushing his already strained luck. 'Imposing? Well, that ain't what we call it round here in Whitechapel.'

'I told you,' snapped Billy.

The Professor ignored the altercation between the two young men. 'I would like, with the young lady's assistance,' he said, addressing the audience, 'to perform an act of true wonder.'

Sorely tempted, Jimmy Tanner restrained himself from making further smutty remarks, knowing the Bury family's redheaded temper to be more than just a rumour: even with Billy, usually the most placid of the Burys, you could only go so far.

'Go on, Ett!' called Maisie in encouragement, 'you let him impose. You assist him, girl.'

Acting as though the audience were behaving with impeccable manners, the Professor continued. He indicated that Ettie should sit on a rough wooden stool at the front of the stage but first, before he allowed her to do so, he brushed the seat clean with his handkerchief. Then, to the approximate sound of a drum roll from the percussionist in the five-piece ensemble, Protsky took a pack of cards and a slate from inside his cape, carefully, rather ostentatiously, placed these to one side, and then took from his pocket a square of blood-red satin.

'May I?' he asked, indicating that he wished to cover Ettie's eyes.

She nodded.

'Is that comfortable?' he asked, draping the veil so that her head and shoulders were completely covered.

She nodded again, careful not to disturb the satin.

'You can see nothing?'

This time Ettie gently shook her head.

The Professor then made a show of adjusting the material once more, ensuring that the audience could see that the cloth was obscuring all light from Ettie's eyes. Then he held up a hand to the musician, indicating that he should lower the volume of the drumming. Next he addressed the now almost silent audience.

'I will now summon the spirits, ladies and gentlemen. I will ask that they enter the mind of this young girl sitting here before you.

'I will ask that they show her what is in my mind.' Again, difficult as he found it, Jimmy Tanner restrained himself from passing the obvious ribald comment.

The Professor took a deep breath, placed an index finger on each of his temples, and made a low, moaning hum. Then, quite suddenly, he snatched up the pack of cards from where he'd left them on the stage, and leapt out into the audience.

'Quick,' he commanded Billy, 'the moment is opportune. Pick one of these cards and hold it up for all to see.'

As he held out the pack of cards, the man's fingers brushed the reluctant Billy's hand. Without even trying to hide his distaste,

Billy drew a card from the pack, staring contemptuously into the Professor's face as he did so.

The Professor held a long finger up to his lips. 'Say nothing, young man,' he commanded, 'merely hold up the card for all of us to see.'

Billy grudgingly held up the card: the two of hearts.

'Higher! Higher! Let all who are here see that the spirits will guide us to the truth.'

Billy raised his arm with a desultory, almost feeble flick.

'Please, keep it high in the air. The spirits are coming, coming to me. I feel them. Hear them. They are amongst us.'

Professor Protsky leapt back on the stage, scooping up the slate as he did so. He placed it on Ettie's lap, making her jump. Then took her hand and placed in it a slender writing implement.

'The young lady will now, with the assistance of the spirits, be able to enter my mind, and then she will write down the name of that very same card which you can all see held aloft by the young man in the front row.'

'Say she can't write?' hollered a wag from the back of the room.

'I can write, ta very much.' Her voice muffled by the satin veil, Ettie spoke for the first time.

'It matters not, sir,' the Professor assured the doubter. 'All that matters is my power of thought-transference, and the willingness of the spirits to assist.'

'Spirits always assist me and all,' chipped in Jimmy Tanner, unable to control himself any longer. 'Especially gin.'

'Please,' the Professor continued, quite undeterred by the hecklers. 'Young lady, write. Write now. Write what you see in my mind.'

'But I don't see noth...'

'Write.' He touched his fingertips to the top of her veiled head, then passed his hands rapidly in front of her covered face.

Ettie hurriedly scribbled something, anything, on the slate.

The Professor seized the board from her and leapt back theatrically to Billy. 'Have the spirits guided us faithfully, young sir?'

With a flourish, the Professor held the slate aloft, next to Billy's aching arm.

'Behold! A triumph for the spirits! The two of hearts.'

Ettie pulled the veil down to her chin and stared. 'Well, bugger me,' she said. Taking the Professor's offered hand, she stumbled down from the stage and back to her seat to the accompaniment of wild cheers and clapping.

When, five minutes later, Protsky finished his act with a mysteriously floating apparition – which could well have been a visitation from the spirit world – he was rewarded with another tumultuous round of applause.

'Thank you, ladies and gentleman,' said the Professor, accepting his applause as if by right. 'And a special thank you to my lovely assistant there in the front row.'

'They're clapping for yer again, Ett,' shouted Maisie over the applause. 'Just listen how they're clapping for yer. Good old Ettie.' She was loving every minute of her friend's success.

'Ettie!' the Professor announced, pointing to her again and leading yet more applause.

'Now see what you and yer big mouth have done,' Billy snapped at his sister. 'The slimy bugger knows her name now.'

'He'd have known it anyway,' said Ettie quietly. 'Cos of the spirits. They'd have told him.'

'Yeah, I reckon,' said Billy angrily.

Everyone looked round at the loud tooting from the back of the room, as Lou the spangled lady announced her return and her intention to usher them out ready to make room for the next house.

Billy immediately scrambled into the row behind and pushed his way into the aisle.

His sister wasn't quite so athletic. 'Come on, Ett, move yerself, girl,' she said, standing up ready to leave but unable to get past her friend. 'Just cos yer a star, I ain't gonna bleed'n carry yer out. And I definitely ain't climbing over no benches.'

Ettie didn't move. 'May, I don't wanna go,' she said.

'Do what?'

'I wanna see the show again.'

'For gawd's sake, Ettie, it's late enough as it is. And yer know I ain't even meant to be here.'

'I know.'

'And how do yer think we can afford another penny? Yer made of money all of a sudden, are yer?'

'We can hide behind that canvas screen and bunk in. No one'll see us.'

Maisie shook her head. 'I'm sorry, Ett. I know yer me best friend and everything, but I can't. Anyway, Bill's waiting and I've got to make sure that that little sod of a Tommy gets out of his fairy frock and back home before Mum finds out what's been going on.'

'It's all right, May,' said Ettie softly. 'I understand. You go on, before yer get trampled to death by the next lot coming in.'

May shook her head, then bent forward and gave her friend a peck on the cheek. 'See yer later then, yer dozy cow.'

'Yeah, see yer, May.'

Ettie let her friend get past her, and watched her join the chattering, excited throng who were filing out of the gaff.

'I'm staying as well, Ett. I'll keep yer company.'

Ettie turned round to see Billy still standing in the gangway between the benches. He was looking at her with great concentration. She stared back at him for a long moment before she spoke.

'That's up to you, Bill,' she said gently, 'but I've changed me mind. I've decided to go home.'

'But yer just said yer was staying for the next show,' said Billy, exasperated. 'Yer don't want me here with yer, do yer? That's what all this is about.'

'It's not that. But do me a favour and leave me alone, Bill, will yer?' She looked down at her hands. 'Anyway, I'm going home to get some money,' she said stiffly. 'Then I'm coming back here to see one of the later shows. That's all.'

22

'Money? From *your* house, yer reckon? Yer've taken leave of yer senses. There's never nothing in your house, yer know that. What's got into yer, Ett?'

'Look, I know what I'm doing. I've decided I don't wanna bunk in here like some daft kid. All right?' She gnawed nervously at her thumbnail. 'I wanna come and pay. Decent-like.'

'Yer not making no sense, Ett.' Billy ran his fingers distractedly through his mop of pale red hair.

'Look, I know how I'll get a few bob, don't yer worry yerself. I'll rob that dirty bastard of a lodger while he's asleep and snoring his stinking head off.'

'Ettie…' Billy shook his head, thought for a bit, then said, 'Look, I'll come home with yer. Just in case. I've heard what this latest so-called lodger of yer mum's is like. May's told me all about him.'

Ettie shot a surprised look at him. So, for all Maisie's bluster, she'd been concerned all along about what a hard time Ettie had been having. She was a good friend when all was said and done.

'I'll be all right by myself, ta, Bill,' she said when she'd recovered from the surprise. 'I can deal with that no-good pig once he's having a kip.'

'Yer don't have to, yer know.'

'I know, Bill, but I want to. Yer know me, I find it hard to be beholding to anyone.'

The difficult silence that followed was shattered by an obviously irritated voice: 'Are you coming, staying, or what, Billy Bury?' It was May, forcing her way back down the aisle towards them, with her little rouged and powdered brother Tommy in tow.

'She's going home now. To get some money,' Billy said, rolling his eyes at his sister. 'Don't want to bunk in like no kid, she reckons.'

'Bloody hell.' May let out a long, slow sigh. 'Yer a dopey mare.' She took a deep breath and tightened her grip on her youngest brother's arm. 'We'd all better be going in any case, hadn't we?' she

23

said, all calm efficiency. 'It's bloody hot and sweaty in here. And, as for you, Tommy Bury, I'm gonna dip yer head in the horses' trough before Mum sets her eyes on yer. Gawd alone knows what she'd say if she saw yer with all that muck on yer chops. Yer look like a bride looking for customers.'

May trailed the wriggling Tommy behind her like he was a sack full of fighting potatoes, the laughing crowd parting good-humouredly to let them pass.

Ettie made as if to follow. This time, it was Billy who was stopping *her* from leaving. He took her arm in his strong, working man's grip.

'Ett, yer do know what yer doing, girl, don't yer? Because, if you ask me, I don't think yer do. Yer don't know nothing about him, do yer?'

'About who?' she said, her chin held high.

'Yer know full well who I mean.'

'I know as much about him as I need to, or want to for that matter, Bill.' She rubbed her hands over her face; suddenly she felt very tired. 'It seems longer, but he's been living in our room with us for a fortnight. That's enough for me to know all about him, believe me.'

'No, not him,' said Billy tensely. 'I don't mean no lodger. I mean this Protsky geezer.' Billy gripped her arm tighter. 'His hands, Ett. I dunno. I didn't like the feel of them. They was all sort of cold and like wax. Horrible they was.'

'What? They ain't all hard and rough like ours, yer mean?'

'Ett, please. Yer don't know what yer messing with.' Trying his last card, Billy added, 'And I think he's foreign or something.'

'Come on you two. Another penny each or yer out.' Lou the Spangled Lady had appeared again and was jerking her thumb towards the exit in an unmistakable gesture of dismissal. 'Now move yerselves or cough up yer money. I've got paying customers waiting to come in.'

Billy and Ettie didn't move.

'And anyway,' Ettie said, trying to release herself from Billy. 'Whatever I do, what have I got to lose eh? Tell me that.'

'Me,' he said quietly.

'Billy,' she said softly. 'I don't know what all the fuss is about. I'm only coming back to see the show.'

'I love you, Ett, I've always loved yer. And I know you ain't happy at home.'

Ettie went to speak, but he wouldn't let her; he was afraid what she might say.

'I could make things all right for yer, honest I could.' The words that had been going around in his head suddenly tumbled from his mouth before he could stop them. 'Is it our Alfie?' he asked. 'Do yer prefer him to me?'

'Wherever did yer get that idea from?' she said, shaking her head and forcing herself to smile. 'Bill, Alfie's me mate, that's all.' She looked away from him. 'And, believe me, Bill, if I had to pick one of yer...'

'Perhaps yer could love me then?' he interrupted.

Ettie didn't get the chance to either confirm or dash his hopes.

'Do I have to tell you two again?' Lou threatened, more loudly this time.

Ettie pulled herself free and walked towards the exit. Billy dodged round in front of her and silently lifted the painted canvas, intending to let Ettie duck out into the corridor. But the authority of the voice coming from the stage behind them stopped them both dead in their tracks.

'Ettie. You're still here, I see.'

It was Protsky.

She spun round to face him. 'Yeah. I wanted to see the show again.' She looked down shyly, paused and then raised her eyes to meet his. 'If that's all right with you, of course.'

–

'Wake up yer lazy, gin-soaked bitch.'

The woman moaned, a low, animal-like sound, as she struggled to bring herself to consciousness. She shifted, lifting her scraggy, aching arm from under the stiff grey blanket. The movement sent an empty bottle crashing from the bed on to the bare, grimy floorboards. The sound reverberated through her pounding skull.

'What d'yer say?' she mumbled hoarsely.

'I said, where is she? Where's Ettie? Answer me.'

'I don't know.' She tried to rub the sleep from her eyes, but couldn't focus in the dim, alcohol-blurred haze. 'She must've gone out, I suppose. I don't know. I didn't feel well, I fell asleep.'

'Asleep? Yer filthy trollop. Yer was out like a light, like yer always are.' He kicked the broken shards of the bottle with his heavy hob-nailed boot, sending the fragments spinning and glinting in the pale light which filtered in through the cracked and filthy window from the court's single gas-lamp.

The woman recoiled nervously, fearing from experience what would come next.

She had every right to be afraid. He tore the thin covers from off her body and looked down at her with disgust.

'Look at yer. Yer make me sick. But yer'll have to do.'

Her throat, already dry from the gin, was now an inferno; she swallowed painfully, watching helplessly as he undid his great buckled belt. All the while, he stared at her with his cold, unblinking eyes.

'She'll be home soon. I'm sure of it,' she croaked.

'Too late. I want it now. I'll see to her later.'

The weight of his big, slaughterman's body was not enough to smother her cries as he pinned her down against the musty dampness of the mattress, and forced himself into her.

'Shut up in there, can't yer?' The angry voice carried clearly through the flimsy wooden partition that separated the room from the family of seven next door. 'There's people in here trying to get a bit of kip.'

'And in here!' The voice from the other side agreed. 'Give her a drop of Satin and keep her quiet, for gawd's sake.'

The laughter from the two neighbouring rooms drowned the woman's pitiful sobs.

Chapter 1

'Thank Gawd above that that's over for another night. Me bleed'n pins are killing me.' Lou the Spangled Lady bent forward and tenderly rubbed her aching legs as she ushered out the last of the stragglers from the final show of the night.

Only Ettie, Maisie, and Maisie's new-found companion – a big, Scandinavian-looking merchant seaman who didn't appear to speak very much English – remained on the bench seats.

'Good night you lot,' said Lou to the three of them. 'I'm off to me bed. His Majesty back there said it was all right for me to leave yer here till he comes out. Mind yer, he never said nothing about no sailors,' she added warily.

'That's all right, Lou, thank you.'

Ettie looked round. Jacob had appeared on the empty stage.

'I'm glad you decided to wait for me, Miss Wilkins,' he said, looking down at her. Still dressed in his black outfit, he looked magnificent. 'But the young man who was with you – he decided to leave?'

'He had to get his little brother back home,' Ettie answered him, her voice low. 'So Maisie here waited with me.'

Jacob nodded. Then he stretched slowly, luxuriously, like a cat. Stepping down into the impromptu front stalls, ignoring Maisie and the sailor, who, in any case, seemed more interested in each other, he reached out his hand to Ettie.

'No, wait,' said Ettie, shaking her head. 'I want to say something. Something I've been thinking about. That's been worrying me.'

'About my asking you to wait for me?'

She shook her head again. 'No.' She paused then, avoiding the powerful gaze of his deep, brown eyes, she said softly, 'It ain't very nice, yer know.'

'Oh? What isn't?'

'Them poor sods yer show in the exhibition out there. The Mountain Maid and that. I'd have thought more from a choice geezer like yer self.'

'This is very unexpected,' said Protsky, unable to hide his surprise at her concern. 'I thought you had enjoyed the show.'

'Well, like I said, I've been thinking. It's the way yer talk and that. Yer should know better.'

'Explain. I'm not sure that I follow your meaning, I'm afraid.'

'And I ain't sure that I follow yours neither.' She hesitated, finding her words. 'I ain't never really had no one talk to me with a voice like yours, see.' She still wouldn't meet his eyes.

Jacob smiled down at her, puzzled yet intrigued.

'Tell yer the truth. I ain't really sure of what yer saying half the time. When you talked to me, when I went on the stage with yer. And them words yer used with the spirits; right fancy words. You know. I got right confused.'

'Then you will simply have to learn to speak like me then, my language. Won't you?'

'That a fact?' she said, looking directly at him for the first time.

'Yes. That's a fact.'

Ettie put her hand on Maisie's shoulder to steady herself and stepped around her and the sailor. 'Mind yerself, May,' she said as she did so, but her friend and the blond seafarer were too preoccupied with their noisy embrace to take any notice of Ettie climbing round them.

Ettie walked forward and stopped a few yards from the foot of the stage. She looked up at Jacob.

'Yer know, the only times we ever hear talk like yours round here is when the toffs come down cos they fancy getting themselves a Whitechapel girl.' Ettie paused, curious to see if he understood. 'If yer catch me drift,' she went on.

He nodded.

'Some of them talk like you. Made me laugh when I first heard them. It's comical sounding to us round here.'

He still said nothing, only raised an inquiring eyebrow.

Perhaps she had said too much. 'Them freaks,' she continued, flustered and pink-faced. 'Whatever yer say. It ain't very nice. It ain't...'

'Dignified?'

'If yer say so.'

'If you learn to look closely, Ettie, you will see that much of what you believe you are seeing is actually illusion. Nothing is what we think.'

'Yer off again. Fancy words.'

Jacob stepped down and led her to the edge of the stage. He wiped the boards with his handkerchief and indicated that she should take a seat.

'Ta,' she said, pleased, despite herself, with the unaccustomed attention to her needs.

Jacob sat down next to her. 'Ettie, supposing the freak show were real, supposing the Hooded Man did exist?'

'But...'

'No, listen. What alternatives would he have, do you suppose? Living in this cruel world where to be different is to be punished. Where not being like one's neighbour is to make one an object of fear and hatred. Would you rather he lived on the streets, scavenging in the gutters for scraps?'

'Yer don't know that's what would happen to him.'

'Believe me, Ettie, I know more about being different than you might imagine.'

'And I know more about living on the streets than you ever will.'

'Maybe.'

'It's all right for you. Yer've got all the words. I only know what I know. What I feel.'

'I could give you the words, Ettie. I could give you words you never dreamed of.'

'Could you tell me how to forget?'

'Forget?'

'Nothing…' Her voice trailed off.

'As you wish.'

'I'd be better off if I was a freak according to you. Then at least I could live in comfort.'

'But you are a freak, Ettie.'

She jumped to her feet and shoved her fists into her waist, confronting him like a plucky little bantam. 'Aw, ta very much, I don't think.'

'You misunderstand me, Ettie,' he said. 'It is your beauty, when compared to the ordinary run of women, that makes you a freak.'

'Cor, hark at him!' said Maisie suddenly. She was nodding towards Protsky and elbowing the puzzled-looking man by her side. She had decided that, language barrier or not, she'd done plenty to persuade the sailor to take her out the next evening when, being off the ships, he'd have a few bob in his pocket.

'How long yer been listening, yer rotten mare?' demanded Ettie, spinning round to turn her anger on her friend.

'Long enough,' beamed May, screwing her eye into a most unsubtle wink. 'Now, mind if me and me young man goes off now? I want to find out where he's berthed, see? Don't want this little fishy to escape, now do I?'

'Of course you must go,' said Protsky. 'Ettie will be perfectly fine with me, thank you for your concern.'

Ettie turned back to Protsky. 'Will yer all stop making up me bleed'n mind for me? I ain't a bloody idiot, yer know.'

'I'll wait outside for yer,' said Maisie, tight-lipped at the reprimand. Then, recovering her composure, she added. 'For five minutes. That's all. Then I'm off. Old blondie here's getting a bit impatient, ain't yer, darling?'

Maisie led the now thoroughly confused sailor out on to the Whitechapel Road.

'I meant it, Ettie,' said Protsky, when May and her catch were out of earshot. 'Your beauty does mark you out from other women. That is the simple truth.'

'Yer know how to turn a gel's head, Professor, *that's* the truth,' she replied.

'Call me Jacob, please.'

'Fair enough – Jacob. Or maybe I'll call yer Jack. That's short for Jacob, innit? What d'yer think of that?' She hoped she was sounding calm and collected, grown-up even, though inside she felt like a silly little girl. A silly, confused little girl. Her head was whirling with questions: what was she doing here? Why hadn't she gone home hours ago? Why had she stayed behind for the three other shows? And finally, did she really need to ask herself those questions, didn't she know all too well? Here, at last, might be the chance she was waiting for – the chance to escape.

'I would rather you called me Jacob,' he replied. 'It is my given name.'

'Eh?'

'You said you wished to call me "Jack".'

'Oh yeah. Right,' she answered distractedly, struck by the thought that time was running out for her to make her mind up. If she didn't get a move on and let May know what she was going to do, May would really be getting her wild up waiting outside.

'I would like you to consider a proposition, Ettie.'

'I should be going,' she said, half-turning towards the way out.

'You don't have to sound so worried,' he said soothingly, misunderstanding her reaction.

'No. I ain't worried. I just wanted to let May know what was happening.'

Jacob nodded. 'Good. I'm glad you're not worried. I thought you had strength. That is why I would like you to consider a business proposition.'

'Do what?'

'I could use an assistant,' he explained. 'Particularly one with your looks.'

'And how about Lou?' Ettie said, forgetting her waiting friend and interested once more only in what this strange, handsome man had to say.

'Ettie, do you really expect me to believe that you don't understand the differences between yourself and Lou? That you weren't aware of the effect you had on the audience tonight? And anyway, you would be assisting me in my act, not taking Lou's role away from her.'

Neither of them spoke for several long moments.

'I ain't never done nothing like no stage work before, you know.'

'I realise that, but I can teach you. What do you think?'

'Would it mean working round here?'

'At first. Then, who knows?' Seeing her disappointed expression, he asked. 'Why? Wouldn't you want to leave here?'

Ettie gave a hollow laugh in reply.

'So you want to leave Whitechapel?'

'I don't know about that, but I know I wouldn't mind getting away from home,' she said. 'It's been a bit hard lately, see.'

Jacob didn't answer, he just continued looking at her, letting her speak.

His expression was so caring – not judging or angry or threatening, unlike the looks she'd come to expect at home. She wasn't used to such treatment from men like him: it confused her. Before she knew what she was doing a hastily censored version of her life story came bubbling out of her mouth, in a rush of partly incoherent, but mostly dejected words.

'Me mum's always had blokes hanging round her,' she gabbled. 'She was a right good-looker before she got the taste for gin. Clever and all. She can even read and write a bit. Not many of her age can do that. She could have made something of herself, yer know.' She stared unseeingly into the far, dark corner of the little auditorium. 'But she likes her drop of gin all right, does Mum. Though there's never enough money, see, to get her all she wants.' She looked round and smiled unconvincingly at Jacob. 'The fellahs are her way of getting a few shillings. So long as she gets her drink she's happy. I don't blame her or nothing – who'd want to exist the way we have to down in them courts? The gin makes it all go away for her. But because we're stuck in that one poxy rat-hole of a room it's too easy for the blokes to...' Ettie paused and drew in a long, slow breath. 'Well, like I said, it ain't her fault, is it? She's in such a state she don't realise what's happening to me, does she?' She paused again, then added sadly. 'Least, I don't think she does. But anyhow, that's how it is, and that's all there is to it.' She hooked a stray curl of her thick dark hair behind her ear. 'And then,' she continued, 'there's the rotten fur-pulling. Gawd I hate that and all. It brings in a bit of money but it's so horrible. Yer wouldn't believe it unless yer had to do it. The bits of fluff get everywhere: in yer eyes and throat, up yer nose, even in yer ears. Terrible it is. And they ain't always gutted out proper neither.' She wrinkled her nose in disgust. 'Then they stink worse than yer could imagine. Specially in the hot weather. And the bloke what collects the pelts, he's a pig and all. Christ, I hate it. All of it.'

As suddenly as the flow of words had begun, they stopped, but her chest continued visibly to rise and fall from the strain of making her revelations.

'Shall I take it then that you are agreeing to accept my offer of employment?' Jacob asked her calmly.

'Do yer mean will I work for yer?'

'Yes. That's exactly what I mean.'

She hesitated for only a second. 'When do yer want me to start?' she grinned.

'Why not immediately?' he said easily, as though it were the most natural thing in the world that she should suddenly take up employment with this strange man she knew next to nothing about.

'But haven't yer finished for the night?'

'Here I have, yes. But there's no reason why we can't begin discussing your new job, now is there? You must come home and stay with me.'

'Eh?'

'Well, you can't possibly want to go back to your mother's room. Not after what you have told me about living there.'

Ettie was not sure whether to be angry with his presumption or flattered by his concern. 'You never said nothing about having to go back to your place,' she said cautiously.

'You have no need to worry,' he said, smiling amiably. 'My intentions are, of course, entirely honourable.'

'No,' Ettie said. 'Thanks all the same, but I have to go back. To sort things out and to see my mum. She'll be worried if I don't turn up.'

'That doesn't make sense, Ettie,' he persisted. 'From what you said she won't even be conscious by this time of night.'

'Don't keep going on at me,' Ettie's voice was tense. 'Yer confusing me. I'll *have* to go home. I can't just bugger off, can I? I'll wait till she's slept it off and then I'll talk to her. I'll be able to come back in the morning, all right?' Suddenly worried that she might have overstepped the mark, Ettie softened her tones. 'I didn't mean to sound so… Aw, I don't know, so…'

In her inimitable style, Maisie broke the tension of the moment by poking her head round the canvas screen – yet again. This time she was not only angry, she was panicking too. 'Now you come on, Ettie Wilkins. This really is me limit. I mean it. *Now.* I'm right pissed off. I said five minutes I'd give yer and that was sodding ages ago. I ain't having no more of it.' She jerked her thumb over her shoulder in the direction of the street outside. 'It'll be bloody daylight in a couple of hours. Me mum's going to love this.'

'I'm sorry to have delayed you. It was my fault entirely,' said Jacob, giving a stiff little bow from his neck.

'Never you mind all that old nonsense,' fumed May. 'I've already risked me mum chopping me up in little bits and feeding me to the rats just by coming here. Now, just for good measure, I've lost myself a right nice geezer and all. Took off, he has.'

Ettie went over to her friend and whispered to her. 'I'm sorry, May, really I am. I'll be with yer in one minute, all right? I promise yer.' Ettie's eyes shone as she lowered her voice to an even quieter whisper, not daring to risk anyone hearing about her luck and stealing it away. 'May, guess what?'

'Surprise me,' said May, sounding more fed up than angry now.

'He said he could use me as his assistant. Me, May. Me!'

'Do what?'

'And he's going to let me stay with him and all.' Seeing her friend's expression, Ettie added hurriedly: 'It's all above board, May. He said so.'

'Ettie, girl,' said May loudly over her friend's shoulder, making sure that her words were aimed directly at Protsky. 'If yer go off with him, yer more flaming barmy than I thought yer were. And that's saying something.'

'Shut up, May, will yer? Keep yer voice down.' Ettie turned to face Jacob. 'I'm just going home for a bit, like I said. To see me mum, sort things out and get some money. Then I'm coming right back. First thing tomorrow.'

'There's no need to go, Ettie,' said Jacob, ignoring the alarmed faces Maisie was pulling at her friend. 'Why don't you stay? Now. You said you hated...'

'Hold on,' May interrupted. She took Ettie firmly by the arm. 'Money? What flipping money?' She was now too concerned – and curious – to be annoyed about the loss of her would-be lover or all the time she'd been kept waiting. 'Yer said that before, to our Billy, about going home to get money. What, have yer come into an inheritance or something? Got a rich auntie have yer?' she demanded sarcastically.

Ettie didn't answer, so Maisie carried on with her interrogation. 'First it's farthings for Tommy. Now this. What's going on? Yer really have gone barmy, haven't yer? Yer going to wind up in a right old mess the way yer performing. You mark my words.'

'I've told you, Ettie,' said Jacob, as though Maisie hadn't uttered a word. 'You don't have to go anywhere.'

'It's nothing for you to worry about, May,' she said, ignoring Jacob's offer out of a practised wariness, but also out of pride. 'I can get some money from home all right.'

'I'm right,' Maisie said, this time addressing Jacob directly. 'She is barmy. Totally sodding crackers. I'm telling yer, yer might as well have a monkey for an assistant. It'd make more bleed'n sense than her.'

Jacob looked at Ettie, then he spoke to May. 'You need have no fears for your friend, Maisie. Ettie can make up her own mind about what she does. I have faith in her. And I will be waiting for her when she returns.' With that he lifted the canvas screen once more and let the two young women out into the corridor. 'Good night, Maisie,' he said very formally. 'Au revoir, Ettie.'

'Do what?' asked May.

'Shut yer gob,' said Ettie, shoving her friend into the corridor and out towards the cool night air.

'Well, he talks funny,' said May, stumbling forward.

'No he don't, it's because he's a gentleman.'

'Gentleman?' snorted May. 'So what makes him so different from any other bloke then?'

Ettie turned to May and smiled dreamily. 'Yer didn't notice, Maise, did yer? How he wiped that seat for me, and the stage, before I sat down. And with his very own handkerchief and everything.' Ettie hugged herself. 'That was as wonderful to me as any magic he could ever do. No one's ever done *nothing* like that for me before. Never.' She pinched Maisie's plump, pink cheek. 'And that's why I'm going to stay with him and be his assistant.'

Maisie rolled her eyes heavenwards. 'Bloody hell,' she said.

Chapter 2

'No more arguments, you will assist me and that is final.'

'No, please, I don't want to. I...'

'Celia, I told you today at the hospital, I'll have no more of your disagreeable wilfulness. I order you. You will assist me. Now put them on.'

He didn't need to shout. The cool, calm authority of his voice was always enough to chill her. He held out the garments.

'You will do as you are told, Celia. Or risk my anger.'

Fighting back the rising waves of nausea, Celia took the stiff, starched dress and the almost rigid cap and apron from his long, strangely delicate hands. She turned her back on him and began to change, doing her best to slip off her heavy woollen dress and put on the cotton clothes before he could see her body. It wasn't even cool for the time of year, yet she shivered.

He took off his black frock coat and placed it carefully in the plain wooden cupboard, so tidily, with an almost obsessive regard for neatness, adjusting the sleeves so that they hung just so. Next he rolled up the sleeves of his pure white shirt, exposing his pale, hairless arms.

The ritual had begun.

Outside the house, in the elegant Belgravia square, it was like any other evening with life going on as usual. But, as she followed her father along the elegantly furnished corridor towards the operating theatre attached to his consulting rooms, she was oblivious to the ordinariness of the world outside. The passing hansoms and the couples strolling by arm-in-arm enjoying the last of the evening's spring sunshine meant nothing to her, nor did the laughter or other sounds in the streets below: they were the commonplace business of everyday life. Life had long since ceased to be in any way normal for Celia Tressing.

As Bartholomew Tressing opened the door and guided her in, no matter how she tried to control her reactions, she couldn't. As always, she gagged. She had become used to the sight of the hinged amputation boards swinging from the operating table. She could almost ignore the box of sawdust, positioned to receive the gory by-products of her father's chosen profession. And the black metal box of shining instruments could nearly always be dismissed by her as being mere craftsman's tools. Even the white jugs of hot water set out by one of the servants, which had acquired their own repulsive significance, could be tolerated by thinking of them in their more familiar domestic setting. But she would never become used to the cloying stench of the carbolic, as her father primed the hand-pump and sprayed a fine mist of the stuff round the big, high-ceilinged room. There was an all-pervasive reek as it danced in the air, settling on every surface in the room – her included, seeping into the very pores of her skin. The worst thing for her was that it never quite managed to cover the real stink of the place, the stink of rotting flesh and coagulated blood that had soaked so deeply into the cracks and very fibre of the scrubbed wooden table and floorboards.

Tressing didn't flinch as the carbolic and mercury solution, in which he cleansed his hands, stung the deep gash on his knuckles. He was more interested in the condition of his well-shaped and manicured nails. Clean, beautifully clean. He took a deep, sighing breath. The final stage in his personal preparation was completed.

'Now, the Venuses.' Tressing moved towards the coffin-like display cases which lined one side of the room.

As Celia followed him, her apron crackled spitefully around her legs and the sound of her footsteps rang out in the otherwise silent room.

Bartholomew Tressing leaned over one of the cases, lifted its glass lid and let down its wooden side to fully reveal its contents.

Inside was a recumbent, lovely young woman, reclining provocatively on a pile of plump, red velvet cushions. Her gleaming, raven hair fell in loose curls around her creamy white shoulders.

And, even though she was naked, save for the single strand of pearls at her throat, she made no attempt to cover her shame, not even the movement of a hand to hide the hair which grew close to her most secret place. It was not modesty she lacked, however, it was life. She was made of wax. An effigy. A sham.

Then came the moment which Celia hated: hated because it both fascinated and disgusted her – both reactions making her feel guilt of the most unavoidable kind. She watched the creature in the case – which was a woman like her, yet not like her – as he reached for that second lid, the lid of the lifeless stomach. He did so with gloating, unconcealed enthusiasm. There, it was done, the lifting of the lifeless lid, which, paradoxically, revealed the replica internal organs, the repository of the mysteries of life itself. The body itself was a case within a case.

Feminine modesty's only representation was in the model's averted gaze: the lowered lids of the eyes contrasting disturbingly with the raised lid of the abdomen.

'We unveil the body,' he breathed, 'and within, behold the mystery which will be revealed through the glory of the triumphs of nineteenth-century scientific discovery, of which I, Bartholomew Tressing, will be the apogee.'

Celia stood quite still and stared at the Anatomical Venus as her father used the model to outline the procedures they were to follow. She knew better than to argue with him, but she wouldn't be forced to listen to his ravings. She blocked out the sound of his voice as he handled the lividly painted uterus, the silent aid to his coarse descriptions of the procedure they were to follow.

'So. It will be clear to you that you are going to assist me in an ovariotomy – if the condition of the raw material allows us.' He replaced the model organs, closed the hinged cover to the abdomen, and then returned the sides and lid of the glass case to the closed position. The Venus was once more at rest in her glass-topped coffin. 'I intend to perfect this technique to a level far

beyond that which that fool Derringer could even contemplate.'
He walked towards the sheet-draped operating table.

Celia followed him, flinching as he went on.

'I am increasingly unhappy to read in the journals how that charlatan is cornering the market in pelvic operations for the idiot, bored wives of rich industrialists. I mean to present a very real challenge to that man's position in the profession, you know. I'll show those frigid bitches how to spend their hundred guineas to provide the answer to their husbands' fading appetites. They'll be queuing up for me to open them up.'

He stopped beside a high side-table where the black box containing the tools of his surgical trade had been placed by one of the servants. Tressing lifted each out in turn, holding the metal objects close to the gasolier, examining first this, then that aspect of its readiness for its task. Sharpness. Strength. Shine. He inclined his head in a gesture of approval for the servant's work. 'I believe that soon Smithson will prove to be as good a surgical assistant as he is a butler.'

Celia was momentarily shocked from her silent dread of what was to come by her father's unaccustomed acknowledgement of another's worth.

'Might Smithson then perhaps take my place...' she began.

The simple act of Bartholomew Tressing raising his hand returned his daughter to her previously mute state.

'Now you will make them ready and I will observe your efforts,' he instructed her.

Celia took a deep breath, fully aware that her failure to remember the exact order in which he expected his tools and materials to be laid out would result in her being punished. His orderliness had become increasingly fanatical since he had become obsessed with the idea of becoming the most eminent surgeon in his field. He seemed to believe that if he had the tools placed correctly, then the technique would follow automatically. Every jar in his pharmacy had to be in its exact position on its shelf. Every book in his library was to be placed in the position he ordained.

Celia had put out every tool except the last two scalpels – was it length or breadth which determined their place in the hierarchy? She almost put the first blade down, then withdrew it quickly and reconsidered. She could feel his eyes boring into the back of her neck. She took a sharp intake of breath and put the instrument on the left hand space, and the final tool in the remaining gap. She closed her eyes and swallowed hard. Waiting for his response.

'Let's see what slum-creeping trollop those fools have found me this time,' he said, apparently totally unaware of his daughter's fear.

Celia let out her breath in a long slow sigh. She was reprieved. The relief of her unexpected respite from her father's anger must have made her momentarily lose her reason. 'They may be poor, Father, but they are not objects.'

'Oh no?' He drew back the sheet, the veil, which covered the body.

She almost swooned at the stink and the sight of the physical degeneration of the corpse which confronted her. Bloated with alcohol, ravaged by poverty and vice, and covered in syphilitic sores, dark stains, a mixture of congealed blood and Thames slime smeared the bare limbs.

'Now,' he said in a low, moaning breath. 'What have those nogoods taken good money off me for?' He selected a knife and slit open the reeking cloth that had once been a petticoat, exposing the naked torso. He swore loudly. 'Another damned abortion, I'd stake money on it. How are we going to stop those meddling women doing this to each other?' He rubbed his forearm over his forehead. 'Damned amateurs taking away trade from us professionals. The bread from out of our mouths.'

Though Celia wanted to vomit, she could not let herself. She could not allow herself to displease him.

He began to laugh, a shallow gurgle in his throat. Celia found his increasingly unpredictable moods almost more frightening than anything else.

'Should be grateful, I suppose,' he said smirking down at the distended form on the table. 'It's their botched handiwork that keeps me supplied with most of the material I work on.' His face returned to its cool expressionless mask. 'But I know I would appreciate the opportunity to work on some fresher specimens. How can I rehearse my skills when all I have to work on are these rotting sewer rats dragged from the mud after two days in the river. But, expecting those Neanderthal morons who supply me to show any initiative would be too much to ask, I suppose.'

'Perhaps the women of the slums could be helped.' Her boldness surprised and horrified her, but it was too late, she had said it, said what she had been feeling for so long.

'What?'

She had gone this far, why not continue? 'If they could be helped in some way, perhaps they would not be in such difficult straits and would not need to resort to such measures.'

He tossed the knife which he had used to cut the petticoat into a metal dish and concentrated on selecting another. 'Are you insane, girl?' he snapped, his lip curling contemptuously. 'Who exactly had you in mind to do such a thing, to *help* such creatures?'

'Someone like me. I should like to help the women of the slums.'

This time he looked at her. 'What do you intend to do: go and cut the unwanted brats out of the whores' wombs yourself? That would be a very charitable cause. I can see the court case being reported in *The Times* now.'

'I did not mean that, Father. I meant that I could help them find a better path in life. That was all.'

'That's all is it?' He shook his head scornfully. 'You really are dim-witted.' As he became more agitated he waved the knife he had chosen closer and closer to her face, emphasising his words with menacing jabs of the glittering blade. 'This country is on the very edge of revolution. Even Her Majesty the Queen isn't safe in the streets today. The squares and parks, even of the decent parts of London, are teeming with labouring classes who labour no more. Then there are the Fenians, anarchists and Asiatics.' He regarded her as though she were an uncatalogued curiosity. 'Are you saying that someone like *you* perhaps wants to go into the slums to help the whores find a better path?'

'Why not me?' she whispered timidly. 'Others have done similar work.'

'You really are mad, aren't you, Celia? I always suspected that there was too much of your mother in you.'

She winced visibly as he mentioned her mother, but didn't dare say a word in either her, or her own, defence. She had already said too much. She shouldn't have said anything.

As though seeing it for the first time, Tressing examined the tool he held in his hand, then discarded it with a loud exclamation of displeasure. 'You are breaking my concentration with your foolish prattling,' he complained sternly, then took up another knife. This time it was a slightly curved, heavier instrument which he selected. He prodded at the bruised, tumid flesh with his long, pale forefinger, looking for the place to begin.

'I don't know what this mania is today for young women having to *do* things. If you really must do something with yourself, then perhaps Bobby Charnsworth would fit the bill. He's not long for this world, that's for sure. And you'd inherit a fair portion, that's for sure too. But,' he turned to her and drew a carbolic-stinking finger down her cheek, 'I'd miss you,' he breathed, 'and that is also for sure. Even if you were away for just a few months.'

He returned to his consideration of the dead woman and, with no warning, plunged in the knife and began the dissection. The pain of the penetration surged through Celia as though he had plunged the blade into her own flesh.

'I...' she began.

'Enough,' he silenced her. 'I don't know why I even mentioned it. Any ideas about Bobby Charnsworth are out of the question. I need you here with me, Celia. This is your place.' He spoke between short grunts of exertion as he cut and pulled at the flesh, all his attention now focused on the body before him. 'Watch, Celia. Watch well,' he commanded. 'It is vital to understand the *meaning* of what one is doing. To understand that there is a ritual

43

to the occasion, as there should be during all times of significance. Note the order of things, the significance of the procedures, the reasons for their existence. Watch, Celia. Watch, and learn well.'

Chapter 3

The two friends walked along the Whitechapel Road, the broad, bustling thoroughfare which linked the entry to the City of London to the routes out to the farming villages of the Essex marshes. They were arm-in-arm as always but, unusually, they weren't speaking. They didn't even share a giggle over the two wild-haired, drunken women fist-fighting over the ownership of a particularly timid-looking little man standing reluctantly next to the brawling pair. The girls didn't even chat or speculate about the day's events in the secret world of the rookeries: the maze of alleyways, courts and narrow, airless streets which was their home; the shadowy world, unknown to strangers, which lay immediately behind the façade of the main highway.

In contrast to the dark, infamous area which lay just beyond, the Whitechapel Road itself was a lively kaleidoscope of sights, sounds and smells which, even at such a late hour – gone midnight, when most respectable Londoners would be safely tucked up in bed – was illuminated by pools of light coming from the fizzing naphtha-lamps that blazed on the street-vendors' stalls, and the warm gaslight radiating from pub doorways and over the archways leading to the uncharted depths of the rookeries. The pavement was alive with people, not only cockneys from the surrounding tenements and slums, but foreigners from off the ships which stood almost empty in the docks beyond.

Food smells permeated everything, masking even the usual stench of the streets. The air was heavy with them: from the sweet, sickly thickness of sugar boiling into toffee in the big copper bowls balanced over fiery braziers, ready to be slapped on to marble slabs to cool and be cut into huge, jaw-aching pieces; to the savoury tang of chilli vinegar lined up next to the salt and pepper pots on the pie-and-eel stalls, there for customers to pour in great, brown pools over their meat pies, stewed eels, mash and liquor that the vendor piled high into cracked china bowls.

The noises were more difficult to separate: street musicians with tin whistles, drums and hurdy-gurdies vied with the screams of laughter, squabbles and shouts from passers-by; horses' hooves, wagon and cart wheels scraping over the cobbles on the uneven, filthy road competed with the endless drone of some unseen machinery in one of the tall, blank-walled buildings which lined the side-streets off the Whitechapel Road. But still Ettie and her friend walked on without saying a word.

It was Maisie who finally broke the silence. 'We're not good enough for yer now, I suppose,' she said self-pityingly.

'Don't be so daft,' said Ettie, flashing Maisie a cautious glance to see if her friend looked serious, or if she was just in a sulk about losing her sailor.

'It ain't me what's being daft,' she said bluntly.

Ettie stopped stock-still in her tracks, jerking her friend to a halt. 'Listen, May, there's no need for us to fall out, is there?'

Maisie shrugged non-committally.

'Have you still got the hump about losing your boyfriend back there?'

'It's not me *boy* friend I'm worried about,' snapped May. 'It's me friend. You.'

'How long we known each other? Since when we was born, that's how long. I thought yer'd be only too pleased to see me making something of myself. And that hardly means losing a friend, now does it?'

Maisie didn't reply.

'You ain't jealous are yer, May?'

Maisie couldn't let that go. Her voice showed her disappointment in her friend; she could scarcely force the words out of her mouth. 'How could yer think that of me, Ett? I'm yer best mate, ain't I? I'm worried about yer, that's all.'

This time it was Ettie who could barely speak. 'I'm sorry, May,' was all she managed.

'This is daft,' said Maisie, trying to sound as though there was no tension between them. Her face brightened. 'Here look, over there, let's see what the future's got in store for yer, Ett.' May tried to drag her friend over to the Romany fortune-teller. Her booth had drawn a lively and mostly good-natured crowd with its tantalising promise to reveal all by the divination of her brightly coloured birds, who were ready to cast a person's fortune with a single peck at a tattered playing card.

'I know yer trying to make up with me, May, but no thanks,' said Ettie, shaking her head vigorously. 'I don't need no crooks telling me what's going to happen to me, thanks all the same. I know what me future is, and it ain't round here. And I can tell yer that without the help of any flaming parrots.' Ettie pulled her arm free of Maisie's and walked smartly away from the seer's stand.

'Ettie!' May chased her as far as the boxing booth where, for two shiny coppers, you could watch the Roaring Girl take on all comers of all sizes in bare-knuckle competition. 'For gawd's sake, slow down, will yer? If yer going off with that Professor bloke, yer don't know when yer might see me again. Let's just have a little look at the stalls for a bit, eh?'

'How about getting home? Myrtle'll kill yer,' said Ettie, walking back to May and linking arms with her again.

'In for a penny,' said Maisie grinning.

They walked along, idly contemplating the stalls and sideshows as though nothing had happened between them, as though the words of distrust, warning and reproach had never been spoken. They paused by a model of Newgate prison with its miniature scene of execution. Maisie made Ettie and the passers-by laugh with her impersonation of its tiny hanged man with the rope still round his snapped neck. Then they moved on and watched disbelievingly at the gulls offering themselves up to be tricked by the thimble-riggers as they foolishly tried to beat the con men at their own so-called game of chance. They were soon back to their old, easy way with each other, but as they looked longingly at a stall selling bright ribbons and pretty feather trims, the friction threatened to return.

'I'll be able to buy all of them one day, May, just yer wait and see if I don't,' Ettie said, running a length of silky, emerald-coloured trim between her fingers.

'That's more like what *you'll* be buying, yer mean,' said May pointing towards the totter's barrow, piled high with barely identifiable rags and tatters. 'Old clothes and cast-offs. That's our mark.'

'Leave off, May.'

'No, Ett, you leave off.' It wasn't like Maisie to sound so solemn. 'Look, yer don't really believe that this Protsky geezer's going to give yer a proper job or nothing, do yer, Ett?'

'I was right,' said Ettie sadly. 'You are jealous, May, ain't yer? But I don't blame yer. I've got a chance to get out and you ain't.' She paused. 'Would you rather I didn't go? That I stayed round here, with all this?'

May looked round her, trying to see the place for what it really was. What she saw was barefoot kids from the gutter selling bits of stolen junk for money to buy a crust; passing hansoms with their customers out slumming, looking to pick up one of the whores who stood on every corner, and drunks arguing and fighting their way along the road. In fact, what she saw was what she always saw: filth and poverty. 'Don't suppose it is much to lose, really, is it?' she said bleakly. 'But you remember Ettie Wilkins, you're a Whitechapel girl born and bred, no matter how much you try and forget it.'

The girls continued their walk in silence, swerving neatly out of the way as a small boy darted out from one of the alleys that lead off the main road. He had dived out after his toy: a football made from a bundle of rags and paper, tied tightly with bits of many-times-knotted string.

'Hurry up with that ball,' shouted his tiny companion, me mum'll be home from the pub soon, and I'll cop it if I ain't indoors looking after the young 'uns.'

'They might not have much, but there's a lot of good people round here, Ett,' said Maisie, trying to find something, anything, to say that could convince Ettie that Whitechapel had something worth staying for. She scooped up the makeshift ball and tossed it to the hollow-eyed child who grabbed it and ran off back to his game. 'Our Billy's a nice bloke. Yer know he is. And he's right stuck on you. Mum reckons he'll make a few shillings for himself one day,' she continued airily. 'You just see if he don't.'

Ettie didn't answer or even look at her friend, although she was actually listening to every word that Maisie Bury was saying. She bent forward, feigning interest in the ill-assorted mess of jumble on a handcart doubling as a market stall.

'He really does think a lot of you, yer know,' May went on, peering over Ettie's shoulder to see what odds and ends were so absorbing her friend. 'He's said as much to me and all. Ever so many times. And yer could do worse than our Billy. A lot worse.'

'I know, May, I know,' she replied, examining a pair of torn lace mitts. 'But I just don't want to wind up like me mum. Stuck in one poxy room, with a rusty, broken bedstead and a buggy, straw-filled mattress. And gawd knows how many kids hanging on me skirts. All having to kip on the floor till they die or disappear one day.' Ettie dropped the ragged gloves back on the heap she'd taken them from and, no longer pretending any interest in the heap of junk on the stall, she turned to face Maisie. 'And having to share one lavvy and a tap with all the rest of the court. Piss-pots under the bed, stinking the rooms out till they're emptied out of the window into the back yard. No firewood to burn cos someone else already had the idea to chop up the banisters before you could get to them. The whole place running alive with fleas, flies and rats. Never mind the drunks hanging round for what they might be able to get off the girls...'

'All right, Ett, all right. For gawd's sake.' Maisie held up her hands to stop her going on any more. 'I *do* know. We might have two rooms to ourselves, but I still live in the sodding courts, don't I?'

Ettie threw a sad, defeated look at her friend. 'Yeah, May, course yer do. And even that rat-hole of a court's better than winding up on the streets like a lot of them poor cows do.'

But Maisie wasn't content to leave it there. 'This Jacob Protsky,' she said carefully. 'Or whatever he calls himself. Yer reckon yer going to stay with him, but he ain't our type, Ett. Yer shouldn't be getting mixed up with the likes of him.'

They walked on, the uncomfortable, unaccustomed silence hanging over them once more. Even the allure of the street vendors couldn't lift their spirits. So it was with real gratitude that they were forced out of their embarrassment by the coarse cries of a particularly loud stall holder.

'Come on, girlies,' he hollered. 'Lovely saveloys, nice and hot. Look at the size of this one!' The ruddy-faced man waved the hot orangey-brown sausage suggestively at the two friends. 'Get yer laughing tackle round that, darling. Go on, treat yerselves!'

The smell was irresistible.

'No ta,' chirped Maisie, her lips tight. 'Everyone knows your grub's all full of sawdust.'

'Cheeky mare, there's nothing wrong with *my* savs. Here.' The stall holder cut a single tantalising mouthful of the piping hot sausage and held it out to her at arm's length, making sure that all the potential customers, who had gathered round to witness the hoped-for row, could see. 'You just try that. Sawdust, my Aunt Fanny!'

He'd fallen for it. Maisie snatched the tidbit from the end of his knife and popped it gleefully into her mouth. 'Bleed'n handsome,' she said, wiping a dribble of grease from her beaming chops. 'Got any more for us, mate?'

'Yer ain't got no money have yer, yer saucy cow?' The sudden realisation that he'd been had infuriated the man. If it hadn't been for the presence of possible customers in the laughing crowd, he would have given Maisie what-for, all right. As it was she was able to stroll casually on, much to the delight of the applauding lads who had witnessed her triumph.

'No matter what yer say, Ett,' said Maisie, pausing only to turn and give the saveloy seller a broad wink and to blow him a kiss, 'this is where we belong. This is our life here. And the court's our home.'

Ettie laughed sardonically, 'Aw yeah, lovely, I don't think. I mean, the whole neighbourhood is so wonderful, ain't it?'

They stepped over a steaming pile of horse muck which added to the overall stink of rotting vegetables and open drains.

'And that bloody stand-pipe ain't been running for ten days now. Why should we have to walk two streets away just to get a bucket of water to drink and wash ourselves in. Eh? Tell me that if yer can. Yer can't, can yer?'

'Well, how about yer job?' asked Maisie, somewhat unconvincingly.

'D'yer know what, May, I'd forgotten all about that. Fancy! How could I forget how much I look forward to scraping fur off them poxy skins day after day? And how I love getting the fluff down me throat and in me lungs so's I can hardly breathe by the time I goes to bed. And, do yer know something else? I'd forgotten how I'd looked forward to spending me old age in the chest hospital cos I can't breathe at all no more. And whatever will all them posh old tarts up West do when they can't get their bit of fur for their new cloaks and hats?'

'Yer don't have to be so bloody nasty, Ett.'

'I'm sorry, Maisie, I don't mean nothing, it's just I don't want to wind up like me mum. Or like them over there.'

Ettie nodded towards two women standing at the entrance to an especially fetid alley. It was difficult to judge their age under the roughly applied layers of powder and rouge: they could have been anything from fifteen to fifty. Their clothes were a strange series of layers made up of petticoats, bustles, skirts, blouses and jackets, topped off with what had once been brightly coloured adornments, but were now greasy feathers, holey shawls and tatty bonnets – all a sad imitation of their previous glory. In between calling out their raucous invitations to any man who passed by, the women sang and danced, laughed and joked as much as their drunken state allowed.

'At least they look like they're having a good time,' said May stubbornly.

'Don't be daft, May. Look at them. Look at them properly.'

'Yer getting a bit toffee-nosed, ain't yer, Ettie Wilkins? Most girls round here have been on the game at one time or another.' She paused, then added quickly, 'And, let's face it, you ain't exactly no lily-white virgin yerself, now are yer?'

'Yer know that ain't what I mean, Maisie. I'm in no position to judge no one. I just want something nice for once.'

Suitably chastened, Maisie tried another approach. 'Yer do know he's a Jew, don't yer, Ett?' she said, glancing at Ettie to catch her reaction. 'That Lou at the gaff, she told me.'

'So?'

'So, haven't you heard all them things they say about them?'

'Like what?'

'Yer know.'

'No, you tell me.'

'Yer just being awkward, Ett, like yer always are when yer ain't getting yer own way.'

Pained, Maisie sniffed and looked away. She was clearly hurt, and Ettie knew why: her best friend was leaving because she couldn't stand living in Tyvern Court any more, so what did it say about Maisie that she was content to stay? But Ettie really didn't want to fall out with her. 'So, what's your Alfie doing with himself?' she asked, changing the subject to the ever-fruitful topic of the goings-on of Maisie's eldest brother. 'I ain't seen him around for a couple of days.'

'He's been lying low. Frightened he'll get done by the coppers again,' said Maisie, sighing loudly.

'What's he done this time?'

'Drunk in charge of his bleed'n donkey barrow, if yer don't mind.'

Ettie let out a splutter of laughter. 'Do what?'

Maisie warmed to her role of story-teller. 'He was driving down to Sclater Street – meant to be delivering a load of songbirds to one of the dealers, see. And he hit a stone or something. The cart went over and all the bleeding birds got out. Well, the donkey took off towards Shoreditch dragging the barrow behind. Right turn out by the sound of it. Anyway, Alfie catches hold of the donkey, grabs it round the neck and kind of wrestles it to the ground. All the fellahs in the market was cheye-eyeking him and taking the right piss. That was too much for him – well, yer know what he's like – went bonkers, he did, and wound up hitting three blokes for laughing at him. By the time the rozzers got there he'd had it away on his toes. The donkey walked home to the yard by itself.'

The two girls burst into uncontrollable fits of laughter at the idea of Maisie's always dapper, yet quick-tempered brother being unable to control the little brown donkey.

'I blame our red hair, Ett. It'd be different if we had dark hair like yours,' said May, trying to recover from her giggles.

'Yer'll have to get yerselves some wigs.' Ettie spluttered the words as she imagined the pale and freckled Bury family resplendent with thick, deep brown hair.

But Ettie's laughter stopped dead as she spotted a big, burly man with steel-grey cropped hair coming round the corner. She wasn't sure if it was him at first, but then he moved into the bluish light cast by a lamp on one of the fruit stalls, and she knew immediately.

'May,' she whispered, 'it's him.'

'Who?'

Ettie grabbed Maisie and pulled her back into the shadows. 'Ssshhh! Keep yer voice down. It's him, me mum's latest.'

'Aw yeah, ugly bastard. Just look at him.'

They watched as the man disappeared into the darkness.

'Come on, May, I want to get home and see my mum while he's out.'

'Mum. Mum.' Ettie shook her mother by the shoulder, but it was no good, she couldn't rouse her. She knew from experience that when she was like this she wouldn't come round for hours.

She peered through the grimy broken windowpane down into Tyvern Court below. There was no sign of him coming back yet. She'd wait for a while longer, she decided. She didn't like the idea of going without seeing her mum. If he came back she could always slip out the back way, into the yard and over the fence, before he even knew she'd been there.

It had been such a very long day. Ettie settled herself down on her bed – a damp, squashed mattress on the floor under the window – and waited. From her ragged place on the bare boards, she could make out the bare dimensions of the filthy room: the narrow cot on which her mother sprawled, the rough, lop-sided wooden table with the quarter loaf of stale, fly-blown bread, the one chair with its rickety legs and, almost as visible, the stink of the piss-pot, the cloying heat and the dirt, the sounds of rowing and fighting from the warren of slums surrounding her, and over it all her mother's snores, swirling, all of them, into one blur of hideous torment.

'Aw no!' Ettie's hand flew to her mouth in horror. It was the sound she dreaded: the heavy hob-nailed boots smashing into the splintered wooden steps which led up to the tiny, cramped hole that was their home.

She couldn't believe it, she must have dropped off to sleep.

She screwed her body into the smallest possible shape, pushing herself tight against the wall. As though that could save her.

At least she'd put out the lamp to save her mum's oil, she told herself. Maybe he wouldn't see her in the dark…

The door crashed back on its single rusted hinge, and hung almost comically at a crazy, drunken angle from the frame.

'Can't yer come in a bit quieter, yer bleed'n nuisance?' echoed from somewhere deep outside in the courts. 'Some of us is sleeping, yer know.'

'Or sodding trying to,' shouted someone else.

The man didn't answer, he didn't care about anyone. He bent forward, took hold of Ettie by her shoulder and dragged her up from the floor. He said nothing. The stench of the slaughterman was all about him: a sickening mix of blood and excrement, the nightmare reminder of the terrified creatures whose throats he slit for his living. The feel of his calloused hands against her made Ettie's skin crawl; the taste of his sour, putrid breath as he forced his tongue into her mouth was more than she could bear.

—

'Hello, May, what you doing sitting out here this time of night? It must be nearly one o'clock. Bugs got too much for yer indoors?'

'Alfie!' At the sound of her brother's voice, Maisie jumped up from where she'd been sitting on the street-door step. 'I'm glad yer back home, I could do with some company. I nearly dozed off, and I promised Bill I'd keep watch for...' But before she could finish explaining who or what she was waiting for, Maisie barged past her brother and began hissing in a loud whisper to someone else. 'And where do yer think you're going?' she demanded. 'I thought yer was at least staying the night.'

Alfie turned round to see who Maisie was having a go at. 'Hello, Ett,' he said, confused. 'What's the matter?'

'I've had enough. I'm off,' sobbed Ettie, shaking Maisie's hand from her arm.

'What's going on?' said Alfie.

'Ettie's going off with some Professor bloke,' said May, as though that accounted for everything.

'Blimey, I've only been away for a couple of days and yer've all took leave of yer senses,' said Alfie, taking off his cheese-cutter cap and scratching his head. 'And what's our Billy got to say about all this?'

'Leave me alone, the pair of you,' gasped Ettie through her tears and ran off sobbing towards the arch that was the way out of

Tyvern Court. 'Never again, May,' she wailed over her shoulder. 'He ain't getting another chance to touch me.'

'Shit!' exclaimed Maisie. 'That bastard must have slipped by me. I've sat out here all this time keeping a look-out and I never even saw him. That's *you* talking to me, putting me off,' she accused Alf. 'Billy ain't going to be very happy, I can tell yer that.'

'Yer going to have to explain, May,' said Alf.

'I told Billy I'd keep a watch out in the court while he went to bed. He's got to get up for work, ain't he?'

'Keep a watch out for *who*?'

'I ain't got time,' said his sister. 'I'll tell yer later.' With that she lifted her skirts and ran off after her friend, but Ettie already had quite a lead on her and May wasn't nearly as lithe as she was. Soon May was panting and puffing like a steam engine, and hugging her aching sides from the effort of it all. She stood and tried to get her breath back, yelling between gasps, 'Wait a mo, Ett, hold on.'

Ettie stopped at the corner and stood in the pool of yellow fight shining from the single street-lamp, her face drained of colour.

'This is it, May,' she called. 'I ain't putting up with it no more. I'm changing me life. I mean it. I'm going on the stage. With Jacob Protsky.'

'But, Ett...'

'I'll see yer later,' she said, and ran off into the night.

Maisie turned and walked slowly back towards Tyvern Court, wondering what on earth she was going to say to Billy.

Chapter 4

No matter how bad it was being forced to help with her father's revolting dissections and experiments, what he did to her afterwards was always worse. Much worse. Sometimes he wouldn't even wait until they were out of that terrible place.

Those times he would moan, 'Save me from the whores, Celia,' as he forced her down on to the hard, unyielding floor of the operating theatre, pleading, 'Don't let me be infected by them,' as he unbuttoned himself. Then, 'Save me with your purity, Celia. Save me.'

The stench of blood and putrefying flesh mingled in her nostrils with the stench of his sweat, his disgusting moans filling her ears – she couldn't escape the sound or the stink of him, the weight of him upon her.

When he had finished with her he would act as though nothing had happened. Some days she almost doubted herself that anything had happened between them, doubted, in fact, her very sanity. But then he would do it all over again. And again.

If she didn't feel so disgusted and dirty she would have prayed for help, but how could she speak those words, even in silent prayer? And to whom, if not God, could she turn? All she could hope for was that he would do it quickly, that he would not hurt her too badly, and that Smithson would not be outside, pressed against the door, hoping to hear her groans of pain and anguish.

Her fear of her father had driven her to become guileful over the years. As she grew older she had become increasingly adept at knowing the moment when she could slip away from the operating theatre at the top of the house and, with a little luck, he might ignore her and choose instead to go to his club with his friends for an evening's drinking and gambling. And, if Piquet or Faro didn't tempt him, and he had decided to stay at home for the evening after all, then occasionally she would dare to stir a little something from his laboratory shelves into his whisky. She couldn't do it too often or he would suspect, but when she did, it was bliss: a whole evening of peace, time to herself without fear.

The whole household knew about it – what he did to her – of course. Servants had a way of knowing everything that went on, but they never attempted to help her. They were too scared of losing their positions with such a fine gentleman. And, as she no longer had a mother, she had to help herself. So she had done her best to make a haven for herself, a little world of her own, a place where she could escape. On those evenings when she dared use a sleeping draught on her father she would wait and then, as soon as he was safely asleep, she would slip away to his library and read. She read anything which could help her make believe that her world was not the sickening place she really knew it to be, anything that could help her deny the vile reality of her life. Books had thus become her one comfort in that hideous place that was her home, the place which should have been her real sanctuary. Those nights when she could sit alone, undisturbed, and read, were almost the only moments of her young life to which she looked forward. And tonight was just such a night.

There he was, slumped like a street drunk in his armchair, his head lolling, his drugged breath coming rasping and sour from his mouth. If only the usually immaculate Bartholomew Tressing could see himself, he would be as revolted as she was by the sight of him.

Celia stood up carefully from her seat opposite his, waiting to see if he would stir. When he did not, she moved quietly from the room, first ensuring that Smithson was not lurking in the hall, and then closed the door painstakingly slowly behind her. Then she made her way as silently across the hall towards the library as her swishing silk skirts allowed.

Once in the refuge of the library, her well-practised routine continued. She would take the work of fiction from the shelf beside the novel she had most recently finished reading, then settle into an armchair by the fireside, close to the lamp she had set on the small side-table to illuminate her reading, and lose herself in the world of the printed page. This made for some strangely eclectic reading, but it was what she preferred to do.

Before developing this habit she had been far more selective, and had deliberately chosen her reading matter, favouring the literature from the particular anti-vice league of which her father was such a well-publicised and eminent member. In reading the society's material she had found a way to help her picture the lives of the women who eventually found their way to her father's dissecting room. She also found a strange comfort, or at least some measure of reassurance, in the content of its pamphlets and journals: seeing the descriptions of the conditions in which the women and girls of the slums were forced to live made her feel guilty and rather ashamed about her own discontent. It made her own situation seem insignificant in comparison, she had reasoned to herself.

But even that pathetic crumb of comfort had been spoiled for her when she had read one particular article by the Reverend W. Arthur in an old copy of *The Sentinel*. In it, the author had stressed that 'In all countries the purity of the family must be the surest strength of a nation.' What could she make of such ideas, when she lived an existence of such base horrors with her father? How could a family such as hers be of any value to the nation? But, as always, she had found a way to compromise her own thoughts, a way to carry on. She did so by deciding that the Reverend Arthur must, of course, know far more than she, and that she must learn to accept her lot. But really it was too enormous for her to continue contemplating – it was all so confusing. So she chose instead to ignore the league's tracts and had begun her systematic working along the shelves which held the novels her mother had so lovingly collected. There was nothing to harm her in those. Or so she thought.

Tonight, Celia entered the book-lined room and stood there in the doorway savouring the isolation, breathing in the fragrance of the leather-covered tomes.

She was currently engrossed in the line of books on the topmost shelves – the works of Sir Walter Scott, whose romantic adventures were becoming a favourite of hers. She pushed the library steps along, letting them glide into place, and then climbed up to reach the volume she wanted. Reaching for the green leather-bound copy of *The Antiquary*, she smiled with anticipation at the thought of becoming immersed once more in its noble portrayal of simple labouring people. But, as she climbed down, some sheets of paper fluttered from between the gold-edged leaves down on to the polished wooden floor below. Celia stepped down, held her skirts to one side, and stooped to retrieve the papers from under the library table where they had settled.

She had to lie on the floor and reach out full stretch to collect the last elusive sheet. Satisfied that she had found them all, she brushed down her skirt and then spread the papers out on the table to inspect the mystery.

Celia let out an almost inaudible whimper of distress. There in front of her, in full, hand-painted colour, were pictorial depictions of those things her father whispered to her when he forced himself upon her.

She grabbed the depraved things – those appalling illustrations of her nightmares – from the table and rushed to the fire. She would destroy them, burn them until nothing but cinders were left. She raised her arm, ready to consign them to the flames. But something made her stop. What would her father do to her if he could not find them? What new punishment might he inflict upon her?

Coldly, she stacked the papers into a neat pile and reinserted them between the now defiled pages of the novel. How could such things exist in her beloved library? Her haven was no more.

She climbed the library steps and replaced the book alongside its companions. She would never take it down again, she determined, but what could take its place? Would anything ever be able to help her escape from the nightmare that was her existence here in this house with her father? And how could she cope with the hypocrisy which allowed such depictions of degradation to exist alongside his pamphlets from the anti-vice society? Her mind swirled with confusion. Somehow, being there on paper, in front her, made those things that he did to her take on a reality that she had always tried to deny, that she had tried to separate from the normal world of young ladies of her age and class: the world of taking tea, choosing dresses, and meeting friends and beaux. In seeing those depictions she now knew that it was the so-called normality of the sun-filled daytime world that was, for her, the lie.

Celia stood quite still, deep in thought, her only movement the rhythmic rising and falling of her chest as she took rapid, shallow breaths. She remained like that for some minutes. Then, quite suddenly, she walked purposefully towards the place where the pamphlets were kept and ran her fingers along the shelves. She knew exactly what she wanted to find, and what she would do once she had found it.

Chapter 5

'I'm going to tell Billy before he finds out for himself,' said May, standing up from the stone step with a decisive gesture which belied the butterflies racing around in her stomach. 'Might as well get it over with, eh?'

She raised her eyebrows to signal that she wanted at least her brother's support, if not his approval for the foolhardy action she was about to make, but Alfie didn't answer. What with Maisie's garbled account of the night's events and how tired he felt, he wasn't really sure what was going on, and the last thing he fancied was a fight with Billy. So he thought it best to just let her get on with it. His only contribution was to edge along the step out of her way so she could get past him and into the passage.

Maisie went into the dark hallway and climbed warily up the bare, creaking wooden stairs. She crept past the half-open door of the room which doubled as the living room and her and her mother's bedroom and gingerly turned the doorknob of the room in which her three brothers shared a bed. She poked her head inside and saw Tommy sprawled out across Billy, the single grey blanket in a screwed-up knot round their feet. Their breathing had the even sound of deep sleep but, with the paper-thin walls, she wasn't taking any chances of waking Myrtle or any other occupant of the two-storey tenement. She touched Billy gently on the shoulder, making him moan irritably and flick at her as though she were just another bug out for a feed on his blood. The sound disturbed Tommy – that was all she needed, her little brother shouting the odds.

'Ssshh, it's all right, Tom,' she whispered. 'You go back to sleep, it's only me.'

Tommy rolled over, pulling the blanket with him and buried his head deep into the coverless bolster which served as the three brothers' only pillow.

'Billy,' she hissed, her lips almost touching his ear. 'Wake up. It's me, May.'

'Whad'yer want?' he mumbled, failing in his sleepy attempt to get any of the blanket back from his snoring, open-mouthed little brother. 'Leave me alone, can't yer?'

'Bill,' Maisie insisted. 'Will you wake up?'

With a loud exhalation of breath, Billy dragged himself to wakefulness. Rubbing his eyes he propped himself up on his elbow. 'What's up,' he said softly, glancing down at Tommy as he stirred luxuriously in the lion's share of the bed.

'I've got some bad news, Bill,' Maisie said sheepishly.

Now she had all Billy's attention: 'Aw yeah?'

'It's Ettie, she's...'

Before she had a chance to finish, Billy was sitting up and had her arm firmly in his grasp. 'What's happened to her?' he demanded to know.

'Nothing,' May said, not very convincingly. 'It's just that, well...' She paused, looking for the right way to tell him. 'It's just that Sarah's lodger's upset her again, and she's...' Maisie bit her lip, not knowing how to put it. Finally she said bluntly, 'Well, yer see, she's gone.'

Billy was up out of bed and on his feet, not caring whether he woke up his little brother, the people across the landing, or even his mother Myrtle herself. Not needing or waiting for further explanation, he stepped into his trousers, had his braces over his shoulders, and was in the doorway before May could stop him.

'Bill, don't. Please. Don't go after him. He'll only hurt Sarah. He'll take it out on her.'

Billy turned and looked at his sister. 'Why don't you shut your mouth?' he spat under his breath. 'And keep yer interfering nose out of it.' Then he was gone down the stairs.

May looked down through the dingy glass of her brother's bedroom window into the court below and saw Billy pushing past Alf.

'What the bloody hell's going on now?' demanded her eldest brother as Billy shoved past him. 'Good bleed'n night and all, I don't think.'

Maisie thrust the sash window up until she could get her head out. 'Shut up, Alf,' she hissed, 'before yer wake the old lady up.'

'And what do yer think'll happen then?' asked a sarcastic voice from behind May. 'When the old lady wakes up?'

Maisie turned round to see her mother standing in the door-way. With the sleeves of her nightgown rolled up to expose her strong forearms, and her fists tucked into her waist, she looked more than ready for battle.

Maisie tried a smile, but there was no swaying Myrtle when she was in full flight.

'Right,' said Mrs Bury, elbowing Maisie out of the way and poking her head through the open window to see Alfie, her errant son, still sitting on the doorstep, a picture of innocence. 'Up here, you. Now. I'm fascinated to know who's gonna explain this little lot.'

–

Dawn still hadn't quite broken and Jacob had to lean forward to find the keyhole.

'When yer said yer'd put me up, yer never told me yer was living near Victoria Park,' said Ettie, impressed. 'I never thought I'd be staying in Bow.'

'Ssshh! You'll wake the neighbours,' hissed Jacob. Then, 'Damn!' as he dropped the key on to the steps.

'Yer'd think there'd be a light outside a nice place like this, wouldn't yer?' said Ettie, tilting back her head to take in the full splendour of the four-storey house.

'Ssshh!' he warned her again as he bent to retrieve the key. When he eventually managed to open the door he ushered Ettie inside. 'Wait here just a moment,' he whispered.

Ettie stood inside the doorway and listened to the muffled sound of his shoes as he walked away from her along the carpeted hallway.

'There.' With a fizzing and popping, he had lit the gas. He flicked the spent match into the grate that was set ready with paper, kindling and logs. 'You can see where you're going now, Ettie. Come in.' He closed the front door behind her and ushered her forward. 'Welcome to my home.'

Ettie walked warily along the corridor and into the high-ceilinged room and gazed around in wonder. The place was crammed with so many things, many of them casting fantastic shadows from the lamplight. It was all very orderly and neat, but everywhere her eyes rested there were books and strange objects, most of which she didn't recognise, let alone know what they were called. Most wonderful of all, the entire floor was covered in rugs.

'So how can yer afford to live here, then?' she asked, looking closely at a mysterious wooden carving standing on a cloth-draped table, then, even before he had the chance to answer, turning her attention to a tall jar fashioned from vivid blue glass.

'I only have the rooms on this floor,' he said with a regretful smile, 'not the whole house.'

'Rooms? Yer mean yer've got more than one? Just for you?'

'I have this one, which has to double as my dining and sitting room, a bedroom, and a kitchen, smallish but very convenient. Although Mrs Hawkins – a charming lady who comes in for a few hours a day to do for me – finds it rather cramped, I'm afraid.' Ettie's chin nearly touched her chest. 'What bank did yer rob?' she asked incredulously.

'I have a little money,' he said, shrugging dismissively. 'Enough for my immediate needs.'

'Blimey,' she said staring around her. Then she turned on her heel and frowned at him suspiciously. 'If yer've got all this, how comes yer working the penny gaffs then?'

'What's so wrong with penny gaffs?' he asked, sounding more curious than defensive.

'Well, they're common.'

'No, Ettie, not common. The gaffs are a world of dreams. Treasure houses of fantasy.'

'They're sodding flea-pits!' she countered.

'They are an escape from the daily grind of drudgery and poverty. A haven. A palace of pleasures for the poor. What is so wrong with that?' He smiled. 'And anyway, you go to them, Ettie.'

'Well, I ain't got no choice, have I?'

'In truth, Ettie, nor have I. For the time being, at least.' Ettie narrowed her eyes, trying to figure out this puzzling man she had put her trust in.

'I've not been in England for some time, so I need to build my reputation here. Gain recognition by preparing a new, exciting performance.'

'Where yer been then?'

'Oh,' he said, running his finger along one of the crammed bookshelves. 'I have been to many places, Ettie. Paris was my last stop.'

'You ain't English, are yer?'

'No,' he said. 'But I lived here once. For several years. I had a house; rather a nice house, in fact. Close to Hyde Park. Most of these things came from there. I left them in storage while I was on my travels.'

'Hyde Park?' Ettie was astounded. 'Yer lived up West? Look, I know Bow ain't as bad as Whitechapel – I don't reckon *nowhere's* as bad as Whitechapel – but whatever did yer come to the East End for? Blimey, I know if I had the chance I'd be bleed'n miles away.'

'Well, we will have to see what we can do, won't we?'

'Eh?'

His expression became intense as he walked towards her. 'Ettie,' he said, 'if you work hard you can do anything. *We* can do anything. Live anywhere we like.'

She held her breath. It was the closest he had been to her since they had entered his rooms.

He hesitated for just a moment then turned towards the grate. 'It may be nearly summer,' he said, his back to her, 'but the early morning air is still very brisk.' He bent down and put a match to light the fire. Then, using a pair of brass tongs from an ornate companion set, he added several large nuggets of coal to the blaze.

Ettie went and stood next to the kneeling man. 'Blimey,' she said, amazed yet again. 'Yer really using all that wood and coal just for one fire? Yer should have seen us last winter. That would have done us for days. No, a week.'

'I understand that for many Londoners it was a bad time.'

The kindling wood began to blaze and crackle, sending dancing shadows round the walls and ceiling of the lamplit room.

'Bad time?' she repeated, stretching out her hands to catch the first rays of heat. 'I should say so. Everyone was cold and hungry. Everyone. Well, everyone round our way was.'

'I read that there was rioting in some parts.'

'That was more up West, near where you used to live. Didn't have nothing to do with that round our way. All I know is that some bastard thieved the banisters out of our stairwell. We didn't even have them left to burn.' Ettie sat down on her haunches by the fire, appreciating the blaze. 'It wasn't so bad when me little brother was around,' she continued, screwing up her eyes in the bright gleam of the firelight. 'He used to nick wood off the barges for us, see. I can't do it, I'm too tall. They can spot me a mile off.'

Jacob moved away from the fire and sat down slightly behind her on one of the big, plump armchairs by the hearth. 'Where is he now?' he asked softly. 'Your little brother?'

Ettie stared into the flames and swallowed hard. 'I dunno,' she said quietly. Then, quite suddenly, she leapt to her feet and spun around to face him, her arms held wide. 'This place!' She couldn't keep the wonder from her voice. 'I ain't never been in nowhere so big and airy. The height of this ceiling...' She nodded towards the closed door at the far end of the room. 'What yer neighbours like then?'

'That room is mine,' said Jacob, without looking round.

'So yer weren't kidding then?' She waited, judging his reaction. 'Yer really have got more than one room?'

Jacob nodded.

'Just for yerself, eh?' Ettie shook her head, still unable to take it all in. She was now grinning fit to burst. She was captivated by it, all of it. She moved around the room again, peering at the wonderful things, like a bee flitting from one sweet-scented, pollen-laden bloom to the next.

'Yer a Jew, ain't yer?' she asked, holding up a small amber jewel, turning it around to catch the firelight.

'And what do you know of Jews, Ettie?' Jacob took a cigarette from an elegant silver box which stood on one of the carved side-tables dotted around the room. He offered the box to her. She shook her head.

'Not much,' she said casually, and raised herself on tiptoe to examine a phrenology skull standing high on a shelf.

Jacob rested his cigarette in the ashtray, stood up, lifted the object down and handed it to her. He sat down again, took up his cigarette and watched her as she examined the china model, turning it this way and that, tracing the painted lines with her finger.

'A Jew woman lived in our court once,' she said, weighing the model in her hand as though it were a cabbage she was being asked to price on a fruit and veg stall. 'Shared a room with one of the Irish families. The others in the court didn't like her, cos of the sweating, see? Not that *she* ever had a sweatshop. She didn't have much of nothing, like the rest of us down there. And anyway, whether they hated the sweaters or not they was always glad enough of the work when they could get it.' She bit her lip, deep in thought. 'But it's a tough way to earn a living. That's why they hate the people who run the sweatshops, see.' Her voice relaxed. 'Well, like I was saying, they thought she should've been with her own kind. So one night she's sitting on the front step sewing. Right clever at it she was. Did all these little lacy stitches. Right clever. And this gang, yer know, the bullies, comes round. One of them walked up to her and head-butted her. Just like that. Split her nose open like a mouth he did. All the blokes in the gang laughed themselves silly. Never saw her no more. Disappeared that night and that was that.'

She felt him staring hard at her. 'I've been going on, ain't I?' she said, embarrassed. 'Me mum's always on at me. "Yer a right little chatterbox you are, Ettie Wilkins." She's always saying that.'

Still he stared at her.

She frowned, and rubbed her face with her ragged sleeve, trying to erase the smuts and streaks of dirt which, she was all too aware, were probably to be found on her cheeks. 'My mush dirty, is it?'

He shook his head, then said. 'Well, a little.'

'So what's the matter, what yer looking at?'

'You, Ettie,' he replied simply. 'You are very lovely.'

'Me?' she laughed, a snorting little expulsion of air.

'Yes, you.'

'Yer barmy.'

Ettie handed the model back to Jacob, who replaced it on the shelf in exactly the spot from where he had taken it.

'Sit down, Ettie. Please.'

'No, the chairs are so nice and everything and me clothes are all… yer know.' She cast her eyes down at her patched and faded skirts. They were stiff with years of ingrained dirt and food, each mark showing its long history of owners. 'It's a smashing place yer've got here,' she said, trying to lighten the atmosphere and cover her feeling of humiliation.

'This,' he gestured dismissively around the room. 'This is nothing.' Jacob stubbed out his cigarette and went and stood at the fireplace with his back to her. His voice sounded oddly strained, distant somehow, when he spoke. 'I have been to places that you could hardly imagine, Ettie. I have seen and done things that most men only ever dream of.'

'Aw yeah?' Ettie was torn between giggling and being scared. 'Like what then?'

'Like...' he paused. 'Many things.' Then he turned and was looking directly at her. 'I have seen the Indian Rope Trick performed,' he said, his eyes shining at the memory. With his fine, long hands he described the images in the air. 'First a rope is uncoiled. Then,' he snapped his fingers. 'Presto! It is made rigid. It becomes a rod of iron.'

'Aw yeah. How do they do that then?' Ettie asked, cynically.

'This action is performed by an Indian man of magic – a fakir,' he explained.

'By a *what*?' she sniggered.

Jacob raised his eyebrows, ignoring her suggestive tone. 'A fakir,' he repeated. 'Then, a small boy clambers to the very top of the rope. Like this, hand over hand. And then,' he snapped his fingers again. 'Quite suddenly he is gone. The boy has completely vanished.'

'Blimey,' Ettie sounded rather more impressed than she had before. 'That's clever.'

'But that is not all. The fakir then takes a huge and sharp sword. A cutlass. Which he then passes back and forth in the air above where the boy was last seen. The child's pathetic cries pierce the eardrums of the awe-struck crowd.'

'I should think so. Poor little sod.' Ettie was now totally absorbed by the story.

'But,' Jacob continued. 'No severed limbs fall to the ground. No blood is seen.'

'No?'

'No. Then the fakir goes to a large basket he has left behind the crowd. He opens the lid. All eyes are on him. And then, out springs the boy, unharmed and ready for the next show.'

'Where d'yer see that then?' she said, one corner of her mouth lifted in an unsure smile. 'Not down the Whitechapel Road, I'll bet.'

'I was privileged to see that wondrous performance in the grand city of Bombay.' Seeing her puzzled expression, Jacob added. 'In India.'

'Aw yeah, right,' said Ettie, still completely in the dark.

'But I have seen equally marvellous things, Ettie, much nearer home. I have seen the Green Man dance in the deep forests of Europe. The followers of his cult, drunk with the fruits of the vine, prancing and carousing, following him through the trees into the secret woodland glades before they...'

She yawned, interrupting him. 'Gawd, I thought I could talk,' she said, stretching and scratching at the back of her now almost unpinned hair. 'But you win the bleed'n prize.' Her eyes had begun to droop – she was tired from standing for so long and the room was unfamiliarly warm.

Jacob smiled. 'I'm sorry, Ettie, you've had a long day. But there are so many things I want to tell you about all the wonders I have seen. And I have seen so very much.'

'Yer sure?' she asked, scratching her head uninhibitedly and trying to hold on to the protective cynicism she had learned in the slums. 'Sounds like yer was half cut to me. Chopping up little boys what come back to life. Honestly!'

'Some might say that what I saw was an illusion. Some might claim that all of us there experienced an hallucination. If so – what of it? Does that make any difference to what I felt when I stood there in that crowd of totally believing onlookers?'

Jacob's long words and his musings were confusing Ettie, and with the discomfort she already felt from standing in the heat, she was beginning to wonder why she had ever come here. Perhaps Billy and Maisie were right after all. What *did* she know about this man? He might even have escaped from somewhere, the way he was going on.

'Why did yer leave Paris then?' she asked as nonchalantly as she could manage. 'That's where yer said yer was, wasn't it? Paris?'

Jacob didn't answer her. He just stood there and stared, far away in the foreign land that was his memory.

'I said, why did yer leave Paris?' she repeated more loudly.

He looked startled, almost as though he were surprised to see that Ettie was in the room with him, but he quickly regathered his composure. 'Paris,' he said slowly, as though the word was an incantation. 'I thought it better to leave that city.'

When it was clear that he had no intention of explaining further, Ettie tried another question. 'Was yer on the stage there? Talking to the spirits like yer do now?'

Jacob's expression changed. He was suddenly animated again, enthusiastic as he'd been before. 'If you are to join me and become a famous medium, Ettie...'

'Me? Famous? A medium?' The growing suspicion that she really was in the same room as a madman was creeping over her like a fever.

'Why not? As I said, if you are prepared to work hard with me, Ettie, then you can achieve anything you want. And I mean anything. The future is ours for the taking. I promise you.'

'I don't really know about that, Jacob,' she said warily.

'I do, Ettie. I *know* what you can be.' A smile played over his lips and his gaze held her. 'You saw what happened back there at the gaff tonight. You have a gift, Ettie, the crowd loved you. You will be more than my assistant. You will be my partner. If you stay with me.'

'Partner?' She looked round the room with a sigh. It was the plushest place she had ever set foot in, but she had to be sensible: she noted that there were two ways out, two escape routes – the door and the window. 'You're kidding me, right? Yer said yer wanted an assistant. Now yer going on about me being a partner.'

With cool deliberation, Jacob said, 'Ettie, I am entirely serious.'

It was a full minute before Ettie replied. 'In for a penny, I suppose,' she said shrugging. Then she shook her head and added, in what she hoped was a light, humorous tone, 'But I still ain't sure that yer ain't half bonkers, if yer want to know the truth.'

Jacob laughed. 'You really are disarmingly honest,' he said.

Ettie shrugged again and tutted loudly. 'It's a right turn out, innit, all this? I feel like I'm dreaming.'

'You're not dreaming, Ettie.' He reached out, took her hand and startled her by shaking it firmly – just like the men in the market did when they struck a deal, except he didn't spit in his palm first. 'And this is business. Our business.' He looked her up and down. 'Now, our first job.'

'Yeah, what's that then?' she said as eagerly as her exhaustion allowed.

'A good night's sleep.'

'What a good idea,' she smiled, full of relief.

'But not like that. We need to clean you up.'

'Bloody cheek! I know me clothes are dirty, but I go down Goulston Street Baths regular,' she said haughtily. 'Tuppence warm, penny cold.'

'And how often do you bathe?'

'Like I said: regular.'

'How often?'

Sheepishly she studied the scuffed and peeling toe of her boot. 'When I can afford it.'

'Well?'

'Like I said, when I can afford it. Water and wood for laundry and baths is a luxury where I come from. Not like you with your gaslight and coal scuttles. We only ever have oil or candles and old bits of wood we can scavenge, down Whitechapel.'

Jacob ignored her sulky pout. 'Your teeth,' he said nodding towards her mouth. 'Let me see.'

'Here, leave off. What do yer think I am, a bleed'n horse?' She wriggled angrily as he took her face in his slender yet powerful hands.

'I'm surprised,' he said, peering into her mouth. 'Your teeth are very good. Especially for someone who's grimy, smelly, and has a head full of lice.'

'What?' she fumed.

'Never heard of tooth powder, I suppose?' he said, still addressing his attention to her wide, full mouth.

'Tooth powder?'

'And you could certainly do with fattening up a bit.' He stepped back and rubbed his chin reflectively. 'That hair of yours will be quite beautiful once it's seen a bit of soap and hot water. Now, get those things off.'

'Aw, I see yer game. Right.' She folded her arms defiantly. 'I should've known. I'm bloody stupid, me. Seventeen years old and I still don't know what's what.'

'Sorry?'

'No, I'm the one who's sorry, mate. Sorry I didn't use me loaf.'

'I don't understand you, Ettie.'

She glared at him furiously. 'Fell for it, didn't I? Yer no different from none of the others, are yer? Least they don't give yer no old flannel first, they just grab yer straight off.'

'Ettie…'

'This what yer want is it?' She grasped the front of her blouse and ripped it open, exposing her greying cotton underthings stretched taut over her breasts.

'Please.' Jacob took a step forward and reached out to her.

The slimy missile hit him in the face before he even realised she had spat at him.

'Yer'll have to carry on wanting, won't yer? Cos yer ain't having it.' She pulled her jacket round herself, covering her body the best she could. 'Now get out of me way before I kick yer in the balls. Yer dirty bastard.'

'Ettie. Please,' he said, wiping the saliva from his cheek. 'You misunderstand my intentions. I merely wanted you to take a bath.'

'Bath? What? In here?' She gestured wildly round the room. 'Where is it then, this bath? Under the table? Yer really do think I'm an idiot, don't yer?'

'No,' he said levelly. 'But I do actually have a small room with a bath and running water. Several of the larger houses in the street have them. That is why I took the lease. I'll show you.' This time it was he who gestured. He pointed towards the door. 'Just along the corridor. And, I assure you, Ettie, it has a lock on the inside.'

—

'You'll be sleeping in here.'

Ettie stood next to Jacob, in the doorway to the bedroom, her body and hair wrapped in big white towels. She felt wonderfully drowsy: not only tired now, but lulled by the absolute luxury of the hot scented bath. She hadn't known that such wonders as baths even existed – but she still had her wits about her.

'What, in the bed?' she wanted to know.

'Of course. You are my guest.'

'And where are you sleeping then?' she asked, suspiciously.

'Back in there. I can manage on the armchairs for now. We'll have to sort out something more permanent tomorrow.'

She sat down gingerly on the edge of the bed. 'Blimey! It's ever so soft.' She made a few experimental bounces on the deep feather mattress.

'You think so?'

'You ain't kidding I think so.' She tried bouncing a bit higher. 'The only bed I've ever had was on the floor with a blanket chucked over me.'

'Well, let's hope that this is the first of many pleasant new experiences for you, Ettie. Now, let's see.' He lifted the lid of a trunk which stood at the foot of the bed and began rummaging through its contents. He produced a lavender-ribbon-trimmed nightgown. 'Theatrical props,' he explained, when Ettie raised a questioning eyebrow. 'Now, if you can stop jigging around and stand up for me.'

Ettie stopped bouncing and did as he asked. She stood very still while he held the lawn nightgown up to her, judging the fit. It was much too short.

'That'll have to do until tomorrow, I'm afraid.'

'*Do?*' Ettie rubbed the soft material against her unusually clean cheek. 'It's beautiful.'

He smiled. 'Do you think you'll be able to find something in there to wear for a day or so?' he said, closing the lid of the trunk. 'Until we can organise some new things for you.'

Ettie clutched the nightgown to her as though it were a talisman. 'New things?' she asked incredulously.

'Of course. You'll need the right clothes if you are going to become a famous medium.'

'Aw. Right,' she said flatly, letting the nightgown drop on to the bed. She stared hard at her clean pink toes. The evidence was all pointing to the horribly clear conclusion that this man was not her saviour after all: he was, as she had suspected in the back of her mind, a raving lunatic.

'Good night, Ettie,' he said very formally, and turned to leave the room.

'Good night, Jacob,' she said as he closed the door behind him.

Jacob turned down the gaslight and settled himself by the fire with a rug over his knees. He stared into the glowing embers and soon he was lost deep in thought: recalling the past and making plans for the future. But his reverie was very soon disturbed.

The door from the bedroom opened.

He looked up.

It was Ettie standing in the doorway with the counterpane draped around her shoulders. 'I ain't never slept by myself before,' she said shyly. 'D'yer think I could sleep on one of the chairs in here with you?'

76

Chapter 6

Dawn would soon be breaking in the square outside, but Celia was still sitting in the deep-buttoned library chair, flicking through the pages of the pamphlets she had begun reading the night before: the literature from the anti-vice organisation of which her father was so publicly a member.

On her pretty, porcelain–doll–like face, there was an unusually determined expression. She had made her decision: seeing those terrible pictures had forced her to decide that she must act at last; she had to do something about the world which allowed such hypocrisy, cynicism and cruelty to exist. And if, to help change things, it meant reading the material which had so perturbed and confused her, then that is what she would do. She could think of no other guide available to her. And what if it did disturb her — it was not for her benefit, it was for others. She had a purpose, though she wasn't yet sure exactly how to go about her campaign. But she knew that she had to learn all she could to arm herself with the tools she needed. She was determined to begin her fight against evil and corruption. And no one, not even her father, would stop her. She took another pamphlet from the pile and began to read, but she was disappointed: all it contained was yet another call to close down the brothels and the invitation to join a midnight protest march. Celia tossed the pamphlet on to the pile of others she had read with a weary sigh. What good would closing down those places achieve? The pamphlets them-selves admitted that as soon as the women were moved from one establishment they simply moved to another, and the men rapidly followed. She was looking for guidance to help her find a way in which she could actually do something, make some contribution to the women's lives that would make them think differently and so avoid taking the path to corruption in the first place. All she had read so far were the usual well-meaning, but hardly earth-shattering, pleas and suggestions. What she was looking for was the merest hint, just a glimmer would do, of how she could make things change. Really change. And that would certainly involve more than taking part in midnight protest marches.

She rubbed her tired eyes and turned to the next pamphlet. This one was illustrated with yet more details of the women's lives and the sensational publications they were reviling. Her cheeks reddened, and she skipped over the more distressing sections.

Then, against all that she had expected, she found what she wanted. It was a closely printed leaflet of just six pages, but it made everything clear in the way she had sought. The author's view was that it was no good condemning and protesting. Action was called for of the most vigorous type to give the young women of the slums an example and inspiration for the life that they could be leading. She looked at the cover for the author's name. There it was, in thick black lettering: the Reverend Roland Stedgely. She remembered hearing the name before – yes, that was it. She had heard it from Sophia, the daughter of one of her father's colleagues at the hospital, one of the few friends he had allowed Celia to keep since her mother's death. It wouldn't do to cause talk amongst one's colleagues, he had agreed grudgingly, and so had tolerated their continued friendship.

Celia re-read the little booklet and its stirring depictions of Stedgely's missionary work amongst the young women of the slums, taking in its vivid portrayal of the crowded courts where the girls lived. Instead of the young women being written off as evil agents of corruption as the other authors had done, the Reverend Roland Stedgely wrote of them as unfortunates who, with the right help, could help themselves from falling into the depths of despair into which their mothers and older sisters had already plunged.

But, as she closed the cover of the little leaflet, as inspiring as it had been, Celia's resolve began to weaken. What could she really achieve when her own life was so imperfect? Tears began to fill her eyes as the thought of her father slumped in the drawing room armchair in his drug-induced stupor made her feel suddenly weak and so very tired. If she were truthful, what hope did she really have of ever finding the strength she would need to carry out such work? On many occasions lately she had wondered if she had enough strength even to complete another day's existence...

Celia picked up the leaflets from the library table. She would return them to the shelves and then perhaps she would turn instead to Miss Austen's *Emma*. It was a book she had read many times in the past, and one she knew had no hidden secrets slipped between its precious leaves. She almost smiled to herself. She would do well to learn the lessons of Emma – another meddling girl. And, who knows, she thought, perhaps her own story would have a similarly comforting ending. But she did not convince herself for even a moment that it might really be so.

As she reached up to replace the pamphlets, she noticed her father's spiky writing in the margins of a well-thumbed booklet which was tucked next to a pile of the more lurid leaflets which she hadn't bothered to take down from the shelf. Curiosity got the better of her and she began to read. First she examined the printed text.

The deformed wizened body of the new-born is a sure sign that the infant is a victim of this despicable condition – an undoubted indication that the infant has suffered for the sins of its parents – that the child is a victim of the so-called Syphilis of the Innocents. The disease as contracted by these guiltless souls is all the more heart-rending and despicable as it is the disease in its disastrous secondary stage when the nervous system is attacked. It is fortunate, therefore, that these tiny hostages to fortune can expect the shortest, though most painful, of existences.

Celia frowned at the abominable words. They held for her a horrid fascination. She was drawn to that word. It was printed there quite openly: 'syphilis'. Her father had said the word in her presence only once, when he had shouted it aloud in his anger. It had happened when the body delivered to him that night for dissection had been diseased with that dread thing yet again. He was angry about the condition of the corpse, complaining that the men had taken good money from him for inferior goods.

And then there was the awful description of the poor afflicted mite.

She turned the slim booklet round, tilting it on one side and holding it closer to the lamp, more easily to read the words which filled the margin, words written in her father's own hand. She bowed her head and a single teardrop plopped on to the paper, spreading out in a creeping, irregular, damp stain.

Her father's description of his son's, her baby brother's, death: the words linking his tiny, malformed body to the pitiable description of the printed words. She gulped hard, taking down great sobbing breaths as she thought of her mother dying so soon after the birth, even though she had been so well. Well, that is, until the baby had died. And then those whispers from the servants about poison, prussic acid. No. She would not believe it. She could not. Her mother with that vile disease, losing her tiny son to its ravages and then being driven to commit the dread sin of self-destruction. And leaving Celia alone with her father.

She felt hot, disordered, sickened. She covered her face with her hands, hiding herself from the appalling words in front of her. But she couldn't hide from the words in her head: her mother had passed syphilis on to the unborn child she was carrying. A disease that she could only have contracted in one way.

Never before had Celia hated her father more, and yet there was something else about the discovery, something that disturbed her in a different way. The terrible madness that came with the disease could, she realised, be the explanation for her father's vile behaviour towards her. She remembered a time when he had been a good and gentle man, caring for her and her mother; the times he would sit in his big armchair by the fire, holding her on his knee and singing to her in his deep, comforting voice while her mother accompanied him on the piano. Her tears ran down her cheeks as she wept for the loss of the father she had almost forgotten.

But she cried too for herself, for she knew that she also might one day show the symptoms of the unspeakable disease that caused its victims to degenerate into madness. She resolved that she would work fast, find the strength no matter how weak she felt, to do some good in the world, lest its dreaded onset prevented her. The strength would come from her love for her dear, dead mother, for the brother she had never known, and for the precious father she now remembered.

At the sound of the library door opening she jumped as though she had been scalded.

She turned to see the butler standing there in his nightshirt, his hair dishevelled from sleep.

'Oh. Oh, it's you, Smithson,' she said, swiftly concealing the pamphlet in the folds of her skirts and keeping her chin down to hide her tears.

'It's your father,' said the butler, not even bothering to conceal the leer which curled around his thin, bloodless lips. 'He's woken from his rest and wants to...' he hesitated, tilting his ugly head to one side, considering the next word. 'He wants to *see* you,' he eventually said.

'Have you no idea of the time, Smithson? It is nearly daybreak. Tell him I cannot,' she said recklessly. 'Say I am in bed. Asleep.'

'Don't be silly, Miss Celia,' he said, and opened the door wider for her.

A moment later, Celia was standing nervously by her father's side as Bartholomew Tressing sipped at his glass of brandy. She usually knew better than to speak before she was spoken to, but she couldn't help herself.

'Father,' she said, her pale lips quivering. 'How exactly did Mother die?'

His hand was slim and manicured but it stung her cheek as harshly as any labourer's calloused flesh could have done.

When he eventually allowed his daughter to go to her room, the sun was shining brightly in the clear spring sky over the square below. Celia washed her tears from her face at the washstand, then sat at the pretty inlaid writing table which had stood at her window since her eighth birthday – it had been her last gift from her mother.

She took out pen and paper and began to compose a letter. It took several attempts before she succeeded in hiding the new horrors which haunted her from showing themselves in her words.

Dear Sophia,

I trust you are well. Yes, I know I have promised to write more often, though I have been remiss. There, I confess. You have a lazy, but loving friend. Not really lazy perhaps but, more honestly, rather preoccupied of late.

I think that my request, however, will make you happier with me, and inclined to forgive my laxity in letter-writing.

I should like to come with you to one of the Reverend Roland Stedgely's League meetings to which you are always inviting me, as I have become very interested of late in the work done by the League. I trust that you are pleased that your request is, at last, granted.

Celia lifted her pen and tapped the end to her lips. How to not make Sophia, so impulsive a girl, ask all sorts of difficult questions? She loaded her nib with ink and continued.

I will come with you, Sophia, but I want you to be clear that my attendance at the meeting is only because I am inquisitive to discover more about them. I do not intend to join the League, as I know that if I do so you will soon become bored, as you have with all your other enthusiasms, and then I shall be left to attend the meetings on my own.

I await your reply with great anticipation. Remember, please, not to make any reference to the meeting in your letter. Father would not approve of my going to places where gentlemen might be present. Instead, suggest we meet for afternoon tea with your governess or something. I know how resourceful you can be, my artful friend.

With fondest regards, from your dear friend, Celia.

Chapter 7

'Here you are, Maise, drink that.' Alfie pushed his way through the busy lunchtime crush of drinkers in the Frying Pan and slid the thick, stumpy glass of gin across the beer-stained marble table towards his sister.

'Ta, Alf,' she said, and drained the glass in one shuddering gulp.

'Gawd blimey, sis, I'd rather keep you for a week than a fortnight. I brought yer out to cheer yer up, not to see how fast yer could pour all me money down yer throat.'

'Sorry, Alf,' said May, wiping her mouth with the frayed cuff of her blouse. 'But I feel right fed up.'

'Yer don't need to tell me, yer've been right humpy.'

Maisie looked round the bar full of laughing, joking people. She swallowed hard before she spoke. 'She ain't even bothered to come back and see me, Alf.'

'So that's it. Ettie Wilkins.' Alf chucked his sister affectionately under the chin. 'Yer can't blame her really, now can yer, May? Wouldn't you get out of here if you had the chance?'

'It's not that.' Alf's affection towards her made it even more difficult for her to hold back the tears that had been threatening to start all morning. 'I'm pleased for her – honest – but... Aw, I don't know. I'm worried for her that's all. She's been gone a whole week now. And as for that Professor Protsky or whatever he calls himself. You never saw him, did yer?' Maisie blew her nose noisily into the grey cotton rag that served as her handkerchief. 'He was a right strange type of geezer. And she didn't know nothing about him, Alf. Nothing. Anything could have happened to her.'

'She'll be all right,' said Alfie, putting his arm round his sister's, broad shoulders. 'And it ain't as though she's miles away is it? She's only down Bow way somewhere.'

'Yeah, according to Jimmy Tanner,' said May, sniffing loudly. 'And yer know what a Tom Pepper he is.' May shook her head sadly. 'And say she really is in Bow. Don't that makes it worse? She could easy have popped round to see me, to let me know how she was. We've always been like sisters, me and her; now it's like she never even knew me.'

Alfie stood up. 'Let's get in another round.' He held up his hand to stop her speaking. 'No. Don't argue. I've got a few bob this week. Let me treat yer.'

At the sound of those magic words, two shabby but gaudily dressed women had shoved their way from the bar and were standing either side of Alfie before he'd even had the chance to move.

'Hello, Alfie, darling,' said one of them, wiping an ingrained finger down his cheek. 'I ain't seen yer for ages, sweetheart.'

'No, not since the last time yer tried scrounging a drink, Flo,' he said, pushing his hands deep into his trouser pockets and rocking back on his heels.

'Did you hear that, Ada?' said Florrie, wide-eyed with offence. 'I can't believe a chap'd talk like that to a neighbour.'

'Come on, girls,' said Alfie, smiling despite himself. 'You can do a better job of cheering our Maisie up than me. Come and sit down and make her laugh and I'll treat the pair of yers to a drop of Satin.'

'Good luck to yer, darling,' said Ada, getting her feet safely under the table. 'Now tell us, May, what's up with yer, me little love?'

Before Maisie could even begin to explain her unhappiness to the two women, Ada was back on her feet waving extravagantly to a man who had just come in the door. 'Over here!' she yelled above the noise. 'Come on. Come and sit with us.'

Maisie looked round to see who was being invited to join them. 'Bill?' She could hardly believe her eyes. 'What you doing here?'

'Aw,' said Florrie, beaming benevolently. 'It's like a family reunion, ain't it? It's nice the way you Burys stick together.'

Billy pulled out the chair next to May and sat down without saying a word.

'Yer never come for a drink of a dinner-time, Bill,' said May, frowning. 'Does your governor know yer here?'

'Yer gonna shut up going on, May,' said Billy bleakly, pushing back his chair. 'Or shall I go down the Alma instead?'

Maisie didn't have the opportunity to answer.

'No, Bill, don't do that,' said Ada. Knowing there'd be more chance of another drink with the table full, she wanted to keep the party going. 'You stay here with us, darling.' She stood up and hollered across the bar. 'Alfie! Alf!' When she'd got his attention she nodded and pointed towards the table. 'Your Billy's here. Get a pint in for him.' She sat down, smiling happily. 'There,' she said. 'That's just the job, ain't it?'

Maisie took her brother's face gently in her big, wide-palmed hands. 'Bill,' she said softly. 'I ain't having a go at yer or nothing, I'm just worried, that's all. Now, what yer doing here?'

Billy brushed his sister's hands away.

Maisie didn't look at Billy as she spoke, she picked at a splinter on the edge of the table. 'It's Ettie, right?'

'I can't get her off me mind, May. I know it's stupid but I just thought she might be here with you.'

'I ain't seen her, Bill.'

Billy raked his fingers through his hair. 'She's never gonna love me, is she? I don't stand no chance.'

'What did he say?' said Florrie, craning her neck to hear.

'Mind yer own,' snapped Maisie at her, then turned back to her brother. 'She's not the only girl, Bill,' she whispered to him.

'She is for me, May.' His voice cracked as he said the words.

86

At the sight of her brother's pain, Maisie could hardly stop her own voice from quavering. 'This ain't like you, Bill,' she said, trying to jolly him along. 'I thought you was tough as old boots.'

'Not where Ett's concerned I'm not, May.'

For nearly an hour the drinks flowed, but the conversation was far from smooth. Florrie and Ada, concerned that the drinks might stop, did their best to keep it going, but after a while neither Alfie nor May wanted to hear yet another tale about the men they'd picked up, nor what they'd been expected to do with them, and Billy wasn't even listening.

'So,' said Florrie, after a lull when they'd all stared morosely into their empty glasses. 'What yer all doing in here of a dinner-time, then?'

Alfie sighed. 'I told yer earlier,' he said impatiently. 'I brought Maisie in to cheer her up. And you two was meant to be helping. Fat lot of good yer've done.'

'No, yer don't look that cheerful, come to think of it, May,' slurred Florrie, stating what was actually patently obvious for everyone to see. 'And Billy looks like he's lost a shilling and found ha'penny and all.'

'I know!' exclaimed Ada, rising unsteadily to her feet and knocking her chair over in a mixture of drunken clumsiness and enthusiasm for the idea she'd just had. 'I'll give yer all a song.'

'Sod me,' mumbled Billy into his chest. 'That's all I flaming want.'

'Patrick. Patrick.' Ada stumbled over to the bar, leant across the counter and began poking the unfortunate landlord in the chest. 'Get on that piano, go on. Let's liven this place up a bit.'

'That's it, I'm off. I'm getting back to work.' Billy took a handful of coppers from his pocket and slapped them down on the table in front of May. 'Have the next round on me,' he said, and was through the door and on his way back to Shoreditch before anyone even had the chance to say goodbye, let alone start singing.

As the first ill-tuned notes of the piano fought against the cracked tones of Ada's teeth-grinding vibrato, Florrie leaned across the table and said to Alf: 'Your Billy'll be upset over Ettie Wilkins. Her buggering off with that strange bloke. Living with him down Bow way, they reckon.'

May's lip began to quiver, but her tears were stilled when her attention was caught by the entrance into the pub of her little brother, Tommy. She sat still until he was in grabbing distance, then made a lunge for his ear. She was right on target.

'Ouch!' he moaned, wriggling vainly to escape her clutches. 'Let go!'

'I'll give yer let go,' said May, giving his ear an extra tweak for luck. 'Now, we're all fascinated to know, what the hell do yer think yer doing in here?'

Alf rolled his eyes and Florrie grinned, pleased with this diversion.

'Are you going to answer me or what?' hissed May through her teeth.

'I ain't doing nothing. Now let go,' complained Tommy; He looked pleadingly at his brother. 'Tell her, Alf.'

'So what are yer doing?' asked Alf. 'What are yer up to this time?' He sounded as bored as he looked at the prospect of yet another family ruck brought on by the antics of the youngest of the Bury clan.

'I'm just getting old Maggie Philpotts her jug of mild,' squealed Tommy, waving the china jug to verify his story. 'She give me ha'penny to fetch it.'

'See, May, he don't mean no harm. Let the kid go,' said Alf.

'You're only sticking up for him cos he's as bad as you was at that age,' butted in Florrie with a happy nod.

May leant across Tommy to get closer to the interfering Florrie and said in soft, menacing tones: 'And you can keep your two-bob's worth to yerself and all.'

Florrie rearranged her ragged shawl pertly round her shoulders. 'Charming, I don't think,' she said, all tight-lipped indignation.

Dragging back as far away from his captor as she would allow, fanning his hand back and forth across his face, Tommy spoilt

May's moment of authority: 'Cor blimey,' he grimaced, 'you stink of gin, May. And I bet Mum don't know *you're* in here either.'

'I think it's time to go, Maise,' said Alf, taking charge of his little brother's now very red ear.

'I had better be getting back,' said May to Alf as she squinted a silent threat at Tommy. 'Mum'll be wondering where I am. Them rabbit skins won't pull 'emselves.' She pushed back her chair, stood up and walked towards the door. 'See yer later, Flo, Alf,' she called, barely able to make herself heard over the increasing din – the result of the drinkers foolishly making the mistake of cheering Ada's first song. She was now in full, throat-warbling flight.

'I'll make sure he gets old Mags her drop of ale,' Alf shouted. 'And that young fellah-me-lad here keeps his trap shut when he gets home.'

—

Billy peered round the open door into the clamour of the bustling workshop. His governor, Cyril Reed, was standing at the big sawbench talking to one of the joiners. Billy took his chance and slipped inside, making for the stairs that led up to the massive timber storeroom which stretched the whole length of the building. He'd nearly reached the top when he heard Cyril's unmistakable holler over the whining of the saws.

'Oi! Bury. Down here.'

Billy dropped his head and climbed slowly back down to the workshop. Nobody stopped what they were doing, but he could feel all his workmates' eyes on him as he walked across the big, high-ceilinged space towards the boss.

'Yes, Mr Reed,' he said politely, as soon as he was within a distance when he wouldn't have to shout.

'In my office, Bury.'

Cyril Reed pushed open the door of his office, in reality little more than a paper-strewn cubby-hole, and nodded for Billy to go inside.

Billy stood, hands behind his back, next to his boss's small wooden desk – a surprisingly ornate Davenport that Reed had made as his apprentice piece many years ago.

'Cuppa?'

'Yes please, Mr Reed.' Billy couldn't believe his luck – he'd thought he'd been in for a right rollicking, and here he was being offered a cup of tea.

'Put the kettle on then, Bury,' he said, pointing at the spirit stove which stood on the sawdust-covered window-ledge. 'I think it's time we had a little chat.'

With a sinking heart, Billy went about preparing the tea while Cyril Reed gave him the benefit of his experience regarding young men's responsibilities to their employers.

After what felt like hours of his governor talking non-stop while they drained two potsful of tea, Billy was relieved that Reed at last seemed to be winding down.

'So I hope yer think I'm being fair, son,' he said. 'After all, I took yer on here as a favour to yer old mum when yer dad, God rest his soul, had his accident down the docks. We was born down the same turning, yer know.'

'Yeah, so yer said,' Billy said, dreading that he was about to launch into one of his marathon explanations of the Reed family history. He would have preferred a straightforward rucking to that, any day.

'But we ain't got time to go over all that now,' said Reed, much to Billy's relief. 'There's too much work out there to be getting on with.'

Billy took his opportunity: he stood up and made his move towards the office door, but he wasn't quick enough.

'Before yer go, son,' said Reed. 'I want to know that yer'll take what I've said to heart. Yer've been a good lad up till now. But I dunno what's got into yer these past few weeks. Yer a grafter, just like yer old man was before yer. So I only hope that yer gonna pull yerself together and follow his example and not take the wrong road and wind up like yer Uncle Davey. And like that Alfie of yours looks like doing.'

Billy shuffled around uncomfortably and ran his finger between his collar and his neck. It was warm in the crowded little room.

'I can see yer hate all this talk about families and turning out right, lad. And that yer reckon I'm making too much of yer going down the pub for a few pints; but if yer don't buckle down, I'll have to let yer go. It'd be the same whether yer was Myrtle Bury's boy or Queen Victoria herself's young 'un.'

'It won't happen again,' said Billy into his chest.

'Well, if I do catch yer slipping off again, me lad, there's plenty as'd be glad of yer job. Especially with work the way it is these days.'

Billy nodded, shame-faced at what he knew was the truth. 'I know that,' he said. 'It really won't happen again. I promise.'

'All right, let's see if yer mean what yer say. Show me yer interested. There's a load of timber been delivered what wants stacking and I reckon my back shouldn't have to put up with all that carrying and loading at my age. If yer fancy earning a few bob extra, get it up to the storeroom before yer catch up with the rest of yer jobs. If yer do it quick enough, I'll see about letting yer do it regular. Go on, get on with yer.'

'Thank yer, Mr Reed,' said Billy. 'I'll get right on with it.'

'And in future yer wanna make sure that yer get some grub down yer if yer going to go drinking.'

'Yer, right, thanks Mr Reed.' And with that Billy was out of the office, into the yard and hoisting the first pile of boards on to his shoulder before Cyril Reed had the chance to offer him any more advice.

He climbed up into the storeroom, heaved the timbers from his shoulder on to the stacks and then took out his handkerchief to wipe the sweat from his face and neck. He walked over to the dusty mullioned window and looked out on to the rooftops of the adjoining houses. A sleek, glossy pigeon with its chest- and neck-feathers puffed out in full courting fettle was striding and bobbing round a female bird. She, however, was determinedly indifferent to the male bird's advances, and continued pecking at some unseen morsel while he wore himself out with his unheeded dance.

'Don't waste yer time on her, mate,' Billy advised the strutting bird. 'She'll only break yer heart.'

Chapter 8

Ettie let out a loud sigh, and dropped down heavily into the armchair. She was eating better than she had ever done before, she was certainly cleaner, and they had sorted out the sleeping arrangements – she and Jacob now shared the big brass bed, with a bolster chastely and firmly placed between them. But after nearly a week of solid learning, she was as exhausted as if she'd been fur-pulling night and day for a month.

'It's me brain, Jacob,' she complained. 'It ain't used to all this stuff. I can't do it.'

'Nonsense,' he said harshly. 'Why do you think I picked you? Now concentrate.'

Ettie rubbed her hands over her face. 'I should've gone and seen May before now,' she said irritably. 'And,' she lowered her voice. 'I'm worried about me mum.'

'I know, Ettie,' he said, less gently than she might have hoped. 'But one thing at a time. Work first, then pleasure.'

'I don't think worrying about me mum's anything to do with pleasure,' she said without looking at him.

'Now guessing the cards. Like the trick we did at the gaff.'

Now she was looking at him. 'So yer mean…'

'Not "yer", Ettie.'

'Oh, all right. So *you* mean it was a trick when I wrote down that it was the two of hearts, then?'

'Of course.'

'So it wasn't magic?'

'No, I didn't say that. It *was* magic, Ettie, real magic, but not the magic you mean.'

'Eh? I mean, I don't understand.'

'Listen, Ettie. People want to believe that magic exists. And, with a little help from me, from us, they can.'

'What sort hof help would that be, then?'

Jacob smiled at her efforts to emulate his speech. 'You are a good student, Ettie, quick.'

'Tell me,' she insisted, flushing happily at his praise. 'Tell me whatyer… what *you* mean.'

'I'll tell you a story,' said Jacob, and squatted next to her chair. As he spoke, he described his visions in the air with his hands. 'There was a famous travelling menagerie. And, throughout the whole of Europe, wherever it stopped, crowds would gather to see the wonders it had to show. But one day the menagerie came to a town which already had a visiting circus camped in the main square. The crowds had had their fill of wild beasts, so the menagerie earned no money in that place. The performers and their creatures went hungry.

'The circus and the menagerie became enemies, keeping their plans secret, trying to reach the next town first.

'Then, one day, the menagerie's elephant died. What could they do? It had been the star of their show. How could they possibly compete with the circus who still had such a creature?

'The owner of the menagerie knew exactly what to do: he had to work his magic on the crowd. He waited until the circus camped in a field on the outskirts of a big and prosperous town. And, as they worked, he watched them. He looked on as they set up their tents and enclosures, listened as the circus people boasted of the enormous crowd they would get that night and how they would earn plenty of money now that the rivalry from the menagerie was no more.

'Then he spied on them as they put up their brightly painted posters around the town, heard them crowing that theirs was the only show with a live elephant. He mingled with the townspeople who cheered as the tumblers rode by on their prancing ponies through the streets, calling to the people that the circus – the only show worth seeing – was in town.

'When the circus parade had finished, the owner of the menagerie went back to his camp and dressed in his finest scarlet livery, then he made his own way through the streets.

'Come and see the only dead elephant in the land!' he called.

'I was working with the circus. And I can tell you that we did no business in that town. No business at all until that great creature had rotted entirely away from its huge skeleton. And even then it was still a major attraction. People paid money to gaze upon the heap of huge bleached bones. I learnt a lot from that experience, Ettie, and so should you.'

Ettie frowned, puzzled by the meaning of his strange story.

He smiled. 'Always find something different, something to tease the wearied appetites of the public. People always want a new sensation, and the successful showman gives it to them. And the public also always wants beauty. So even if we have holes in our boots, Ettie, we must weave our magic and let them see only what they want to see. Beauty, that is what they want.'

'Least I've got something right,' she said, and held up her legs, showing Jacob the almost entirely worn-out soles of her boots. 'Bet yer ain't seen no holes like these 'uns.'

'I only meant metaphorical holes, Ettie.'

'Gawd, I don't know if I've got any of them,' she said warily.

'You don't need them, Ettie,' he said, not unkindly. 'We'll go out and buy you some new ones.'

'What, proper new, or off-the-boot-doctor new?'

He laughed. 'Proper new. Now, go and find yourself a cape from the trunk, and we'll see what we can buy for those feet of yours.' Ettie didn't need a second chance. She was in the bedroom before he had even finished speaking, all thoughts of missing her friend and worrying about her mum forgotten. She knew exactly which cape she would wear. She had been through the piles of clothes several times, admiring their faded beauty, planning which skirt would look pretty with which bodice.

Within moments she was standing by the front door, impatiently waiting for Jacob to pick up his hat and dandified cane. 'We going or what?' she yelled along the hallway.

Jacob pulled on his gloves and closed the door behind them. 'A lady never acts in such a manner, Ettie,' he reminded her. 'Don't forget what you have been learning. Modulate your tone. Please.'

'Certainly, sir,' she said grinning happily, and dropped a wobbly curtsey.

In the street, Jacob held out his stick and hailed a passing hansom.

Ettie was so dazzled at the prospect of riding in a cab that she didn't utter a word, modulated or otherwise, while Jacob instructed the driver through the trap-door in the roof.

'Marshall and Snelgrove, thank you driver.'

With a click from the cabman's tongue and a shake of the reins, the hansom jerked away.

'I ain't never been in no cab before,' she whispered to Jacob.

'You don't have to whisper, Ettie. But,' he gestured slightly with his hand, 'remember you don't have to bellow.'

'Yer can afford cabs,' she said quietly. 'Yet all this week yer ain't done a stroke. Not a single show in a gaff or nothing.'

'I told you, Ettie, I have a little money. Enough for our needs.'

'Then what we doing all this work for?'

Jacob answered her slowly, an unmistakable tone of irritation in his voice. 'I told you, I want to build a reputation here as good as the one I had in Paris.'

'If yer was doing so well over there, why didn't yer stay in Paris then?'

Jacob drew in an impatient breath. 'I also told you that I had to leave Paris in a hurry.'

'But yer never said why.'

'Have you ever been to Marshall and Snelgrove's store, Ettie?'

'Yer know I bleed'n ain't,' she said, deliberately choosing her words to make him wince. Just as he had deliberately changed the subject yet again.

–

'All this cloth yer've bought me is so lovely, Jacob,' Ettie said under her breath. She was intimidated by the splendour of the shop and had waited until the shop assistant had left them to return a bale of muslin to the shelves before she had dared to speak.

'I'm glad you approve,' said Jacob, fingering a swatch of lemon-yellow watered silk.

'And don't think I ain't grateful, but what am I gonna do with it all?'

'The intention was for you to make something decent to wear. You cannot perform without the appropriate props. And, lovely as you look in those, they do not give the impression of success that we need to convey.'

'Sodding hell,' she said more loudly than she'd intended. She looked around sheepishly and dropped her voice to a hoarse whisper. 'I was hoping you wasn't going to say that,' she said glumly, and sucked on her teeth.

'Why is that? Is something wrong? Don't you care for the colours? The fabric?'

'They're all handsome. Honest.' She looked round to see if anyone else was in earshot. 'Look, I know it's stupid, but I can't sew.'

Jacob gave her a disbelieving look. 'You can't sew?'

'I never had no need to, did I?' she said, her voice rising in volume with anxiety. 'Only thing I ever did with a needle was darn me drawers. I never had nothing except what Mum got from the toot stall. And then I didn't always keep it for very long. If it was any good, it wound up down the pawnshop, to pay for her gin.'

The horrified expression on the returning shop assistant's face was enough to prevent Jacob from uttering another word.

Chapter 9

'I didn't think you were ever coming, Celia,' pouted Sophia grumpily. 'Do you realise how long I've been waiting for you?'

'I'm sorry,' panted Celia, patting the rise and fall of her chest with her white-gloved hand. 'I had to wait until Father left for his club. I thought he'd never go.'

'I accept your apology. And you're here now – I suppose that's what matters.' Sophia consulted the marcasite fob-watch pinned to her bodice. 'Come on, we should go in. It'll be starting soon.' The friends stepped from the bustling street, busy with the evening homeward-bound traffic, into the cool, marbled entrance hall of the meeting rooms. Their silk skirts rustled expensively as they brushed past the rows of chairs in the crowded, yet hushed auditorium.

'I love your bonnet, Celia,' trilled Sophia, as she nodded her thanks to the admiring, sober-suited gentlemen who gave up their seats for them. 'Very pretty with your fair curls.'

As they edged along into their seats, Celia put her finger to her lips indicating that Sophia should lower her voice.

No sooner had they taken their places than everyone around them rose to their feet and began clapping enthusiastically.

'What's happening?' murmured Celia, nervously avoiding the frantically pumping elbows of the man next to her.

'We're in luck,' beamed Sophia, craning her neck to get a better view. 'That creepy old man mounting the platform is the Reverend Roland Stedgely. The League's star. A real fanatic.' Remembering the inspiring words of the pamphlet he had written, Celia frowned at her friend's mocking tone.

Stedgely raised his bony hand and the applause gradually subsided. The audience took their seats and he began to speak.

'We would have much to fear if the slum-dwellers of the East End were left to their unholy ways,' he intoned in his booming Scottish base. 'We who know better must lead them towards the path of righteousness. Innocent lambs they may not be, but we can change those who are young enough to have still pliable minds. For our work we need more funds, and more volunteers to dispense the farthing breakfasts that attract the urchins to our missions. I call upon those here to devote their time and money to the cause. And mark that I will accept no weakness. No males over the age of twelve years shall be admitted to the breakfasts.'

He leant forward, clasping the lectern with his gnarled, mottled hands; his voice took on a shuddering, ominous rumble.

'Even though they will try to slip in, but we must resist them. They are beyond redemption. Let them go to the Jew's soup kitchen or the Popish mothers' meetings for their crusts of bread. We have no use for them. It is the young girls that we must redeem, be they willing or not.'

He quelled the rapturous response to his words with a finger jabbing heavenwards.

'Do not think it will be easy. Our missionaries have been attacked in the streets by wild women with matted hair, their faces and hands ingrained with dirt, their breath stinking of the demon liquor, refusing to allow their daughters to listen to our Truth. But their wrath is a small price to pay for the souls of their young!'

Celia joined in with the new burst of applause, but Sophia just rolled her eyes and looked languidly round the wildly cheering room.

Stedgely, staring with his hooded eagle eyes around the packed room, nodded his acknowledgement of the energetic reception his words were receiving. Then he slammed his hand down hard on the lectern, making the dust fly up and dance in a gaslit halo around his grey head, and continued with his diatribe against the slum-dwellers of the East End.

Apart from Sophia, the whole audience was enraptured by his preaching about hellfire and redemption, and after a half an hour of his ranting, she was far more interested in her friend's hat.

'Do tell me, Celia,' she said, moodily swinging her legs, 'where exactly did you buy your bonnet?'

'Stop prattling on, for goodness' sake, Sophia,' snapped Celia. Then she gave out a little gasp of pleasure. She fussed with her ringlets and straightened her skirts. 'Look. The reverend gentleman is coming over here. To us.'

Ignoring the clamouring crowd that had gathered round him, Stedgely stopped in front of Celia. He looked steadily into her eyes, as though he could penetrate her very thoughts. 'I trust that we shall be seeing you at future meetings, Miss… ?'

'Taylor,' said Celia impulsively.

Sophia's jaw dropped.

'Miss Taylor,' he repeated with a brief nod.

'Goodnight, Reverend,' said Celia, putting out her arm for the dumbfounded Sophia, and leading her friend out into the cool night air.

'The evening is quite lovely,' observed Celia. 'Even though there is a nip in the air. How wonderful nature is.'

'Celia! What's happened to you? You lie about your name. You've gone all poetic. And your cheeks are positively glowing.'

'I can't think what you mean,' answered Celia, as they made their way along the quiet residential streets.

'Why did you tell him your name was Taylor?' Sophia shook her head making her curls bounce around her pretty, wide-eyed face. 'It makes you sound like a parlourmaid.'

'I would rather my father didn't know about this evening.'

A look of understanding came over Sophia's face; she was a well-practised deceiver of her own parents. 'But the way you looked at old Stedgely,' she said, ducking in front of Celia, making her come to halt. 'I can't imagine why you did that.'

'It was you who kept asking me to go to a League meeting with you, Sophia.'

'I wanted to have some fun,' said Sophia impatiently, her voice rising to a squeak.

Celia took Sophia's arm in hers and hauled her along in the direction of Belgravia. 'Stop raising your voice, Sophie, you're making a spectacle of yourself.'

'Me?'

This time it was Celia who stopped, causing a couple out for an after-dinner stroll to have to step into the roadway in order to pass the two squabbling friends.

'I was very moved by the meeting, Sophia. And I intend to go to another one.'

'Celia!' Sophia threw up her hands in despair. 'What's got into you?'

'Don't you care about the unfortunates who are living on the very doorsteps of our homes?' Celia scolded her.

'How could I help but be concerned?' mocked Sophia. 'Belgravia is simply bursting with the poor.'

When Celia didn't respond to her teasing with her usual giggles, Sophia gave up. 'Oh, have it your own way, Celia,' she snapped. 'Go out and save the ridiculous girls from themselves. Go and get your throat cut down some dingy alleyway in Whitechapel, or wherever it is that Stedgely and his cronies hang around at night.'

Slowly the smile returned to Sophia's face. 'We could go to the East End now,' she suggested. 'We could go to the music hall.'

'No, Sophie, we couldn't. We shouldn't even be out.'

'At least I came to the meeting with permission,' scowled Sophia. 'Mama thinks it's good for me to take an interest in charitable matters.'

—

Celia walked confidently to the front of the hall and took a seat near the speakers' platform.

'Aren't you the brave one?' Sophia taunted, trailing after her. 'Where's the little mouse who used to hide at the back of the hall?'

'I want to be able to hear properly, Sophia. That's all,' said Celia, tucking her skirts neatly around her.

'You want to be closer to that raving evangelist, more like,' giggled Sophia.

'Sophia,' Celia replied, her voice cool but her cheeks burning. 'The Reverend Stedgely is a very good man.'

'You're so innocent, Celia.' Sophia sounded bored. As far as she was concerned, this fourth visit to the League was definitely one too many. She looked vaguely round the room hoping, not very optimistically, for a diversion.

Celia looked far more content as she settled herself in a demure, straight-backed pose and waited bright-eyed and eager for the meeting to begin.

A whey-faced woman, dressed in the dullest of grey serge costumes, strode purposefully on to the stage, Bible in hand, and started off the proceedings.

'It is but a few short years since the League began its crusade against the twin demons of drink and lust.' She spoke in a chant-like dirge, waving her Bible for emphasis and throwing back her head so that her deep-set eyes rolled even more deeply back into their sockets. 'But we have come far in our noble campaign to return decency and Christianity to our once great metropolis.'

As the woman took a great wheezing intake of breath, ready to begin her next onslaught, Sophia almost burst from suppressing her giggles. There, round the woman's nostrils, clear for all in the front rows to see, was the unmistakable crust of dried snot.

Celia turned and glared at her companion.

Oblivious to her inadequate nasal hygiene, the lady in grey continued. 'Now, without delay, I would like to introduce the man responsible for our success.'

Thunderous clapping drowned anything further she might have said, but gave Sophia the chance to whisper to Celia. 'I'm never sure why he's a reverend, you know: no one ever mentions a parish or anything. Or even…'

Celia's look was enough to rebuke Sophia into silence.

As Stedgely mounted the platform, he made his usual, seemingly self-deprecating gesture of raising one hand, indicating that he was unworthy of such an ovation. But, also as usual, this merely had the affect of whipping the audience into even more fervent applause and cheers of support for their leader. He was in every way, except in the matter of dress, just as much a star turn as anyone who trod the boards of the music hall.

At the first utterance from his lips, the noisy acclaim immediately came to a halt.

'In this, the beginning of our fourth year of missionary work,' he began. 'I want you all to renew your commitment to our task.'

He waited for the unrestrained shouts of willing agreement to cease. 'It is in the knowledge that we have right on our side that we must keep entering those streets of shame. We must not be weak, nor flinch in horror from what we see there: the depravity that begins at such an early stage in those young girls' lives.'

'Praise be!' came the cry from several members of his enraptured audience.

He brought his bony fist down hard on the lectern, thumping it with surprising force for such a long, gangling man. His strange, undefinably coloured eyes held the gaze of everyone – Sophia included, despite her earlier cynical comments – as he stared about him. His stringy hair and gaunt, graveyard features seemed unimportant to those who felt themselves in the presence of an other-worldly power.

'And now,' he boomed, 'a new madness has entered the streets of this city. Women, carrying the disease which has been sent to them as a warning from God Himself, are still carrying on their filthy trade.' He challenged a blushing woman sitting near Celia with an unblinking stare. 'We cannot close our minds to the existence of such things. We need to know our enemy.'

The woman swallowed hard and tried to regain her composure.

'The festering dung held tight in the cauldron of the slums beneath the lid of secrecy would shock you far more than my words telling of that dread disease. In this once fine city of ours,' he continued, pointing at the now totally discomforted woman, 'young women, barely more than children themselves, become mothers and then kill their own offspring.' He nodded his head at the disbelieving woman. 'I have proof. Oh yes!'

The gasps of horror from around the packed hall were confronted by a question shouted in a bold cockney voice from near the back. 'Proof of what?' asked the not-quite-adult voice.

Angry murmurs came from all round the room.

'Sit down!' someone shouted.

'No, throw her out,' yelled another.

'You get yer hands off,' she demanded, pulling herself free and shaking her fist at Stedgely. 'You listen to someone else for a change. What mother would kill her own baby if she could provide for it, eh? You tell me that.'

The young woman was shoved down roughly into a chair by two men dressed in black imitation of Stedgely, who was now speaking loudly over her complaints.

'We will rid the streets of vice by saving them while they are girls. Even if it is too late for the likes of her, we will carry on!' he roared, pointing towards the pitiful young woman who was now surrounded by accusing faces. 'We will force out the corruption and make this city safe once more for decent people.'

The girl tussled with the two men and struggled to her feet. 'I said get yer hands off me. And I *won't* be shut up again. I come here to tell you lot what's what, and that's what I mean to do.'

'Disgraceful!' tutted a middle-aged woman from the audience.

'And *you*,' the girl shrieked, jerking her head towards Stedgely. 'Yer no different from yer mate Charrington. Yer might not come in and close down the case-houses like he does, but yer still poking yer noses in where yer not wanted. And yer driving the customers away and us girls out on to the streets, just the same as him. That's what yer doing.' She shouted louder, raising her voice over the growing protest. 'Instead of them coming to us, we have to go out and look for geezers now, out into the streets and alleys. Yer've made us fair game for any bloke what wants to hurt us or rob us. Do us in, if he feels like it. Who's gonna look out for us on the streets eh, you tell me that?'

The objectors' voices rose in waves of fury.

'Sit down!'

'Throw her out!'

'Stop her filthy tongue!'

'Don't let her blame you, Mr Stedgely. She doesn't *have* to walk the streets.'

Stedgely never replied, he just watched, observing impassively, as the room exploded in self-righteous surges of indignation.

'Shut up, all of yer,' the young woman yelled with a force which surprised them. 'Yer reckon I don't *have* to walk the streets, do yer? Well, how d'yer suggest us brides makes our living, then? Cleaning big houses for the likes of you, so's yer old man can get us in the family way, and not even have to pay for the privilege of giving us one?' She poked the chest of the astonished woman who was cringing in the chair next to her.

'There are places you can go for help,' the woman remonstrated weakly with the filthy-looking girl.

'And where's that then?' demanded the now enraged cockney.

'There are, I don't know, provisions.' The elegantly dressed woman was close to tears, her chest hurt, and she was humiliated. The thought spun around in her mind: did this person actually know about her husband and their recently dismissed parlour-maid, or was it just an unfortunately accurate generalisation?

'Well, the bastard Relieving Officer won't help yer. Yer can take me word for that. I know. Yer don't get nothing till yer prove yer've sold everything you own. Till you ain't even got a pot left to piss in. And then yer have to sell the only thing what's left. And that's just what I'm doing, ain't I? Selling meself. The last thing I've got.'

Sophia burst into a fit of nervous giggles.

The girl rounded on her. 'And you can shut up, yer silly tart.'

A man sitting near Sophia, who had been admiring her all through the meeting, saw his opportunity to impress her. He stood up and strode resolutely towards the object of the room's contempt. Seeing his determination, the appalled yet exhilarated crowd made room for him to pass. On reaching the young woman, he seized her brutally by the arm and dragged her screaming and kicking through the big double doors which opened on to the street.

He reappeared without her and slid the bolts firmly behind him. The cheers and hurrahs drowned her bashing at the wooden doors.

'The sinner is thrown out,' he said simply, and returned to a seat much closer to Sophia's than before.

Celia didn't notice the new seating arrangements: all she was aware of was Stedgely speaking again, and the feeling that his eyes were burning into her, as though he were addressing her alone of all the people present. He spoke with a fervour which filled her with a determination to do whatever he wanted. She would join his crusade. She would make sure that no other young girl need ever again fall from grace. She would join in the campaign to make the streets a better place for womankind. She would be his disciple.

'Women such as that whore,' he roared, 'will never labour honestly when money is to be had so easily from their corruption of hapless young men.'

'Can't those "hapless young men" control themselves?' an elderly lady demanded indignantly.

'Once a young man has been tempted by whores—' Stedgely replied — 'and from Adam onwards, the Bible tells us it is his nature to be so — then the viper of lust is in him. Only if he is fortunate enough to contract a Christian marriage might he be released from the poison which would otherwise suck away his very flesh.'

'And what makes these "whores" different from any other woman here?' the elderly woman continued.

'Virtue has no meaning for them. They, in their ignorance, choose to indulge their desire for drink, fanciful dress, and the *Hell* of unbridled sexual passion. They do not even experience the misery of their fall, as any decent woman would. They exult in vice and corruption.'

'And men cannot resist them?' The woman's voice was heavy with sarcasm.

'It is not the fault of decent men when the lower orders are given attractive physical form with which to tempt them. It is merely another test in the travails of life, to which some poor souls succumb.' He drew himself up to his full, gangling height and looked down his long thin nose at her. 'It is only by the intervention of the League that the young girls of the slums can learn to reject the life their mothers would force them into.'

The elderly woman rose unsteadily to her feet with the aid of her stick. 'So not only do you condemn the public women, sir, but you actually blame them when they are blessed with God's gift of beauty.' She gave a snort of derision. 'Surely even one as slow-witted as you cannot believe that they have taken to the work they do...'

'Work?' He said the word incredulously, looking to the audience for support.

'Yes,' she said slowly. 'Work.' With considerable effort the woman looked about her. 'What sort of charlatans are you? You profess charity, yet actually you are thrilled by the horrors you claim you wish to heal.' She would not be silenced by the audience's angry denials. 'I know your type,' she sneered. 'I have witnessed the so-called charitable ladies when a slum is not so terrible as they had hoped. "Can you show us nothing worse?" they beg, disappointed that they have seen nothing bad enough to make them of interest at their next soiree.'

'Wait! I know her.' A stout, ruddy-faced man stood up and pointed an accusing finger at the elderly woman. 'I've seen her. Handing out leaflets claiming that the whores are poor, misunderstood maidens, sacrificed by wicked men.' He pushed his way along the row till he was standing in front of her. 'I'd know this creature anywhere.' He turned to Stedgely. 'She smokes cigarettes and wants the vote!'

'You protest too much, sir,' she countered. 'Do you have a secret of your own to hide, perhaps? Maybe you pay visits to the brides yourself.'

'Get her out of here,' the man bellowed, his face drained of the blood which moments before had reddened his cheeks.

'Does female emancipation frighten you so very much?' she asked, a challenging smile playing round her lips.

'Go and join the other whores.' The offended man's eyes bulged with fury and he raised his hand as if to slap her. 'You're no better than the rest of them.'

With no thought for the risk to her balance, the elderly woman set about the man with her cane. 'Threaten an old woman, would you? Take that, you so-called Christian. You know nothing of the way of God. Nor of women.'

While several men surged forward to help their fellow philanthropist in his struggle, Sophia hugged her aching sides, almost beside herself with laughter, delighted that the meeting was proving so amusing after all.

Next to her, Celia sat absolutely still, save for her head which she turned back and forth to catch each development in the amazing spectacle which was unfolding around her. The whole place was in uproar. The woman in grey who had opened the meeting only added to the general melee by re-mounting the platform and leading the front few rows in a rousing chorus of 'Shall We Gather at the River?'.

Sophia turned her attention to the man who had earlier gone to her rescue by throwing out the prostitute. She accepted sweetly as he offered her his protection against the growing rowdiness of the meeting, but would have been furious if she had known what she was missing while she smiled into his pale grey eyes. Having decided to leave the hall before any damage was done to his person, Stedgely walked swiftly past the front row and, as he did so, he discreetly pressed a note into the astonished Celia's hand.

Celia unfolded the paper and read the hastily composed words. They invited her to join him in private prayer for the unfortunates who chose to corrupt their daughters into walking the streets of the night.

She glanced to her left. Satisfied that Sophia – who was even now accepting her new companion's help to clamber on to her chair so she could get a decent view of events – would not miss her, Celia slipped away to follow the departing figure of Stedgely.

Roland Stedgely opened the door to his luxurious set of rooms which were connected to the League's meeting hall, and let Celia into his inner sanctum. She passed by him with a shush of apricot watered silk, but even the sound of her expensive skirts was not able to veil the drumming of her pulse beating in her ears.

'It has been remarked to me, Miss Taylor,' he began. 'Or should I say Miss Tressing?'

Celia opened her mouth to speak but he raised his hand authoritatively to silence her.

'Do not be surprised that I know your true name,' Stedgely continued. 'I know many things about many people.'

Celia bowed her head to hide her embarrassment at her lie being exposed then whispered: 'Do you know anything about the disease which the brides pass on, sir? And of the consequences for those they infect?'

Stedgely's dry-lipped mouth cracked into a leering smile. 'You need have no worries about such things, Miss Tressing. Our work does not expose us to such risks. Syphilis is not a problem for the likes of us.'

Celia felt the flush of embarrassment creeping up from her throat.

'It has been remarked,' he went on, seeming not to notice her discomfort, 'that you have become a regular, and most enthusiastic, attender of our meetings.'

Celia looked up at him through her lashes. 'This is my fourth meeting.'

'And I have been watching you, Miss Tressing. I know that you can be a power of good in our battle.'

'Me?' Celia could barely raise her voice above a cracked whisper.

'Yes, Celia. You.' His thin, scrawny hand reached out to her, the desiccated old man's flesh of his fingertips catching on the silk of her sleeve. 'You are a most handsome young woman,' he said. His voice began to quaver in the way it did when he was preaching. 'You are a girl who could surely stir the souls of even non-believers.'

Celia grew alarmed as his breath began to come in short wheezing rasps – a sound so like that which her father made when he... But no, she thought frantically, he couldn't be like that. Then a new horror as Stedgely fell to his knees, threw his arms round her ankles and began mewling and moaning at her feet.

'We can do so much together, Celia,' he groaned from the floor, 'but I need your strength.' He lifted his head and clawed at her skirts.

Celia was horrified to see the trail of spittle running from the corner of his old, cracked mouth.

'I need your strength, Celia,' he whimpered. 'Your youth. Help me.' Then, without any warning, he thrust his hand up under her skirts.

Until that moment Celia had felt herself without power, unable to speak or move. But the fury she now felt gave her all the power she needed. She drew back her hand and brought it swinging round in an arc, striking him directly above his ear. She had contact with his head for just a moment, but his straggly grey hair left a greasiness on her palm which, even in her terror, made her shudder with disgust.

She took a long, slow breath and spoke to him as calmly as she could manage. 'Take your hand from me,' she insisted. 'And get up from your knees and open the door.'

Stedgely collapsed sideways on to the richly carpeted floor and rolled into a tight foetal ball, hugging his knees. 'You don't understand,' he whined. 'It is an honour I am bestowing upon you. Only a few are admitted to my inner circle.'

'Stand up,' demanded Celia, her fear now completely supplanted by cool anger. 'I can hear someone outside.'

With astonishing agility Stedgely sprang to his feet and rushed to unlock the door.

As he pulled it open Celia saw the hymn-singing lady in grey standing in the doorway. No longer a composed, tight-lipped figure, her wiry, unravelling locks flopped about her face.

'Someone summoned a police constable and he has called for reinforcements,' she cried wildly. 'Oh Reverend Stedgely, please, come and do something.'

The woman at first appeared to be completely blind to anyone but Stedgely, but as soon as he had pushed past her to return to the affray, the woman strode over to the still stunned Celia.

'Do not think you are in any way special, young woman,' she said contemptuously. 'There are those who have been here before you, and there are others who will be here in the future. Being chosen is an accident of nature – your youth and lack of disfigurement is what makes you different: nothing else.'

Celia shook her head in horrified incredulity. 'You think I succumbed to him? You think I let him touch me?' Celia raised her chin and looked down her fine, aristocratic nose at the now rather uneasy woman in grey. 'I understand exactly what goes on here now, and I am appalled. You think you are, but you are no better than that girl they ejected from the hall this evening.'

Celia pushed past the open-mouthed woman and went out of a side door which opened on to a long corridor. As the door closed behind her, she lifted her skirt and ran as fast as her layers of petticoats would allow, almost skidding to a halt as she realised that she had re-entered the hall by a back door. She skipped nimbly around the loudly arguing groups of League members and police officers, managing to avoid Sophia, who anyway seemed happily preoccupied with the man whose acquaintance she had so recently made and, with a final dash for the double doors, found herself in the freedom of the street outside.

She leant against the sooty brick wall to regain her breath, her chest heaving with the unaccustomed exertion of running.

A plane tree, planted in the wide pavement, was just coming into leaf. She looked up through the branches into the deepening blue of the evening sky and saw a beady-eyed blackbird balancing on a slender twig, going through its last trills and warbles of the day. Something suddenly made it take fright and it flew hastily away from whatever danger it had seen.

As Celia watched the bird winging away from her, tears flowed uncontrollably down her cheeks. With a great deal of effort, she pushed herself away from the wall and began walking slowly along the road in the direction of Belgravia. She could no longer trust anyone but herself, she thought, the despair almost choking her. She was alone in the world and, no matter what, she would have to make up her own mind about what was right and what was wrong.

Chapter 10

'All these fancy frocks and posh manners,' she sighed. 'I wish me old mates…'

'Friends,' Jacob corrected her as he came into the bedroom. He looked over Ettie's shoulder at her reflection in the cheval looking-glass. 'You're pleased with the seamstress's work?' he asked.

'My old friends won't know me,' said Ettie, twirling around the room admiring her new outfit. 'Yellow and grey striped satin, eh? Who'd have thought Ettie Wilkins would ever wear something like this?'

'Anyone who had really looked at you, Ettie, could have seen past your poverty, and could have recognised you for what you really are – a beautiful, clever and wonderful girl.'

'You've quite turned my head, Jacob Protsky,' she said coquettishly as she walked over to him and put her hand on his arm. 'You'll have me actually believing all your pretty words before you know it.'

Jacob didn't move away from her, but neither did he respond to her touch.

'In these couple of weeks you've shown me how I can be a lady, Jacob. And I feel as good as anyone now. Thank you.'

'You always were as good as anyone, Ettie. It was just that you weren't aware of it before.'

'It really, I don't know, it amazes me, that a geezer…' she laughed happily. 'A gentleman, I mean, should sort of *like* women like you do. It's kind of, well, funny, don't yer think?'

'Funny? In what way funny?'

'To like us, not just to want to, you know, do it with us.'

'I learnt many things whilst I was in France, Ettie. Many funny ideas, as you put it.'

She turned back to her reflection in the mirror and primped at her hair. 'Yer never did tell me, Jacob,' she said matter-of-factly. 'Why did yer leave Paris if it was so good?'

'"You", Ettie, "you". Not "yer". Your voice, concentrate.'

'Just who d'yer think I bloody am?' she demanded, angry at his continual evasion. 'A sodding princess?'

'Princess or not, Ettie, we have work to do. We are becoming dilatory, we must proceed with our plan of action.'

'If you like,' Ettie said.

'You sound reluctant,' said Jacob.

'If that means I'm fed up with being taught table-knocking, ecto-bloody-plasm appearances, trances and all the other rotten tricks of the trade, then yes, I bleed'n am reluctant.'

He took out his gold half-Hunter watch from his waistcoat pocket. 'Oh, Ettie, I'm sorry. It's almost five o'clock. We've been working for hours. I've been very selfish. Shall we go for a walk? Or would you like some tea?'

Ettie put her hands on her hips and narrowed her eyes at the man she found fascinatingly handsome, but whose face was now crumpled with concern for her. 'You know just how to get round a girl, don't you, Jacob? You're such a bloody good actor. I must be bonkers, but come on then, let's get on with it. What do you want me to do next?'

'Get into the box,' he said, his enthusiasm returning immediately. He drew back the muslin curtain covering the front of the three-sided cabinet which stood in the corner of the bedroom and indicated that she should enter. 'Mind your head. You're a bit taller than my last assistant.'

'Oh, is that right? Who was she then?'

She should have known better than to have asked. As usual, he did the trick he did best of all: that of changing the subject whenever he chose not to answer her questions.

'Is your mother tall?' he asked, friendly and kind, helping her into the seat at the back of the black painted box.

'Not especially,' she answered tersely, settling back.

'Your father, then?'

She laughed. 'Who knows? He could have been a bleed'n giant for all I know. Or care.'

'Look,' he said, concentrating on fiddling with a small brass eyelet on the side of the box. 'This is where I fix the string that allows you to move the spirits around the room.'

'But that's so obvious. They'll see it's all done with tricks.'

'Oh no. The spirits can only commune in the dark, Ettie. Our earth light hurts their ethereal bodies. Watch.' He turned the gaslights down to the faintest glow and began mumbling incomprehensible phrases. Then in a loud, clear voice he called on the spirit world to join them, there in the room. 'I can feel them with us, Ettie,' he moaned, and began panting alarmingly. 'Yes! Yes! Oh yes! They're here.'

Ettie could see both his hands on the table, in full view, but she could also see a hand – not Jacob's – reaching up from under the table and waving its frightful fingers in her direction.

She screamed.

'Please! No!' Jacob groaned as though he were in great pain. 'The spirits will be afraid. Oh,' he moaned. 'Too late. Too late. They have departed. They have left us.' His voice took on a saddened, disappointed tone. 'Please, turn up the lights, Ettie.'

Ettie took a deep breath and levered herself out of the box. Feeling her way across the room and only turning her back on the hideous apparition of the hand at the last possible moment, she turned up the lamps to shed their full light. Then she swallowed hard and turned her wide-eyed gaze back to the table where the vile thing rested. She burst out in loud, relieved laughter.

'You're a bloody… Aw, I dunno, but you are one.'

Jacob was still sitting at the table, waggling his hands high above his head. One of his legs was also raised so that his foot rested on the table top. And there, clear for her to see, was the spirit hand, a luridly coloured rubber confection, which he had slipped neatly over the toe of his boot.

'Easy,' he said grinning, 'all you have to do is cross your leg and bend your knee, and,' he lowered his voice to a slow, dramatic growl, 'up pops the spirit.' He resumed his normal, persuasively gentle tone. 'And putting a shoe on your hand and brushing it over the sitters' heads in the dark gives a wonderful impression of flying spirits.'

She laughed until tears rolled down her cheeks. She hadn't admitted it, even to herself, but she was falling in love with him: a rogue. But such a handsome one; such a charming, funny, kind, con man.

—

'And now,' trilled Lou. 'The first ever performance in England of the World Famous Silent Beauty!'

'Well I ain't never heard nothing about her,' shouted a wag from the back of the penny gaff.

'How yer gonna hear about someone who can't talk? Yer dozy great nit,' Lou hollered back at him.

Satisfied that she had confused the heckler enough to silence him, Lou flipped her train to one side, treated the front row to a slow wink, and then wiggled away behind the curtain, leaving the makeshift stage clear for Jacob and Ettie.

Within moments of taking their first, introductory bow, Professor Protsky and the Silent Beauty had the audience totally captivated, and Ettie was enjoying every moment of being on the stage, just as Jacob had promised her she would when she had said she could not go on in front of everyone. Now each face in the audience was turned eagerly towards her, hoping above hope that the spirits might have a message just for them. It didn't matter whether the message was good news of a fortune to come, or a warning of possible danger: the fact they were singled out was all that mattered, exactly as Jacob had said.

During the next few weeks, they worked almost non-stop. By night they played the penny gaffs, with Jacob always making sure that they didn't set up too close to her old haunts: he wanted her to make a clean break with her old life. And, during the day, they worked on practising the more sophisticated patter and tricks for a new act intended for a very different audience to that of the East End. They laboured ceaselessly. Sometimes they would return from a penny gaff and fall asleep in their clothes, but still they worked.

Jacob taught her all about melodrama, the importance of fanciful rituals and the use of ambiguity. He showed her how *someone* in an audience would always respond to a message – so long as it came from a spirit with a common enough name, of course.

Even as they ate their breakfast he instructed her.

'People will always hear what they want to hear, Ettie. Remember only that which matters to them,' he said, slicing at the cold mutton that Mrs Hawkins had set out for them the night before. 'And they simply forget any message without significance for them. Believe me, we *all* only hear what we want to.'

Ettie was doubtful. 'I know people can be daft, but they aren't that stupid, Jacob,' she said, taking the plate he held out to her.

'Oh, but they are,' said Jacob, joining her at the table. 'We see it every night in the gaffs.'

'Yeah, well, the gaffs are one thing, but this new act…'

'Not only the gaffs, Ettie. Think of those crowds who flocked for the Jubilee,' he said, swallowing a mouthful of meat. 'They forgot, they *chose* to forget, for that day how much they resented the privilege of the crown. They ignored the discomfort as they stood and waited for the parade to pass by. Took no note of the stink of the bodies pushing against them, as though none of it existed. Forgot even the calls they had made for so long for the monarchy to be destroyed once and for all. And now they only recall the wonder of seeing their beloved Victoria. People act like stupid fools, Ettie. No, worse, they *are* self-deluding fools.'

'It's all right for you to say all that, Jacob, but I ain't the bloody Queen, now am I? Girls like me are a penny a dozen. We don't ever really get out of the East End.' She concentrated on her plate as she spoke, as though it held all the answers to her confusion. 'See, no matter what you do, it'll always be in me. Always. The people who you're aiming at with all this new stuff, they'll never believe that I'm anything special. Not little Ettie Wilkins from Whitechapel.'

Jacob gulped at his coffee and shook his head. 'You are wrong. So very wrong. They will believe in you, Ettie, they will.'

Ettie carried on eating in silence.

'Don't fail me now, Ettie. Don't lose your nerve.'

She set down her knife and fork very deliberately, wiped her mouth on the napkin in the way he had shown her, and put it beside her plate before she spoke. 'Jacob,' she said, levelly. 'I'll tell you the truth. I'm scared. I've heard about those blokes who deliberately go spirit-grabbing for a laugh. Say they do that to me? Say I get caught tricking them and they call the coppers?'

'Ettie, they do those things when amateurs make it obvious that they are trying to gull the sitters. When they have their cheap pieces of cloth dipped in substances to glow in the dark, and give themselves away by forgetting that their hands too will be stained. They make mistakes. We will make none. We will be professional. The best. I have so much knowledge, so many skills.' He clasped his hands in tight fists and threw back his head. 'Ettie, we will become the greatest.'

He stood up and moved round the table towards her. She sat very still, bewildered and threatened by his sudden passion.

He stood behind her, looming over her. His breathing slowed, and he placed his hands gently on her shoulders.

'I have seen what people are prepared to do to have proof of the spirit world, Ettie. I have seen the lengths to which they will go to convince themselves that this world,' he gestured wildly around him, 'is not all there is. People want to believe in anything that gives meaning to their dull, inconsequential lives. Let me show you something.'

Jacob held up his hand to indicate that she should remain sitting while he took down a leather-bound book from the shelves. He held the spine towards her.

'Memoirs of Extraordinary Popular Delusions and the Madness of Crowds' he recited from memory.

'Blimey, what an 'andle,' said Ettie.

Jacob was too obsessed with finding the page he wanted to reproach her for her relapse into her old way of speaking. 'Listen. The man who wrote this – Charles Mackay – certainly knew man's folly for novelty, Ettie. He tells, here in these pages,' Jacob held the open book towards her, 'how on the continent men were once prepared to kill one another over tulip bulbs. Can you imagine?'

Ettie shrugged, discomforted by his excitement. 'Can't say as I can, really. No.' She paused. 'So, what's a tulip then?'

'A flower.'

'And they went mad over these tulips, did they?'

'Yes. They were the latest wonder, just as you shall be, Ettie. The rarest bloom. The wonder whom everyone desires to meet and possess.'

'If you say so,' said Ettie dubiously.

'Let me read you what he says about the tulip bulbs. No, let me read first what he writes on the pursuit of fortune-telling.' He flipped eagerly through the pages. 'Right, this is it: "Upon no subject has it been so easy to deceive the world as upon this." And he's right, Ettie. We can do it. Together.'

'I don't know about all this, Jacob. I didn't realise it was going to be so serious. I thought we were going to do a few shows round the gaffs and then maybe the music halls when we'd practised enough.'

'Would you object to providing a little amusement in the drawing rooms of the idle rich who have nothing better to do with their time and money?'

'It ain't – isn't – that. I just haven't got the experience of nothing like it. How will I know what to do? I know you've been teaching me and everything, but I don't think I could swing it, Jacob. I really don't and that's the truth.'

'I have all the experience we need,' he assured her, his face lighting up as he told her how the public could always be persuaded to want what they never knew they needed. 'Guaranteed cures from wonder drugs,' he said, laughing loudly. 'Gladly purchased after rumours of fever scares had been spread, of course. Games of Three Card Monte and Thimble Rigging in shabby market places in order to get the stakes for bigger games, where rich men can't wait to throw their golden guineas in my direction. Promises to relieve rich curse victims from certain death.'

'What curses?' Ettie wanted to know as she grew increasingly tantalised by his enthusiasm.

'The curses I convinced them were on them in the first place.'

She couldn't help laughing out loud. Her fears were not entirely forgotten, but she was now excited as well as intrigued. Her head spun as Jacob became more animated in his recalling of his exploits in his journeys around the world.

'And, the wiles I learned from two women from the United States of America – the big one that we can do, Ettie. The Pow-Wow.'

His eyes glowed with promises of future glory. Ettie could only stare.

'It's so simple, Ettie, just like I've shown you. The seances. They love them. The trance. The distorted voice. Messages from the spirits. Vague words which have significance and meaning for almost anyone. They love the flattery, thinking that the spirits have come to give a message just to them.' He threw back his head in the uninhibited way which always alarmed her. 'Ettie, Ettie. We can do what we like. Forget the penny gaffs, they are in the past. We can do anything.'

'Say they don't believe in us?'

'I've told you, Ettie. They will.'

'Say they don't?'

'Then we blame them. Say it is their fault. They don't have sufficient faith or mental powers to assist the spirits in their return journey to this plane. Nobody likes to be a failure, Ettie. It's foolproof. We can never be proved wrong. By the time we have prepared them, with ritual and mystery, they will believe anything we say.'

He went and stood in the corner of the room with his back to her. Then he suddenly turned round, his chin low to his chest, his eyes hooded.

'There must be no animals within ten yards of this room,' he chanted. 'The spirits must not be disturbed. No green silk can be allowed. Oh,' he moaned in agony, 'please, your scarf, remove it, madam. For all our sakes.'

'What?'

'Mystery, Ettie, mystery,' he said in his normal voice, flashing her his most appealing grin.

'Bloody nonsense, more like.'

'So what? So long as it detracts from what is really going on, and builds up the anticipation that something is about to happen.'

'Whatever would my old mum make of all this, eh?' said Ettie grinning back at him, but shaking her head as though she really didn't know what to make of it all either.

Chapter 11

'Myrtle. Myrtle, you in there, girl?'

'Who is it?' Myrtle called, leaning over the banister and peering down into the dark stairwell below.

'It's me, Sarah,' the slurring, disembodied voice replied. 'I wondered if yer might have a drop of broth or something I could have. I'm a bit short, to tell yer the truth, and I've missed the soup kitchen and all.'

'Sleep, were yer?' Myrtle Bury asked coolly.

'No. I didn't feel well,' Sarah shouted back miserably. 'The lodger'll be home soon. He'll be hungry. And I ain't got nothing to give him, Myrt.'

'Come on up,' said Myrtle wearily.

Myrtle stood at her open door and waited for her neighbour to puff her way up the stairs. As Sarah dragged her way on to the landing, Myrtle let out an unintentional gasp and an uncharacteristic expletive. 'Bugger me, Sarah, whatever's happened to yer?'

Sarah ducked her head and shielded her bruised and swollen face with her hand. 'I told yer, I ain't been feeling too good. I had a bit of a fall,' she said, keeping in the shadows away from the window so that her neighbour couldn't get a look at the real extent of the beating she'd taken.

'Sit yerself down,' said Myrtle, gesturing with her head to one of the matching wooden chairs that stood either side of the little firegrate where a cast-iron pan of bubbling stew was suspended over the glowing embers. 'And I'll dish yer up a drop of this sheep's head broth to take home with yer.'

'Gawd love and bless yer, Myrt. I smelt that soup from the other side of the court and I knew yer wouldn't let yer old mate down.'

Myrtle busied herself wiping out a crackle-glazed china basin, then filled it with steaming, delicious-smelling stew from the big pot.

'Yer must miss your Ettie,' said Myrtle, taking down a ragged white cloth from the string washing-line stretched across the chimney breast.

'You ain't kidding,' said Sarah, sniffing greedily at the big pot over the fire. 'That bloody lodger of mine wants it off me morning noon and night now she ain't there to look after him.'

Myrtle shook her head in disgust and tipped the contents of the basin back into the big pan. Sarah's look of disappointment soon changed to one of incredulity as Myrtle used the cloth that she'd intended to cover the basin with to lift the cooking pot from the grate. She thrust it roughly at Sarah, not even caring that she spilt some of it on to the floor.

Sarah's eyes widened to slighter larger than their usual puffy slits. 'What?' she gasped incredulously. 'The whole pan full?'

'Go on, take it,' barked Myrtle.

Sarah took the brimming pan and ran her tongue around the rim and up the side, catching every last spill of the hot stew.

Myrtle could barely contain herself. 'Get out, Sarah. Now. Before I say or do something I might regret.'

Sarah looked at her benefactress, trying to keep her eyes in focus and smiled. 'As yer like. Ta Myrtle, I'll fetch the pan back tomorrow.'

'There's no rush,' breathed Myrtle, keeping her hands behind her back to stop herself from picking up the breadboard and smacking Sarah Wilkins round the head with it. 'Now, if yer don't mind, I've got me jobs to get on with.'

Myrtle stood at the window and watched the woman who had once been her friend stagger across the court towards the dark hallway of Number Twelve under the weight of the pan and the influence of at least a half-bottle of Jacky. Myrtle sat herself down on one of the wooden chairs by the grate, stared into the fire and remembered the old Sarah who had made her laugh with her daft carrying on, and made her proud to call herself her friend when she'd done such a good job of bringing up her baby single-handed. It was different now the drink had got hold of her: to see how Sarah had wound up made Myrtle cry. Two fat, salty tears trickled down her cheeks, but at the sound of footsteps on the stairs she hastily went over and stood by the table and rubbed her eyes dry with her apron. Myrtle wasn't one to let anyone see her upset or sitting idly by the hearth when there were jobs to be done.

'Watcha, Ma,' said Billy as he came into the little room. He went straight over to the fire and dumped down a pile of timber offcuts he'd brought home from the workshop. 'Wasn't that Sarah I saw wandering about with a big pot of something out there?' he asked over his shoulder as he piled the wood neatly into piles by the grate.

'Yeah,' Myrtle said flatly. 'It was Sarah.'

'What a state,' said Billy, sadly. He stood up and stretched. 'So what did she have to say for herself?'

'Nothing about Ettie if that's what yer want to know.'

Billy didn't answer. He sat down in the chair that his mother had just left and started to roll himself a cigarette.

'Driving her own kid away like that,' Myrtle hissed through her teeth as she sawed angrily at the bread on the table, taking her anger out on the loaf. 'She was such a good girl to her mum and all. Did all she could for that selfish bitch.'

Billy looked up at his mother's unfamiliarly harsh words.

'I'd like to have seen you settled with young Ettie Wilkins,' Myrtle said, setting about attacking the next slice off the loaf.

'Me and all, Mum,' Billy said softly, tucking his tobacco pouch into his trouser pocket.

Myrtle handed him a tin plate with two slices of bread scraped with marge. Billy took it silently.

'I give that wicked cow all the stew. Don't know what I'm gonna give Alfie and Tommy when they get in.'

'I'll send the little 'un out down Sclater Street for some pie and mash, Mum, don't upset yerself.' Billy stood up and put the untouched bread and marge down on the table, then he put his arms round his mother and kissed the top of her head. 'Yer've always been soft, ain't yer?' he said gently. 'Yer wouldn't care if yer starved as long as us lot had some grub in our bellies.'

'You're a good boy, Bill,' Myrtle said fondly.

Billy blushed, thinking about the talking-to he'd had from Cyril Reed only a few hours before. 'Tell yer what, Ma,' he said. 'Soon as that room downstairs that the landlord was talking about comes up, you tell him we'll have it.'

'Do what?' Myrtle pushed Billy away from her and stared at him as though he'd suggested moving into Buckingham Palace. 'But how can we?'

'I had a chat with the governor today,' he said, editing the events for his mother's benefit. 'He's offered me a bit of overtime. Regular if I want it.'

'Billy.' Myrtle buried her head in her son's shoulder and thought how blessed she was and how proud his father would have been to see him looking after her so well. 'Three rooms, all to ourselves.' She lifted her chin and looked at him. 'No. We don't need all that. You keep a bit for yerself, yer work hard enough. Put a bit by.'

Billy opened his mouth to interrupt.

'No, son, I won't hear another word. Yer'll find yerself a nice girl to settle down with, you see if yer don't. Then yer'll need a few shillings to set yerself up in a place of yer own.'

This time Billy couldn't find the heart to answer her.

Chapter 12

A new phase of even harder work had begun for Ettie. Jacob expected so much of her. If Ettie had been tired before, now she was exhausted. She learnt codes: complicated combinations of words; questions; even different tones of voice and sneezes. Sometimes she would lose patience, being unable to believe that she could learn another thing, or could cram another idea into her aching head. But, by the time the cold winter months had taken a grip on the London streets, Ettie could 'read' Jacob's mind. She had become a wonder of telepathy – a sure way to convince even the most sceptical. And she knew how to pick up the slightest cues from an audience, how to fit them into stories which they could – such wonders! – associate directly to their lives. And, even if no one responded to a message, Jacob assured her, it would still work: she would simply point to one of the more timid-looking individuals and say in a low, serious voice: 'I want you to promise me that you will find out about this. It is very important. The message is very important indeed.'

After a particularly tiring day of learning and more learning, Ettie went out for a walk, supposedly to buy a newspaper, but really needing to clear her head. Jacob had not seemed to mind that the local agent hadn't tipped him off about vacant premises for them to set up a penny gaff that week. Lou and the rest of the acts weren't too pleased about it, but Ettie was delighted, as it meant that the evenings were her own, to do as she pleased, for seven whole days. She wanted no more than to settle down with a pot of tea, a plate of cakes from the baker's shop on the corner, read for a while, then have another gloriously early night.

Jacob had recently moved a fold-away cot into the bedroom, but Ettie was still allowed to keep the big brass bed, even though she was the shorter of the two of them by several inches. Jacob didn't seem to mind discomfort. And Ettie didn't plan to argue: she loved that bed more than any other change that had occurred in her life over the past few months.

With the newspaper under her arm, Ettie walked up the steps to what had become her new home and let herself in, pulling off her jacket almost before she was inside the front door, and throwing it on to a chair in the sitting room. She still wasn't used to having a place to hang her clothes, as Jacob was always keen to remind her. She kicked off her shoes, and sat at the table to read the paper.

'Is the kettle boiled?' she asked Jacob.

'Yes, madam,' Jacob called from the little bathroom. 'Tea will be served as soon as I finish in here.'

'Cheeky bugger,' she scolded him with a laugh.

Ettie followed each line of the newspaper stories with her finger. Her reading was now much improved, but still she silently mouthed each word.

'Bloody hell!' she shouted, bringing Jacob rushing in, his chin still half soaped from his incomplete shave.

'Whatever is it?'

'Listen to this,' she squealed, her voice quavering out of control. 'A woman in Mile End Old Town has been sent to prison. A month's hard labour, Jacob. Just for telling some girl's fortune for a tanner. A bloody tanner. What the sodding hell have you got me involved in? If they do her for asking for a tanner...'

'Don't concern yourself with such matters, Ettie,' he said, waving his cut-throat blade around with airy indifference. 'I will be careful to indicate to our–' he paused – 'fellow investigators into the spirit world, that we do not ask for payment, merely that they should contribute some small donation, perhaps, to enable us to carry on our work. And with your charm and beauty that should prove to be no problem at all.'

Jacob didn't notice the frown of concern which, though barely discernible, clouded Ettie's face for a brief moment.

He seemed so caring and gentle, and genuinely to like her, but Ettie was increasingly bothered as to why Jacob had never made any attempt to touch her – other than a brotherly pat on the arm, a chivalrous helping on with her coat. The worst part of it was that, against everything she would have believed only a few months ago, Ettie wanted him to touch her. Wanted him to touch her very much. She had always believed that the only man who would ever make her feel like that would be Billy; that one day her life would simply sort itself out and they would wind up together, happily married with a whole brood of red-haired babies. Even though they had never even kissed, she had always just taken it for granted that she loved Billy, and that he loved her. Maybe that had been the problem: she had taken too much for granted. And now she hadn't only admitted to herself that she was falling in love with Jacob, a strange, enigmatic man from who-knew-where, but she had developed a physical desire for him as well.

Not for the first time in the last few months, Ettie wished that she could talk to Maisie. She always had a way of making her feel better, of making her laugh at herself. But knowing how Maisie had also expected her to pair up with Billy one day, she didn't know if her friend would ever want to see her again. It seemed unbearably sad to her, that that part of her life might only be a memory, that it was behind her.

Jacob came into the room, concentrating on fastening his cape round his shoulders. 'Are you ready?' he asked, but as he raised his eyes to look at her all thoughts of his cape left him. 'You look so beautiful, Ettie,' he murmured. 'Truly beautiful. Every man in the restaurant will envy me.' He touched her hair, taming a wayward, shiny black curl with his sensitive, magician's hands. 'Tonight, as we make ready to enter 1888, we will be celebrating more than the beginning of a New Year, we will be celebrating a new you. You have been a wonderful student, Ettie. Wonderful.'

'Ta,' she said before she could help herself. 'Thank you, I mean.'

He smiled, his eyes crinkling with amusement. 'You have learnt well, Ettie, but I think it might be better if, for a while, until we train your voice properly, you maintain a mysterious silence during our performances. Yes. Silence.' The idea inspired him. 'Mysteriously silent. That's good. Very good. We will cast a veil over your identity. Instead of a new name, you will have no name! You will be the mysterious, silent beauty. "Watch her!" I will command them. "Watch her! Death itself has whispered in her ear." Ettie, the world will be at our feet.'

'Oh yes, you're a real genius, you are,' said Ettie casting her eyes heavenwards. 'So how do you think I'm going to give the messages out if I'm silent?'

Jacob shook his head in admiration. 'Ettie, you are not only beautiful, you are clever as well. And sensible. I become carried away with my schemes and you bring me back to reality. But don't worry, I'll think of something.'

'I bet you will,' she said simply.

'We'll go far, the two of us, Ettie. We can't fail.'

—

Jacob and Ettie stood outside on the pavement, hoping somehow to attract a cab to join the crowds of celebrating Londoners who were heading towards the West End. There was expectation in the air, the feeling that something momentous was about to happen.

'You've grown very quiet, Ettie. Is something wrong?'

'I feel, I don't know. Sad. And guilty, I suppose. It's so long since I saw my mum.' She looked up into Jacob's face. 'Before you say anything. I know what I told you about her and how she treated me, but she is my mum. And she wasn't always like she is now. She was different once. She did the best she could.' She sighed loudly. 'And I miss my mates. I know, I know,' she said wretchedly, before he could object. 'My friends.'

'Let's change our plans. Instead of going to supper at the restaurant, we'll go to Whitechapel to see in the New Year. I think I owe you that.'

Ettie's face brightened. 'Owe me? Why?'

'For many reasons, but one very good one is that you stayed with me at Christmas instead of going to your mother.'

'Mum was all right. She doesn't know one day from the next, long as she's got her bottle.'

'I still appreciated it. Even though I don't celebrate the festival, it would have been very lonely up in those rooms without you.' Ettie looked hard at Jacob, trying to see if he was mocking her, trying to see beyond his sophisticated, cultured exterior into the mind, and maybe into the heart of a caring, sentimental man who could surprise her even after she had shared his home for nearly seven months.

'Are you sure you don't mind going down there?'

'Of course I don't. And I will be intrigued to see how cockneys celebrate their New Year.'

'We can go to the Frying Pan,' she said excitedly. 'That's our local: me and the girls used to have a right old time down there. And me mum's always in there. You see, we'll have a right old time and all.'

Jacob smiled to see her look so happy, even though she had slipped so easily back to her old way of speaking. 'And I'm sure it'll be a sight safer than the West End tonight,' he said. 'There's been a bad feeling since that fellow was killed in the riot.'

Ettie's smile disappeared. 'It makes me wild. All them people on the streets for his funeral, all weeping and wailing. It was one bloke what died. One. Do you know how many people die every single day on the streets in the slums? How many babies starve to death?'

'Ettie, that's…'

'Different?' she almost yelled. 'Is that what you were going to say? Different because he died in the West End?'

'No, Ettie, it wasn't. I was going to say that one man dying in his protest against poverty has seemed to touch the hearts of the privileged in a way that nothing else has. It's brought it to the attention of people who were ignorant of the truth.'

'I'm sorry, Jacob. I shouldn't have shouted like that. Let's leave it, eh? Not tonight. Don't let's spoil everything.' She tried a small smile. 'I'm looking forward to seeing Mum.' Then even the small smile disappeared. 'We are still going, aren't we?'

'Yeah, darling,' said Jacob in a very creditable imitation of a cockney twang. ''Course we are.' He held out his arm to Ettie and winked broadly. 'Shall we be off then, me old duchess?'

She took his arm and squeezed it.

'What's so funny then, cocker?' asked Jacob.

'You,' she said. 'To think I once believed you had special powers.'

'Maybe I have,' he said, reverting to his usual polished tones. 'In that case, show us how you can get a cab, eh? I'm freezing me arse off standing here.'

Within fifteen minutes they were in Thrawl Street, and Jacob was handing over the fare to the cabman.

'Watch yerselves,' called the driver from his perch, tipping his hat before pocketing the coins Jacob had just handed him. 'This pub ain't really the place for the likes of ladies and gents like yerselves, yer know. Take care, won't yer? And Happy New Year to both of yer.'

'There's one fellow who's convinced you're a lady,' said Jacob as the cab pulled away into Brick Lane, leaving them standing outside the Frying Pan. 'Now let's see what your mother makes of you.'

Chapter 13

'Well, bugger me, look at her ladyship!' shrieked Florrie as she dragged Ada in a beeline across the pub, through the throng of laughing and singing merrymakers, towards the door where Ettie and Jacob had just come in: Flo and Ada knew the look of a soft touch when they saw one.

'Hello, girls,' smiled Ettie, trying to hide the fact that she'd wrinkled her nose at the now unaccustomed stench of unwashed clothes and bodies. 'Jacob, these are my old pals, Ada and Florrie.'

'Long time no see,' said Ada, looking Jacob up and down. 'This the fancy man we've heard so much about? A crook or something, ain't yer mate?'

Ettie's mouth dropped open, but Jacob took the question in good part.

'A very successful bank robber actually, madam,' he said, taking off his tall hat and bowing low to the two brides. 'Now, may I spend some of my ill-gotten gains on buying you charming ladies a drink or two with which to see in the New Year?'

Florrie nudged Ada sharply in the ribs. 'We've got a right one here,' she giggled.

Ettie did her best to keep up with Jacob as he worked his way through the crowded room to the bar. She got there just as he was handing over a handful of coins to the landlord. Ettie stretched forward and took back a florin.

'Yer know we don't do our own round here, Patrick,' she said, handing the money back to Jacob.

'Sorry, sweetheart, didn't know he was with you,' said Patrick in his soft Irish lilt, shrugging happily before getting on with serving the line of customers vying for his attention.

Jacob laughed and picked up the glasses from the beer-stained counter as Ada yelled across that she'd found them a table.

Holding the glasses high above his head, Jacob led Ettie through the crowd to where Ada and Florrie where now ensconced in the corner of the room near the door.

'I'll drink this, then I'll nip over and fetch me mum,' Ettie said, licking the thick, creamy foam that the porter had left on her lips.

'Yeah, you do that, Ett,' said Flo, flashing her brown, gap-toothed smile at Jacob. 'We'll look after yer friend here for yer, won't we, Ada?'

'Certainly will,' beamed Ada.

'How charming of you ladies to offer,' said Jacob, flashing his own, white-toothed smile in return. 'But I think that I should accompany Ettie if she has to go outside – especially on an evening such as this.'

'Couldn't yer just eat him up?' said Ada, pinching Jacob's cheek between a filth-ingrained finger and thumb. 'Yer a lucky mare, Ettie Wilkins.'

'Here, look what the cat's dragged in,' said Ada, gesturing towards the door with her already half-empty glass.

'Yer can see she's been on the turps already,' smirked Flo.

'Cor, you ain't wrong there,' sneered Ada. 'Yer can smell she has and all. I thought you ponged bad enough, Flo, but she stinks.'

'Thanks very much,' said Flo good-naturedly, and sipped delicately at her gin.

'Look at the state of her,' continued Ada with a disgusted shake of her head, and gulped down the last of her drink.

Ettie took a deep breath, stood up, and walked over to the barely sensible woman who had just stumbled into the bar.

'Ettie?' Jacob scraped back his chair, unsure where she was going and whether or not to join her.

Ettie swallowed hard, took the inebriated woman's arm and said gently, 'Hello, Mum. How yer been?'

The pub's drinkers were now in almost full celebratory flight: the piano was going non-stop, songs were being sung, and the occasional knees-up was beginning to break out. In the corner by the door, Ettie had wedged her mother between her and Flo to keep her upright, while Jacob and Ada made sure that drinks were fetched at increasingly frequent intervals from the bar.

'Mum,' said Ettie earnestly, as she tried to keep Sarah upright, 'please, let me get yer a different place to stay. Somewhere near me, over by Vicky Park, then I can look after yer.'

'Bow?' She almost spat the word out. 'Leave off. What do I wanna go and live in that shit-hole for?'

Ettie winced. 'Well, if I make sure yer have enough money for... for whatever yer need, at least promise me you'll get rid of that lodger.' Ettie went to put her finger to the deep bruising on Sarah's otherwise whey-coloured face, but her mother brushed her hand away.

'Yer don't know nothing, you. How d'yer think I'd do that, eh? He likes hurting people, see.' Sarah's eyes swum in and out of focus.

'You wouldn't have to worry about that. I'd make sure someone'd get rid of him for you, Mum.'

'Maybe I like having him around,' challenged Sarah, holding up her empty glass to whoever was interested.

Jacob took it from her and went to the bar.

'Yer all right, buggering off with yer fancy man, but how about me, eh?' Sarah went on, her logic as well as her speech confused by the drink. 'Who's meant to give him what he wants every minute of the night and day?'

'Shut up, Mum. Yer not making any sense.' Ettie's face was flushed as much from embarrassment as from the stuffy atmosphere in the over-crowded pub. 'Do you wanna get rid of him, or what?'

'Aw, belt up yerself,' slurred Sarah.

'Do you think that your mother should be getting home to bed?' asked Jacob quietly as he handed Sarah the drink and watched her pour it straight down her throat. He'd done as Ettie had asked and had told Patrick to cut her drinks with water, but she was still knocking back enough to lay out a six-foot docker.

'Don't wanna go to bed,' mumbled Sarah, belching loudly. 'I wanna dance.'

'Mum…' said Ettie, and tried to restrain Sarah, but she'd somehow got her second wind. She staggered to her feet, sending the table and her chair crashing to the ground.

Jacob picked up the table, then collected the broken glasses and took them over to the bar while Ettie tried to calm her mother. But before Ettie could stop her, Sarah had lurched her way into a little knot of drinkers, who willingly made a space to watch the spectacle of the drunken woman dancing a wild jig. Much to the amusement of her audience, she bent over and flung her skirts over her head, showing her torn and hole-ridden drawers to anyone who cared to look.

'Go on, why don't yer get 'em down, Sarah? Go on, girl, show us a bit more of what yer've got,' one of them mocked, while the others held their noses and grimaced at the sight of the woman making a show of herself.

Ettie squeezed between two of the whooping, jeering men. 'Stop it!' she yelled, with tears streaming down her face, hammering her fists on the chest of one of her mother's tormentors. 'Leave her alone!'

The man looked down at Ettie and grinned. 'Take after yer mother, do yer darling?' he smirked, grabbing hold of her wrists. 'How about it then? I could fancy a good-looker like you.'

'Let me go,' screeched Ettie, squirming to break free of the man's grip.

'If yer know what's good for yer, yer'll do as the lady says.'

The man let her go.

Ettie dropped her fists to her side and turned to see Billy Bury, arms folded, chin in the air, his stare threatening any of them to disagree. Behind him stood Alfie, a bottle held ready in his hand like a cosh.

'Go on,' said Bill, 'all of yers. On yer way. There's plenty going on down the Butcher's. Get yourselves down there.'

With much mumbling and complaining, the little group did as they were told: there might have been six of them and only two Burys, but the odds were still against them coming out on top.

'Ta, Bill. Alf,' said Ettie, and tried to take her mother by the arm.

'Piss off,' hissed Sarah, shoving Ettie back against the bar. She swayed towards the door. 'Yer've forgotten how to have a bit of fun, that's your trouble, girl,' she called over her shoulder. 'Yer've turned into a right little snot-nosed bitch.' She opened the door and spat violently on the pub floor, then disappeared into the night.

'Ettie?' Jacob pushed through the crowd at the bar and touched her on the shoulder.

'You took yer time showing up,' sneered Billy. 'Frightened yer might get that pretty face of yours kicked in if there was any trouble?'

'Who's this then?' asked Alfie. 'Out slumming, are yer mate?'

'He's with me, Alf,' said Ettie impatiently, making her way towards the door. 'Can't yer all keep yer noses out for once? You've made Mum go off gawd-knows-where.'

Outside on the pavement Ettie didn't know whether to head for Tyvern Court or the Butcher's Arms. Her chest rose and fell as she leaned back against the soot-covered wall of the pub, not bothering about her new dress any more.

'Ettie, I had no idea you were in trouble. Believe me, I wouldn't have left you. You know that.'

She turned to see Jacob standing beside her, his face creased with concern.

'Do me a favour,' she said wearily. 'Go back in and have a drink, will yer, and leave me alone for a bit.'

'But it isn't safe…'

'It weren't exactly safe in there just now, was it?' she interrupted him. 'Now please, leave me alone.'

'I told you, Ettie. I didn't realise what was happening.'

'*Please*,' she said, and turned her back.

'As you wish,' he said coldly.

Feeling a pressure on her arm, Ettie spun round ready to shout at Jacob to leave her alone, but the words dissolved in her mouth. 'Billy,' she said. 'I didn't expect it to be you.'

'Like the old bad penny, ain't I, Ett?' he said, smiling gently. 'I keep turning up, don't I?'

'Thanks for helping us back there,' Ettie said, doing her best to return his smile. 'I couldn't believe it, Bill. She was never as bad as this. She's changed so much.'

'She ain't the only one,' he said, raising his eyebrows at her elegant, candy-striped skirt and bodice.

'These are just clothes,' shrugged Ettie.

'Just clothes?' Billy said incredulously.

'You know what I mean, Bill,' insisted Ettie. 'Me mum's changed deep down. She's different.'

Billy didn't say anything, he just stood quietly by her side, rolling himself a cigarette and watching the revellers make their rowdy way up and down Brick Lane.

'Least *they're* having a good time,' Ettie said eventually as one particularly boisterous crowd wove its way past them.

There was another pause, then Billy said over the din: 'I heard yer was in the Pan, that's why I come down here, to see yer like.' He didn't look at her as he spoke, but kept his eyes on the pavement as he ground out his cigarette butt under his boot.

'I'm glad yer did,' answered Ettie, glancing sideways at him.

'Didn't think there was gonna be no rows though.' Billy laughed. 'Just like old times eh, Ett? When me, you, May and Alfie used to go out for a few. We had some laughs, didn't we?'

'How's May doing?' asked Ettie, turning to him.

'She misses yer,' said Bill, still staring down at the flagstones.

'Where's she tonight, then?'

Billy grinned. 'Gone and got herself a boyfriend, ain't she?'

'Yeah?'

'Yeah. Funny-looking geezer from down Union Street. But he's a good un. Got himself a fruit stall down the Lane.'

'Myrtle'll like that.'

He looked directly at Ettie. 'Yer right. And looks ain't everything, are they, Ett?'

'May always wanted to find herself someone steady,' said Ettie. 'I hope she's happy. Give her my love, won't yer, Bill?' As she spoke she shivered.

'Yer cold. Here.' Billy slipped out of his jacket and Ettie let him drape it round her shoulders. She didn't move or pull away when his hands brushed against her throat as he straightened the collar.

'Ta, Bill,' she whispered, looking up into his eyes. 'You always was good to me. Ta.'

Billy gulped and started staring at his boots again, but he quickly looked up. 'I forgot!' he exclaimed, and suddenly started rummaging around in the jacket pockets.

'Here! What's your game? Get yer hands off,' said Ettie, pulling away. 'Whatever's got into you, Billy?'

'This,' said Billy, handing her a little leather pouch that he'd taken from the inside jacket pocket. 'I got something for yer, look.'

Ettie frowned at him. 'I thought yer'd taken leave of yer senses,' she said, pulling the coat round her.

'Go on, open it,' he urged her.

Ettie pulled open the drawstring fastening and shook the contents out on to her palm. 'Bill!'

'Do yer like it?'

'I dunno what to say.' In her hand was an oval, golden locket and chain. She held it up to the light coming from the pub window. On the front of the locket was the letter 'E' engraved in fancy script. 'It's ever so pretty, Bill,' she breathed. 'But yer shouldn't have. Yer shouldn't waste yer money on me.'

'I'm glad yer like it,' he said, and took the locket from her hands. 'Turn round and I'll do it up for yer.' As he fiddled with the delicate fastener, he spoke to her over her shoulder. 'I'm doing right well for meself at work, Ett. Things went wrong for a bit but I've sorted meself out now. I've even been able to put a few shillings by and pay for another room for Mum. And buy yer this necklace.' He stood back a little. 'There.'

Ettie turned back to face him. 'Well,' she said, rearranging the chain in the pin-tucks of her blouse. 'What d'yer think?'

'I think yer look like a proper princess,' he said.

'Ta, Bill,' she said.

'Yer keep saying that tonight,' he smiled.

'And I mean it,' she said. 'But, honest, yer shouldn't go spending yer money on me.'

'I couldn't help meself,' he grinned. 'Soon as I saw it in the pawnshop I knew yer'd like it. So I put down a deposit on it, then paid it off over a couple of weeks. I've been keeping it for yer ever since. Cos I knew yer'd come back, Ett.' He leaned closer to her. 'Cos yer a Whitechapel girl, ain't yer, like Maisie always said.'

'That don't mean I have to stay in this hole all me life,' said Ettie faintly.

'No, but it means that yer know what's what. What's important in life. Yer've seen it all if yer come from round here.' He looked into her eyes and, even in the gaslight, Ettie could see that he'd blushed crimson. 'That's one of the reasons I've been working so hard. I figured out what matters and I've been saving see. For us. Waiting for yer to see sense and come home. We belong together, Ett, you and me.'

The smile vanished from her face. 'I think yer've got it all wrong, Bill,' she said. 'I ain't come back. Not like you mean.'

'Yer mean yer going back with him?' Billy shook his head disbelievingly. 'After what happened in there, when he left yer to let all them blokes start on yer?'

'Don't exaggerate, Bill. Nothing happened in there and you know it.'

'I know you was glad enough to see me and Alfie.'

'Jacob just didn't notice, that's all.'

'He didn't *wanna* notice, yer mean.'

'Oh leave off, Billy,' she said, turning her back on him. 'Can't yer stop going on?'

'Yer making excuses for him, that's all. What's so special about him anyway? You don't know nothing about him. Or where he's from. Nothing.'

'How do you know what I know about him?' said Ettie, spinning round, her face almost touching Billy's and her voice rising to a yell.

'Well, yer didn't know that the bloke's a bleed'n coward, did yer?' Billy hollered back at her. 'That was sodding obvious.'

'Is everything all right out here?' At the sound of Jacob's voice, Ettie and Billy leapt back from each other.

'It was, till you showed up,' muttered Billy.

'Shut up, Bill,' hissed Ettie, hastily turning away from them both. She tucked the locket down inside her blouse, hoping that Jacob hadn't noticed it.

'Is something wrong?' Jacob asked.

'No,' she snapped. 'Why should there be?'

'Is this why you asked me to leave you alone?' he said evenly. 'So that you could be alone with your friend?'

'What're yer letting him speak to yer like that for, Ett?' Billy demanded to know. 'You don't have to answer to no one.'

'No. And you don't have to poke yer nose into my business. Now why don't yer piss off, both of yer. Just leave me alone. And yer can take this back and all,' she shouted angrily, throwing Billy's jacket down on to the damp pavement.

'I'll forget what yer've said tonight, Ettie. I don't think yer really meant it,' Billy said, picking up his coat and shaking it. 'I'll put it down to yer being upset by yer mum and everything. But I'm telling yer, I meant every word I said tonight.' He put on his jacket, walked off down Thrawl Street towards Commercial Street, and quickly melted into the shadows.

'What did he say that was so momentous?' Jacob asked, looking in the direction in which Billy had disappeared.

Ettie was just about to open her mouth and hope that some convincing story about what Billy had said would come out, but she didn't have to worry. Suddenly the sound of chimes and peels rang out, competing with the wild yells from the pub and the crashing of saucepan lids and kettles from the surrounding streets.

'Eighteen eighty-eight,' said Jacob.

'Happy bloody New Year,' said Ettie.

PART TWO

Spring 1888

'But Jacob, say no one comes?' Ettie threw her gloves on to the chair and flopped down on the bed, her energy drained by anxiety. 'This is my one big chance to do something right. I couldn't bear it if it all goes wrong.'

'Don't worry, Ettie.' Jacob spoke to Ettie, but he was looking into the cheval looking-glass, contemplating his immaculately pressed and brushed outfit. 'All the posters and the leaflets have been distributed,' he said, picking at an almost imperceptible speck of fluff on his shoulder. 'And the tickets for the first show have been sold out for a week. So don't worry. Just remember what I told you. Relax and think of it as just another performance.'

'I don't know why you're so calm,' she snapped, her fear making her aggressive. 'It's hardly a penny gaff, is it?' She stared hard at the ceiling. 'Till the rehearsals I hadn't even been inside a posh theatre before, let alone done a show in one.' She rubbed her hand over her face then turned over to face him. Propping herself up on her elbow she asked, 'Say they don't like me? You should have got Lou to help you with the new show, Jacob. She's a pro, not a know-nothing like me.'

'They'll love you, Ettie, believe me,' he said, squinting over his shoulder at his reflection and trying to see if his back view was as fetching as that of his front.

'And I keep thinking about that woman who got nicked for fortune-telling. I might have done a lot of things but I've never been nicked.'

'I'll explain again,' Jacob said, his voice beginning to betray his diminishing reserve of patience. 'We are not fortune-tellers, Ettie. Nor do we claim to be. We are researchers conducting investigations into the spirit world. If we *do* offer any clairvoyant guidance, then that will be done in private sittings and for a contribution – a donation – certainly never a fee.'

'I don't think I wanna do this,' she whined, curling up and hugging the pillow to her chest. 'I really don't.'

Jacob walked over to the bed and pulled her up roughly by the arm. 'Ettie, pull yourself together. I believe that you are actually doing this deliberately. Do you want to go back to that hovel in Whitechapel? Do you want to have a string of babies and die before you're thirty from the sheer wear of it all?'

Ettie sank back down on the bed and rolled over, turning her back to him.

'Get your cape and hat, Ettie. Now. We have to leave.' He grabbed hold of the door-handle and pulled it open with unnecessary force. 'And for God's sake take care with your voice. You sound like a guttersnipe.'

'Billy never talked to me like that,' she said pathetically.

'Billy had no cause to,' he snapped back. 'He had nothing to offer and nothing to lose.'

Dry-mouthed with fear at what was to come, and too scared even to feel fury at his harsh words, Ettie sat rigidly and silently next to Jacob in the back of the cab. She heard nothing of his final instructions for the performance. All she wanted was to be sick. The rocking of the hansom as it sped over the uneven cobbles of the road, combined with the smell of polished leather and sweating horse-flesh, made her feel even worse. Perhaps she really did want to be back in Whitechapel – still be anonymous little Ettie Wilkins, pulling fur for a living and meeting Billy Bury for a drink or two in the Frying Pan. He was a real nice lad, Billy, she thought – secretly putting her hand to where the locket he had given her nestled beneath her blouse – everyone said so. And he could have been hers. So whatever was she doing being driven along in a cab, dressed up like a Christmas parcel and kidding herself that she could put on a show in front of hundreds and hundreds of people with some posh geezer who didn't give a damn about her? It was almost funny: only a few months ago she'd never even been in a cab, and now she was wishing she could get out and walk.

'I can't do it, Jacob,' she said into her lap. 'I'm sorry, but I can't.'

'Too late,' he said simply, 'we're here.'

'You hard bastard,' she mouthed to herself.

She allowed Jacob to lead her past the front doors of the theatre, too numb to object. She didn't even notice that a long queue had already formed at the box office.

Jacob pushed her firmly and wordlessly into the side alley which led to the stage door. The stale smelling, enclosed space was curiously comforting in its cosy familiarity. If it had been just a bit grubbier and dingier, with a few more dusty weeds growing up between the cracks, it would almost have been like the entry into Tyvern Court, where she had once lived what now seemed a blissfully uncomplicated existence.

Jacob walked closely behind her, herding her towards the warmly lit door like a shepherd guiding a recalcitrant sheep from the hillside.

As they mounted the worn stone steps, the doorman greeted them with a cheery welcome. 'Never seen nothing like the business the box office is doing for this little lady,' he said to Jacob, his face wreathed in smiles and his red cheeks shining. 'All of London's gone spirit-mad I reckon.'

Ettie managed a nervous smile in return. 'Will the house be full, do you think?' she asked him timorously.

'To bursting, little lady. To bursting,' the jolly-faced man reassured her. 'They can't wait to get their minces on yer!'

Ettie took a deep relieved breath. 'Thank you,' she said, and walked briskly towards the dressing room.

Jacob handed the man a coin. 'Thank you,' he said. 'She needed that.'

'Yer welcome, sir,' said the man, winking broadly and touching his finger to his forehead in a little salute. 'Don't want to see the little lady get all excitable, do we now? I'm used to the theatrical temperament, you see.' He bit the coin automatically before he pocketed it, then handed Jacob a small stack of envelopes. 'Letters, sir,' he explained to the puzzled-looking Jacob. 'I wasn't telling no lies to the little lady. There's plenty of interest in the show, all right. Them posters of yours have been bringing 'em in and no mistake.' He chuckled. 'The ghosties and spirits always gets 'em going.' He winked again, squeezing his watery old eye tight. 'Yer on to a winner if ever I saw one, guv.'

The old stage doorman would have done well to have started in the clairvoyance business himself: his prediction for the success of the show proved entirely accurate. Ettie and Jacob were a sensation. From the moment the lights were dimmed and Jacob drew back the veil covering the cabinet of mysteries, the audience were in the palm of his hand, ready to be amazed and bewildered.

'Ladies and gentleman, I must ask that everyone remains silent until I say otherwise.' Jacob stabbed a finger towards the gallery. 'Even that gentleman up there in the front row who is missing his watch.'

The thunderous applause in response to Jacob returning the duped man's property, via a series of eagerly helpful hands, was well worth the florin Jacob had slipped the front-of-house usher for his help before the show in purloining the timepiece.

'To begin the demonstration, ladies and gentleman, I shall walk amongst you. I will ask that the person whose shoulder I touch shall stand up and hold aloft a personal item. If it pleases the rest of those here present that that person be selected for the experiment, then a rousing "Yes" must follow. If that person is not to the liking of the rest of those present, then the response I would ask for is a loud "No". Is that clear?'

The audience roared their affirmation that all was indeed clear, then they sat on the edges of their seats in awe-struck anticipation of what was to come.

Ettie sat impassively on the stage, her eyes fixed on an unseen distant image as she supposedly fell deeper into the trance in which Jacob had put her.

It was fortunate that the theatre was so large, or they might have heard her muttering under her breath as she concentrated on making the links with Jacob's patter and the code he had so painstakingly taught her over the months.

With all the items spectacularly successfully identified, and Ettie even deeper in her state of trance, the spirits began to float and the messages began to flow. By now, even the most cynical member of the audience was captivated and enthralled by Ettie's mysterious powers. She glowed with success, dazzled them with her loveliness, and shone with the power she had over the witnesses to her triumph.

'You were magnificent!' said Jacob, releasing the cork which left the bottle with an exuberant rush of exploding bubbles, hitting the far wall of the shabby little dressing room. 'This, Ettie, is the first of many, many celebrations. We'll go from success to success. We'll get bigger rooms: a proper apartment with live-in staff. We'll get you a dozen new hats. New everything.'

Ettie sipped the fizzing wine and grinned. 'I *was* good, wasn't I?' She closed her eyes and held her hands at arm's length. 'I can feel the spirits,' she moaned sensually. 'I can feel them. They are here. They are giving me a message. A message for someone called, Alfred. Is it Alfred? Or Albert? He has seen a loved one pass over recently. The departed one wants him to know that you are forgiven and that you mustn't blame yourself for what happened...' She flashed open her eyes and gave Jacob a cheeky grin. 'Good, eh?'

'Good indeed.' Jacob clinked his glass against hers. 'Carry on like this and you'll be able to have everything your heart desires.'

'Everything?' Ettie looked him up and down and winked. 'We'll have to see about that, won't we?' Then she flicked her skirts to one side and went over to the window. She leaned on the window- ledge and looked down on the scene in the street below. She drew in her breath with delighted excitement. 'Oh, Jacob, come over here and look. Just look at them.'

'That's what I like about you, Ettie Wilkins,' said Jacob, walking across the room to her. 'You're never afraid to express pleasure.' He stood behind her and rested his hands lightly on her shoulders. 'Now let's see what's caught your fancy this time?' Ettie pointed down to the scene below, where a line of carriages was parading along the gaslit street past the appreciative men who strolled by or stood waiting in the shadows. A young woman, dressed in a striped scarlet and black costume, complete with matching feathered bonnet, driving a beautifully turned-out phaeton, headed the parade. To complement her outfit, the gleaming black pony carried a single scarlet plume, which bobbed between its pert little ears.

Ettie sighed in undisguised admiration.

'Ettie!' Jacob seized her hard by the shoulders and spun her round to face him. 'Those women. Surely you know what they are? They're whores. They are out there parading for customers.'

'I know,' she said, turning round and gazing fixedly down at the brazen procession below. 'They're only earning a living – just like Ada and Flo and the other girls. And at least they're honest about what they're doing. *And* they're not beholding to no one.' She paused, then added, 'Maybe they didn't have brides in Paris or wherever it was you run away from.'

Jacob frowned and went to sit at the narrow dressing-table. He smeared cream over his face, then began wiping off the thick theatrical make-up from his cheeks. When he spoke, his tone was flat and expressionless. 'I need to go to the dressmaker tomorrow,' he said, indicating the marbled, leather-bound notebook. 'To collect some of my designs I've had made up for you.' He lifted his chin and tilted his head from side to side, checking his reflection for any remains of powder or greasepaint. 'I'm sending a letter to confirm your first performance in a private house for next month. You'll need to look the part. Those clothes are all very well for the theatre, but for close-up work, you'll need something decent.'

'You haven't mentioned any of this before,' Ettie said excitedly, and skipped over to him, the parade below and any difficult questions about Paris instantly forgotten.

'It was meant to be a surprise.' His voice was cold.

'More new clothes!' Ettie put down her glass on the dressing-table, stood behind him and hugged him. She looked at the seriousness of his reflection in the glass. 'Blimey, cheer up, Jacob. It might never happen.'

He ignored her attempts to make him smile. 'We'd better be getting back to Bow,' he said, pulling away from her. 'You need to get some rest and I have to look over the accounts and receipts. And reply to all your correspondence.'

'Suit yourself,' she said, matching his coldness. 'I could never do with moods and sulking myself, but if that's how you feel.'

'I'm not sulking and I really am going to be very busy tonight. The letters are pouring in. There are a lot of lonely people out there looking for answers.'

'There's one here and all,' she said quietly to herself as she slung her cape carelessly round her shoulders and went to stand by the dressing-room door. 'Well, come on. You was the one who wanted to get off home.'

The next day, Ettie woke late to find that Jacob had already gone out. The performance must have taken more out of her than she had realised. She slipped into a cotton housecoat and went into the little kitchen to make some tea.

She was on her second cup of dark brewed Assam – a taste she had acquired since meeting Jacob, and very different from the brew made from the almost leafless powder that she had been raised to drink – when she heard the key in the lock.

'That you, Jacob?' she called, determined not to let him carry on with his sulks. 'There's plenty of tea in the pot.'

Jacob walked down the hall to join her at the neatly laid oak table. 'See if there's anything there that you care for,' he said, thrusting a huge brown paper parcel at her.

'The new clothes?' she asked eagerly, and dashed off to the bedroom before Jacob had even had the opportunity to nod his agreement.

As Ettie sorted through the new clothes, holding them up to herself in the mirror, she looked critically at herself. She was a grown woman now, good-looking too, yet still Jacob showed no interest in her – not in that way. They had been sharing the same bedroom for almost a year, but still they changed and bathed separately. Jacob's lack of interest certainly wasn't what she was used to. Since she was barely fifteen years old, she had had her mother's various lodgers forcing themselves on her. She had spent all those sleepless hours dreading the return of her mother's latest 'friend'; she thought then that she would never want another man to touch her ever again. Although there were always the very special feelings she had had for Billy – but they had confused her, and she'd been shy, not knowing how to react.

But now she was older, more confident, with a mature longing for Jacob that she certainly understood, even if he so obviously failed to share her feelings. That was how it was, whether she liked it or not.

She sighed and returned, with only slightly spoiled pleasure, to the clothes.

'Mind you don't tear anything, Ettie,' he called from the sitting room as he poured himself another cup of tea. 'Some of that cloth is very delicate.'

'Delicate! Yer bloody telling me it's delicate,' Ettie shrieked back at him through the door. Excitement, like tiredness, still made her lapse into her old familiar way of speaking. 'Look at it, it's beautiful.'

She came dancing into the sitting room, still dressed in her night things, holding up to her a pale blue silk and lace dress.

'I loved what you gave me out of that trunk of yours, and then them things you got made for me before. But this...' She twirled around the table for Jacob to admire her. 'These make all the others seem, I don't know, ugly. It's like the sun's come out when you look at this.'

Jacob looked at her through impassive, narrowed eyes. 'I'm glad you approve,' he said.

Ettie had enough enthusiasm for both of them. 'Hold this a minute,' she said, pulling her nightgown over her head. She was about to step into the dress, but impulsively she changed her mind and just stood there, naked except for the gold locket and chain at her throat, the blue gown dragging on the rug like a broken doll.

'Don't you think I look nice like I am, with nothing on?' she asked.

'Of course I do. You are very lovely. That's why I chose you.' He stood up and moved towards her.

Ettie felt herself begin to tremble.

He reached out but, instead of taking her in his arms, he lifted the locket, looked at it and said, 'That's a very attractive piece. I didn't know you possessed such a thing.'

'I don't understand you, Jacob, I really don't,' she screamed at him.

She hoped desperately that he didn't realise she was crying as she ran into the bedroom, slamming the door behind her.

Chapter 14

'Hello, little legs,' said Billy, bending down and ruffling the hair of his little brother who was parked on the street-door step. 'What you and yer mates been up to while I've been at work? Been a good boy for Mum, have yer?'

'I reckon I have,' said Tommy, hardly able to speak through the bread and scrape he had jammed in his mouth. 'I've been out playing all day.'

Billy laughed. 'That's a good kid. Keep out from under her feet, eh?' He put his arm on Tommy's shoulder. 'Shove over, let's get in.'

Tommy leaned sideways to let Billy into the hallway. 'Hang on, Bill,' he said, swallowing the remains of the bread. 'Guess what's been happening over there.' Tommy nodded towards Number Twelve.

Billy stopped where he was, half in, half out of the passage. 'No, you tell me.'

'There's been murders over there,' Tommy said, eyes wide. 'Yer should have heard it. Sarah Wilkins and that big ugly lodger of hers.' He shuddered. 'Horrible geezer. At it hammer and tongs they...'

Billy didn't wait to hear the end of the tale, he turned and started sprinting across the court. 'Go and fetch Alfie,' he shouted over his shoulder. He'll be down the Pan or in the Butcher's. Go on, move, yer lazy little sod.'

Billy stood outside Sarah's room; he had to make his mind up what to do. If the bloke was still inside, his only chance was to surprise him – he'd make two of Billy and he was a mad bastard by all accounts. He knew, from how lop-sided it looked, that he'd have to either lift the door to open it or kick it in. He decided on the latter. He leaned back against the banisters and shoved the full force of his hob-nailed boot into the centre panel. He needn't have bothered using so much effort. The only remaining hinge gave way and the door fell flat to the floor, making a dull thud on the filthy bare boards inside.

'Shit!' he gasped and slapped his hand over his mouth. The stench from inside the room was unbearable: it was like something had crawled in there and died. But at least no slaughterman the size of a barge had rushed out to murder him.

He squinted, trying to accustom his eyes to the gloom. In the corner, he could just make out the shape of a bed.

'Sarah?' he called softly. Then louder. 'Sarah!'

'Bill?' The voice wasn't Sarah's, but Alf's calling up the stairs. 'You up there?'

'Yeah, up here, Alf. We're too late, he's gone.'

Alf took the stairs two at a time. 'What happened...' His words came to an abrupt halt. 'Jesus Christ! The stink in here.' He blundered his way over to the window and tried to force it open. All he succeeded in doing was breaking one of the panes. 'Least it's a bit of fresh air,' he said, gasping in a lungful through the gap. 'I dunno how...'

'Sssh, Alf, listen.'

A low, pathetic moan came from the corner.

'Sarah?'

'Who's there?' The words were barely audible.

'Myrtle's boys,' said Billy, swallowing back the bile that was rising in his throat at the thought that he might have to go near her.

'I'm hurt,' she whimpered, her words coming in short rasps as she took shallow, agonising breaths in between. 'The bastard's bashed me up again.'

'I'm sorry, Bill,' said Alf, still with his head to the broken window. 'I don't think I can handle this.'

'Yer ain't alone there, Alf,' said Billy. 'I'll fetch Mum, she'll know what to do. And we can go down the yards and see if we can get hold of the slimy... We'll show him what it feels like to get hurt.'

'Right,' said Alf. 'We'll show the no-good bleeder.' Relieved to escape, Alf was out of the room and down the stairs to fetch Myrtle before anyone changed their mind.

'He won't touch yer no more after we've finished with him, Sarah,' promised Billy as he turned to leave.

'No,' gasped Sarah. 'Don't do nothing to him. Yer don't know him. Don't get him wild with me.' Her voice was barely audible. 'He don't really mean it.'

Billy turned back towards her. He could have walked out without saying anything, and he certainly wasn't one to hurt someone when they were down, but this time he couldn't help himself. 'Like he didn't mean it when he did them things to Ettie?' he said quietly.

'That was her fault,' snivelled Sarah. 'She led him on, she...'

'You disgust me,' sneered Billy, and leapt down the stairs and into the court outside before he did something he'd regret.

Chapter 15

After the debacle in which Stedgely had been exposed in his true colours, Celia knew she no longer needed the likes of him to tell her what to do. *She* would decide what was of most use in improving the lot of the poor and ignorant. She would make secret excursions into the East End; be brave like the great women explorers venturing into the Dark Continent, making her mark on the map of the slums of London. Her savages would be the slum-dwellers of the tenements. She would show no fear. Fear was for hypocrites who said one thing but practised another – like that charlatan preacher. It was not his example she would follow, but the courageous example of the elderly woman who had spoken out so bravely at the meeting. The woman was obviously misguided in her views, Celia knew that, but she did have tremendous spirit. Just as Celia had spirit. She was proud of herself, proud that not even her father, not Stedgely, nor any number like them could destroy her resolve to do good.

Mercifully, for the third evening in a row, her father had been involved in committee meetings at the hospital. As was his habit on such occasions, he would stay behind with his colleagues; then they would go to dinner at one of their clubs, probably spending the night there. There would be no silent meal shared with him, no dissections, and no being forced to do the unspeakable things with him afterwards. She was free – for a few hours more, at least.

'Is my father home, Smithson?'

The butler stood in the doorway of the drawing room, swaying from the effects of helping himself to his master's brandy. His physical appearance, his movements, even the very sounds he always made Celia think of him as an overgrown, bloodless grasshopper.

'No, Miss Celia,' he snarled. 'The master's not dining in tonight. Club with his colleagues.'

Celia stood up, smiled, and walked towards the door, trying to hide her impulse to recoil from his presence, but refusing to let him block her way.

'I think I'll take a turn round the square, Smithson,' she said airily. 'It's such a lovely evening.'

Smithson didn't answer her immediately, nor did he attempt to move from the doorway to allow her to leave the room.

'Was there something else, Smithson?' Celia asked as lightly as possible, hoping that she was succeeding in keeping the tremor from her voice. She never found it easy to speak to the butler, let alone act confidently with him. He was a leering, difficult man, who only ever remembered his position when her father was present.

'I'll call one of the maids to accompany you,' he said.

'No, no, there's no need, Smithson.' Celia held her breath to avoid the alcohol fumes, and brushed past him into the freedom of the large, marble-floored hall. 'I won't be very long. Fresh air, you see. Such a lovely evening.'

'The master won't be best pleased.'

'Why ever not?' She hoped that the crack in her voice sounded like a playful giggle rather than the fear he was managing, merely by his presence, to instil in her.

She took the stairway to her room as quickly as her full skirts and tight corset would allow. Her plan was to collect her cape, a bag, and some money, and then flee from the house before the butler could put any further difficulties in her way.

At a safe distance from the square, Celia raised her hand to hail a passing cab.

'Where to, miss?' asked the cabman, respectfully averting his eyes as he looked down at her through the hatch.

She was already feeling extremely daring: never before had she travelled alone in a hansom. 'Take me to the docks, driver,' she said, confidentially, but without looking up at him.

'Docks? You sure, miss?' Now he certainly *was* looking at her. From where he was sitting she looked every bit the well-to-do young lady; nicely spoken, too, and in a good neighbourhood – she was hardly a brass pitching for sailors. 'You sure?'

'Quite sure. Thank you.'

'Which dock was it you were wanting then?' he asked warily, not bothering to hide his doubt as to the wisdom of what she was asking him to do.

This was something Celia *hadn't* prepared for. 'I'm sorry?'

'Well, what road was yer wanting, then?'

She thought for a moment. 'Any one with tenements or slum-housing surrounding it,' she answered non-committally. Then, searching her memory for a name from one of the League pamphlets she said suddenly: 'The Ratcliffe Highway. Do you know the place?'

'Do what? The Highway? You must be mad – begging your pardon, miss. Do you have any idea what it's like down there?'

'I understand that it has some of the very worst slums.'

'And some of the very worst coshings and all. I'll take you as far as the edge of St Katherine's, and drop yer near the dock gates, but no further. This is a new cab, this is.'

'I'll make it worth your while,' she said, nervously looking back towards the square for any sign of Smithson or one of the maids. 'Or would you prefer me to take another hansom?' she added recklessly.

'Suit yourself, miss. But to tell yer the truth, I don't think yer'll find no one from these parts'll risk going down there. Not unless they belong there themselves. I ain't getting my hansom bashed in and nor will they. It's by St Katherine's or nothing.'

'Close by St Katherine's will do very well then. Thank you,' she said primly.

'And I wouldn't venture no further down there if I was you, miss.'

'I'm quite capable of deciding where I go, thank you, driver.' Again she flashed a nervous glance back along the street.

'Long as you knows what yer doing,' he said, shrugging, then closed the hatch, shook the reins and clicked his tongue, urging his big bay mare forward. Women, he thought to himself. He'd never understand them. He shivered, and drew his rug closer round his knees. What had been a lovely day was now growing chill in the cooler evening air. Nice young ladies going down to the docks. Whatever next, he wondered? The world was going mad and that was the truth. And the traffic, that was another thing, that was getting worse every day. Some days he just didn't know why he drove a cab.

'St Katherine's Dock,' the cabman called down through the hatch.

With all the dignity she could muster, Celia paid the man his fare and, chin held high, stepped down on to the slimy, cobbled roadway. For the last part of the journey she had felt as though she were entering another, previously unknown world, but she was determined not to let the patronising driver see how disturbed she was by her strange surroundings.

She looked round. The roads around were lively with the business of the docks and the river, but the side-streets were darker than any outdoor place she had ever seen in a city. It was as though the scene melted away into blackness. At the sound of the cab pulling away, she turned round and raised her hand to hail the driver, to call him back, to take her home. But she was too late. He was speeding off back to the civilised world she had left. Celia was alone.

Here the river had its own sounds and smells; it couldn't be more different from the pleasant, grassy-banked Thames only a few miles up-river where, in distant, happier days, she had gone boating and picnicking with her parents. This was a place of foghorns and stale fish, spices and timber, shouts and whistles, tall cranes and the swirling, dank river mist. It was all such a shock. She had never imagined anything even remotely like it. All her senses were alert and prickling to the unexpected sensation of disgust mixed with terrified excitement.

Celia raised her skirts as far as she dared to avoid them collecting up the worst of the filth and, keeping as far away as the traffic would allow from the threatening shadows of the high, blank walls of the warehouses, she walked gamely on – further into the Ratcliffe Highway.

She kept her eyes demurely lowered, yet still attracted the calls and shouts of passing dock-labourers, who made various, but all astonishingly low, offers of money for her favours. As soon as she was able, she took a side-alley away from the main thoroughfare. She wanted to see slum housing, not the busy commerce of the Empire.

She took a gulp of air and plunged into a narrow gap between two of the huge repositories which held goods she would never see, that would be traded with lands she had never heard of.

Scuttling noises accompanied her unlit progress, but Celia chose not to think about the source of the scratching and scraping sounds. At the far end of the alley, a gas-lamp burned, giving off a pool of dull yellow light. Quite suddenly the passageway came to an abrupt end. There was no railing or guard to prevent her fall; the ground simply stopped. Her chest rose and fell with the shock of what might have been. Only the gaslight had saved her. Gingerly she edged forward to look over the precipice. She blinked hard, as though her eyes were deceived by the dim illumination of the single lamp, but no, she was right. Incredible though she found it, she was actually standing at the head of a stairway, a flight of steep stone steps, leading down to the muddy banks of the Thames. She had nearly plummeted down on to that disgusting, dark grey sludge. The thought sickened her. For a moment she thought she might faint, but then, at the foot of the stairs, a sudden movement accompanied by sucking, slurping sounds, made her throw herself back against the side wall. She kept her feet firmly planted, but leaned forward as far as she dared to see if she could discover the source of the disturbance. There, far below her, she could just make out the silhouette of a small, crouching figure, groping in the slimy muck below her.

'Child, what are you doing?' she demanded firmly.

'What's it gotta do with you?'

Celia moved closer to the edge of her vantage point beneath the gaslight and looked more carefully. She could just make out the stunted, prematurely aged features of a malnourished boy of about seven years old.

'Don't be afraid,' she said more gently. 'I only want to know what you are doing.'

'What's it worth?'

'Whatever do you mean?'

'You want information – so how much is it worth to yer?'

Celia couldn't help herself, she laughed out loud at his audacity. 'How much do you think?'

The boy could hardly believe his luck. 'Penny?'

'How about tuppence?' she said, desperately trying to control her ill-mannered amusement.

The words had barely left her lips before the boy had clambered up the steps and was standing by her side. His bare feet and legs were covered in a layer of shiny grey river mud right up to his waist, dotted here and there with unidentifiable bits of detritus. The smell which radiated from him was equally indefinable, but probably resulted from a long-term combination of river water, effluent and the innumerable discarded sweepings of the metropolis.

'Deal!' he said in his serious little voice, spat on his palm, and held out his absurdly dirty hand for Celia to shake.

With some difficulty, Celia overcame her reluctance and touched her gloved hand to his filthy fingertips. She would throw the gloves away at the first opportunity.

'Now,' he said, very businesslike, 'what do yer wanna know?'

'Well. Where do these steps lead, for a start?'

'Waterman's stairs, these are, lady. So's the blokes can get up and down from their barges and that. Otherwise it's a bleed'n long

159

way to jump when the tide's out.' He let out a loud, spluttering, coughing laugh at his joke.

'You have a chest complaint?' asked Celia solicitously, making sure that she stood well back in case of infection – she had learnt some useful things from her father.

'All of us mudlarks gets bad chests. It's the damp, see. Ain't so bad when it's warm. We do a bit of penny-diving then and all.'

'Penny-diving?'

'Yeah, me and the other kids dive in the river for coppers what gentlemen and ladies like yourself throw in for us. Trouble is, when it *is* warm the whole place stinks something rotten. Worse than indoors then, it is, and that's saying something. You should smell the pong in our room. Horrible!' He laughed again, a racking, rattling wheeze that made him hug his sides with the pain.

Celia put out a tentative hand of concern. 'Are you all right?'

'Never better, lady,' he said, winking broadly as he kissed the two penny-pieces she had given him for his tale. 'It's the winter that's the bugger. I'm glad that's over. Freezes yer arse off that do, missus. Next time I'm planning to go into the House of Correction, I am: that's me plan for this winter. Do something a bit naughty,' he smiled cheekily, 'if yer gets me drift, and I'll be set up for the winter then, won't I? Snug as a bug. A set of clothes and a bit of grub. What more could yer want?'

'But how about your family?'

'They'll just have to manage without me, won't they?'

'You mean *you* help finance your family?'

'Do what?'

'Ermm, nothing.' Celia was confused. 'Well, no. What I actually meant was, don't your family support you?'

'Yer've not been round here before, have yer?' he said, his wide grin showing more gaps than teeth.

'No. No I haven't as a matter of fact.'

'Well, lady, yer take me advice and don't hang around here too long. It ain't safe for the likes of you.'

'Thank you for your concern.'

'Any time!' He kissed the pennies again and slipped them into a pouch hidden inside his ragged trousers. 'Cheerio, missus,' he called, and was back over the side and on to the muddy bank before she could stop him. 'I've got to get on,' his little voice called up in explanation. 'The tide'll be coming in soon.'

Celia walked back along the alley towards the Highway, not sure where she was going, just walking. But when she reached the main road she turned on her heel and hurried back to the stairs. She called down into the gloomy shadows below. 'Do you live here?'

'No, I bleed'n don't,' came the reply. 'I lives in Whitechapel, missus. Near Flower and Dean Street. I only comes down here for me work.'

'Will you take me there?' she asked the disembodied voice.

'Do what?' he asked, suddenly suspicious, wishing he'd never mentioned Flower and Dean Street. She might be one of them do- gooders that sometimes came round, ready to split you up from your little brothers and sisters and send you away to some horrible place in the country. He'd heard all about them from the other kids.

'Please,' she persisted. 'Show me where you live.'

'Why?'

'I'll give you a shilling.'

Almost immediately he was up the steps and had reappeared by her side. 'Let's see the colour of yer money first, then,' he said, still sceptical.

Celia handed him a shiny coin which he examined closely.

'Seems all right, I suppose,' he said paying her the same close attention as he had to the shilling piece. 'Yer ain't from no workhouse or orphanage or nothing are yer? Me mum'd kill me if yer was.'

'I promise, I'm nothing to do with such a place.'

'Yer'd better be telling the truth,' he said firmly. 'Or me mum'll kill you and all,' he warned. 'With her bare hands. Yer ready, then?'

'Do you think you might leave that here?' she asked, indicating the grisly remains of some long-dead animal he was holding.

'You bonkers? That'll boil up lovely for a nice bit of stew.'

'Would another shilling make you leave it here?'

He looked at her with raised eyebrows, confounded by such profligacy. 'If yer like.' He took the money from her warily, not sure how to treat this obviously mad woman, and then carefully secreted the putrid haunch of meat by the steps. 'I'll come back for that tomorrow. If yer don't mind, that is.'

'I don't mind,' Celia said. 'But won't the rats get at it?'

'Probably,' he said simply.

Once they were away from the river, the scrawny child lost his fear that she was either going to kidnap him, bash him over the head, or do some other unspeakably horrible things to him. He actually became quite jaunty walking along by her side, his little body swaggering like a bantam cock strutting round its coop.

'Joe's the name, missus,' he piped up suddenly. 'Joe O'Meehan.'

'How do you do, Joe. I'm Miss Tre... Celia,' she corrected herself. Now it was she who was wary of being compromised.

He led her through a maze of grim, narrow streets towards the place he called home. Now and then he'd burst forth into a flow of barely intelligible phrases. The language was English, but for Celia the speed and accent with which he spoke made the meaning almost incomprehensible.

'Me granny saw someone hanged, yer know,' he chirruped quite suddenly, with no reference to anything he'd said before, but obviously feeling that he had to entertain his paying companion.

'I'm sorry?' Celia thought that she must have misheard the child.

'At Newgit. Public hanging. Right lark that must've been. Wish I'd been there. She sold pies to toffs like yerself, something for them to nosh, see, while they watched. Earned a right few shillings she did and all. Told me all about it. That's what yer have to do if yer wanna make a good living, boy, she always said to me: earn off the toffs. Hanged 'em, they did.' He made a macabre pantomime of the act of execution. 'Like that. By the neck till they was goners. There's a good model of it on one of the stalls down the Whitechapel Road. I'll take yer to see it if yer like.'

When they eventually crossed yet another wide and noisy thoroughfare, and entered yet another network of innumerable vile-smelling courtyards and alleyways, crammed full of cheap tenement lodgings, Joe became silent and watchful. The further they went into the labyrinth, the more sensitive he seemed to become to his surroundings and to the sporadic comments from passers-by about his strange companion. Not once since they had entered the world of ill-lit, insanitary byways, had anything like a proper road intersected their path.

He suddenly indicated for her to duck down, and then scampered ahead of her into a brick tunnel, not three feet wide and barely five feet high. When she was finally able to raise her head again, she found herself in a cramped yard scarcely fifteen feet across, with a cracked gutter running its length, and incongruous dusty weeds flowering between the filthy cobbles.

Bernsley's Court, said the rusted metal street sign. All the doors to the houses which lined the four walls of the court were open to the world, the elements and the neighbours. But she could not make out anything of the interiors, as the hallways were far too dingy, although she was all too aware of the vermin which were everywhere. Only one corner of the court had anything other than a tenement: the side entrance to an alehouse. From its peeling door wafted the smell of stale beer; the sounds of an ill-tuned piano, accompanied by cracked, smoke-coarsened voices, drifted out on the thick, rank air.

All the buildings had wooden shutters totally devoid of paint, most of which hung tipsily from their rusted hinges. What windows there were were mostly mended with paper or stuffed with rags. Plucking up her courage, Celia peered through one of the few remaining panes of glass in one of the windows.

When her eyes grew accustomed to the shadows within, she let out an involuntary gasp. She could not believe it. It really was far worse than the pamphlets had even begun to suggest.

'What the hell d'yer think yer doing?' A gruff, tobacco-roughened voice snarled from inside the dark room.

'I'm sorry,' said Celia, devastated to be caught prying into the woman's home. 'This young lad brought me. I was hoping to speak to some of the women and girls who live here.'

'What young lad?' the disembodied voice wanted to know.

Celia looked round the court. 'He was here a moment ago.'

'Aw yeah? Go on, get off with yer. Yer another one of them bleed'n missionaries, ain't yer. All Bibles and hallelujahs. We want grub, not sodding God. Now go on, bugger off.'

'No, please. You don't understand. I only want to talk.'

'What about?' The woman's voice now took on the suspicious tones Celia had heard earlier from her young guide.

'About your lives here.'

'How much?'

'As much as you feel able to tell me.'

'No yer stupid cow, how much yer gonna pay me to talk to yer?' Celia remembered her deal with Joe: she should have realised that it appeared to be the custom in these parts. 'Oh, yes of course. What do you think?' She still had a lot to learn about negotiating with East Enders.

The woman turned to an invisible companion and whispered something. Her voice was kept low but she was hardly able to conceal her glee at having caught herself a real live one.

'I'm Ada,' the voice said suddenly, in what were now very friendly tones. 'If yer take me and me mate Florrie here down the Frying Pan for a couple, then we'll both talk to yer. How will that do?'

'That will be perfect,' said Celia, unsure as to exactly what the Frying Pan might be, and totally unaware of the interested crowd which was gathering behind her.

The two women stepped into the court from the passageway to a mixture of derisive snorts and hollered comments. But Celia ignored all the noise: she was too taken aback by the sight of the two women. At first she could hardly take in what she was seeing.

Their dull tangled hair was scragged back, exposing lined faces, deeply ingrained with dirt. They could have been any age from thirty to sixty. Or any other age for that matter. Each had a clay pipe stuck in the corner of her mouth.

Florrie was wearing a crushed straw hat, which might once have been a black bonnet, with a wretched bent feather sticking up from the brim. Ada had on a man's flat cap, pulled well down over her ears. Both wore shabby men's boots laced up with string. Shawls that were more holes than wool were wrapped round their plump shoulders and crossed over their abundant chests.

'Ready?' the one with the flat cap asked. Then, without waiting for a reply, she continued, 'I'm Ada and this here's me mate Florrie. This way, dearie. Come on.'

Celia walked out of the court flanked on either side by the women – they had no intention of letting such a potentially valuable source of gin escape them. Much to Celia's relief, save for a few ribald remarks, her companions loftily ignored the cheye-eyeking of the women who were sitting in the evening air outside the court's depressingly dark houses on old kitchen chairs.

'So who's yer fancy friend then, Flo?' one of them yelled.

'Look at the duchess with Ada and Florrie,' another hollered. 'Who's she think she is, then?'

Celia wasn't so impressed when they turned out of the court into a maze of narrow streets, the women blithely choosing to ignore a street fight. A bulky brute of a man was viciously laying into a tall, wild-haired, bare-breasted woman.

'Shouldn't we do something?' Celia asked frantically, all the time trying to avoid staring at the woman's semi-nakedness. 'Why doesn't someone intervene?'

'You don't mess round with big Katie Nolan,' said Ada, nodding wisely. 'Specially when she has the drink in her.'

'But that beast is taking off his belt to her.' Celia flinched as visions of her father's brutality crowded her thoughts.

'Don't yer worry yerself about Kate,' grinned Florrie, her pipe bobbing as she laughed. 'She'll come off best. She always does.'

As they rounded the corner and went down an almost pitch-dark alley, which led them into a court almost identical to the one they had just left, a howl of pain and rage was heard from behind.

'Hark, that'll be that old bugger getting what-for,' Florrie added sagely.

'Bleed'n good job and all,' said Ada, with evident satisfaction at the outcome of the fight. Then she touched Celia's arm, guiding her round a hole in the broken pathway. 'Watch yerself on them stones. Now through here, girl, and here we are.' She pointed to a pub across the road. 'The Frying Pan. Our favourite, innit, darling?' she said fondly to her friend Florrie. 'Good for business and all,' she added, tipping her a sly nod.

The Frying Pan, standing at the corner of Brick Lane and Thrawl Street, was crowded with rowdy drinkers, both men and women. Some were standing alone, others were in noisy groups, shouting and laughing to one another across the cramped counter. In the big, mottled and cracked looking-glass behind the bar, Celia could see reflected a huddle of men standing in the corner, buying and selling goldfinches in tiny wooden cages.

'Find us a table then, Ada,' commanded Florrie. 'We don't wanna stand around all night, do we? The lady wants to talk to us, remember?' She poked her friend hard in the ribs. 'And she wants to buy us a little drink.'

'I don't think I could do that,' said Celia, panicking at the idea of having to approach the bar with their order.

Ada quickly came to the rescue. 'Don't worry yourself, dearie, I'll do it.' She turned haughtily to her friend. 'And yon, Florrie. *You* can find us a table.'

Unaware of the potential row which was brewing, Celia held up her bag and took out some coins. 'How much do you need for drinks?'

'That'll do!' said Ada, snatching a half-crown from Celia's hand. She raised her eyebrows at Florrie in wonder and delight, and made her way over to the bar.

Florrie glared at a quiet little man sitting inoffensively at one of the beer-stained tables. She stood there, hands on hips, staring silently at him until he had no choice but to move, forced to do so by the sheer discomfort of being the object of her menacing attentions.

'Sit yerself down, dear,' Florrie instructed Celia, all smiles again.

Ada came back from her errand at the bar and slid a glass in front of each of them. 'Get that down yer neck!'

Celia choked over the raw, unrefined gin. 'Whatever is it?' she gasped.

'Satin. Jacky. Mother's Ruin. They calls it all sorts,' said Ada, sniffing loudly and wiping her mouth on her greasy sleeve. 'But it makes no odds what they call it. It all tastes the same going down yer gobhole, don't it?'

The taste of the gin might have been appalling but it was less sickening to Celia than the air which swirled around her, thick with the sweaty stench of unwashed bodies, the pungent smoke from the clay pipes and the unbearable heat given off by the wood-fuelled fire which blazed in the grate. Good works were going to be considerably harder to carry out than she had imagined.

–

'You claim you all live in that one basement room? Your whole family?' Celia said, still sipping at her first drink, while Flo and Ada swallowed their sixth – or was it seventh – shot of gin. She felt that she might be going mad. The rules which usually applied to the world were all being turned on their head.

'That's right,' Ada told her for the third time. 'I told yer. All the houses round here are divided up into rooms like that.'

'But the ceiling can't be as low as you suggest.'

'Look, I'm telling yer. Me oldest boy's not head and shoulders higher than me, and he can't stand up straight.'

'That's right, dear,' said Florrie, ostentatiously playing with her empty glass. 'Ada's boy can't stand up.'

'What do you do for washing and cooking? Do you have separate facilities?'

'Don't rightly know what "facilities" are, but I don't suppose we've got 'em,' laughed Flo. 'But I do know we ain't got no proper place to cook, not in Bernsley's Court we ain't. Except the range in the downstairs back of Number Four.'

'That's right. If we ever gets a bit of scrag-end down the market, the old girl in there does it for us.'

'I love a bit of scrag-end stew,' said Florrie, licking her chops. 'I could murder a drop now.'

'Or the baker lets us stick our bit of grub in his ovens when he's finished baking for the day. But me and Florrie usually get's a bit of hot something or other from down the soup kitchen or one of the missions.'

'How ever do you cope?' Celia was beginning to realise the enormity of any ambition to start a project to help these women. What could one person do?

'A drop a gin helps,' said Florrie craftily, looking sadly at her empty glass.

Celia handed over more coins for another round of drinks, remembering to refuse a refill for herself.

As Florrie slid the drinks across the table, she flashed a warning look at one of the other brides to keep out of her territory: she wasn't about to share a find like Celia. 'Yer musn't think we don't have nothing,' she said proudly as she slid on to her seat. 'We do have the stand-pipe for water. That's turned on most of the time.'

'Leave off!' said Ada. 'Most of the time it's a trickle of rusty brown piss.'

'Still better than having a scummy tank like some of them have to put up with in the Buildings. *And* every house down our court's got its own lav for the tenants' own exclusive use.'

'Aw, pardon me,' mocked Ada, her tongue loosened by the gin. 'I forgot we lived in a bleed'n palace.'

'At least we've got a roof over our heads. I ain't been near the spike for months,' said Florrie haughtily.

'The spike?'

'For them what can't even afford the common lodging-houses, dear. Bloody bug-holes, the lot of them. Shake whole box of Keating's over them beds and they're still running alive. And them spiteful, slave-driving bastards what run 'em. I hate them. Only half a step away from being stuck in the workhouse proper, they are.'

'I've wound up in there more than a few times in the past,' said Ada, surprisingly quietly. 'And it made me appreciate the lodging-house I was in afore I got me room in the court, I can tell yer.'

'But the court's our home now, ain't it, Ada?' said Florrie.

The thought of anyone speaking fondly of Bernsley's Court astonished Celia. She could hardly make sense of this bewildering world where such a place was thought of as home. And then there were the horrors of the spike – whatever that was. For want of knowing what to ask next, Celia suggested the two women might like another drink. They agreed all too eagerly, and Ada was up at the bar almost before Celia had drawn breath. By the time the drinks had been bought and they were all settled once more around the table, Celia had thought of another, she hoped less silly, question.

'As you share your room with your families, and you have no separate kitchens,' she said, her brow creased with concentration. 'Where do you keep your food?'

Unfortunately this question was greeted by the two brides with astonished laughter.

'Keep our food? Never been in the position to have enough to keep,' Florrie finally managed to answer. 'We goes round the corner for whatever we can afford, see? As we earn a bit we go round Ma Johnson's. Screw of tea and a bit of sugar a couple of times a day – we have that with a bit of bread and scrape. Then taters and maybe a bit of gravy of a night. And like we said, perhaps a jug of soup from the kitchens, if it don't run out before they get to yer in the queue.'

'Yer can keep hard biscuits for weeks if yer ever have the means to get any,' added Ada, looking at her again almost empty glass and deciding it was wise to be helpful. 'They lasts, they do. Yeah, yer can keep them. Under the bed's the place.'

'Yeah, but then the rats have a go at 'em,' said Florrie, sighing at the problem posed by it all.

'That's true. But anyway, we can never afford more than we can eat at one go, so what's the odds?'

The two women laughed good-humouredly, displaying their tobacco-stained and broken teeth.

Celia took another tiny sip of the clear, sticky liquid. She shuddered. Even that foul brew couldn't take away the taste of the deprivation of which the women spoke so matter-of-factly.

'Mind yer, if I comes into a bit of luck, like,' Florrie nudged her companion hard in her ample side and winked coarsely, 'then I can have a walk along the Mile End Waste and buy a nibble of whatever I fancies off the grub stalls. Pigs' trotters; plum duff; baked taters. Handsome!'

'How do you "come into a bit of luck"?' asked Celia, sensing that here perhaps was what she was looking for: the way in which she could assist the women to improve their terrible lot. Maybe she could see that they had more "luck" than usual.

This time the women didn't even bother to hide their amusement; they could hardly contain themselves. 'Blimey, gel, where have yer been all yer life, up a bleed'n tree?' Florrie hooted.

Celia blushed at their raucous laughter and at her own stupidity.

'We earn enough to treat ourselves at the grub stalls by going walking and getting ourselves a big spender. That's how,' Ada explained slowly, her cap bobbing around as she nodded for emphasis.

'Walking? You mean...' Celia wasn't sure of the appropriate term.

'Whoring,' Ada said amiably, keen to be of assistance.

'It's that or having lodgers,' added Florrie. 'And yer never know if yer can trust strangers, now can yer?'

'Yer right there, Flo,' said Ada. 'Look at the state Sarah's got herself in with that big bastard.'

Celia had to interrupt. 'Lodgers? But where would they sleep?'

Florrie leaned across the beer-sodden table towards Celia and held out her hand. Using her fingers to mark off the points in her explanation. 'Look, it costs eight pence a night to rent the room for me and me kids, right?'

This was all new to Celia, but she nodded anyway.

'So, *we* sleeps in the bed.'

'What, all of you?'

'Christ, girl,' said Florrie, her eyes rolling at Celia's unbelievable stupidity. 'I've only got three kids. And it ain't like I've got an old man, like Ada here.'

At the mention of her husband, Ada mouthed a foul curse under her breath.

'There's sodding nine of them all together in their room,' explained Florrie. 'But me, I've got room see. So if I likes, I can let me floor out to a couple for the night. That brings in a few pennies.'

'But doesn't it concern you, with your children there, having people, well,' she paused delicately and lowered her voice, 'sleeping on the floor?'

'They don't see nothing they ain't seen before, that ain't the problem. No, it's like I said, yer ain't always sure who they are. So, if the truth be told, I'd rather get a few bob from going out walking. It's safer that way.'

'Tell me,' Celia spoke in a low, conspiratorial voice. 'How did you first begin walking?'

'Me mum,' said Florrie proudly. 'Taught me all she knew. Good old girl she was.'

'Your own mother?' Celia was doing her best not to pass judgement on these extraordinary women. 'How old were you?'

'Twelve, thirteen, I suppose,' said Florrie looking at Ada for some sort of confirmation.

Ada shrugged. 'Don't rightly know, to be honest, Flo. Don't even know how old I am meself.'

'Well, about twelve,' said Florrie. 'That's the usual age.'

'I started when I was older,' said Ada. 'Cos it was something I could do of an evening if I wanted, when the kids was asleep. Most times they don't even know I'm gone. And it means I don't have to lock 'em in the room, see. That's what I like. I used to have to lock me nippers in till I got back of a night. Had to do it for their own safety. Me old man never bothers about 'em, and they'd have wound up gawd-knows-where if they was left loose.'

'Soon stopped that though, didn't yer, Ada?' chimed in Florrie. 'When Marie's kids got burnt up?'

'Terrible that was,' said Ada shaking her head sadly at the memory.

'Burnt up?' Celia repeated quizzically, thinking that they were speaking in slang.

'Yeah, they reckon the candle burnt down and set light to the blanket they had slung over 'em,' Florrie explained. 'Poor little buggers.'

'God rest their souls,' muttered Ada. 'I tried everything when I gave up sweating,' she continued. 'I earnt a decent couple of bob down hopping, but that's only once a year, so it don't last long. And there's no charring round here to speak of, so yer have to go up to the City. It ain't that far, but I couldn't manage that walk and the work on an empty belly. By the time I got up there I was worn out. Then the thought of the walk back after all that scrubbing… Specially when it's dark and icy of a morning.' She shuddered at the thought of it. 'So it was the workhouse or going on the game for me.' She grinned contentedly. 'I ain't never looked back, have I, Flo?'

When it became clear that Celia was not intending to buy them any more to drink, the women became restless and eager to go. Celia took the hint and stood up to leave.

'Will you escort me to the main road?' she asked, pulling on her gloves without remembering how the mudlark had soiled them. 'I'm afraid I could never find my own way back.'

'We'll walk yer as far as the Waste. For a tosheroon,' said Florrie, her eyes swivelling from all the gin she had swallowed.

'How much is that?'

'Half a crown, dearie. Two and a tanner. Half a dollar,' Ada translated for her.

'And yer can get us a pie and all, if yer like. Me belly thinks me throat's been cut.'

Celia looked at the fob-watch pinned to her jacket. 'Goodness, it is very late. Will there be somewhere open?'

'What, on the Waste?' crowed Florrie, her voice becoming extremely loud. 'Open all night, darling, then they still don't close, case someone wants a bit of breakfast.'

'Yeah, nice hot pie and a penn'orth and 'appence, that sets yer right up, that does.'

Celia was feeling extremely hot. The atmosphere in the noisy crowded pub, coupled with the women's rapid, impenetrable slang was making her dizzy. 'Penn'orth and...' she trailed off hopelessly.

'Penn'orth and 'app'orth,' explained Florrie, rubbing her broad middle. 'Penn'orth of rum and 'app'orth of milk. No finer start to the day.' She grinned at Celia. 'Or end to the night.'

Celia stood back and waited for Ada to lead the way out of the pub. She held her head high, ignoring the remarks tossed at her from the crowd as she made her way to the door. During the evening she had become almost used to such familiarity from strangers, had even grown to expect it. But, as she went out of the door, she hadn't expected to find an almost naked child sitting huddled on the pub step. 'I'm sorry,' shrieked Celia, nearly toppling over as she narrowly avoided treading on the little girl.

'She'll be waiting for her mum.' Florrie nodded at the little scrap and tousled her unwashed hair affectionately.

'Come on. This way.' Keen to get to the pie stall, Ada hurried Celia away from the hollow-cheeked youngster.

As they scuttled along Brick Lane in the direction of the Whitechapel Road, Celia was scandalised to see so many children out so late, apparently unaccompanied. They were either sitting apathetically on the kerbs, or scavenging in the gutters under the gaslit stalls for rotten fruit and vegetables. A woman with a frail-looking baby at her breast pleaded with Celia for a few coppers for a night's lodging.

'*She* ain't fussy about going in the spike,' said Florrie, looking down her nose at the desperate woman.

'Better than carrying the banner all night,' said Ada pragmatically.

'The banner?'

'Walking the streets cos she ain't got nowhere else to go,' Ada explained, and flashed a knowing look at Florrie that spoke eloquently of her contempt for Celia's stupidity.

'And better than winding up dead like that poor bastard, whoever she is,' said Florrie, nodding towards the newspaper man who was shouting the sordid details of the latest gruesome crime: yet another body with its throat slit had been found floating in the Thames.

Celia stood quietly by the pie stall while Ada and Florrie ate their fill. The women licked every scrap of the rich, greasy gravy from their lips before wiping their mouths with the back of their grimy hands.

Celia did her best not to show her distaste for their uncouth manners, continually saying to herself that it was all a matter of ignorance. She smiled warmly at them. 'I really must be going now. I'm sure I can find a hansom so near the London Hospital.'

'What? No rum and milk?' complained Ada loudly, spraying Celia with fragments of pie as she spoke.

'I'm sure that you ladies are anxious to get home.'

'Bollocks!' shouted Ada, made louder than usual by all the drink that Celia had bought her.

'Yeah, yer just another snotty-nosed bitch when it comes down to it, ain't yer?' Florrie was incensed that something seemed to have gone wrong and it was beginning to look as though they might lose their mark and miss out on clearing every last copper coin from the stupid woman's bag. 'Just sniffing round here for a few cheap thrills, then clearing off when yer've had yer fun. Well, yer know what yer can do, don't yer?'

Celia looked shame-faced. 'I sincerely hope I haven't offended either of you. I only meant to come here to see if I could be of any help. You must forgive me.'

A woman running a nearby seafood stall called over to them. 'Here you are, darling. Come over here if yer wanna help someone. See if yer can help this gentleman. He's having a bit of trouble getting his winkle out, ain't yer lover?'

Celia was hurt when Ada and Florrie joined in the mocking laughter, but she was determined not to be put off from carrying out her good intentions. 'You can laugh and you can doubt my purpose in being here, but I will return to help in whatever way I can. I promise I will help you.'

'What? Whether we want yer to or not, eh girl?' the winkle woman roared, accompanied by more ribald remarks from her customers.

'I can help you find a different path in life,' Celia said. She could hear her voice rising to an ineffectual squeak. 'A path of decency.'

'A decent path eh?' Ada shouted dramatically, enjoying all the attention. 'Gawd blimey girl,' she roared. 'I ain't been decent in me whole life. And I don't mean to start now.'

'Life doesn't *have* to be like this, you know.' Celia's tone betrayed her desperation. 'There *are* other ways in life.'

'Maybe we like things the way they are,' said a garishly made-up woman as she swaggered menacingly over to Celia from the pub doorway where she'd been leaning. She looked more than ready to raise her fists by way of protest.

'Yer don't understand, do yer?' said Florrie. As she spoke, she glared at the mouthy interloper to warn her off. She was actually starting to feel sorry for Celia – she *had* treated them all night, after all. 'See, it's like… It's like running that pie stall over there. So long as there's customers, it's worth baking pies. No customers, no business, no pies. See, so long as the blokes come round, then we bake 'em more pies.'

'Bleed'n hell!' said Ada, not having any idea what her friend was talking about. 'Hark at her.'

The woman who had been ready to slug Celia earlier had lost interest in the chance of a fight and, instead, wove her way across the wide road to the railings outside the hospital, where she might draw a bit of late-night trade.

'Don't look so upset, darling.' Florrie was now trying to comfort Celia. 'I'll give yer this, yer ain't as bad as some of 'em what come round here poking their noses in.'

This was a line of thought that Ada could follow. 'Yeah,' she said. 'You're right and all there, Flo. Them lady rent-collectors are right hard cows. Chuck you and yer kids out for owing 'em just a couple of coppers they would. Least you talk to us.'

Celia stared down at the dirty flagstones, trying to find the words to explain to them, to convince them that she meant them only well. She *knew* she could do something for them. She could help them and she would. She would do something worthwhile in her life. And she wouldn't let this one evening be the end of everything just because she'd made a few silly mistakes. She'd have to learn, that's all there was to it.

'I'll be back,' she said finally. 'To help you.' Then she walked swiftly off towards the hospital to hire a cab.

'Make sure yer bring plenty of dough with yer, dearie,' Ada called after her. 'We'll make a night of it.'

Chapter 16

'It's remarkable how well you have fitted into this new life, Ettie. I always knew you'd do well, no matter how doubting you were. But even I have to say how impressed I am with your progress.'

'I wonder if my mum would be as impressed?' Ettie put the toast back down on her plate and pushed it away from her.

'Not hungry? I thought you'd be famished after doing the show last night.'

'I can't eat when I feel like this.' Ettie wrapped the fine lawn housecoat round her more tightly. 'Do you know I haven't set eyes on my mum since we went down to Whitechapel for New Year's.'

Jacob poured himself more coffee. 'I thought that after the way she treated you that evening, you wouldn't want to see her again for a very long time.'

Ettie stood up angrily, knocking over the milk jug. The thick yellow liquid spread slowly through the linen cloth. 'So? She's me mother, ain't she?'

'You mean "isn't she", not "ain't she".'

'I mean what ever I bloody want? All right?'

'You're losing your temper again, Ettie.' Jacob picked up the milk jug and put it to one side. 'Is something wrong?' he asked her, without looking up.

'Not with me there ain't,' she snapped. 'Perhaps you want to ask yourself what's wrong.'

'Why don't you sit down, finish your breakfast, and talk to me about whatever it is that's worrying you.'

'Stop being such a bloody saint, Jacob. You're getting on my rotten nerves, you and your Mr Nice act. Do you understand?

You're such a sodding gentleman all the time. It's driving me flaming barmy.'

'Would you rather I was like your friend Billy? All brute strength and beer on my breath?'

'At least he'd know how to make me feel like a woman.'

'Ettie.' Jacob stood up and pulled her chair out from the table. 'Come on, please, sit down. Don't let's argue. Talk to me.'

'That's all you ever bloody do, talk.' Ettie, still standing, picked up her cup and swallowed the last of her coffee. 'Lucky we ain't got a show tonight, because I'm off out.'

As Ettie turned into the court where she had once lived with her mother, she became very aware of the stylish outfit she was wearing. It was different at New Year, the streets had been full of people wearing fancy clothes, but this was just another ordinary morning in the slums. At least she had put on the dark green taffeta. Putting on her new yellow silk dress with the matching bonnet really would have been a mistake.

'Hello, Ruby,' she called as she walked towards a tiny little woman sitting sowing sacks on the front step of Number Twelve. 'Do yer know if Mum's lodger's gone to work?' She was glad that, as usual, the little woman was on sentry duty – she didn't fancy coming face to face with the big slaughterman.

'Gawd love us and save us,' said Ruby, letting out a long slow whistle. 'Is that you in that posh frock, Ettie Wilkins?'

'Course it is, Rube,' said Ettie. 'Now, tell me, is he out or what?'

'I'd heard yer had a fancy man, but sod me!'

Deciding that the conversation was getting her nowhere, Ettie plucked up courage, took a deep breath and said, 'Mind yourself, Rube.'

She stepped over the hunched figure and found herself looking into the dank and depressing interior of Number Twelve Tyvern Court. She didn't wait to hear the rest of Ruby's comments, but instead went straight up to find her mother.

'Mum?' Ettie called softly into the dark back room at the top of the stairs. 'You there?'

A groan which Ettie recognised as her mother's voice welcomed her back to the family home. It was even worse than she had feared. Although it was mid-morning on a bright spring day, the room was in darkness. The few windowpanes that weren't covered with paper or stuffed with rags, still couldn't let in any light because of the brick wall which threw the whole of the building into deep gloomy shadow at that time of the day. There was no lamp lit, but the stink of urine-sodden bedding drew her towards the shapeless heap in the corner which she knew would be her mother.

'Mum, it's me, Ettie.'

'What?'

'Ettie. I've come to see you.'

'Leave me alone,' she moaned. 'I'm tired.'

'Mum, please. Wake up.' The stink of ammonia mixed with the fumes of gin on her mother's breath all but overpowered Ettie as she knelt down next to the bed. 'How about coming out for a walk or something?' Ettie was getting desperate for fresh air. 'We could go and get a bite of something. You'd like that, wouldn't you?'

'I told yer, I'm tired,' Sarah mumbled listlessly, the words coming out in short, almost disconnected rasps. 'And I don't feel well. Don't feel well at all.'

'I know, Mum,' said Ettie gently. 'But I've come to see you. To see what I can do for you. Don't you want to talk to me?'

As Ettie's eyes grew used to the gloom, she made out the swellings and cuts on Sarah's once lovely face.

'Come back later, eh love?' she gasped. 'When I've had me little rest.'

Ettie stood up, ashamed to feel so, but relieved to be away from the stinking bed.

'I'll leave you some money, Mum,' she said, opening up her bag and taking out everything except a few shillings. She put the money on the table. 'That big geezer, the slaughterman, still staying here, is he?'

'I know yer don't like him, Ett,' her mother murmured. 'But he helps out with the rent and that. And he ain't too much trouble.'

I can see by the look of that black eye, thought Ettie, but she didn't say it out loud. Why should she rub it in? Her mum had enough trouble.

'I've put the money on the table,' said Ettie. 'Make sure you put it away before he gets in tonight.'

'Ta, darling. Yer a good girl for yer old mum.' She struggled for a moment to gain her breath. 'I know yer don't think I've always treated yer right, but things wasn't always easy, yer know.'

Ettie knelt back down next to the bed. 'I know, Mum, and we had some good times, didn't we? You used to call me "your little doll", remember? You was right proud to take me out with you, showing me off to all your mates down the market. And when they used to give me an apple or something, you used to say: "Just this once; us Wilkins can pay our way."'

Sarah mumbled something incoherent and settled back down into the heap of rags.

'We could have them good times again, Mum. You don't have to stay here. You know that.' Ettie's voice was faltering. 'I told yer that at New Year's.'

Sarah lifted her head weakly. 'Yeah, and I told you what yer could do with yer fancy new ways and yer poncy boyfriend, didn't I, Ett?' Her chest wheezed and crackled with thin laughter.

'You did that all right,' said Ettie, trying desperately to laugh with her, to stop the tears from flowing. 'In front of the whole bloody pub and all. I don't reckon there's anyone in Whitechapel didn't hear you hollering at me that night.'

'Drunk as a bloody sack I was. Out for two days, they tell me.' Ettie was shocked to feel her mother take her hand in hers. Shocked, because gone was the firm, strong grip of a working woman she remembered, and in its place was the clasp of a frail, icy claw.

'Don't let yerself wind up like me, Ett. I was pretty like you once. Though no one'd believe it.' Another rattling cough worked its way up from her lungs. 'Look, I'm tired now, sweetheart. I'll close me eyes for five minutes. You go and see May. She was asking after yer the other day. Their Billy's doing well for himself, yer know. He's a good un, their Bill. Been good to me, he has. So's his mum and all.'

Ettie took deep gulps of air. Even the atmosphere of dirty old Tyvern Court seemed like sweet country air compared to the decaying stench inside that top room in Number Twelve. She felt disloyal, but she was still glad to be outside. Choked with emotion and with the foul taste of squalor on her lips, Ettie walked towards Brick Lane to see if she could find Maisie in the Frying Pan. The local girls usually gathered in there after the Saturday morning market.

Within five minutes, Ettie was poking her head round the door of the Frying Pan. Across the crowded room she saw Maisie sitting at one of the little round tables.

'May.'

'Gawd help us, it's Ettie Wilkins!' Maisie called back. 'Hello, darling. How are yer?'

Ettie waved in reply.

'Just look at yer,' shouted Maisie, unperturbed as to who was listening. 'All done up like a dog's dinner, but yer face looks like yer lost a tanner and found a farthing. Whatever's the matter?'

Nearly every head in the pub turned to see what was going on, but seeing that it wasn't a row or a fight brewing, most of them went back to what they were doing.

'Nothing, May,' Ettie said sadly, not even bothering to have a go at the ones who were still staring as she pushed through the noisy bar and settled herself down next to her friend. 'It's good to see you.'

'Well, it's good to see you and all,' Maisie grinned. 'I was gonna give yer a right rucking when I saw yer. But how can I? I'm that pleased to see yer. But I ain't glad to see yer looking so rotten miserable. If I had a frock like yourn, I'd be smiling me bloody head off.'

'It's me mum, May,' said Ettie, speaking as easily as though it was only a few hours rather than months since she'd last seen her friend. 'I want to get her somewhere decent to live. I can't stand seeing her in that dump. But she says she won't let me. I don't know, she doesn't seem to have any life left in her somehow.'

May chose her words carefully, then said. 'Do yer really think moving her would make any difference?'

'Not really, May, no. But it'd make me feel better. Like I was at least trying to help her.'

'She's real bad now, ain't she, Ett?' Rather than face her friend, Maisie was looking fixedly at the table.

'Yeah, real bad,' said Ettie flatly.

'Funny, ain't it,' sighed May. 'All them wicked things what she's done to yer over the years, and yer still care about her.'

'Bloody wish I didn't sometimes. But I still can't help remembering the things she did for me. How she never let them take me away. She tried, May, even though everything was against her.'

'Aw, don't start grizzling, Ett,' said Maise, putting her arm round Ettie's heaving shoulders. 'Yer'll start me off. Come on, get yer wongers out and buy us some drinks. Before all the others get here, or they'll all want a drop and all.'

'I haven't got much on me, to be honest, May. I left most of it with Mum.'

'Blimey, I hope yer hid it well. Or that bleed'n great bastard'll have it off her.'

Ettie stood up to go to the bar, but then stopped. 'I was thinking about paying some of the boys to go round and sort him out, May.'

'It's a thought,' said May, non-committally.

'But I don't know if him going would make her any happier. He pays his way, so she reckons.' Ettie sniffed. 'I hope she gets something out of him. I know he scares the shit out of me.'

'Yer know that if ever yer do want him sorted out, our Billy's the one. He'd do anything for you, Ett.'

'I know he would, May, but I wouldn't want Billy getting involved in nothing like that. That's more your Alfie's game.'

'Yer right, I suppose,' said May. 'Billy's changed a lot lately. He's settled down. Got a nice little spot for himself up at Reed's. Their blue-eyed boy he is. Earning a fair whack. But if *you* was to ask him, he'd pull down the bloody moon on a string for you.'

'Don't be daft,' said Ettie. 'Now do yer want this drink or don't yer?'

'I don't think yer'll have to bother, girl,' said May, leaning sideways and talking to somebody behind Ettie. 'Always turn up, don't yer?' she said. 'Got the knack, you have.'

Ettie turned round to see who she was talking to.

It was Billy Bury. 'Hello, Ett,' he said. 'How yer doing?'

'Hello, Billy,' she said shyly.

'Yer can still make one another blush,' said Maisie, laughing and slapping her broad thighs. 'Like a pair of great big kids.' She grinned and looked from one to the other. 'Well? What yer waiting for? Save Ettie going up the bar, Bill. Get us both a drink. Go on, we'll keep a seat for yer.'

She winked broadly at Ettie as he went up to the bar. 'Like I said, he's doing very well for himself. They're right pleased with him at the workshop.'

'I can see,' said Ettie, studying the surprisingly well-dressed figure leaning against the bar, chatting with easy animated charm to Patrick. 'I'm glad he's sorted himself out. I thought at one time he was set to follow in your Alfie's footsteps.'

May tutted. 'Thank gawd he ain't. But I ain't so sure about that little sod of a Tommy. He worships our Alf.'

'What's Alfie doing now?'

'Looking out for some of the big boys' business over by the Old Nichol.'

'Bloody Hell,' said Ettie. 'I hope Myrtle don't find out. She won't be best pleased.'

'You'd be surprised,' said May cynically. 'She don't seem to mind what either of them's doing, now they're bringing home so much dough between 'em.'

'Mothers, eh?' said Ettie with a weak smile.

'Yeah, right proud of her two boys she is. Yer ought to see her old bounce when she walks down the street with one of them on her arm.' May laughed. 'You'd look right good on Bill's arm yer know, Ett. Yer'd make a right good pair, you two with all yer fancy gear.'

Ettie changed the subject hurriedly: she knew from experience that Maisie was relentless once she got on to the topic of matchmaking Ettie and Billy. 'Who's that sitting in the corner?' she asked, hoping to distract her.

'Some posh tart with plenty of money to chuck about, been hanging around with Ada and Florrie. Yer know, another one of them do-gooders. From the Mission, I suppose.'

'That explains it,' said Ettie, laughing to herself. 'I wondered why they never came over here on the scrounge when they saw Bill come in.'

'Talking about that,' said May, standing up. 'Oi! Billy. You gonna bring us them drinks over or what. We're bleed'n gasping.'

'I was waiting for you pair to stop rabbiting before I brought 'em over. Yer was going ten to the bloody dozen.' He walked over and put the three glasses down on the table. Then he slipped a coin into his sister's hand. 'Go and get us all a pie, May.'

'What did your last servant die of? Overwork? Get yer own bleed'n pie, yer lazy great sod.'

'No.' He winked at May and jerked his head towards the door. 'You go and get us all a pie. And take as long as yer like.'

'Aw, all right,' said Maisie cottoning on to his meaning at last. She stood up and sauntered over to the door. 'I ain't sure how long I'll be,' she said, returning her brother's discreet signal with her own far less subtle bat of an eyelid, and stepped out into the street.

They sat in silence sipping at their drinks. Billy studied his hands, his glass, the table – anything rather than look directly at Ettie. She stared into her lap.

'Still wearing the locket I got yer, Ett?' he asked eventually.

'Sorry?'

'The locket. Yer still wearing it?'

'Oh, yeah. Course.' She reached into the neck of her blouse and drew out the necklace for him to see. 'I'm sorry, Bill, I was miles away.' Ettie sipped at her gin and looked round the cosy, fuggy interior of the pub. 'I was thinking about me mum, how she used to be, and remembering the first time I ever came in here. I was just a little girl. Least, I think it was the Frying Pan; it might have been some other place.' She closed her eyes and took a deep breath. 'But the smell was exactly like in here – all beery and spirits and smoke, all mixed up and sort of,' she tried to find the right word, 'sort of comforting.'

Billy took a swig from his glass and wiped the foam from his lips. 'I know what yer mean,' he said. He looked deep into her eyes, but she didn't seem to see him.

'I knew that smell: it was so familiar from all the time I'd spent sitting outside on the kerb, hoping that Mum would come out soon. But it was so much stronger the first time I actually went in. Mum pushed back the velvet curtain over the door and we stepped inside.' Ettie smiled at the memory. 'She held my hand. She didn't do that very often.' After a moment she continued. 'I thought it was so beautiful. There were bright gaslights glowing around the walls in shiny brass fittings. Thick red velvet drapes keeping out the cold night air, and everyone was laughing and happy. A man was playing the piano in the corner. I can't remember the song but it was so full of life. Fun. A really pretty girl came over to me and Mum and she lifted me right up in the air for everyone to see. "Look at this little pet," she said. "She's my little doll, ain't yer?" my mum said. And everyone looked at me and smiled and cooed. That night was like magic. They passed me from table to table, petting and fussing me; they called me "sweetheart" and gave me little sips of their drinks. I didn't like the taste, but I didn't want to spoil it by making a fuss or nothing.

'Then they sat me down on a big chair and called for Mum to sing them a song. "Go on, Sarah," they said. "Sing us one of the old ones." I'd never heard her sing before. It was lovely. Everyone clapped.'

Ettie didn't notice the tears flowing down her cheeks.

'They clapped my mum. Then she come and sat down with us at the table. I felt so proud. They were all talking and laughing. But then it got serious and the laughing stopped. One of the women said to Mum, "How yer gonna manage, eh girl? It ain't easy keeping a kid with no bloke, especially not now yer in the club again."'

'Me mum looked at me and she smiled. I can see her face now, so clear. "We'll manage, won't we, Ett?" she said. "Me and my little doll. You just see if we don't. We'll manage," she said. Now look at her.'

'Bloody Hell, Ettie, what's up with you? Yer better not have been upsetting her, Billy.' May put down her steaming parcel of newspaper-wrapped pies on the table and sat next to Ettie. With her arm protectively round her friend's shoulders, she said, 'What's up, darling?'

'Nothing, May,' she sniffed. 'I was getting a bit sentimental, that's all.'

'Oh, "a bit sentimental",' mimicked Maisie, trying to make her smile. 'Hark at her, Bill. Right Lady Muck, ain't she? Yer'd get on well with that woman hanging around with Ada and Florrie. She's right posh and all.'

'Shut up, May,' said Billy, staring into Ettie's eyes.

'So where's all the girls got to today?' asked Ettie, feigning enthusiasm. 'Not still sleeping off last night, surely?'

'They've all gone down the docks,' said Bill, still not shifting his gaze. 'Mad Milly come legging it down the market about an hour and half ago, hollering that a big Yankee ship had come in. They've all gone down there. See if they can do a bit of business.'

'That's nice. I was waiting for them in here and all,' said Maisie angrily.

'They knew yer was at the funeral with Mum,' said Billy, calming her down. Still he kept his gaze on Ettie, as though he were worried that she might try to escape.

'Oh, May, I'm sorry. I've been going on about my own worries. Who's died?'

'No one,' said May laughing. 'She's a right caution, our mum. Even though Bill and Alf are helping her out with money now, she still can't resist a good funeral. Still hangs round the cemetery gates to see if she can scrounge herself a drop of something at the do afterwards.'

'Still the same old Myrtle Bury,' said Ettie, laughing through her tears. 'One rule for how everyone else should go about their business, and another rule for her, eh? Some things'll never change round here.'

'One thing has changed,' said Billy, suddenly serious.

'Yes?' said Ettie.

He tried to say what was on his mind, but couldn't talk with Maisie around, so he decided to leave it. He changed the subject to the latest bit of gossip doing the rounds. 'The girls are having a bloody hard time round here,' he said. 'That's why they all shot down the docks so sharpish.'

'What? No business?'

'No, it ain't that,' said Billy, turning round and holding up his empty glass to Patrick and gesturing for him to bring them another round of the same. 'It's that Charrington geezer, him and his flaming good works. He's causing murders round here.'

'How comes?' said Ettie.

'Closing all the case-houses, that's how,' Maisie chipped in. 'All the working girls are being driven out on to the streets. No, nothing. Having to do it in the alleys and under the railway arches like the right old whatsits. Right dangerous it is, if yer ask me. And all cos of that interfering bastard.'

'Alfie and a few of the boys have been seeing what they can do to keep him and his cronies away, but that Charrington's got some powerful friends. Nasty bit of work, he is. Reckons he's doing it for the girls' own good, but that's a load of bollocks. Buying up property or something, so I've heard.'

'There's a lot of 'em doing right bad round here, Ett. Things have never been harder for some of the poor sods. But our

Billy ain't got nothing to complain about, have yer?' said Maisie, steering things back towards her favourite subject. 'Man of means now, ain't yer Bill?'

'Good to see yer, Ettie girl,' said the landlord in his soft Irish brogue as he leaned over and put down the glasses on the table in front of them. 'Good for trade to have beauties like you in the Pan.'

Ettie smiled and nodded her thanks at Patrick for the compliment and the drink, picked up her glass, and downed it in one. Then she looked at Billy. He still wasn't conventionally handsome by any means, but he'd grown into an attractive, well-built man.

'Cat got yer tongue, Ett?' asked May, looking from her friend to her brother and back again.

'What?' said Ettie, frowning.

'You,' she said slyly. 'Yer staring at our Billy and yer ain't saying a word. What's up with yer?'

'Leave off, May,' warned Billy.

Ettie pushed back her chair and stood up. 'I'll have to be going,' she said.

'What? Getting back to the Professor are you?' said May, suddenly sarcastic.

Billy glared at his big-mouthed sister as he stood up next to Ettie. 'I'll walk yer,' he said casually.

'No. It's all right, Bill,' she said resting her hand gently on his sleeve.

'What? You ashamed to be seen walking along the streets with the likes of me?' Billy's face was growing red, and May was looking outraged.

'Don't be stupid, Bill,' Ettie said softly.

'Aw, too stupid for yer now, are we?' butted in May.

'Leave off, the pair of yer,' shouted Ettie, her sense of hurt getting the better of her.

All heads were turned, but Ettie disappointed them by rushing towards the door, almost knocking the drink out of an elderly man's hand as she did so.

Billy dashed after her and stopped her in the doorway. 'Don't go, Ett. Not yet.'

'I've got to.' She grabbed the door-handle. 'Please, leave me alone, Bill. I'll see you around some time.' With that she slipped out of the door and into the unexpected chill of the early evening air.

As the door shut behind her, she was about to turn and go back in, but then she heard Billy's voice call out, 'What's yer fancy man got to say about yer locket and chain, eh? Tell me that? Or is he used to men giving yer presents?'

Ettie ducked her head down and began running along Brick Lane towards the Bethnal Green Road. She didn't care who she forced out of her way. She just wanted to get out of Whitechapel and back to Jacob. She didn't want people to see she was crying again – crying for her mother, for herself, and for the home where she felt she no longer belonged.

Chapter 17

As Celia walked along the now familiar streets of Whitechapel towards Brick Lane, she grew more and more despairing that she would ever be able to do anything of any use for the poor women she visited during her secret excursions into the East End. She was becoming almost resigned to being useless, accepting that her role of observer was as good as worthless to those whose lives she watched, although they assured her that they appreciated her greatly when she handed out money for drinks. At least, she reasoned with herself, being in the pub kept them off the streets and out of harm's way for a few hours. But she couldn't deny her disappointment. She had seen this as an opportunity to prove that she was of some consequence, that she had real worth, and that her life wasn't just a meaningless round of abuse and fear.

So concerned was she with her thoughts that she didn't notice the cattle until it was almost too late to get out of the way.

'Watch yerself, yer dozy bitch!' yelled the big, burly man as he drove the herd of terrified beasts on their way to one of the dozens of slaughterhouses in the area.

Horrified, Celia pressed herself flat against the wall as a living tide rushed by her in a blur of wild-eyed animals, closely followed by eager, whooping children, rushing to keep up so that they wouldn't miss the popular diversion of the wretched creatures meeting their bloody end at the sharp point of the slaughterman's knife.

A more familiar sound attracted Celia's attention from the gory spectacle: Ada, hollering at her usual full blast, 'It's her, Florrie, ain't it? Look, over there by the wall.'

Ada and Florrie came weaving along the street towards her, excitedly, indifferent to the steaming piles of dung left behind by the frightened animals.

Celia was used to the signs by now: they were obviously both much the worse for drink.

'How about buying us a few drops of Satin, eh girly?' Ada asked her in a pathetic, wheedling voice.

Celia nodded her terse assent, hoping that if she didn't speak, she would be able to keep the sickly aroma of the cattle-befouled road from entering her mouth.

She didn't say a word, in fact, until they were safely inside the Frying Pan where, almost unbelievably, she found the stench of stale beer and tobacco acceptably familiar. She handed Ada some money for drinks – she still didn't like going up to the bar – and sat down with Florrie at one of the little round, marble-topped tables.

As usual, Celia did her utmost to bring the conversation round to the two women's way of life and her endless, hopeless list of alternatives.

'Here she goes again,' said Ada. 'Same old song. Don't yer know any new tunes? I'm fed up with hearing yer go on at us.'

Florrie flashed a furious look at Ada, warning her not to upset their gold mine – good booze-providers like Celia didn't grow on trees.

Ada took the hint from Florrie and modified her tone. 'But I don't know why yer worry yerself so much about us, Celia. At least yer know we're decent girls.' She tipped back her gin glass and swallowed the fiery liquid in a quick, single gulp, then screwed up her eyes as it hit her throat and took a long pull at her glass of stout to soften the effect. 'Least we don't go in for no coshing like that mob up the Old Nichol,' she gasped, her voice coming out in a fume-filled gush that made Celia wince.

'That's only cos they've got no choice,' said Florrie, surprising both Ada and Celia. No matter how bad their reputation, Florrie felt a personal link with the women from round those parts: her only surviving sister lived there. 'They have to do what they do. The bully gangs'd do the girls over good and proper if they didn't bring in the marks for 'em to rob.'

'And it's better than starving to death, I suppose,' said Ada philosophically, conceding to her friend's wisdom.

'Is there really *no* gainful employment in which you might find occupation around here?' asked Celia, still persisting in her attempt to put the women back on the Right Path.

'If yer mean, can't we earn an honest shilling no other way, then the answer is, yeah,' said Ada, still serious from the thought of the women having to somehow get by in the Old Nichol. 'Sometimes we can.'

'But when there is work it's so bleed'n horrible that *I'd* rather walk the streets, for one,' said Florrie, also uncharacteristically solemn. She leaned forward and tapped on the table, marking each alternative as she spoke. 'See, there's yer sack-making – that rips yer fingers raw. Then there's fur-pulling–that ruins yer lungs. Sweating's no better than slave labour, and more often than not yer get told there's no money till the end of the following week, so you have to live on air pie and windy pudden till yer get paid. Scrubbing freezes yer to the bone and gives yer screws in yer knees and back. Taking in washing needs money for firewood before yer can even *start* thinking about that.' Florrie looked up and grinned at Ada. 'Mind, there's nothing wrong with mangling – except it kills yer from overwork!'

The two friends laughed loudly and uninhibitedly as Florrie finished reciting what had become a familiar list of possible employment to Celia.

'And the pay from them jobs. That'd make yer laugh and all,' said Ada, barely able to control herself from screaming with laughter. 'Times I've gone without to make sure me kids have had something in their bellies, then been too hungry to go to work the next morning.'

Celia couldn't understand what was so funny, but then she didn't understand much at all about these two women and their lives, which were as exotic to her as any mountain dweller's in the furthest-flung reaches of the Empire.

'That's the choices *we* have, dear,' said Florrie, wiping the tears of laughter from her eyes with the back of her hand. 'So we choose to walk the streets.'

'So you see doing this "work" as actually a type of freedom, do you?' Celia really did want to understand. Even if she had to ask them to repeat themselves every day for a year, she'd understand; even if it was the last thing she did.

'Freedom?' Ada was now almost beside herself. 'Leave off, will yer, or I'll wind up pissing meself.'

'Freedom from what?' said Florrie. She had stopped laughing. Inside she was feeling angry – what did this woman from up the other end know about anything? – but she wasn't stupid, she wasn't going to let this meal ticket go, not by rowing with her. So she said, slightly sarcastically, but pleasantly enough, 'What, from starving to death in the gutter?'

Now Ada had stopped laughing too.

'I'm sorry, that was insensitive,' Celia apologised. 'I really am sorry.'

'Don't you go feeling sorry for us,' said Ada, tucking a greasy lock of hair primly behind her ear. 'We don't want yer pity. Pity never helped no one.'

'Well, tell me,' said Celia earnestly, leaning forward in her seat: maybe here was the answer to what she could do for them. 'What *would* help?'

'A bit more consideration from some of the bloody landlords, that's what.'

'That's enough, Florrie, we don't need nothing from the likes of them, or her.' Despite her resolve to keep Celia sweet, the topping up of gin and ale had brought out Ada's aggressive streak. 'If we was lucky enough to get ourselves one or two decent big spenders, we'd be well away. It's a bit of luck we need, that's all. And we ain't got much of that lately. We even missed that bleed'n Yankee ship what come in the other day. Could have made a nice few bob if we'd have known.'

'Aw yeah, and we could get ourselves a nice little gig and go riding through Vicky Park!' hiccuped Florrie, her mood swinging back to amiable good humour. She drained her glass and held it up expectantly to Celia. 'Like proper ladies.'

'Is that what you both want from life?'

Ada shook her head, as though she had been confronted with teaching a particularly stupid child to unravel an especially complicated puzzle. 'Yer still ain't got a single idea what walking the streets is really about, have yer? Get 'em in and let me tell yer about it.'

Celia handed over more cash.

—

'Like I told yer before,' said Ada, handing round the glasses, and wagging her head up and down for emphasis. 'Me old girl put me on the streets when I was a youngster. And I've had to go with all types in me time, believe you me. Horrible, diseased old bastards. Raving nutcases with right funny ideas about what they want and how they want it. I've got meself up the duff gawd knows how many times when me little ways have let me down.' She noticed Celia's expression. 'Aw yeah, we do have our methods, but they ain't much use half the time.' Ada took Celia's untouched gin and knocked it back.

'Yer hear all sorts of stories,' said Florrie, taking up the story from her friend. 'Kids born all sick and that 'cos of what the mothers have tried to do to themselves to get rid of it. And there's women what smother or drown their babies in a bucket.' She lowered her eyes. 'What else can yer do? When yer life's all about being exhausted, cold and hungry; or exhausted, sweating and drunk? In the end yer do what yer have to.' She lifted her chin and looked Celia straight in the eye. 'Walking's a job like anything else.'

Celia shook her head. 'But surely...'

Ada held up her hand and butted in. 'There's no need to look at us like that. Every city has its business area, and always will have when there's still men around. But it's easy for the likes of you, ain't it? You can just keep away if yer don't like it. Run off home to yer posh house.' Ada's voice was growing tense. 'But for us it's a totally different story. We have to stand all the shit being thrown at us. "Dirty, no-good whores," they say. But we don't do no harm to no one. Don't even disturb them, unless they comes round here looking for trouble. Then they get what-for.'

'Do the police come if there's trouble?'

'Some of our best customers, darling,' sniggered Florrie.

'The police?'

'Yeah. And why not?' Ada wanted to know. 'They're blokes, ain't they? And just cos yer don't see your sort of fellah hanging about round here much, don't think that they ain't our customers. Your type of bloke might live with his wife, but it's us they turn to when they fancy a bit of company.'

'Can't blame the wives, mind,' said Florrie. 'If I didn't have to, I'd never look at another geezer again. Who wants to get knocked up every few months and wind up having to roll around while some dirty-pawed old girl pours muck down yer throat and rams something up yer fanny to get rid of it?' She smiled fondly at her friend. 'I'd rather a girlfriend any day of the week, wouldn't I, Ada?'

'That yer would, Florrie. Best way to get a bit of love in yer life, eh gel? Come on, give us a kiss.' Ada leaned drunkenly towards Florrie, her lips pursed.

'Could I have a drink of water, do you think?' asked Celia. 'Water!' Ada sounded affronted that such a thing should pass someone's lips in the Frying Pan.

'Reckon our chat's warming up yer blood, eh gel?' giggled Florrie. 'Feeling a bit randy are yer?'

'It's the heat. It is a very warm evening.' She lowered her voice and placed her hands over her abdomen. 'I can hardly breathe.' Florrie nodded knowingly. 'That'll be yer underthings, girl. That's what'll be wrong with yer.'

'She's right,' agreed Ada. 'You go round the back and get 'em off, girl. Yer can't wear tight stays in this weather.'

'I really don't think I could,' said Celia tersely, blushing a deep crimson. 'It's all very well for you: such matters do not seem to concern you.'

'Different for us?' Ada's tone had become harsh. 'Yeah, yer right there. We can't afford poncey underthings like youm – so we don't wear any at all.'

Celia's face was now burning. 'But wearing no underthings inflames men's desires, surely?'

'I hope so!' spluttered Ada, her mood forgotten as she showed her unconcealed amusement at the stupidity of the young woman. 'How else would I earn me living?'

'Perhaps you could buy a second-hand garment in the market?' Florrie couldn't make it out. Celia was more shocked by the revelation that they didn't have their bodies strapped up in a harness than by what they did down the back alleys with them. She did her best not to laugh in the young woman's face. 'Listen, girl,' she said. 'Having a corset holding yer tits up and yer belly in ain't gonna stop geezers' desires, as yer put it so nicely, now is it? Matter of fact, one of Big Bella's regulars loves 'em. Likes 'em laced right tight so's she can hardly breathe. Pays her good money for that and all.'

Ada nodded her drunken agreement. 'Right good money.'

'There must be something that can be done. I don't mean about underthings, but about…' Celia flapped her hand around, taking in the pub and everyone in it. 'All this. All of it. It's all very upsetting.'

'Sorry, I'm sure,' said Ada sarcastically. 'But I'm afraid it's our life, girl. And whether yer like it or not, there's no other bugger gonna feed our kids, now is there?'

'There's no need to trouble yerself about it,' said Florrie, glaring at Ada to warn her that she was going too far. 'It's just the way things are, see?'

'Trouble herself? Her? Disgust her more like,' said Ada. 'Look at her, nose in the air. We ain't throwing ourselves at the geezers, yer know. They come to us cos they wants us.'

Celia opened her mouth to speak, although she wasn't sure what she was going to say. But she was saved from offending the women further by a bare-footed child rushing into the pub and yelling for help. He was followed by a wild-eyed, distressed man, who stood in the middle of the pub pleading with someone, anyone, to give him money to pay for a doctor to help his sister.

'We told him, he won't get no doctor to go down *there* without money up front,' said a small, dumpy woman who followed them in.

'Can I help?' asked Celia standing up. 'I have some medical knowledge.'

'Yer don't know where he wants yer to go, love, do yer?' said Florrie, grimacing and holding her nose. 'Their place is right dookie. I ain't the fussiest one around, but it ain't very nice where they're from.'

But the man didn't need a second chance – he saw the possibility of help for his sister and he grabbed it. He grasped Celia by the arm and dragged her frantically to the door. Never one to miss the opportunity of having a lark, Ada and Florrie rolled their eyes, gathered up the crying boy, and followed rapidly behind.

The man lead them into the maze of courts and alleyways similar to those with which Celia was already becoming familiar, but then he ducked into a low tunnel known only to the dwellers of the squalid hovels that had been built by the desperate inmates of the hellish inner sanctum of the rookery. Even the tenement and court dwellers thought twice about going into the jerry-built hutches and lean-tos constructed from old packing cases and other leavings of the more fortunate.

As Celia lost all sense of direction, and with it any semblance of normality or familiarity with the neighbourhood – if it could be called that – she became increasingly nervous, wondering what on earth she was doing following this strange man in the company of two prostitutes and a howling, filthy child. She pulled back from the man and stopped dead when they came to a dark archway between two quite solid-looking brick buildings.

'Go on, yer all right. We're behind yer.' It was Ada, urging her on – they'd left the comfort of the pub and had come this far, she didn't intend missing out on the last act of this little drama.

The man's desperate expression beseeched Celia to follow him and, before she had the chance to reconsider, he was directing her over the doorstep and into a totally black passageway leading into one of the buildings.

Celia gasped. 'God, what's that smell?' she gasped, gagging at the stink.

Ada spoke through her shawl that she held up to her mouth. 'It's the cesspits. The ones round here are open. Down in the cellars.'

'Hold something up to yer face,' mumbled Florrie from behind her sleeve.

'She's in here,' said the man's voice from the gloom.

Celia wanted to hold her breath, never to take another mouthful of that disgusting air, but she had to speak. 'I need some light,' she gasped.

A piece of candle was produced by one of the inquisitive bystanders who had gathered to see what the to-do was all about.

The pale glimmer of light was enough to show Celia that she was in an almost derelict room. In the shadows she could see that there was no furniture, save a market basket which had been up-ended to serve as a table, and a bundle of something by the empty hearth to serve as a bed. A small child, hollow-eyed from malnourishment, sat in the corner of the putrid chamber and stared. The object of its gaze was a woman, possibly its mother, but whoever she was she was almost lifeless, stretched out on a fetid pile of rags, a dark stain of blood spreading out beneath her, soaking into the already stinking bedding.

'The old girl upstairs tried to help her out,' explained a small thin woman who was standing, arms folded, watching in the doorway. 'She's had too many got rid of in the past, if yer ask me,' she said, and bent forward to scratch at an ulcerated sore on her leg. 'Her insides couldn't take no more messing. And the state of this place.' She looked round the dingy room. 'Too much on-the-door nosing to bother to keep her room tidy, that one, if yer wanna know.'

Celia flashed a look of contempt at the woman and her uninvited comments, and then knelt down, unconcerned now about spoiling her fine dress on the bare, unwashed boards: her whole being was consumed by the sight and stink of the miserable soul before her.

'Will someone take the children out of here?' she said quietly.

'Come with me, darling,' said Florrie, and scooped up the little girl in the corner.

The older child, who had gone to the pub to ask for help, silently refused to leave. He knelt down next to Celia and watched as she held the woman's hand while the life ebbed away from her.

'I'm sorry,' whispered Celia through her tears. 'There's nothing anyone can do. I'm sorry.'

As she stood outside, Celia closed her eyes, but the sight of the man rocking the dead woman in his arms was burned into her soul. And the silence of the boy had been almost more terrible than the man's sobs.

The little girl who Florrie had been minding looked up at Celia crying and pulled free of Florrie's hand. She ran inside, crying out for her mother, who now lay dead in the hopeless depths of what the child knew as home.

'This can't carry on. I won't let it,' Celia vowed as she walked numbly along beside the now entirely sober Ada and Florrie. 'I'll find a way to do something useful round here. I swear I will.'

'Yer wanna do something useful round here?' said Ada, clinging on to Florrie's arm for comfort. 'Find a way of helping out poor cows like her. That'll be doing something all right.'

Chapter 18

'Watch her carefully. Pay attention to her every move. She has chosen to spend her everyday life without speech but, when the spirit moves her, she will speak directly to me.' Jacob pressed the fingertips of both hands to his forehead. 'Her words are appearing in here. She has the gift to transport her thoughts directly into my mind.' With his arm at full stretch, he described a sweeping arc around the room. 'Death itself has whispered in her ear.'

Jacob, with his usual calm pragmatism, had decided it would be better after all that, when they entered the homes of society ladies and their indulgent husbands, Ettie should be the enigmatically silent beauty. With her recent moods of dissatisfaction, he had concluded that it was too risky to allow her to speak: she might so easily, when in one of her ill-humours, show far too many rough corners. And he didn't want to risk her snagging them on the sensibilities of the upper classes. She had to remain credible to her audience, and the reality of her background would be an immediate dampener to their belief.

In the faint red glow of a silk-draped lamp, the semi-circle of sitters watched, enthralled, as Jacob moved to the back of the room. He stopped by a tall wooden box standing on a small raised platform. Both box and dais were painted with arcane designs and mysterious cyphers in rich, jewel-like colours. The more imaginative among those present might have believed the cabinet to be an up-ended coffin.

Jacob raised his arm and, with a flourish, pulled back a flimsy veil of silky cloth; and there sat Ettie – eyes closed, chin high, hands resting lightly on her muslin-clad thighs, her chest rising and falling with deep, even breaths.

Murmurs of excitement drifted around the darkened room.

'Please, I must insist. Absolute silence. She is communing with the old souls. The departed ones. The messages come through to me on planes of pure thought. To disturb her would be dangerous.'

Ettie began moaning sensuously. Several gentlemen who had come along to the meeting to pacify their wives were finding the proceedings far more interesting than they had expected, although they were also beginning to find that their collars had become excessively tight.

'The messages are coming through,' Jacob intoned in a loud stage whisper, the cue for Ettie to begin a slow, eel-like writhing, although still within the confines of her box.

'Yes, I have the first message coming through. Someone in this room knows of a man called William. A man who suffered much but who suffers no longer. A man who has joined with the blessed spirits on the other side.'

Eager to be part of the proceedings, the sitters racked their brains for recently deceased acquaintances of that name.

Jacob stood with a dignified serenity, waiting for the first response. He did not have to wait long.

'Yes. William. Yes. That's right. It's come to me.' A fur-caped woman in the inner circle of sitters raised her hand like an eager schoolgirl who knew the correct answer to her tutor's question. 'The under-gardener. Frightful accident.'

Jacob smiled inwardly. Perfect. He had his mark. With that single raised hand, Ettie was launched on her career as a private clairvoyant.

Ever the showman, Jacob was careful not to have too long a period without a fresh sensation to titillate their audience. Giving out names and messages were all very well, but the hostess had paid dearly to have the seance conducted in her drawing room, and Jacob intended her to feel she had had value for money, as well as the prestige that staging such a private event brought to society ladies.

Mixed in with his effortless flow of patter, Jacob gave Ettie the secret code words, and within moments a series of waxy faces – spirits from beyond – had appeared on either side of her in the dim recesses of the box.

The sitters craned forward, trying to suppress their gasps of astonishment. Jacob had instructed them well: they knew that too much sound and the apparitions would dissolve like so many snowflakes on a lamp-warmed windowpane.

'I hear you. I hear you,' Jacob moaned, closing his eyes and drawing himself up to his full height. 'The spirits want to move amongst you. I must ask that no one moves. The lights must be dimmed completely. Only the red lamp may burn above the cabinet.'

Jacob then made a melodramatic progress around the sumptuously appointed room, instructing the footman to turn down each gas-jet in turn. Then he directed the servant back to his post by the door with a hushed, 'That will be all,' and hoped that Ettie had remembered the lay-out of the furniture.

As Ettie stepped out of the cabinet and wandered ethereally amongst the enraptured sitters, she left behind her the unmistakable smell of sweet roses, which she had sprayed liberally over her gown before leaving her seat. She brushed her hands near the heads of the sitters who felt both honoured and privileged to be touched by the spirits.

From the safety of the darkness, Jacob smiled to himself. Ettie was doing her work well, he thought, very well. He had been right about her from the first time he had seen her. He congratulated himself that his experienced eye had seen through the surface grime of the grubby little street urchin at the penny gaff to the beauty who was waiting there to be discovered.

He heard her return to the cabinet and take her seat.

'The lights,' he instructed the now terrified footman, who was more than keen to return the room to even the low level of illumination acceptable to the spirit world.

'Are the spirits happy?' Jacob asked.

He could barely suppress his desire to applaud her expertise as Ettie answered the question on behalf of the departed ones with some impressively loud raps, produced by the well-practised technique of striking her bare big toe against the hollow dais on which the cabinet stood.

'Thank you for that sign. Can I now ask a final favour?'

Three resounding raps echoed around the otherwise silent room.

'Give us a token, a sign, for the believers here gathered, from the other side.'

The hostess gave a whimper of pure pleasure. This was even better than she had hoped. Her friends would trample over one another to get an invitation to her next soiree.

Ettie stood up in her coffin-like confinement and deliberately ripped shreds from her muslin robe which she then handed to Jacob.

Unable to control himself, a puce-faced man at the front let out a strangulated, 'Oh I say!' at the thought of the silent beauty actually disrobing herself so passionately before his very eyes. He was to be disappointed, in that at least.

Jacob took the strips of muslin and handed them out to those he had correctly assessed as being the most important guests. The favoured few accepted the talismans with evident delight.

There was, however, to be a final treat for everyone. With a startling flap of her arms, Ettie stepped from the cabinet, her robe whole again, her head high, her breathing rapid and loud.

Obviously exhausted, Ettie staggered back and dropped down on to the seat in the tall chest.

'We must finish now,' said Jacob, as Ettie's head flopped forward. He lowered the curtain across the front of the box, and indicated for the footman to dim the lights again.

'Silence, please.' Jacob reached out and extinguished even the red glow above the chest. 'She is gone!' he said simply.

By the time the lights were turned up once more and the covering applause and excited chatter had died down, Ettie had indeed gone – out of the room, out of the front door, and out of the neighbourhood entirely; running as fast her trailing cape permitted.

–

'Ettie, we are going to be the darlings of the drawing room.' Jacob rushed into the room like a Dervish. 'The celebrities of the salon.' He had just arrived back from the seance, and was still buzzing with the excitement of their success.

'I'm very pleased,' she said flatly, pulling a shawl round her. 'Shut that door, I'll freeze here in my nightdress.' She turned her back on him and began aimlessly examining the bookshelves.

'Ettie, what's wrong?'

She didn't face him. 'You've been long enough, haven't you? I've been back for hours.'

'I had to stay and talk. They expected it.'

'So I noticed.' She pulled the shawl round her more tightly. 'I saw the way you played up to the women. It was bad enough when we met them before the sitting. You laughing at their stupid stories. But what I *really* hated was the way you kept sending all the men over to me.'

'You didn't have to say anything to them,' said Jacob, resenting her spoiling his elated mood. 'You have it easy.' He smiled coldly. 'You only need to converse with the spirits.'

'Bloody lucky for them toffs,' she said, and turned round to face him, her face pale with anger, "cos I'd have told them their fortune good and proper if I had have spoken to them.'

Jacob unwound his long silk scarf and took off his cloak. 'Ettie, it's important for the audience to meet us, an important part of the act.' He threw his things on to a chair. 'It's the way we ensure good donations and gifts.'

'Hypocrite.'

'What do you mean?'

She nodded towards the cloak. 'If I do that you go barmy.'

Jacob smiled, more warmly this time, pleased at the easier atmosphere. He picked up his things and put them on the hall stand.

Ettie followed him into the little kitchen. Something was obviously still worrying her. 'When I did my disappearing act, I watched you for a bit, you know. I opened the door, just a crack, and watched you.'

Jacob turned on her, the kettle in his hand. 'That was absolutely stupid, and you know it. What if they had seen you?'

'I ain't stupid, and they didn't see me. Anyway, it's me who should be angry. You were all over them women.'

Jacob looked at her, puzzled. 'Don't get so upset, Ettie. I hate repeating myself, but it *is* part of the act.'

'It's different when you have no choice,' she said, spitting the words out at him. 'But it's not right when you don't have to do it.'

Jacob slammed down the kettle and strode back into the sitting room. He sat down in one of the armchairs by the hearth and indicated that Ettie should take the other one. 'I know we're both very tired, but I think we should talk about whatever it is that is making you so unhappy.' He took the cigarette case from the side-table next to him and struck a match. He was being infuriatingly calm. 'It would be unfortunate to ruin what would otherwise be a very successful collaboration between us.'

Ettie slumped back in the chair, watching him begin to smoke the cigarette. With her pouting lips, long bare legs stuck out in front of her, and thick dark hair falling loose about her shoulders, she looked every bit the sulky child.

'The girls round Whitechapel don't exactly like what they do, you know. They do it because they have to. Like I said, *they* have no choice.' She said the words slowly, quietly, as though she was thinking carefully about what she was saying.

Jacob's reply was a barely raised eyebrow.

'When things are bad and there's nothing coming in, what else can they do but go out walking?'

Jacob shifted in his chair and then leaned towards her. 'Your mother?'

'Don't stare at me like that,' she said. 'She always said it wasn't so bad. And it was honest.' Ettie suddenly buried her head in her hands and began softly weeping. 'Least it was better than what that dirty bastard of a lodger did to me.'

Once she had begun her story of abuse and deprivation, Ettie couldn't stop herself. Out it all came, not just the parts she had told him when they first met at the gaff, but all of it – like a swollen river bursting its banks.

By the time she had finished, Jacob was cradling her in his arms. 'It's part of me,' she sobbed, 'part of what I was. What I am.' Jacob let her go and stood up. He bowed his head and then he too began to weep. 'Ettie. I knew you had suffered, but, God forgive me, what you have told me now, it's like a madness overtaking me.' He turned and fell on his knees at her feet. 'I can't stand it, Ettie, I want you. I've tried to avoid this moment, to stop myself telling you because I know you must hate…'

Ettie took his head in her hands and kissed him. She pushed him back with her kisses until they fell back on the rug. 'It's OK, Jacob. It's OK,' she murmured. 'I want it too.'

They made love the first time with a wild urgency, taking off and undoing only what would have prevented their coupling; unaware of anything but the need to satiate their desire. But then they discovered a fresh appetite, a need for a more intense and deeper exploration of each other.

They lay spent, wrapped in each other's arms, staring into the grey embers of the fire.

'Ettie, everyone will love you,' he said, kissing the tip of her nose, an affectionate, easy gesture that just a few hours ago would have been unimaginable. 'How could anyone fail to love you? You will be the biggest star ever to appear in London. In Europe!'

'D'yer reckon?' She snuggled her head deeper into his chest. He levered himself up and, resting on his elbow, traced the outline of her face with his fingertip, admiring her beauty. 'You palmed that cut-up cloth from the robe absolutely brilliantly. Do you know that? You're quite a conjuror. And a very good actress.'

'Yeah, I am,' she giggled playfully. 'Well, come on, I'm getting on for nineteen. You can't expect someone from round where I was brought up to be little Miss Innocent, now can you?' She stretched luxuriously. 'You might have done and seen a lot, Jacob, but you've still got a lot to learn.'

'So I see.'

She hadn't noticed his change of tone. 'For instance,' she made herself cosy against him. 'If you want to see a real bit of conjuring, you want to see how the brides can make a bloke think that they're, you know.' She bit her lip, suppressing a laugh.

'Think they're what?'

'Think they're still pure little virgins. The girls all do it – well, when they're still young enough to get away with it. They earn more money, you see.'

'I don't understand.' His voice was increasingly cool, but Ettie was too relaxed, too happy to notice.

'Blood soaked sponge, shoved up inside them. Works every time, they reckon. The posh ones pay a lot for...' She felt his body move – just a fraction – away from her. She turned and looked up into his face. 'What are you looking at me like that for?'

'Like what?'

'Like I'm rubbish or something.'

He said nothing.

'You knew I wasn't no lady when you picked me up.' Ettie stared at him as though he was a stranger. 'I might know all about what the girls get up to, and I might be the daughter of a brass, but that doesn't make me a bad person.'

'I know. But I hadn't realised that you would talk of such things with such good humour.'

'What, d'yer prefer me crying?'

Jacob remained silent.

'I told you, living in Whitechapel's all about survival, all about...' She hesitated, then, struggling free of him, she stood up and raked her fingers through her hair. 'You just imagine, Saint bloody Jacob, living in a world where going with some stinking drunken no-good is most women's best chance in life. Then get on yer high horse about selling yerself.'

'Ettie, please. I didn't mean that. I just thought that you would be different.'

'You, you…' She could hardly speak with anger but the contempt in her voice was clear. 'I met you in a poxy penny gaff, remember, not in a posh theatre up West. Life gave me the worst deal it could, but I didn't lay down and die, I didn't just take it. I wouldn't. D'you hear me? No, don't you dare turn away. Look at me!' She stood over him, naked and beautiful. 'I ain't no one's victim. I choose what I do, *and* who with. And I don't have to stay here neither. I can sort meself out. Right?'

He just lay back on the rug, looking up at her.

'I'm yer equal, Jacob Protsky, whatever anyone might think. Even if I ain't posh. It's only cos yer've had chances that I ain't. That's the only difference between you and me.'

'Have you finished?' he asked, his voice icy.

'No, I ain't. Just you listen to me. What difference is there in what the brides do, to what most so-called ladies do every night of their married lives, eh? What difference? It's all about surviving the best you know how. And yer was all right just now, wasn't yer? I was good enough for yer then. And least I ain't no liar. Least I ain't had to run away from no Paris.'

He rolled over, turning his back to her. 'Your voice, Ettie. Remember your voice.'

'Bollocks to me voice!' she screamed at him.

Jacob spoke very quietly. 'Ettie, will you come into the bedroom with me?'

She followed him through without speaking.

Chapter 19

When Celia eventually crawled into bed, she didn't find the comfort of sleep: the face of the young woman she had, only a few hours ago, watched die from the bodged abortion came back to haunt her, as did Ada's words: 'Yer wanna do something useful round here?' she had said. 'Find a way of helping poor cows like her. That'll be doing something, all right.'

Ada was right, being 'helped' was what the women in their dreadful poverty really needed and, by the time the dawn was breaking, Celia's mind was made up: she would save as many others as she could from needlessly early deaths caused by the ignorant ministrations of untrained old women with their gin and rusty knitting needles. Celia had the skill and the knowledge, she would be the one to give them what they wanted in as safe a way as possible.

Over the next few days, she made herself ready. She pored over the relevant passages in her father's anatomy books; she pilfered spare instruments and medicines from her father's store-cupboards, packing them away in a black leather bag which she kept hidden at the back of her wardrobe.

Even pretending to be pleasant to her father was easier now she had determined what to do. It was as though she had found a real strength at last, as though she could separate herself from what, in his sickness, he was doing to her, hardly cringing when he stroked her arm or whispered to her how lovely she had become. She even tried to forget how, one day, she too might sicken and lose her reason.

The first opportunity Celia had to leave the house was almost a week after the young woman's death. Her father was at a hospital meeting and afterwards going on to his club, and Smithson was harassing the parlourmaid. Celia slipped quietly out of the front door and hastened from the house in the direction of the East End.

With mounting anticipation, she made her way to the Frying Pan, but when she entered the familiar bar she suddenly felt unexpectedly deflated – she realised that she didn't actually know what to do next. Patrick, the landlord, had acknowledged her with an unceremonious but friendly enough nod of his head, and the other customers hardly turned a hair at seeing the now common sight of the well-dressed young lady sitting in the corner. But, when all was said and done, she was still an outsider. She could hardly stand up and make a public announcement that she was prepared to perform illegal operations on pregnant women. So it was with relief that she saw Florrie come flouncing into the bar.

'Hello, ducks,' Flo called, extricating herself from the clutches of a bulky man dressed in the collarless shirt, stock and waistcoat that was almost the uniform of the market costers. Florrie wouldn't need his trade now that Celia was here to provide her with gin.

The man didn't seem to resent Florrie's disloyalty, however, and he soon found himself some more willing company to take his arm.

Celia gave Florrie a welcoming smile and some change to buy herself a drink.

Holding her glass carefully so as not to spill a precious drop, Florrie slid along the bench, made shiny-smooth from years of being polished by customers' backsides, and settled herself down next to Celia. The close proximity of a slum-dweller still made Celia gasp for fresh air, but she was becoming better at hiding her distaste at their lack of personal cleanliness. She knew that it wasn't going to be easy – raising the subject of her helping local women – but if anyone would know what to do it would be Florrie.

The two women were soon chatting amiably about this and that, with Florrie willingly filling Celia in on any local gossip that Celia might have missed since her last visit.

Celia grew restless. She was anxious to get to the subject that she really wanted to talk about: how she could help the court-dwellers. 'Do you know a small boy who makes his living collecting whatever he can find from the banks of the Thames?' asked Celia – her first step in drawing Florrie away from her rambling tales about the men she and Ada had met at the docks.

'How many mudlarks d'yer want?' asked Florrie, concentrating more on the string of mutton she was trying to prise from between her teeth with a grimy fingernail than on Celia's question. She unearthed her prize and examined the piece of meat closely before wiping it down her greasy bodice. 'There must be hundreds of the little sods working down the Thames. They can be a right nuisance sometimes with their hollering and hooting – puts some of the customers right off doing the business.

'Is there nothing to be done for the families who cannot feed their children?' Celia could feel she was getting closer to the subject she really wanted to discuss. 'Ignoring the workhouse of course,' Celia added. She had learnt something from her trips to the slums.

'How many times do I have to tell yer?' said Florrie impatiently. 'Will you never learn nothing? It's their *mothers* what wants the help. If they didn't have to have the kids in the first place, then there'd be no need for 'em to go mudlarking, now would there?'

Celia bit her lip: she had to find the right words. There could be no mistake this time.

'Mind you,' Florrie went on, oblivious to Celia's growing tension. 'Speak as I find, we was all right impressed when yer went down and tried to do something for Dirty Percy's sister. That showed yer mean well, more than well. There's not many would have done that.' She threw back the last of her drink. 'Mind yer, shame yer couldn't have helped her a bit earlier, eh girl? Then she wouldn't be Uncle Ned now, would she?'

'I'm willing to use my medical knowledge to help the local women,' said Celia quietly, averting her gaze from Florrie's suddenly pop-eyed stare. 'If you really think that that is what is needed.'

'Bleed'n hell,' said Florrie. 'Hark at you. Yer've changed yer tone a bit, ain't yer?'

'Maybe.'

'Well come on, then,' said Florrie, slamming her empty glass down on the table. 'No sooner said then done.'

Within minutes of her making the offer, Florrie was dragging Celia with great enthusiasm up the back stairs to one of the rooms above the pub.

'I've got just the girl for you,' said Florrie, throwing open a flimsy wooden door.

Inside, the walls of the tiny room were decorated with tawdry drapings of cheap, plum-coloured velveteen with gaudy gold-brocade trimmings, garish even in the dull lamplight. The only furniture was a narrow bed adorned with ragged curtains. On it reclined a pallid young woman, drenched in sweat and thin to the point of emaciation.

'Thank gawd it's you, Florrie,' the girl breathed, looking up at them listlessly. 'I thought yer was another customer. 'Who's she?' Her expression changed to one of concern. 'She ain't a customer, is she?'

'I don't think she's like that, worse luck,' chuckled Florrie, looking thoughtfully at Celia. Then she turned back to the girl on the bed. 'But she wants to help yer out in another way.'

The girl pulled herself up to a half-sitting position and rubbed her cheeks with red, work-worn hands. She looked scared. Celia noticed the tell-tale green mark left by a brass ring on the girl's finger – a mockery of the symbolic purity of the gold wedding band affected by many of the so-called brides.

'Where's your husband?' Celia asked her gently.

'Dunno, miss,' answered the now terrified girl. 'Whatever he's done, honest, I don't know nothing.'

'I'm sure he hasn't done anything to concern you,' said Celia, feeling more and more out of her depth. Then she swallowed

dryly and said. Will he mind if you decide not to have the...'
Celia pointed clumsily towards the girl's gently swollen belly. 'If
you decide not to continue with...'

Florrie replied on the girl's behalf with a hollow peal of
laughter. 'Yer a funny bleeder, Celia.'

When Florrie eventually led the exhausted Celia back
downstairs to the bar of the Frying Pan, it was with genuine affection that the Whitechapel prostitute brought her now undeniable
friend a glass of much appreciated brandy.

'There y'are, girl,' said Florrie, handing her the glass.

Celia took it from her with shaking hands.

'That was a good job yer did there, girl. The difference
between life and death, the state she was in.'

Celia gulped at the tawny liquid, ignoring the smears and
chipped edges of the glass.

'Just let anyone in Whitechapel take the piss out of the way you
speak ever again, that's all,' Florrie whispered respectfully, 'and
they'll have me to reckon with.'

–

Jacob's and Ettie's days and nights had soon developed into a
continuous round of practice, work and then love-making – with
Jacob seemingly inexhaustible in all the three spheres of their life
together.

When they had first met, Ettie had become so worn out by
his desire for perfection that she had despaired of ever being able
to meet his ambition of turning her into the most sought after
medium in London. She would go over and over the complicated
codes time and time again, and practise the painful toe-tapping
techniques and the rapid sleights of hand which could give them
away if she moved just a fraction in the wrong direction. But since
they had first made love, his professional demands on her had
become almost ceaseless. Then, at night, when they went into
the bedroom which they now shared in every sense, he turned
from being her rigorous mentor in control of everything they

did, into a fiercely demanding lover so full of desire and craving that all thoughts of tiredness were driven from her. Afterwards, she so wanted him to show that she had pleased him, for him to take her in his arms, but he never wanted to discuss what they did together, never wanted to be affectionate or playful like Ettie craved him to be. It was as though another person took him over when they lay together. There was Jacob and then there was the man with whom she shared her bed.

It was beginning to make her feel even more lonely than she had before he had ever touched her.

Chapter 20

'Who has written to you, Celia?' Bartholomew Tressing put down his knife and fork and watched his daughter slit open the envelope as he refilled his coffee cup.

'Sophia, father,' said Celia, keeping her gaze fixed firmly on the letter. 'She wants me to attend a League meeting with her.'

'A lovely girl,' he mused. 'And no harm mixing with someone from that family.' He wiped his mouth on his napkin. 'I don't see why you shouldn't go.' He poured himself more coffee. 'You may attend.' He looked at her over the rim of his cup. 'So long as you don't speak with any male members of the League. And providing, of course, that I'm at my club, and don't need you here.' Celia swallowed hard at the unspoken understanding as to what his needing her entailed. 'Thank you, Father,' she said. It was ironic, she hadn't dared mention any interest in the League meetings before – when she was genuinely attending them – but now they would prove useful cover for her other, far more important, expeditions. She was a little surprised at her bravery, but now she had taken the first step by 'helping' the young woman to whom Florrie had introduced her, she was becoming more daring.

When he had finished his breakfast, her father rose from the table, kissed her – mercifully perfunctorily – on the cheek, and left for the hospital. Celia remained where she was and, while the maid cleared away, took up her letter again to read the interesting part of what Sophia had actually written.

> *I know that, for some inexplicable reason, you do not care*
> *to attend the League meetings any more. (Let me surmise,*

might a certain reverend gentleman be the cause of your dislike, perhaps?) But please, Celia, do make a particular effort to meet me outside the meeting hall tomorrow. My mother is dropping me off there before going on to dinner, but I have something far more exciting planned for us. Something that will be tremendously wonderful fun. Say you will come, please. Please, say yes. You shall be my alibi and my companion!

As Celia walked along towards the hall, she saw the usual crowds gathering and chattering outside in anticipation as they waited to go into the meeting of the League.

Sophia rushed up to her, all breathless and bouncing. 'Celia, you've come. I'm so pleased to see you.' Sophia touched her lips against her friend's cheek. 'I thought you had gone into hibernation, it's been so long since we last met.'

Celia narrowed her eyes. 'I sometimes think you could persuade me to do anything you set your mind to, Sophie,' she whispered, hoping that she would take the hint and lower her voice. 'You really are the most dreadful exploiter of friendship.'

Keen to placate her, Sophia said in a melodramatic hiss, 'I'm taking you to see something a lot more entertaining than what goes on in there.'

'I don't think they come here for entertainment, Sophia,' said Celia primly. 'And must you always be counted on to say something outrageous?'

'Outrageous?' said Sophia, gesturing with her parasol towards the League members. 'If you want to be outraged, just look at those old fools and their ludicrous goings on.'

'Sophia!'

'Celia!'

Much to the annoyance of those around her, and against her better judgement, Celia began to giggle. Sophia really was infectiously badly behaved.

'So where are we going?' asked Celia, joining in Sophia's conspiracy despite herself. 'To a white-slaver's den?'

'No,' she replied, her eyes bright with the connivance. 'We're going to a seance.'

'A what?'

'Ssshhh!' Furiously accusing faces turned to look at the girls.

'It's all very respectable,' said Sophia under her breath, all the while smiling sweetly at the disapproving woman standing next to her. 'Lots of very learned gentlemen go to them. It's like...' She searched for an appropriately innocent-sounding description. 'Scientific research,' she declared triumphantly.

'Sophia, this is the most ridiculous of all the schemes you have come up with yet. Whatever are you thinking of? Scientific research?'

'Truly, Celia, it is. You wait and see.' Sophia beamed artlessly at her friend, her dimples puckering her pretty cheeks. 'And it's sure to be the best fun.'

'If I went with you, Sophia, you'd only get us into all sorts of trouble.'

'Celia. Please.'

'No. It really would be a mistake.'

'But why?' Sophia whined pathetically.

Celia racked her brain for an argument to convince Sophia. 'For a start, the League is totally opposed to any kind of fortunetelling. You know that.'

'What, you'd let a boring old hypocrite like Roland "Let me get my hands on your pretty arm" Stedgely tell you what to do? I can't believe it.'

'What do you mean, Sophia?' Celia's eye grew wide and her cheeks flushed as she remembered his repulsive touch. She had had no idea that Sophia had known what had happened.

'I mean that the whole League is like a ridiculous and unpleasant joke. And you know it as well as I.' She touched Celia gently on the shoulder and said more softly. 'Don't worry, your secret's safe with me.' Sophia turned and smiled prettily over her shoulder as two young men raised their hats as they passed by. 'Anyway,' she said, turning back to Celia, 'it's obvious that you're just making excuses because you're scared to go to the seance.'

'Never mind the seance,' said Celia under her breath. 'Do you mean that you...' She paused. 'That you know about what happened with that, that terrible man, yet you still go to the League meetings?'

'Of course, I do. Mother insists. Thought I'd meet "decent girls, keen on good works", that sort of thing. But, if you ask me, it's really because she was fed up having me around the house when her lovers called.' She shrugged. 'But it suits me too. It gives me the opportunity to get away from home for a few hours. God, I could die of boredom sometimes, listening to her giggling about the house while I have to stay in the drawing room pretending to practise the damn piano or my rotten sketching.'

'Sophia!'

'What? Are you so *very* shocked? Poor little Celia. You're so sheltered.' Trying her wheedling voice again, Sophia pleaded with her friend: 'Come on, let's have some fun. Come with me.'

Seeing that Celia was apparently resolved to stand her ground, Sophia played her trump card. 'If you don't go with me, then I shall have to go by myself. And just think what might happen. You know the sorts of scrapes I get involved in. You'd feel so guilty if I found myself in trouble.' She looked imploringly at her friend. 'You're always so sensible, Celia. You could look after me.'

'Sophia,' Celia said sternly. 'Don't ask me to do this. Please.'

'It's sure to be the best fun.'

'Why does everyone want to persuade me to do things I don't want to? I've been trying so hard to make up my own mind about things.'

'Well, why don't you come and do exactly that then? Make up your own mind and have fun at the same time.'

'Everything's fun to you, isn't it, Sophia?'

'I knew you'd agree!' Sophia took Celia's arm and, much to the relief of the incensed, elderly members of the League, dragged her protesting friend off along the road. 'You wait and see. You'll love it. She's meant to be marvellously entertaining. Simply everyone's talking about the Silent Beauty.'

Chapter 21

Ettie clasped the bed-covers to her chin to stop Jacob dragging them off her. 'Five more minutes, Jacob, please, let me rest. I'm ever so tired.'

'You've got to get up, come on: you've been asleep all afternoon.'

'That's only because you kept me up all night.' She smiled and reached up for him. 'There's no stopping you once you get going, is there? Now why don't you come back for a cuddle?'

Jacob pulled away. 'There's no time for that now.'

'There's never any time unless you say so, is there?' Ettie dragged the covers back over her head. 'Always what you want,' she mumbled through the eiderdown. 'Bloody selfish you can be. Why is it all right to do it when you say?' She rolled over, pulling the bedclothes tighter round her. 'And how you always want it.'

Jacob ripped the covers from her. 'I don't like it when you talk like that.'

'You bloody hypocrite,' she snapped at him. 'Why can't you just show me some affection for once? Why is it always what *you* want?'

Jacob rubbed his hands over his face. Ettie could see the beads of sweat on his top lip. 'I'm sorry, Ettie, if that's how you feel,' he said coldly, walking towards the door. 'I'm sorry.' Before he shut the door he looked over his shoulder and murmured, 'I'll let you get dressed.'

Ettie sat up in bed and touched the locket which nestled between her breasts. She thought about Billy when he'd given the necklace to her. And about Maisie – her words, which lately had begun to haunt her. 'Jacob Protsky—' she'd said his name so venomously – 'or whatever he calls himself. Yer don't know nothing about him, but I know he ain't our type, Ett. Yer't get mixed up with the likes of him. Our Billy's the bloke for you.'

Maybe Maisie had been right about one thing: what did she really know about Jacob Protsky? And what else was there to find out about him leaving Paris like that? She lay back down on the pillow and stared up at the ceiling. Why did everything have to be so bloody complicated? Some days she felt just like she was a character living out one of the stories she used to love at the penny gaffs – the poor little maiden in the hands of the evil genius…

She dragged herself out of bed. She knew she had to get ready for tonight's performance. Jacob had been going on and on about how important it was going to be for weeks. It was going to be a small gathering of influential people at an exclusive address in Mayfair. People who were influential in the sense that, if they liked what they saw, Ettie and Jacob would be assured of a very profitable season of bookings as a result. Perhaps she shouldn't be too hard on Jacob, she thought, as she stared at her reflection in the looking-glass, examining her creamy, ivory skin. He'd given her a chance that she would never have imagined would come along for her, little Ettie Wilkins. And he was right: this was a special evening, she should be making an effort. But she couldn't help it, she still kept getting the feeling – more and more, if she was honest with herself – that she was uncomfortable with him. But why? She knew there was some secret that Jacob kept from her and that kept them apart. It was a barrier, that was it, that prevented her from really knowing him. She might share his bed now, but she certainly didn't share his thoughts. And even their time together in bed wasn't what it had been.

She sighed deeply. She'd have to try and pull herself together.

'Ready,' she said simply, standing in the bedroom doorway, arms outstretched, waiting to be admired. But Jacob didn't go through the usual ritual of reassuring her how lovely she looked, and how she would woo the sitters into believing everything she said. He was still cold with her after their row. Instead, he went on and on about concentrating on one elderly man who would be sitting at the centre, opposite the cabinet. He was to be their ticket into this circle, and Ettie wasn't to make any mistakes that he was their mark.

As they waited for a cab, Ettie didn't go through her customary stream of chatter and jokes to stop her from feeling nervous. Instead, she just stood there next to Jacob in a determined, tight-lipped, silent sulk. God she hated all this. What she actually hated most wasn't having to keep quiet for once – difficult as that was – but the fact that Jacob didn't even seem to notice her mood. He just stood there, as silent as her, in his own private world, where she was beginning to think she would never be allowed to enter.

The house was indeed very grand: more sumptuous in every way than any they had visited so far. It was all Ettie could do to prevent herself from gawping.

They were shown into an elaborately decorated salon, rich and heavy with fabrics, paintings and ornamentation of every kind: the room which Jacob had chosen as being most suitable for their trickery and the one which, he had explained when he had called on the hostess the previous week, was the most auspicious place for their performance.

Although there were many servants on hand, Jacob refused all offers of help, insisting that he was the only one who could arrange the room in a way of which the spirits would approve. His efforts were watched eagerly by the assembled guests, who whis-pered excitedly, speculating on the nature of the demonstration, as he carried out exaggerated yet actually minor adjustments to the position of everything from an ormolu clock to a Worcester art pot containing a luxuriant fern. Ettie was grateful that she was the Silent Beauty and could sit on the sidelines in a large wing armchair in splendid isolation: they could stare and goggle at her all they liked – she was used to that by now – but the thought of having to talk to these people in the mood she was in was too much for her even to contemplate.

She studied the people in the room with little enthusiasm. They were the usual type: past their youth, concerned to be reassured that there would be something for them in the Great Beyond when they departed this world, and with more money than sense.

With all she had on her mind she couldn't have cared less about the performance: in fact, she was growing bored with the idea of Jacob repeating yet another series of mistily ambiguous details to a group who would prove to be as easy to fool as all the others. So she was pleasantly surprised to see two much younger women come into the room. Ettie ran her eyes knowingly over their outfits – they were both fashionably dressed and moved with the effortless grace of the privileged classes, the way Jacob had so painstakingly taught her. The dark-haired one was chattering away like an over-excited schoolgirl, while the blond one, who was perhaps a few years older than Ettie, was less talkative and seemed more interested in looking round to see who was there. Maybe she shouldn't be here herself, thought Ettie perceptively. Then she looked at her more closely. She was sure she recognised her from somewhere. But where? Maybe she'd been at one of the other meetings, but she didn't think so – another thing Jacob had taught her was the importance of having a good memory for faces: it wouldn't do to give the customers conflicting messages on different occasions. After all, even Seekers After Truth weren't as stupid as all that.

Her speculations about the pretty fair-haired young woman were interrupted by Jacob telling Ettie to take her position in the cabinet and for the guests to be seated.

The buzz of anticipation was halted as Jacob introduced the proceedings. He ran through the usual instructions not to touch the spirits if they decided to move through the room. He warned about possible manifestations, and asked any persons of a nervous disposition to leave before the demonstration began. All in all, he soon had them eating out of the palm of his well-manicured hand. If asked, most of those present would swear on oath that they had already felt something unearthly enter the room. Even Ettie, foul mood though she was in, had to admit that his power to persuade was as masterly as ever.

Ettie looked at the sitters through her lowered lashes – she was meant to be preparing for her trance state, but she was fascinated by the pretty blond girl with the talkative friend. If only she could remember. There was definitely something familiar about her. But who was she? Whoever she was, Ettie didn't need the skills of perception that Jacob had so painstakingly taught her to see that she was troubled in some way: that much was obvious to anyone who cared to see.

Jacob finished his preparations and lifted his hand to indicate that the footman should lower the lights ready for the demonstration to begin.

With the lamps lowered and the shades draped in red silken cloths, the room was filled with a warm yet mysterious glow. In the complex code he had developed, Jacob told Ettie to ignore the blond girl on her left, and to keep her gaze on the stout old party in the middle. *He* was their special mark for this evening. Not only was he a Member of Parliament and extremely rich, but he was also very influential and could prove a useful ally should anyone decide to make life difficult for them in the future.

Ettie did as she was instructed but, even while she concentrated on the job in hand, she still couldn't get the girl's haunted features out of her mind.

Jacob, on the other hand, was now well into his stride. He played the audience like a well-tuned instrument, and they loved him for it. As their astonished gasps and cries of wonder – more eloquent than any written testimonial could ever be – filled the room, a feeling of excitement rose in Jacob's chest. He and Ettie were a success in the place where it really mattered.

His timing was perfect: using the old showman's trick of pretending to finish at just the point when the audience was clamouring for more, Jacob teased them that it was all over; until the moment that he would decide it was right to give them the final something special. So, immediately after the muslin robe had been shredded into tokens and then made miraculously whole again, he announced that the evening's demonstration was at an end as the medium was completely exhausted.

There was much murmuring of disappointment, but lots of wildly enthusiastic applause. Jacob bowed low from the waist. He was well satisfied. He knew that when they did the final beguiling disappearance, the marks would be his for the taking. After tonight's performance, he and Ettie would be able to name their own price.

But, with the serious-faced girl sitting before her, Ettie didn't share his pleasure. The girl's look of being somehow trapped reminded Ettie too much of the way she had felt back at Tyvern Court, feelings she wanted to forget but which were now unpleasantly close to those she was beginning to feel about living with Jacob. Quite suddenly, and with no warning whatsoever, Ettie stood up and stepped out of the cabinet. Startled, Jacob spun round to confront her. What the hell was she playing at? Thoughts of panic raced through his mind. He had just been about to tell the footman to turn up the lights and then announce that the Silent Beauty was gone, that she had disappeared into the ether with the spirits. Thank goodness he hadn't opened his mouth.

Then the unthinkable happened. Ettie pointed to the blond young woman and began to speak.

'I know you are troubled,' Ettie said carefully.

The audience were stunned. What was happening? The Silent Beauty was speaking, and in her own voice, instead of communicating directly into the mind of the Professor in the language of the spirits.

Jacob did his best to hide his fury, to keep some sort of control of the situation; and at least, he reasoned to himself, she was speaking in the voice he had taught her to use, not the cockney slang of the back streets.

'I have a message to give you,' Ettie continued, moving in a slow glide towards the young woman, her muslin robe floating out behind her in the breeze from the French windows – the windows that Jacob had carefully made sure had been opened, intending them to be her escape route for the disappearance.

Everyone was staring.

The girl's fidgety, noisy friend was almost beside herself with delight that her companion was the object of so much attention, although the girl herself looked deeply concerned, her pretty brow creased in a tormented frown.

'You must do what *you* feel is correct,' Ettie intoned, using words that would, in fact, have comforted her, had someone cared enough to say them, and hoping as she spoke that her vague message would be of some comfort to the, obviously distressed young woman. 'Follow your conscience. Do not let others make you do things against your will. But even if they succeed, they cannot hurt you, not deep down in your innermost self. Believe, and you will find the answer to the path that you must take.'

The girl herself was now standing, oblivious to those around her. She wanted to say something, to speak to this marvellous apparition who had found her voice merely in order to give her a message. But her intention was thwarted by Jacob. He went over to her and gently but firmly made her take her seat again, then hurriedly indicated to the footman that the lights should be dimmed immediately. He then began to speak, giving Ettie the coded, but to her very clear, message that she had better stop whatever it was she thought she was up to, right now, instantly, at that very moment.

His voice sounded calm to the audience, but Ettie knew him better: she could tell that he was furious. And she could guess exactly why he was so enraged – their sensational finale, her disappearance at the end of the act, was now completely out of the question, ruined by the audience's exhilaration at being witnesses to the Silent Beauty's discovery of the gift of speech, and their clamouring for more direct messages from the mouth of the medium herself. She could see by the way he looked at her what he was thinking: that if the audience were going to be so exhilarated, it should have been because he, Jacob, had decided to make them so, not because Ettie had taken it in her head to act out this pathetic little melodrama of her own devising.

Jacob might well have been furious over what she had done, but the circle of sitters were plainly completely captivated by her performance, and most affected of all was Celia. She was stunned – stunned by the message that the Silent Beauty had given her.

At that moment, Celia knew that she had to meet her privately, she had to, because here was the very first person who had ever understood about her suffering and about what she was trying to achieve.

Chapter 22

'A cab for the hospital, Smithson,' Bartholomew Tressing said as he buttoned his frock coat.

'Will you require dinner tonight, sir?' the butler inquired, unlocking the big front door.

'No. Not tonight,' said Tressing, consulting his pocket-watch. 'I'm dining at the club. I shan't be home till tomorrow evening.'

As she heard her father speak those words, Celia could have cried out with joy, but she knew better than to draw attention to herself, so instead she sat quietly at the breakfast table and waited until her father had left the house.

She had arranged with Sophia that if she could get away from home that morning they would meet at the hat shop currently favoured by her friend. The moment Smithson closed the door behind his master and went to eat his own breakfast below stairs, Celia raced up to her bedroom, had a quick wash, and grabbed her outdoor things.

'Celia,' wailed Sophia, turning round in her seat. At the sound of the jangling bell above the door, she had known it must be her friend entering the exclusive little milliner's shop, as that particular establishment off Bond Street only entertained customers by prearranged appointment. 'You must help me. I'm absolutely desperate.'

'I have assured the mademoiselle,' said an elderly, over-made-up and apparently French woman in a red dress with a too-tight bodice, 'all of them look divine on her.'

Celia didn't join in the petty squabbling. She just sat quietly on the little velvet upholstered gilt chair that a timid-looking young man had rushed to bring her.

Sophia studied her reflection, tilting her chin this way and that. 'It's no good, they are both hideous. I look a complete frump.' She dragged the offending straw creation from her head and tossed it petulantly to one side. 'Have you nothing new? Nothing special?' Sophia turned her round brown eyes on the now extremely anxious milliner, her voice was sharp rather than cajoling.

The shop owner replied in a babbling amalgam of broken English and French, and disappeared into the work room at the back of the shop, where she could be heard berating her minions in an indiscreetly loud cockney accent.

'Yer'd better get yer bleed'n ideas bucked up out here,' they heard 'Madame' yell at her unfortunate workers. 'Or yer'll all be back on the sodding streets where I found yer!'

'Very "continental" behaviour,' Sophia said sarcastically, and picked up one of the hats she had earlier tossed aside.

'Will you look at this, Celia?' she demanded. 'Whatever is the woman thinking of?'

As she perched the offending article on top of her elaborately dressed hair and pouted at herself in the looking-glass, she caught sight of Celia's reflection. She was furious to note that Celia still wasn't giving her the attention she wanted.

'Celia, for goodness' sake, stop staring about the room and help me.'

'I'm sorry, Sophie,' said Celia. 'I was thinking about something else.'

'That much was obvious,' scowled Sophia.

Celia chose to ignore her friend's tone. 'That girl,' she said evenly. 'The one at the seance.'

'You're not still going on about her, are you?' Sophia twisted round on her seat and faced Celia. 'Once you get an idea in that head of yours…'

'I knew it,' said Celia sharply. 'You've forgotten, haven't you? All you care about is yourself.'

Sophia rolled her eyes in exasperation and dug around in her bag. 'No, I haven't forgotten actually. I didn't want to give it to you while Madame was in here.' She gestured with her bag towards the back room where the woman could still be heard at whoever was unlucky enough to be in there with her. 'Some of us,' she added, handing Celia a folded slip of paper, 'like to help our friends when they ask.'

Celia tucked the paper safely away in her bag. 'Will you come with me?' she asked, her face furrowed with seriousness.

'Just try and stop me,' grinned Sophia in reply. 'I wouldn't miss it for the world. How about this evening? I can get away then.'

With much amusement, Sophia watched Celia anxiously check the piece of paper on which the address of the so-called medium was written for about the twentieth time since they'd met earlier that evening. Sophia was enjoying herself hugely: it was all proving to be much more fun than she could ever have hoped for when she had first planned the expedition to the seance.

–

'This is the place,' said Celia, stepping back towards the kerb so that she could get a proper view of the house.

'Do you think that she and the Professor, you know,...' said Sophia raising her eyebrow. '*Live* together.'

'I'll ignore that,' said Celia, gathering her skirts and walking up the steps to the front door. She straightened her hat, took a deep breath, and knocked firmly on the door.

After what seemed like ages, an elderly woman in a clean white apron answered them with a friendly smile.

'I wish to inquire if Professor Protsky is at home to visitors,' said Celia, not quite sure what to say in the unaccustomed circumstances of arriving at someone's house without a formal invitation.

'I'll go and see,' said the woman pleasantly. 'Won't yer step inside the hall, miss.'

In her eagerness, Sophia shoved her friend aside, and so was the first to see that Jacob was already coming towards them along the hallway.

'It's all right, Mrs Hawkins,' he said, looking questioningly at the two young women. 'I'll deal with it. You get back to your chores.'

'As yer like, Professor,' said the elderly woman as she went off to her duties, singing a tuneless little song in a cracked vibrato voice.

'Now,' said Jacob, 'of what service may I be?'

'I understand that you are prepared to conduct private readings,' said Celia, her words coming out in a breathless whisper.

Jacob nodded. 'That is correct.' He looked at Sophia. 'Your friend here contacted me after the party last month.'

'You have a very good memory, Professor,' said Sophia flirtatiously. 'And you must meet so many people in your line of work.'

Jacob smiled a broad, easy smile, showing off his handsome features to perfection. 'How could anyone forget such lovely young women?' He gestured towards the stairs. 'Please, won't you come in?'

Jacob instructed Mrs Hawkins to fetch tea for the two young women, and then left them in the sitting room while he went to the bedroom to speak to Ettie.

'We have some unexpected guests,' said Jacob, sitting on the bed where Ettie was still tucked cosily under the covers.

'Who? No one ever comes here.' Ettie sat up, frowning.

'Calm down, nothing's wrong. You've got yourself that private reading we were expecting, that's all.'

Ettie groaned and rolled over. 'That's all I could do with. I thought I was having a rest this evening. Can't they come back tomorrow?'

Jacob didn't answer her. Instead he got to his feet, scooped her up in his arms, and dumped her unceremoniously on the stool in front of the dressing-table.

'Mustn't let the customers down, now must we?' glowered Ettie. She sighed, then picked up her hairbrush and began raking it through her thick, glossy, brown curls. 'Go on, go and tell them I'll be out in a minute.'

When Ettie entered the sitting room five minutes later, the two young women let out little gasps in surprised unison. It wasn't only her unusual tallness which made her stand out, it was something about her: her dark hair that fell in loose curls about her shoulders, and the vivid contrast it made with the pale creaminess of her skin; the quite shocking informality of the white floor-length silk robe that was tied about her waist with a ribbon, the colour of which matched almost exactly the deep, ocean blue of her eyes. She looked, in every way, magnificently exotic.

'Good evening,' said Ettie, dazzling them further with the broad, welcoming smile that only she and Jacob knew to be an artifice.

Celia bowed her head as she spoke. 'I am delighted you have had your speech restored,' she said.

'Yes,' said Jacob, flashing a surreptitiously sarcastic look at Ettie. 'Praise be. That was something of a miracle, wasn't it?'

Sophia didn't join in the conversation: she merely smiled and simpered girlishly, enjoying every moment of this unexpectedly enjoyable diversion.

It was Celia who spoke next. She looked at Ettie but was clearly addressing Jacob. 'Do you think that it would be in order for me to be alone with…' She paused and looked at Jacob.

'With Miss Wilkins?' he prompted her.

She nodded.

'Why not?' Ettie answered for him. 'I'm sure Professor Protsky can entertain your friend.'

Sophia giggled coquettishly and, putting her empty tea-cup on one of the side-tables, stood up to follow Jacob.

'I'm afraid that we are rather limited for space,' said Jacob, gesturing gallantly for Sophia to go in front of him. 'We shall have to wait in the kitchen. It's a small, but very cosy, room.'

Sophia answered him with yet another giggle, and flounced out of the room leaving Celia and Ettie to their own devices.

'Now,' said Ettie kindly, settling herself on the chair which Sophia had just vacated. 'I see that something is worrying you badly.'

Celia blinked her eyes, making a teardrop spill on to her cheek. 'Is it so very obvious to you?' she asked her in a small, quavering voice.

Ettie took her hand – it was cold and trembling, even though the evening was warm, almost hot for the time of year. 'You don't have to be afraid,' Ettie reassured her. 'Whatever you say or ask will be known only to us.' Then she added hurriedly. 'And to the spirits, of course.'

Celia looked at Ettie, her face a confused mask of desperation. 'My father,' she said starkly. 'The way he...'

'Yes?' said Ettie encouragingly.

Celia studied her hands as she wrung them round and round in her lap. Then she looked up at Ettie and shook her head. 'No. That doesn't matter,' she said calmly, 'I won't let it. Not now.' Her gaze returned to her lap. 'Please, tell me what you feel about babies.'

'Babies.' Ettie nodded. Now she understood what was going on: the girl was pregnant and too scared to tell her father. Ettie had known as soon as she'd seen her at the seance that something was preying on her mind. She still wished she could remember where she'd seen her before, but that would have to wait: what she had to do now was to try and make her feel better, help her sort out her life and realise that life went on, no matter how terrible things seemed at the time. 'All babies have perfect little souls,' Ettie began kindly, and then went on to do her best to reassure Celia that all babies, even before their birth, were complete spirits, and were only waiting for their chance to come to earth; that they brought great joy to all who were lucky enough to have them, whatever the circumstances in which they had been created. That seemed to upset Celia, so Ettie tried another, more direct approach, and told her that those who were privileged to be able to give their little ones all that they could ever need or desire should have particular reason to welcome them, and that they should think themselves blessed that they were not like the unfortunate women of the slums who didn't have such luck and couldn't even feed themselves let alone another hungry mouth.

Celia seemed heartened by that, and soon the tears poured more slowly down her cheeks. Ettie stood up and pronounced the reading over.

'It's incredible how much you see,' sniffed Celia. 'So reassuring to hear your words. I had made my decision already, but you have confirmed everything for me. You have been a great help.'

Ettie handed Celia a handkerchief. 'Take this,' she said, putting it gently in her hand, 'and I'll show you to the bathroom so you can wash your face.'

With Celia safely in the bathroom tidying herself up, Ettie went to the kitchen to speak to her companion.

Standing in the doorway Ettie said, 'I'm afraid that your friend became quite emotional. I think she could do with a bit of comfort.'

Sophia giggled.

Ettie knew it was none of her business, but she didn't like this frivolous young woman. Her friend needed help, and all she could do was flirt with Jacob.

But the smile was suddenly wiped from Sophia's face. Her jaw dropped as she focused on something behind Ettie. 'You look frightful,' she squealed, as though the sight of her friend's tearstained face were a personal affront to her pleasure.

'I'm sorry,' whispered Celia hoarsely, dabbing at her eyes on the handkerchief that Ettie had given her.

Jacob, in his usual quest for control in front of paying customers, turned his attention towards Celia and addressed her in his firm, bass voice. 'You have been moved by the spirits, I see,' he said, reaching out and taking her hand.

Celia nodded silently.

Sophia stared for a moment at Jacob touching her friend, and then leapt from her seat at the little kitchen table. She placed herself between Celia and Jacob and began pulling on her gloves. 'I'm so sorry,' she said, flatly, 'but we have to go.' Then she shrugged her elegant little shoulders at Jacob, flashed a quick, insincere smile at Ettie, and made for the door. 'So sorry about the rush.'

They heard the front door open and Sophia slamming it behind her.

'Well. Goodbye, and thank you again,' Celia said, collecting her things. She paused just long enough to say to Ettie. 'I hope to see you soon.' Then she disappeared into the hallway after Sophia, calling out behind her, 'Thank you so much for the tea.'

The door slammed shut for the second time, but even from inside the kitchen they could still hear Sophia's unmistakably trilling tones as she called to her friend, 'Celia, hurry up, I'm not waiting for you. This is *Bow*, for God's sake.'

Jacob settled himself down at the table and poured himself a cup of tea. 'That spoiled young lady paid you adequately for your time and wisdom, I trust?' he said, holding up the pot to offer Ettie some tea.

She shook her head in disgust. 'How can you sit there and drink tea like that? What's the matter with you? You're meant to be such a fine gentleman, but you're just a bloody insensitive, no good...' Ettie's anger made her at a loss for words. In frustration she slammed her hand down on the table, making the tea-cups rattle. 'All you care about is whether she paid me enough, when you could see the poor cow's obviously in trouble.'

'And you, the blessed St Ettie, helped her I suppose?' said Jacob sarcastically.

'Yes, I did as a matter of fact, you flash bleeder. I made up a right load of old nonsense to try and make her feel better, cos that's what I'm good at. It's what you taught me to do.' Ettie slumped into the hard, high-backed chair. 'The stupid mare's obviously got herself involved with some bloke who's got her up the stick.'

There was a look of loathing on her face as she stared across the table at Jacob. 'Ain't you got no heart?'

'Watch your language, Ettie,' he said, and calmly sipped at his tea.

'I swear, if you say that to me *once* more.'

'What? What do you swear, Ettie?'

'Oh, bugger you, Jacob Protsky. Bugger you.'

Chapter 23

Celia tried to catch up with Sophia, but she was moving remarkably quickly despite her long, cumbersome skirts, and quickly disappeared from Celia's view down one of the many side roads leading away from Victoria Park.

Sophia quickly regretted the temper tantrum that had prevented her from waiting for her friend, however. She didn't even see where they came from, but suddenly she found herself surrounded by a crowd of terrifyingly wild and dishevelled children. The urchin who had first spotted Sophia had come rushing out of an alleyway, and he was soon joined by a straggling, malodorous mob who bounced around her, begging for farthings.

Sophia panicked. She had no idea what to do. She was alone in a disgusting street, in a dreadful, totally unfamiliar part of London, the sky was now almost dark, and there were children all around her: vile urchins with no shoes, filthy dirty and smelling of heaven-only-knew what, grasping and tugging at her sleeves.

Frantically, Sophia looked about for assistance, but nobody seemed even to notice her, let alone help her. She had had enough; she would have to deal with it herself. She raised both hands to chest height, then shoved the smallest child as hard as she could, sending him tumbling to the ground in a sprawl of limbs and rags. She lifted her skirts and rushed off in what she could only pray was the general direction of Belgravia -- or at least of a main thoroughfare where she might get a cab. Her thoughts were not solely on her safe escape, however, she was also concentrating on exactly what she would say to the unfortunate Celia Tressing when they next met.

Celia was far less perturbed when she lost sight of her friend: she simply made her way determinedly towards another part of the East End – Whitechapel.

In the shadows of the railway arches near the top of Brick Lane, Celia stopped to catch her breath. As she stood, her chest rising and falling from the effort of breathing, she saw a group of well-dressed men walking along towards her. Her breathing almost stopped entirely when she recognised the group as colleagues of her father. Terrified that they would see her and betray her secret mission to her father, she pressed herself back against the wall. Her heart was pounding so loudly she was sure they could hear it.

She could hardly contain herself when they stopped only a few yards away and stood illuminated by a pool of light cast from the windows of a pub. She could hear them clearly and see that they were addressing a tall man who was standing with his back to her.

'What's it to be tonight, old man? Fat? Thin? Red head? Blond?'

'A girl? Or how about a young boy?' another man asked him.

'There are some pretty ones on the street tonight. Come on, tell us, what do you fancy? Maybe an oriental lovely?'

'Yes, come on Bart,' the first man persisted, 'tell us. You're the expert on what's to be had round here.'

'In this world,' Bart replied, 'there are many delights. Prostitution is normal, a way of life enjoyed by most of the inhabitants of these parts. Their breeding makes them animal-like in their passions. No different from the beasts of the field.' 'Pity some of our ladies aren't more like that, eh Bartholomew?'

'God help us if they were,' guffawed a short, rotund man. Celia could see his fleshy jowls quiver as he laughed. 'Imagine being worn out by a wife, and not having the energy to sample wider pleasures, eh, old chap?'

'No problem for you, Bartholomew. From what I've heard, you'd have the energy to satisfy a dozen a night.'

'A dozen? Damn it, my reputation must be slipping!'

As their laughter echoed around her, Celia flattened herself even closer against the wall, not caring that the bricks were running with slimy water. Her mind was filled with confusion. How could he, her own father, continue to do this, even if his mind was blighted with the sickness from that terrible disease? Celia felt a wave of nausea rise to her throat.

She rubbed her hands over her face trying to clear her head. The message from the spirits that Ettie had given her, telling her that helping these women was right, didn't seem so convincing now. But no, she would not waver, it *had* to be right if the spirits had said so, and she had seen for herself how innocent babies would suffer if nothing was done.

Celia slumped against the dripping wall of the arch, her head buried in her hands. Perhaps she too was going insane, the poison of syphilis even now surging round her body and eating away at her mind.

She leaned forward cautiously, peering out from the darkness, as one of the men's voices became increasingly agitated.

'Come on, Bart,' he was saying excitedly, 'what's it to be?'

'Might as well take a tart, I think. Good for research.'

'Funny sort of science, Tressing,' laughed another man.

'No, not at all. It's rather an elegant procedure. Almost a cycle of events. You see, you get one of them pregnant, then the other whores use their barbaric ways to try and rid her of the bastard. That all goes wrong and she finishes up on the dissecting slab. More dead meat for us to cut up.'

Celia drew in her breath at his foul words.

'No, you're misguided there, Tressing,' one of her father's colleagues protested, his voice rising above their ribald laughter. 'It's not good enough having these outsiders involved in surgical procedures. They're learning too much about the techniques. We in the medical profession need to protect ourselves.'

'Jackson's on to his favourite subject,' mocked one of the others. Tressing held up his hand to stay the man's laughter. 'I must say, Derringer, that I agree with Jackson there.'

'Don't encourage him, Tressing,' said Derringer, sneering at his competitor.

'You can laugh, Derringer,' continued Jackson, never one to be silenced. 'But if we don't fight to keep out these amateurs, we are going to lose more than a bit of business. Our whole professional mystique will be eroded.'

Tressing opened his mouth to offer further support, but Jackson was not to be interrupted so easily.

'It's not good enough to let outsiders think the work is easy,' he continued, addressing his companions as though they were sitting in their West End club after an agreeable dinner rather than standing in a dark and dangerous street in the East End. 'Savvy? Otherwise every man-Jack'll be at it. And, when all's said and done, it must be worth a half-guinea or so for these harlots to get rid of what they don't want. And that soon...'

Celia's father *had* to interrupt him there. 'A half-guinea! How do you suppose these creatures could find that much money? A half-crown if they're lucky, more like.'

'Well, you'll just have to pay a bit more for your fun then, won't you old man?' said Derringer, anxious to get on with the evening's entertainment and to get one over on Tressing – who, as all his colleagues knew, was Derringer's acknowledged rival for the role of being the most popular surgeon with bored ladies whose husbands had more money than sense where their wives were concerned. 'Good for business all round.'

'A better idea,' said the short fat one, aroused by the turn things were taking. 'Why not do a straight swop? It's a brilliant idea. You could offer the operation in exchange for a...'

'That's enough, Walter. Come on, or you'll get over-excited and spoil your evening.'

Celia watched as though in a dream as a ragged, tangledhaired boy sidled up to them.

'Sir, sir. Gis a penny for a hot dinner, sir,' the child whined as he dragged on her father's sleeve. His little bare feet were ingrained with the grime of the streets, and his frail body, with its bones jutting out, looked like the split carcasses hanging in a butcher's window display.

'Gorn, sir, please. Only a penny. I'm starving, sir.'

Bartholomew Tressing looked down disdainfully at the persistent waif and attempted to swat him away as though he were an inconvenient flying insect spoiling a summer's picnic.

But the hungry child was too desperate to be put off so easily. 'Please, sir? Go on. Please.'

Bartholomew calmly raised his silver-topped cane and struck the pathetically skinny child a sharp blow across the side of his head.

Celia smothered her cry with her gloved hand as the boy fell senseless to the ground. She stood there, horrified, yet unable to move or even look away from what she was witnessing. Her father, using the toe of his boot as a lever, rolled the boy over.

The child's arms flopped about across his body like the limbs of a broken doll.

'Shame,' Tressing said, wiping clean the bloody end of his stick on the child's ragged shirt. 'He had an appealing little body.'

'Come on, Bart,' said Derringer, 'even you can't be that heartless.'

Tressing raised an eyebrow. 'Squeamish?' he said with a half smile. 'Come along, gentlemen, we have the whole evening before us.'

Glad to leave such a potentially incriminating scene behind them, Tressing's companions followed him hurriedly along Brick Lane towards the Whitechapel Road. All their voices, except Tressing's, were decidedly subdued.

As soon as she dared, Celia came out of the shadows and rushed over to the injured child. Kneeling down in the gutter beside him, she took his bone-thin hand in hers.

'Can you speak?' she whispered.

The boy lifted his lids slowly and met her gaze with large, staring eyes. He moved his lips; his voice was so weak that she could only just make out his words. 'Help me,' he moaned.

'I'll help you,' Celia said, dabbing at the blood flowing from the side of his head with Ettie's tear-dampened handkerchief. 'I'll fetch someone. Where do you live?'

'Street,' he gurgled, as blood bubbled from his lips and nostrils.

'You have no one?'

The orphaned child managed to shake his head.

Celia pulled off her cloak and draped it over the boy. 'I'm going to find someone,' she said, standing up. 'I'll be back. As soon as I can.'

She ran along towards Thrawl Street faster than she would have thought possible, ignoring the calls of passing men, not caring what anyone said or thought. She had to get to the Frying Pan: someone there would know what to do.

It was with relief that she found Ada chatting at the bar with Patrick.

Ada was soon standing next to Celia, looking down at the pathetic, half-naked child. Even though Celia had left him for only a few minutes while she fetched help, her cloak had been taken, as had the boy's own tattered shirt.

'It's Timmy Blake,' Ada said with a sigh, sitting herself down on the damp cobbles and brushing back the boy's blood-matted fringe from his forehead. 'Least it was Timmy Blake.' Ada gently drew down the boy's eyelids.

She looked up at Celia. 'We're too late to help the little mite now.'

'My God,' wailed Celia self-pityingly, 'can I do nothing right?'

'Don't you blame yerself, love,' said Ada kindly. 'Been on the streets since Iris, his ma, passed away last Christmas. Terrible death she had. In labour for five days before her and the baby died.'

'Oh, Ada, all this has got to stop,' wailed Celia. 'The lives these people lead. Children dying. Something must be done.' She dropped on to her knees next to the filthy woman.

'Maybe if there'd have been someone like you around to help her stop having more babies... who knows, perhaps then this little fellah might have had a better chance.'

Celia buried her face in her hands. 'But is it right, Ada? Is it?'

'Ssshhh, don't upset yerself.' Ada put her arms round Celia, and rocked her while she sobbed into the bride's putrid-smelling shoulder as though she would never stop.

PART THREE

Summer 1888

It was a gloriously sunny, truly beautiful summer's day. Ettie stood by the window looking down at the laughing groups of young men and women parading through the park. She sighed deeply, blowing out her breath through pursed lips. She was fed up. And the thought of another evening spent moaning and swaying in that wooden box, in front of a circle of open-mouthed, enraptured dupes, was more than she could endure.

'Jacob,' she said, turning away from the window to talk to him.

'Mmmm?' He didn't look up, but continued writing in the leather-bound notebook on his desk.

'You busy?' she asked, hoping that her cajoling tones would at least gain his attention.

'Mmmm.' Still he continued writing.

'Fancy coming for a walk?' she asked, all bright smiles – although she actually felt ready to slap him for being so neglectful of her.

'You go,' he answered, then paused while he recharged his pen. 'But don't be late: we're working, remember?'

'How could I forget?' she mumbled to herself.

Disappointed, but not surprised by his reaction – she had grown used to him only ever being interested in her when it suited him – Ettie jammed her hat on to her mass of glossy dark-brown curls, stamped out into the hall and slammed the door behind her.

He probably didn't even notice her go, she fumed to herself. What did he think she was, a marionette? A wax doll from one of his freak shows? It was all right for him: he was happy to work all the time. Apart from the times when they made love, work was all that he seemed interested in – that and his rotten books and ledgers. But *she* didn't feel like working today. She wanted to go out and have a laugh, like she used to. She thought of Maisie and the other girls. She missed them, all of them, with their easy companionship and raucous laughter. They knew how to enjoy themselves all right. And she couldn't remember the last time she had seen her mum. She thought about Billy: pulling the locket and chain he had given her from inside her blouse, she kept her hand on it for a few moments as though it were a good-luck charm.

Glad of the chance to enjoy the fresh air and sunlight, she strolled along, not realising how far she had walked: lately she'd spent most daylight hours indoors practising, or asleep recovering from work the night before. All that was missing, she thought to herself, was a bit of company. Beautiful summer days were meant to be shared.

As she got near the Poplar Recreation Ground, she heard loud hurrahs and cheering: before her was all the company she could ever want. There was a huge crowd of milling people, all laughing and pushing forward, all intent on having a good time. Ettie tucked her locket safely inside her blouse, held on to her hat, and raced towards the park. She'd always been quick on her feet, and she didn't intend missing out on a bit of fun.

'What's happening?' she asked a young lad who was giving out leaflets to passers-by, her breath coming in short, panting gasps. 'What's going on?'

'It's a hot-air balloon, miss. A great big bugger of a thing, it is. Gonna fly right up in the air. No one ain't never seen nothing like it never before. Look at it!'

She squinted into the sun, looking in the direction of the boy's pointing finger. She shaded her eyes with her hand, making out the immense shape of the brilliant, multi-coloured dirigible being inflated ready for flight. 'Who's in it?' she asked the child, still staring at the immense expanse of billowing material. 'Who's going up?'

'There's a pilot to drive it, and what they call "four local notables". Ain't yer heard nothing about it?'

'No.' She shook her head as she answered the boy, but her attention was still focused on the air-filled wonder.

'No.' The boy chuckled to himself. 'Course yer ain't. A posh lady like yerself's hardly from round these parts.'

Ettie frowned and looked down at his grubby, eager little face, searching for a clue about herself. Had she really changed so much?

'Wish it was me going up there,' he said, pointing up into the clear blue sky. 'Know what I'd do? I'd fly right up in the air, right away from this shit-hole – begging yer pardon – if I had the chance. It's so beautiful, ain't it? Like yerself, miss.' The boy smiled cheekily and handed Ettie a leaflet.

'There yer go, miss. Have a butcher's at that.'

She returned his smile and pushed forward, joining the queue as it snaked into the recreation ground.

As she waited, she looked at the paper the child had given her. It read:

> Today only! An extraordinary performance of a wondrous phenomenon. The ascent of the famous Dalling Brothers' hot-air-filled balloon. Thrill to the spectacle of men in actual flight.
>
> The ascent will be followed in the afternoon by a concert featuring popular songs and dancing. Dramatic interludes of a most fascinating nature will be enacted by the celebrated Dalling Brothers' theatrical troupe – see moments of melodrama and excitement, romance and fear. The Dalling Brothers' noted dog and monkey circus will be performing tricks such as have never been seen before. Slack and tightrope acts of great daring will continue throughout the day and evening. The grand finale

will be a spellbinding display of fireworks, the like of
which has never before been created in England.

Admission sixpence to include view of the ascent.
Threepence after the balloon has gone up.

Ettie laughed, thinking how Jacob would approve of such showmanship. There she was, pushing through with all the others to
pay her tanner, yet the balloon could be clearly seen above all their
heads, straining on its ropes, ready to be released. She would have
to remember all the details to tell him. It was a shame he wasn't
there, she knew he'd have loved it.

A shout suddenly went up: 'All in the park that wants to see
the ascent.'

Ettie was shoved unceremoniously through the gate with the
last of the stragglers at the end of the line. Once inside she
clambered on to the already packed stand to get the full, sixpence-
worth of view. What she saw and heard was a great roar of flame,
nearly, but not quite, matched by the roar from the excited,
cheering on-lookers. The fire seemed to shoot up into the gaily
coloured cloth of the balloon; somehow it didn't burn it, but just
made it flap and billow as though it were alive. The cloth dragged
at the basket, which in turn bucked and reared like a startled pony
as the belly of the balloon swelled and stretched, showing the full
exuberant glory of its elaborate patterns and jewel-like colours.

The horde of small boys who rushed forward to grab the
sandbags which the pilot was tossing on to the ground from the
wicker gondola, were chased back by two of the showmen waving
long, knobbly sticks in warning.

Then, in a split second that everyone somehow seemed to miss,
the balloon was suddenly free of its moorings and up and away it
went, beginning its ascent into the sky. Once they realised what
was happening, a great whoop went up from the spectators as
they cheered it on its way. They intended to enjoy every farthing's
worth of the sixpences they had parted with.

Along with the rest of the crowd, Ettie craned her neck and
watched as the balloon went higher and higher, floating away into

the cloudless blue of the afternoon sky. As Ettie squinted up into the heavens she remembered the leaflet boy's words. 'I'd fly away, if I had the chance,' he'd said.

And that's what she had done, she'd flown away. The child was right, she didn't belong in the East End any more. She was no longer the grubby, ragged Whitechapel girl. She'd changed, she was different. So what was she doing back here? She'd only been kidding herself when she said she was going to see her mum. Look at her: here she was in the recreation ground. She wondered if she'd ever really had any intention of going back to Tyvern Court. But where did she belong now? She bit her lip and looked around her at the shouting, roaring crowd. It was then, at that moment, that she knew she had been stupid ever to think otherwise – the only place she belonged now, the only place she wanted to be, was with Jacob.

—

'You'll never be able to guess what I've seen. Never.' Ettie slipped through the door, past Jacob and into the sitting room. 'You'd have loved it, real showmanship, just like you're always rabbiting on about.'

She unpinned her hat, pulled it off, and shook her hair free, then turned round to him, grinning with delight.

'Where have you been, Ettie? I've been desperate.' His face was passive, belying his words.

'Were you?' Her grin faded to a frown as she plonked herself down inelegantly in one of the armchairs by the hearth.

'Yes, of course I was.' His voice had taken on a harsh, angry tone. 'We were meant to be working tonight. Remember?'

Ettie stood up, folded her arms and rocked back on her heels. Regarding his stern expression, she said, 'You mean *I'm* working tonight, don't you?'

'Well, it was you who chose to speak out and give personal messages,' he said, his face now uncomfortably close to hers as he loomed over her. 'It was you who decided to stop being the Silent Beauty and take over the whole act.'

'Well, I am the one with the talent,' she said, determined to meet his gaze without flinching.

'I don't think I'm sure what you are implying, Ettie.'

They stood there, confronting each other, like boxers making ready to begin the first round.

Ettie felt uneasy. She dropped back down into the armchair, crossed her legs and jiggled her raised foot, making her petticoats – swish rhythmically.

'It's no good,' she snapped. 'I try to talk to you, and you don't listen. I saw the most wonderful thing today, I wanted to tell you all about it, share it with you, and you had to go and spoil it. All you want to go on about is work.'

'If we didn't work, Ettie, you would have no money to spend on seeing whatever frippery you're jabbering on about, now would you?'

'Don't you have so bloody much of it.' She practically spat the words out. 'Frippery?' She concentrated for a moment on picking at an imaginary loose thread on her bodice, then she spoke. 'You've changed,' she said quietly.

'So have you, thank God.'

She looked up at him standing over her. She thought that he looked so serious, so cold. 'You don't seem to like me very much any more, Jacob.' She said the words sadly.

'It's time you were getting ready,' he said, going over to his desk and opening one of his notebooks. He ran his fingers down the page of neatly entered appointments. 'Celia Tressing is due here for a private reading in a little more than half an hour.' He didn't look up as he spoke. 'Then we are expected at the Brownlows'.'

'I said, I don't think you like me any more.' Ettie stood up and went over to him. Very gently she touched the back of his neck. She wouldn't let him ignore her.

But he pulled away from her, making her feel that her touch might somehow taint him. He might as well have struck her.

'Ettie, stop being so melodramatic.' He stood up from the desk to confront her, but she turned her back on him. She couldn't let him look at her. She was humiliated.

'You know, I was wondering today about where I belonged,' she said, biting back her tears. 'I thought I knew. I thought I belonged here with you. But I'm not so sure any more.'

'Ettie, don't.' He raked his fingers through his hair. 'Now you really *are* being ridiculous. Do you want to go back to those slums I dragged you from?'

'No. No I don't,' she said, sniffing back her tears. 'But you just remember I can always earn my living if I want. I don't need the likes of you.'

'And I need you, do I?' He was shouting now, something he rarely did. 'Girls like you, Ettie, are ten a penny. I don't need anyone. Do you understand? And, even if I did, I could find a replacement whenever I wanted.'

'Good.' Her voice shook with emotion. 'And why don't you just do that, eh? You go and find someone else. Cos I'm going to see me mum. I'm going to move her out of that bug-hole and find somewhere nice for the both of us. You might think I'm worth nothing, but at least I can afford to get us a decent place to live. I can afford that all right.'

'I won't dignify that remark by asking you how you can afford it.' His face looked ugly and strained with temper. 'I think you planned to argue with me this evening, Ettie. That you want an excuse to leave now you are a success.'

'Don't talk such rubbish.' Her voice was sneering.

'It seems lately that you think everything I say is…'

'Shit?'

'What?'

'You heard, Professor Protsky.' Her lips curled in contempt as she jabbed him sharply in the chest with her finger, emphasising each word as she spoke. 'Shit. Want me to spell it out for you, do you?'

As she slammed the front door, Ettie, and all the tenants in the house, could hear Jacob yelling after her. 'Go on, go back to the gutter where you belong. You were right when you said it: you'll always be a Whitechapel girl; you'll never get it out of you. Never. Get back to where you belong.'

It was as though Ettie had never been away as she stood in the shadows of the archway leading into the court and watched the scene before her. It was dusk, but the light had an unnaturally vivid quality and the grubby evening air felt more than usually oppressive, made heavy by the threat of the storm which had been gathering since the afternoon. A pair of scrawny hens pecked idly round the broken flagstones at the dusty weeds, pausing occasionally to turn their heads to one side to regard, with their black, beady eyes, the half-naked children with whom they shared the little open space in the centre of the court. A tiny boy sat thoughtfully absorbed in his task of collecting drips in a rusty can from the communal stand-pipe. When his tin was half full he carried it carefully to the other children, who mixed it with dirt making a thick, sticky mud which they fashioned into crumbling pies. Every so often a sudden, vicious but short-lived squabble broke out over the ownership of the piles of discarded oyster shells with which they decorated their muddy creations.

Around the edges of the court, the women were gathered. They either sat on chairs brought out from their rooms, or perched themselves on the warm stone street-door steps. All fanned themselves with the hems of their pinafores, as they chatted and half-heartedly scolded their offspring. Now and then a child would be cuffed round the ear for overstepping the unspoken rules of life in the court, but more often than not the adults didn't bother, having been made too sluggish by the heady mixture of sultry summer heat and gin.

Ettie stood there and watched. Her mother had claimed she couldn't move away because she would miss the company of these women who she called her dearest friends. But she wasn't out with them now, of course, because, as she and Ettie both knew, for the last year or so she had hardly bothered to leave her bed – except to buy her supply of gin or to get a jug of soup from the mission kitchen.

Ettie closed her eyes. She felt exhausted, as though everything had become too much effort. She felt as though she could sit herself down on one of the steps and let everything just wash over her. If only she didn't care about her mother. But the trouble was, no matter how cruel and negligent Sarah had been, Ettie still did care what happened to her.

But it still took every bit of her strength to push herself away from the wall of the arch and step out into the court itself.

'Come on girl,' she said to herself. 'Move your lazy self.'

It was hard coming back, but she knew she had to make a determined effort to try and persuade her mother to move before it was too late.

'Hello everyone,' Ettie said, trying a smile on the assembled women, hoping she sounded brighter than she felt. 'How are you all doing? All right, are you?'

A woman sitting in the far corner looked up briefly in Ettie's direction, then turned back to her lap and carried on with her poorly paid piece-work of shelling peas into newspaper. 'He's in there, yer know, love.'

'What, Mum's lodger, Nora?'

'That's the bloke. And he's right pissed and all. I'd be careful if I was you, girl.'

'Ta.' Ettie didn't move. She stood there and thought about what she should do next. 'Maisie Bury about?' she asked.

'Down the Frying Pan with the others,' Nora replied, still mechanically splitting the pods and extracting the tender peas from within.

'Ta,' said Ettie again. 'See you.' And turned to walk back out of the court. As she did so she heard the women's voices behind her.

'Fancy telling her that. Toffee-nosed cow like her. Yer should have left her. Let her go in and have him give her a seeing-to. She deserves it, leaving her old mum while she goes off with her fancy. Poncing about in all fancy gear. That frock'd keep me for a year.'

'Aw, shut up,' said Nora wearily. 'I wouldn't wish that wicked bastard that Sarah's got herself hiked up with on no one.' She waved a pea-pod at her neighbour. 'And nor would you if yer told the truth.'

'Leave off, Nora. You saying it's all right for him to do that to her mum, but not to her? What's so special about that little madam, then?'

'Yer just bleed'n jealous,' said Nora, still getting on with her work.

'Jealous? What, of that little tart? You *are* having a laugh, ain't yer? At least the gels round here are honest whores. Not like that little hypocrite.'

Ettie couldn't make out Nora's reply because of the other woman's hollow, spiteful laughter that echoed round the court. But she'd had heard more than enough anyway.

–

'Ain't seen yer round here for a while, girl,' called the bride known as Mad Milly, as she waved extravagantly to Ettie from across the bar. 'Come over here and see yer old mate.'

'Thought yer'd had enough of these parts,' said Florrie, hurriedly downing her drink before she joined them at the table in the hope of a free refill. 'What yer doing back here, then?'

'She's come back to earn a few bob, ain't yer, Ett?' Milly gave Ettie a big, friendly wink and shoved her matily in the ribs.

Ettie returned her smile easily; she felt comfortable back with these women and their uncomplicated ways. 'It's good to see you, girls,' she said. 'Now, first things first. Who's having what?'

The three women were soon laughing and joking, sitting there as though it was the most natural thing in the world for Ettie to be dressed up to the nines while she chatted away with her old mates. Florrie and Milly filled her in on what had happened to everyone since Ettie had last been in Whitechapel, and had her almost collapse with laughter as they told Ettie about Ada's latest escapades with the local constabulary: the story concluded with

Ada blacking a young constable's eye and getting locked up in the local nick for her trouble. But the women also talked about their more serious concerns about life in Whitechapel – the growing unemployment, the general, worsening, lack of money, the hated Charrington's campaign to drive the girls off the streets, and even their fear of anarchists, riots and Fenian bombs. But, for all their breathless chat, not once did either of them mention Sarah Wilkins. The two women knew that the increasingly downhill path Ettie's mother was taking was not a topic for light bar-room conversation – there were some things that were too painful to discuss in public when you were sober. That could wait for a more suitable time.

As Ettie sat down and began dishing out yet another round of drinks, Milly jumped up and waved at someone coming in the door. 'Look,' she called out. 'It's Maisie. Over here, girl. Over with us.'

Ettie left the table and went over to greet her friend. She held out her arms and hugged her.

'I saw yer walking past in the court,' May said coldly, holding her cheek away from Ettie's proffered kiss, and looking pointedly at Ettie's fine clothes. 'So long since we've seen yer round here, I was surprised I recognised yer. Thought yer'd forgotten all about us lot.'

'Course I haven't forgotten you, May.' Ettie pulled up a seat for Maisie from the next table.

'Could have fooled me,' said May, settling herself down. 'And yer mum.'

'Shut up moaning, Maisie,' said Florrie, flashing a warning with her eyes.

'No, Florrie,' said Ettie. 'Yer don't have to defend me. She's right. It has been a long time – too long – since I've been back.'

'Be a bleed'n sight longer if it was me,' said Milly, belching loudly. 'Yer wouldn't catch me hanging round here if I had any choice.' She shook her head vigorously. 'Wouldn't see me for sodding dust, yer wouldn't.'

'How about some more drinks?' asked Florrie, cheerily. The conversation was all getting a little too close to the bone for her liking: she didn't want Ettie getting herself all upset and doing a daft thing like leaving the pub before she'd spent all her money on them.

'Yer on, Florrie,' said Ettie, smiling as she looked knowingly at her own suddenly empty glass which she'd only just had refilled. 'Let's have ourselves a little party, shall we?' She looked anxiously at Maisie as she spoke.

'Go on then,' said May, and sat down, only a little grudgingly, next to Milly.

Ettie squeezed through the crowded bar to the counter. While she was waiting to be served she called to her friends over her shoulder, not caring who heard her. 'I've missed you lot, you know. All of you. And everything else round here.' She paid the landlord, soaking her sleeve in the puddles of beer on the counter. 'Well, maybe not everything, eh Patrick?' she said, shaking the drips from her arm and laughing as she made her way back to the table, balancing the glasses on a tin tray.

'There you are ladies,' she said, with a mock genteel curtsey. 'Get that down you.'

'I was just trying to think what exactly it was yer could have missed round here,' said Milly, frowning and shaking her head. 'I'm buggered if I can think of anything.'

'Well, apart from you mob, of course,' Ettie said, then she thought for a moment. 'And I've missed the laughs and when we used to go down the market together.'

May stared pointedly at Ettie's dress, with her eyes narrowed and her lips pursed. 'Don't look like yer need no market to me,' she said.

'It's having a good old rake round the barrows that I miss,' she said, her face as bright from the happy memories as from all the gin she'd drunk. 'You remember, May, when we used to see what we could get for a farthing? Buying a bit of trim to go round our bonnets. Wondering for ages what colour ribbon to buy. And remember that peacock feather I got once?'

'Yeah, yer mum went flaming potty, didn't she?' said May sourly. 'Made yer throw it out in case it brought yer's all bad luck.'

'You know I never did throw it out. I kept it hidden under me bedding. It's probably still there.'

'Well, it ain't done yer no harm so far, Ett,' said Florrie, draining yet another glass. 'If what yer've got is bad luck, than let's all have a bit, eh girls?'

'Ain't done yer mum much good, has it?' said May spitefully. She fiddled unnecessarily with her hair, pushing pins back into place that hadn't even moved. 'Now my mum's a different matter. With our Billy doing so nicely for himself, she's doing very nicely out of it and all. Doing her right proud he is. She wants for nothing. No wonder he's got so many girls after him. Lining up for him they are.'

Ettie nodded silently and gulped at her drink.

'Why don't you shut up, May?' said Milly. 'Yer right getting on me tits. There's hardly any comparison, is there now, between how Myrt's treated you lot and how Sarah's treated Ettie.'

Florrie was looking worried: if a fight broke, it would spoil what promised to be a long night of free drinks, so it was with real relief that when the door opened she saw a big strapping lad with red hair come in through the wreaths of blue tobacco smoke. With him was a tall, skinny chap of about the same age.

'Look, May,' she said, nudging the stem-faced Maisie. 'Here comes your Billy boy. And he's got that dozy Cecil with him from the wood-yard.' Florrie leapt to her feet and shouted: 'Play us a song, Cec.'

'Yeah, go on, Cec,' Patrick called from behind the bar. 'Get this lot dancing and make 'em good and thirsty for plenty more of my beer.'

With much cheering and back patting, Cecil and Billy pushed their way over to the girls. Billy stood behind Milly, facing Ettie. Cecil stood next to him.

'If you girls'll do us a dance, I'll play,' said Cecil, holding up his battered concertina and grinning his great gormless grin.

'Well, if that's all yer want off us,' beamed Milly. 'We'll have to see if we can oblige.'

'Righto!' Cecil pulled the little handles of the mother-of-pearl-inlaid squeeze-box and stretched it to its wheezy full width. Then, with a flash of his hands, the music started.

Florrie was first up, sending her chair crashing to the ground as she leapt forward and began skipping around the circle of drinkers who had stood back to watch the show. Soon even Maisie had joined in with the others as they laughed and whooped, jigged and leapt to the wild playing and clapping of the drinkers. They held hands and pulled out in a ring, their skirts flying, their feet whisking up ever bigger flurries of sawdust from the floor as Cecil urged the squeeze-box into ever more complicated tunes and rhythms.

When he stopped for a brief swig of his beer, Ettie took the opportunity to grab his arm. 'Cecil, is it?' she gasped.

'That's right,' he said, grinning with pleasure at being spoken to by such a pretty girl. 'I'm a mate of Bill's, from work.

'Well, I'm puffed out, Cecil,' Ettie told the still-beaming young man. 'I haven't been dancing for months, see, and I'm that tired. Here, I've got a few bob left, get in a couple of quart pitchers of beer between us.'

'Patrick,' called Milly to the barman, her booming voice unaffected by the dancing, 'sing us one of them sad songs, while we all have a blow. Go on.'

Urged on by his customers, Patrick leaned on the counter and began to sing, in his sweet, mournful tenor, songs from his childhood of the hills and green of the home he had left behind across the sea.

A barmaid helped Cecil carry the big glass jugs of foaming beer over to the girls and Billy, who had sat himself next to Ettie. They plonked the pitchers down on the stained and ringed wooden table top that was already awash with spilled ale.

Tears filled Ettie's eyes as Patrick's songs, combined with the drink, took their effect. She turned round as she felt something brush her arm.

'Yer still wear it then, do yer?' Billy asked quietly.

Ettie touched the locket at her throat. 'Yes,' she said. 'I never take it off.'

'Speak up you two,' snapped May. 'I can't hear yer.' She leaned closer to her brother. 'Or have yer got secrets yer wanna keep, Bill?'

'Fancy some fresh air, Ett?' asked Billy, ignoring his sister.

Ettie nodded and stood up, letting Billy guide her towards the door.

As they stepped out on to the pavement from the warm fug of the bar, she shivered. 'I didn't realise how hot I was in there,' she said, avoiding looking into his eyes.

Billy took off his coat and put it round her shoulders.

'Yer did that for me once before,' she said in almost a whisper.

Billy sank his hands deep in his pockets and leaned against the pub wall. 'Yer looking good, Ett,' he said gazing aimlessly up and down the street.

'Ta.'

They stood quietly, not speaking. Then Billy suddenly called a brief, 'All right, then?' and nodded at a man passing along the other side of the road.

The silence fell between them again.

'This is very smart,' said Ettie, stroking the strong tweed of the jacket – as much for want of anything better to say as any comment on Billy's dress sense.

'I ain't doing too bad for meself,' said Billy, kicking at a stone – anything to avoid meeting her eyes.

'So May was saying.'

'I'm earning all I need and I've still got plenty to take home for Mum. We've got them extra rooms now, yer know. The whole top of the house and one downstairs.'

'I'm glad, Bill,' said Ettie. 'I bet she likes that.' She sighed sadly. 'I was hoping to do something like that for my mum one day.'

'She's in a bad way, Ett, your old mum.'

'It's that bloke she's got there. He frightens the life out of me.'

'Yer know yer can always depend on me, don't yer, Ett? If yer want him sorted out or anything. I'll get Alfie and we'll go up there and show him what's what.'

'To tell you the truth, Bill, I don't know what I want. Part of me says, yeah, just get the no-good bastard out of there. But last time I suggested it, Mum wouldn't hear of it. I was going round there tonight anyway to try and persuade her again, but Nora told me he was indoors – that's what I'm doing here. I was scared, like a stupid bloody kid.'

'I meant what I said, Ett. Yer ain't gotta be scared of no one while I'm around.'

'Ta, Billy, but that last time I talked to Mum, she as good as told me it was nothing to do with me. Him being there is what she wants – so she reckons.'

'Whatever you decide, Ett, I'll be there for yer. I mean it, I'll sort out anyone, no matter how tough he thinks he is. And that goes for that Protsky geezer and all. He don't impress me.'

Ettie couldn't bring herself to meet Billy's urgent stare.

'Ett. What is it? He's not upset yer or nothing, has he? I'll kill him if he has.'

'No,' Ettie snapped. 'He ain't. What makes you say that anyway?'

'Nothing. I just wondered why yer was really here, that's all.' The man Billy had acknowledged earlier had come back. He was standing across the street looking over at them.

'How do you mean, why I'm really here? I told you – I came to try and sort out my mum.' Ettie glared at him, her face flushed with anger and embarrassment that he could read her feelings so easily.

Billy sounded agitated. 'Look, I know this ain't exactly the right moment to go off, but I can't explain all the ins and outs, Ett, I've just gotta go. That fellah over the road has been pulling some strokes or other with Alfie, and now Alfie's gone and got himself well into debt with him. I'm gonna sort it out before it gets too out of hand. If it wasn't important...'

'You always was the sensible one, Bill,' said Ettie tenderly. 'Sensible or not, I know I wanna get all this sorted out and this bloke out of the way before our Tommy gets wind of it – yer know what a big shot he thinks Alfie is. I don't want him getting no ideas.'

'From what May said, I thought you'd be too busy fighting off all the girls to worry about your brothers,' said Ettie.

'I dunno what's got into that gel, Ett, honest. She lives in a bloody dream world, that one.'

'You don't have to explain yourself to me, Billy.'

'I know I don't, but I want to. I don't want yer thinking I was up to anything dodgy.'

'I know that's not your way, Bill.'

The door opened behind them, making them both jump.

'Yer must have a bad conscience you two,' said May, poking her head round the door. 'Now, are yer coming in for another drink or what? We'll all be going home soon.'

'Ettie'll be there in a minute, May. We're just having a little chat then I'm off to see a fellah about a bit of business.'

'Suit yerself,' said May. As she let the door slam, the music faded again to a muffled beat.

'She doesn't approve of me any more,' said Ettie, handing Billy back his jacket. 'And to think she used to be my best friend.'

Billy flicked his coat over his shoulder, his finger hooked under the collar. 'She's jealous, that's all, that she ain't a beauty like you,' he said. 'That's what it is.' He smiled and chucked her gently under the chin. 'I've gotta get off, Ett, but promise me yer won't be a stranger and that yer'll let me know if yer need any help.'

'Ta, Bill. I will. Night night.' She swallowed hard, it was more difficult saying goodbye than she would ever have believed. 'See you next time I'm over?'

'Try keeping me away.' He studied the ground for a moment then said, 'If yer get fed up – yer know, with what yer doing – I'll be waiting here for yer, Ett. I'll always be here for yer.' Then he leaned forward and kissed her softly on the lips. Before she could say a word he'd sprinted after the man who was just disappearing down Flower and Dean Street.

–

'That's me cleaned out, girls.' Ettie put down the tray of drinks and tossed her empty purse on to the table.

'We might as well go when we've finished these then,' slurred Florrie. 'That old bastard never lets yer have nothing on the slate,' she complained loudly, making sure that Patrick's stony-faced wife could hear her. 'How yer getting home, Ett?'

'Don't know, but I know I can't go back to Jacob like this.' She giggled tipsily. 'I think I'm a bit pissed. I'm not even sure I'd be able to find him if I wanted to.'

'Blimey, Ett, how can yer be pissed? Yer've hardly drunk enough to wet yer whistle.'

'I know, Mill, but I've not had no booze for so long and, anyway, Jacob's not used to seeing me like this.'

'Well, yer can't come home with me,' said May primly. 'Me mum wouldn't like it, having an unexpected guest.'

'Hark at her!' Milly shrieked with laughter. 'What, d'yer need an invite to stay round yours now?'

'I'm not *asking* you to take me home,' said Ettie, trying not to laugh as she attempted to focus on the tight-lipped Maisie.

'Good,' snapped May, glaring at the still almost hysterical Milly.

'But I would like to know what's got into you, May. You used to be my best friend. Remember?'

'She's only jealous,' said Florrie. 'It's obvious. Don't let her upset yer.'

'That's what Billy said and all,' sighed Ettie, 'that yer was jealous, May. Is it true?'

'Is it true? *Me*, jealous of *you*? Maisie almost exploded from her seat. 'Who the bloody hell do you think you are?' she fumed, leaning across the table, her finger pointing into Ettie's face.

'I'm Ettie Wilkins,' giggled Ettie.

'That's right,' yelled May. 'Ettie Wilkins, a Whitechapel girl, just like the rest of us.' And with that, Maisie stormed out of the pub, leaving Ettie unsure whether to laugh or cry.

'Looks like it's kipping under the arches for me tonight,' Ettie said eventually, leaning drunkenly against Milly's shoulder.

'Not with us around yer, Ett.' Florrie poked Milly in the side. 'Whip round,' she informed her, nodding at the empty glass she was holding up. 'Chuck out yer mouldies.'

Florrie and Milly rummaged through their pockets, dug out some coppers from somewhere, and tossed the farthings and half-pennies into the glass.

Florrie counted out threepence three farthings on to the table. She stood up, staggered over to Cecil, and grabbed him by the shoulder. 'Leave off that row for a minute,' she said snatching his squeeze-box from his hand. 'And give us a farthing.'

Cecil smiled dozily and handed over the money without a qualm. Florrie nodded her thanks. 'All right, yer can get on with yer playing again now, sweetheart,' she said, and made her way back to the table with her spoils. She flopped down on to her seat. 'Gawd alone knows how that dozy great streak of nothing manages to play that music,' she said, shaking her head in wonder. 'Still, he's got a good heart, and he must be all right if he's a mate of Bill's.' Then she handed the money over to Ettie. 'There y'are, darling. Plenty. Yer can spend the night in Thrawl Street if yer game.'

'I've kipped in the common lodging-houses plenty of times before, Flo, when Mum's booted me out. It definitely won't be the first time, but,' she looked sadly towards the door, 'it is the first time Maisie's ever treated me like that. Good job I've still got mates like you two, eh?'

Florrie gave her an angelic, gap-toothed grin. 'I think I might join yer. I don't feel like going home tonight.' She winked at Milly.

'Yer on, girl,' said Milly, repaying her with a suggestive smile.

Ettie sighed, with the maudlin self-pity brought on by all the gin and ale she'd swallowed. 'You're good friends to me, you two.

The best friends anyone could ever have.' She looked towards the door again, thinking of May. 'I hope we'll always be friends.'

'Time we was leaving,' said Florrie, heaving herself to her feet. 'It's been a right good night. Don't let's get all miserable now.'

Milly took Florrie's arm and walked out of the pub ahead of Ettie. Their procession across the bar was accompanied by loud cheers and ribald remarks.

'Yer only jealous cos I've got meself a lady friend,' responded Florrie from the doorway, and treated them all to an obscene gesture and a loud beery belch as she stepped out into the street, her head held high and her bonnet tipped rakishly over one eye.

'I'm glad yer've cheered up, Flo,' said Milly, admiringly, patting Florrie on the arm. 'You had the right hump earlier when yer posh mate didn't show up tonight.'

'Who's that then?' asked Ettie, swaying slightly as she spoke.

'No one,' grinned Florrie.

'Some posh tart, a nurse they reckon, hangs round here sometimes.'

'Oh yes?' said Ettie suggestively, getting into the mood for teasing Florrie.

'Our Flo thought she was well in there and all, didn't yer Flo?' said Milly.

Florrie shrugged non-committally.

'Patrick said he saw her earlier. She went in the pub, looked round, and then run out again. Funny cow she is, Ett. Gawd knows why, but she helps the brides out. Gets rid of their trouble for 'em. She could work in some nice clean place, but she comes down here. Half barmy, if yer ask me.'

'That's a good 'un coming from you, Mill,' said Florrie affectionately. 'Bleed'n raving, you are.'

With their arms linked as much for support as friendship, the three women managed to walk in a reasonably straight line towards the common lodging-house at Number Eighteen Thrawl Street. They swerved now and then to avoid bumping into the brides who, with hands on hips and the flash of an occasional ankle, lounged against the walls.

'There's so much life here,' said Ettie, growing increasingly sentimental. 'So much going on, even this time of night. It's like a bloody church where I'm staying.'

'And I bet yer ain't got nothing like that in Bow neither,' said Mad Milly, pointing along the road to the hurdy-gurdy player. 'Time for another little dance, I think, girls.'

But Florrie was having none of it. 'Come on, Milly, hear that clock striking quarter past? That miserable bastard of a deputy'll have let all the beds if we don't get a move on.'

'Can't wait to get in bed, eh darling?' said Milly, elbowing Florrie and almost knocking her into the gutter.

Although so close to the pub, it was just before one when they eventually got to the common lodging-house in Thrawl Street. They stumbled to a halt and bashed on the heavy cast-iron knocker.

'Come on, open the bleed'n door and let us in, yer miserable old sod,' bellowed Milly.

Florrie put her finger to her lips. 'Ssshh, not so loud, Mill, he won't let us in.'

The door creaked open and there, standing in front of them, was the deputy. He was a fat, ugly man who seemed to thrive on the misery of others. He smelt of a mixture of stale food and wood-smoke from the hours he spent sitting in the little side room which served as his office, watching the comings and goings of the unfortunate lodgers, eavesdropping on them as they sat huddled in groups in the big, dank communal kitchen, listening for any information to use against them.

For a moment he was stuck for words, and just stared in surprise at Ettie's fine and comparatively spotless clothing. Then he shook himself like a big, tangle-coated dog. 'Yeah,' he snarled as he wiped his nose on the back of his broad, hairy hand. 'What d'yer want?'

Realising the impact she'd had on him, Ettie drew herself up to her full height and, chin in the air, she used her finest tones as taught to her by Professor Jacob Protsky: 'We are seeking lodgings for the night, my good sir. Now, kindly show these ladies and myself to our rooms.' With that she brushed past the open-mouthed deputy and into the passage. But it wasn't going to be as easy as that.

'Hold on,' he growled, grabbing her shoulder in his great furry mitt. Where d'yer think you're going?'

'We do have the price of a bed,' said Florrie, in a comic imitation of Ettie's diction and brandished the coppers they'd raked up between them in the reluctant deputy's face.

Without another word, the malodorous man snatched the money from Florrie and stomped away along the dark corridor.

'Yer wouldn't think he had a living to earn, miserable old bleeder,' complained Milly, as they went down the unlit wooden stairs to the cavernous kitchen in the basement. 'Bet the owners don't know he gives everyone such a hard time. They'd have him out of here right on his arse, if they did.'

'Ignore him. Let's have a cuppa tea and get off to bed,' said Florrie, flopping down in a chair next to the big cast-iron range. 'Blimey it's hot,' she protested, rubbing her scorching leg as her skirts touched her calf.

'Then move, yer dozy cow,' said Milly, spinning the chair round on its back leg, with Florrie still sitting on it, and drawing it up to the big scrubbed pine table standing in the centre of the flagstoned basement.

Ettie watched the two women teasing each other: seeing how they cared for each other made her feel very lonely.

'Now then,' said Milly, rubbing her hands together as she surveyed the room. 'Who wants to club in a bit o' tea and sugar with us?'

Two elderly women proffered blue paper screws of tea dust, which they dug out of their layers of tattered clothing. They said nothing, just gathered eagerly round the table near the three newly arrived women.

'Lovely,' said Milly, adding her own and Florrie's stores of tea, and then tipping their combined rations in the big earthenware pot.

'I've got a drop of milk to share,' said a young woman. She was really no more than a girl, but was obviously in an advanced stage of pregnancy. 'And some sugar.'

'Ta, sweetheart,' said Milly, taking the milk can from her. 'But yer be careful. Yer don't wanna go giving all yer stuff to strangers. Yer look after yerself.'

'When are you having your baby?' asked Ettie, pulling a chair out for the girl to join them.

When Ettie spoke, the girl first looked surprised, then suspicious. 'Blimey, the way yer talk. Yer ain't from round here, are yer?'

'Aw yes she is,' laughed Florrie. 'She's a Whitechapel girl through and through, but she's got herself a fancy fellah and some education, ain't yer girl? Tell her about how yer went on the stage.'

Milly scowled at Florrie and gestured with her head towards the two elderly women.

Florrie understood immediately. 'And don't bother trying to rob her when she's asleep,' she called in their direction, jerking her thumb at Ettie. 'We did all our money in the boozer tonight. Got it?'

Ettie instinctively put her hand to her throat where her necklace nestled safely beneath her blouse. But the elderly women didn't notice; they were too busy mumbling about Florrie's unfair accusations, though they didn't push their luck arguing with her, especially not with Mad Milly around. And anyway, they were as keen as the young girl to hear Ettie's story of how she had met and moved in with her fancy man – they thought they might pick up a few ideas themselves.

'It's like something out of a book,' said the girl, putting her thick china mug down on to the table, when Ettie had finished her story. 'I wish something like that could happen to me.' She looked down and stroked her swollen belly. 'Ain't much chance unless I get rid of this,' she said ruefully.

'Wasn't there anyone who could have helped you?' asked Ettie. 'No one you could go to?'

265

'What d'yer think she's in here for?' rasped one of the old women. 'Cos her maid's got the night off?'

'I didn't think. I'm sorry.' Shame-faced, Ettie poured the girl some more tea.

'Oi, fair does, gimme some of that. Don't let her have it all.' The other old woman shoved her cup towards Ettie.

'I'm sorry,' she said again. 'It's a while since I've shared like this.'

'Well, get back where yer belong,' she hissed, leaning over Ettie and spraying her face with saliva thick with tea and pipe tobacco.

'Shut yer gob, granny,' said Florrie in a low warning voice. 'This is where she belongs, with her own. With her friends.' Then she turned to the girl. 'And you sit back down and all, darling. Don't let that old cow frighten yer.'

Knowing that Florrie and Milly weren't to be messed with, the two women filled their cups and retired to a bench near the range.

'Thank the girl for her milk,' Florrie instructed them.

The old women mumbled something which might have been their thanks.

'Take no notice of them old bats,' said Milly, patting Ettie's shoulder. 'It's being hungry: gives 'em the hump.'

'I *do* remember what it's like, Mill,' said Ettie, staring into her tea. Then she looked up at her two friends. 'I don't know what to do about Mum,' she said suddenly. 'It's so stupid. Now I've got the money to help her she won't let me. There's something wrong. She must be scared of him. Really scared. She's never cared before who stayed there, so long as she got her gin money. She knows I'll give it to her but she still won't get shot of him.'

'I've heard a lot of talk about him,' said Florrie, more seriously than she ever usually spoke. 'He's a strange one and no mistake.'

'You don't have to tell me, Flo. I lived there with him.'

'Flo's right though, Ett. I ain't being nasty or nothing, and no disrespect to Sarah, but what does he want yer mum for? Be honest, love, she ain't no beauty no more, is she?'

'Milly!'

'It's all right, Flo, Milly's only telling the truth. And it's what everyone thinks anyway,' said Ettie, embarrassed at her friend's discomfort. 'Mum's in a real state. I know that. The only thing I can think of is that he must want a place where he can do as he likes. Where he can lie low. Somewhere that no one bothers him.' Ettie shook her head, refusing Florrie's offer of a pinch of snuff. 'He knows she's too weak to sort him out.'

'Well, why don't yer get someone to chuck him out?' asked the girl.

'I've gone over all this before,' said Ettie, smiling kindly at her. 'Believe me. But she refuses to let me do anything. Up till now, anyway.' Ettie searched up her sleeve for her handkerchief. The girl's eyes widened at the pretty lace-trimmed square as Ettie dabbed at her nose. 'She actually spat in my eye the last time I tried to persuade her to let me get rid of him.'

'At least yer tried,' said Florrie, soothing her.

'Not hard enough though, Florrie. Why doesn't she want me to help her?'

'It's no good crying, Ett. Be honest with yerself,' said Milly, tenderly. 'She's too far gone for anyone to do anything. She's been knocking it back for so many years her brain must be pickled by now.'

'I know, that's why I'll have to do something,' Ettie said. 'Get my courage together and go there, whether that bastard's there with her or not. I'll have to get to the bottom of it.'

'Why don't yer ask Billy to go with yer?'

'I've thought of that, more than once, and he's offered to go with me; but when I said to Mum I'd get rid of the lodger – I told yer, she went barmy.'

'I reckon she's scared he'd come back when there's no one there to help her and finish her off to get his own back,' said the young girl. 'Sounds like she wouldn't be free of him unless someone does for him good and proper.'

'We've all thought that,' said Milly, angrily. 'But none of us was stupid enough to say it, was we, when we could see Ettie's so upset?'

The young girl blushed and dropped her chin to her chest.

'Leave her alone, Milly,' said Ettie. 'It ain't her fault. And she's right in a way. Murdering the bastard's probably the only way to get rid of him for good. And Billy'd sort it out for me as well, if I asked him. He's got the connections.' She laughed wryly. 'Good job I'm not the type to take advantage of my friends, eh?'

'So yer do still *like* Billy, then?'

'Yes, Flo, I do. But it's not so simple. And now I'm living with Jacob...'

'How about if we go with yer to yer mum's?' asked Milly, brightening at the thought of a row. 'He could hardly take on the three of us, now could he?' She studied her nails casually. 'I've got rid of one or two fellahs in me time.'

'I could help,' said the girl, sensing an opportunity to get herself back into their good books.

'Even if we was planning to do anything as barmy as Milly here's suggesting, we wouldn't let yer come. Not in your condition,' said Florrie gently. This is a right hard bastard we're talking about. Knock a man down with one blow, let alone a little scrap like yerself.'

Ettie took the girl's hand. 'Ta, it was a kind thought, but like she said, this one's no ordinary bloke.'

Living up to her nickname, Mad Milly suddenly lifted her skirts and scrambled across the table top. 'Look who's here,' she shrieked, and grabbed hold of the woman who had groped her way down the dark stairs and into the basement. Milly waltzed her wildly round the room. 'It's Polly Nichols, as I live and breathe,' she said when they finally came to a stop. 'I ain't seen yer for months, girl. How are yer?'

'Pissed as a pudden!' leered Polly giddily, swivelling her eyes as she tried to fix her stare on Milly.

'Yer all know Mary Ann – Polly – Nichols, don't yer?' said Milly, showing off her friend like she was a prize exhibit at a cattle show.

'All too well,' said a voice from the stairway. It was the deputy.

'I don't know how yer got past me this time, Nichols, but I'll tell yer again, yer ain't staying till I've seen the colour of yer money. Got it?'

Polly swayed towards the man and threw her arms round his neck.

He shied away from her boozy breath. 'Gawd help us, woman, yer'll suffocate me.'

'Can't I give yer the money tomorrow, darling?' she rasped in what she thought was a seductive lisp. 'When I've done a bit of business. I'm dead on me feet.'

'No money, no bed. Now out.'

'Let me...' Ettie began to offer her the price of a bed for the night, then remembered that she wasn't even paying for her own lodging.

'Go on. Yer know she'll be good for it in the morning, yer bloody tight sod,' shouted Milly. 'Let her stay.'

'Aw no. I know her of old,' he said firmly. 'And she's got more chance of being asked to kip in the bleed'n palace with the Prince of Wales himself than of staying here for the night. And any more out of *you*, and you can piss off and all,' he threatened.

The two elderly women sat on the bench tutting disapprovingly, while thoroughly enjoying the free entertainment.

The deputy stuck his hands on his hips. 'So, what's it to be? Fourpence or out?'

'We can't help yer, Polly, sorry,' said Florrie shrugging, 'We're boracic, the three of us.'

'It's all right,' hiccuped Polly, 'I'll soon earn the money for me bed.' She sashayed round the room, flicking her skirts at the pucefaced deputy. 'Look how lovely I looks tonight. She tilted her black straw bonnet to a more saucy angle on the side of her rat's nest of tangled brown hair.

'Lovely? She must be drunker than she looks,' sputtered one of the elderly women. 'She looks a right bleed'n wreck.'

Polly scoffed at the elderly women while scratching savagely at her bodice, doing her best to get at the fleas which fed beneath her thick layers of clothing.

'I already told you once to shut up and mind yer own business,' warned Florrie, pointing at the old woman who'd foolishly made the comment about Polly. Then she turned to the deputy. 'I suppose it's all right if we give her a cuppa tea before she goes?'

But Polly didn't wait for the deputy's answer. 'No thanks all the same, girl, I'll have to go and have me bit o' jolly before I passes out.' She screwed up the side of her face in a drunken attempt at a wink and went staggering towards the stairs which led up to the street. 'Jolly Polly, eh girls?' she called over her shoulder as she grabbed hold of the rickety banister rail.

'Leave some of yer things with me, I'll look after 'em for yer,' one of the old women from the bench croaked at her.

'That's bleed'n right,' Polly shouted from the head of the stairs. 'And have yer nick me drawers?' She stumbled back down the stairway and into the kitchen so that they could all get a good view, then she lifted up the skirts of her brown linsey frock, exposing her grey woollen petticoat and flannel drawers. 'Only got these the other day. Nearly new they was.' Then she did a groggy little jig, striking the metal tips of her boots on the bare flagstone floor, then tottered up and away again, into the darkness of the streets on the look-out for the price of a bed for the night.

–

The women sat talking for a while longer, going over yet again what could be done about Sarah Wilkins' lodger. But still they came to no solutions. No matter what they suggested, Ettie wasn't convinced that anyone could do much, with her mum or with her lodger.

'It'll be a bit of a comfort to know that you two were at least keeping an eye on her for me,' said Ettie wearily. 'I'll treat you both.'

'We'll do what we can,' said Florrie doubtfully.

'Maybe I should chuck it all in and just come back home,' said Ettie despondently.

'I thought I was the one who was meant to be mad,' chuckled Milly. 'Don't act so flaming daft, Ettie Wilkins. What good would that do – both of yers being in the shit?'

They sat in gloomy silence for a few long minutes, then Florrie said, 'Well, the tea's all gone,' and upended the pot to prove her point. 'Who's for bed then, girls?'

They made their way to the dormitory with Florrie and Milly walking ahead, arm-in-arm and talking in low, affectionate whispers. Behind them, they heard the rough, familiar voice of one of the other local brides who had just come in after her night's work. She was shouting, in a drunken, loud-mouthed holler, at the deputy who had stayed in the kitchen to make sure the oil-lamp had been put out and the fire damped down for the night.

'I saw that Polly Nichols on me way round here,' they heard her say. 'Pissed as a fart, she was. I tried to get her to come back here with me, but she wouldn't. Said you'd told her to bugger off. But she said to make sure I told yer that she was gonna do well for herself tonight and earn a right pretty penny.'

'She was well gone when she left here over an hour ago,' they heard the deputy reply. 'Gawd knows what state the trollop's in now. Who'd be interested in going with her when she's like that?' The woman spoke again. 'I dunno. And that's why I said to her, "Yer barmy," I said, "working in that state." I mean, anything can happen to yer, can't it?'

–

Celia flinched as her father told the butler to fetch a second bottle of claret from the cellar – alcohol made his moods even more unpredictable than usual. When supper was over and he insisted she accompany him to the drawing room, where he drank several glasses of brandy, her nerves were on a razor's edge.

She had been hoping that he would go out and leave her alone, but he had been insistent that she go with him. But at least evenings spent in the drawing room didn't usually finish in the same grotesque way as those in the operating room. More often than not, he wanted his daughter as nothing more than a target at which to fling all his opinions, invective and general bile about what he considered to be the ills of modern times. This night proved to be no exception.

He waved the newspaper angrily at her before tossing it indignantly to the floor.

'Unemployed?' he fumed. 'Unemployed? Bloody newspapermen. Why don't they say what they mean? Why not tell the truth for once? Why make up a new word when it's just another damned fancy term for idleness? Damned do-gooders interfering with the natural order of things. Going where they have no business, stirring people up.'

He reached down and picked up a random loose sheet from the paper and waved it menacingly at Celia. 'Homelessness? Poverty?' He screwed the paper into a rough ball and flung it across the room. 'Drunken beasts, more like. Of course they're poor.' His voice was rising to an alarming pitch. 'Who'd give work to those miserable creatures? The constabulary would have done us all a favour if they'd have finished off the lot of them when they had the chance last year in Trafalgar Square. When I walk to the bloody club they're there in front of me. Sleeping in the park, if you don't mind. The *royal* park. How's a man expected to walk the streets to his club in peace?'

He stood up, swayed unsteadily, and stumbled over to the bell set in the wall to ring for Smithson.

'Fetch my malacca cane,' he instructed the ferret-faced man when he arrived in the drawing room. 'The pearl-topped one.' He paused and frowned, staring fixedly into the middle distance. 'I'm off to the club. The vermin won't stop me going out for the evening.'

'Shall I summon a hansom for you, sir?' asked Smithson, inclining his head obsequiously.

'No!' he turned on the butler, his face vicious. 'I intend to walk there. To stroll at my leisure. I won't be driven off the streets of my own city by scum.'

Smithson nodded and smiled ingratiatingly as he left the room.

Tressing kicked out at the screwed up ball of newspaper, but missed it and fell forward at a stumbling run.

Celia didn't even think of laughing.

The butler returned with the cane and handed it to his master.

Bartholomew held it at arm's length and grasped the ornate, pearl-topped handle. Then he withdrew the long slender blade from its secret sheath in the cane and ran his thumb along its length to test its edge.

'Needs sharpening, man.' His words blasted out at the butler. 'Can you do nothing without orders?'

When her father finally left the house, Celia went to her room on the pretext of retiring for the night. She sat patiently on her bed, filling her journal with the day's trivia, until she was sure that Smithson had started on his own pastime for the evening: his goal being to empty down his throat the contents of the brandy decanter which the eagle-eyed butler – and Celia – had noted her father had forgotten to replace in the Tantalus.

With her blond hair hidden by her hood and her bag of instruments and medicinal compounds secreted under her cloak, Celia slipped out of the front door and into the night, an anonymous figure in black. She waited until she was two squares away from her house before she stopped a hansom.

'Where to, miss?' asked the cabman, touching his finger to the brim of his hat.

'Whitechapel,' she answered simply.

Chapter 24

George Cross yawned as he dragged himself along on his way to work. Half-past three in the morning, what a bloody life.

'Shit!' he swore loudly to himself as he tripped on something. He couldn't make out what it was he'd fallen over, Buck's Row was blanketed in the shadows cast from the tall warehouse walls, the only light coming from the single gas-lamp at the other end of the street.

'Bad enough I've gotta go to poxy work this time of the morning.' He kicked out angrily at the bundle of whatever it was that had tripped him.

'Christ.' His earth-soiled hand flew to his mouth and he leapt back. It was a person lying there in front of him and he'd kicked the poor sod.

It was only the arrival in Buck's Row of another market porter on his way to work that brought Cross back to his senses and made him move into action.

'Here, mate,' Cross called urgently. 'Come and help us. This woman's pissed and I've fallen over her. She might be hurt or something.'

The other man ran over to Cross and knelt down. He looked at the woman then touched her cautiously. 'She's right cold, but I'm sure her heart's still beating,' he said. Then, before he stood up, he adjusted her clothes, pulling her skirts and underthings down over her legs to restore a modicum of decency to the prostrate figure. 'I wouldn't want no wife or sister of mine showing herself like that,' he explained to Cross. 'Looks like someone might have, you know, had a go at her.'

'Yer mean she ain't just drunk?' Cross began to panic. He'd been the only one there a few minutes ago. They might think he had something to do with it. The times he'd been pulled in by the law – for everything from illegal trading to being drunk and disorderly – flashed through his mind like newspaper headlines.

'I dunno, moosh,' said the other man. 'But we'd better find a copper.'

It was too late to pull out now. Cross and the other man ran to the end of the street, calling for the officer on the beat, one of them hoping more than the other to see the familiar gleam of the police constable's bull's-eye lamp coming out of the early morning gloom.

If it hadn't been so dark, they'd have seen the remains of the life blood of poor Polly Nichols flowing out from her.

–

Celia had never dared to stay out so late before, she had always returned from her efforts in the slums soon after midnight. The dawn was already lightening the sky, but she kept close to the railings, feeling safer in the protection of the dying shadows. The time had dissolved, she hadn't realised how quickly it could disappear. She was tired and she was dirty. All she wanted was to have a bath and go to bed and sleep. The idea of sinking in the deep feather mattress, with its clean linen sheets and pillows, was blissful. She had it all planned: when her father returned from his club she would pretend she felt ill and sleep in until late. She would not only get the rest she craved, but she would not have to spend time with him at the table or in that dreadful room.

As she turned into the square she whispered a soft prayer that, with her father at his club, the servants would still be in bed and she would have no awkward questions to answer, no Smithson to face. But her prayer went unanswered. She couldn't believe it. Not even the shadows could protect her now. From the street below she could see the lamps burning in the operating room at the top of the house. She hadn't expected him to be home, let alone working in that place. He'd been so drunk the night before, she was sure he would stay the night at the club. What had made him come home? What could he be doing this time of the morning? She simply had not planned for this, her father being there in that room. She whispered another prayer – that he hadn't noticed her absence.

She stood on the corner thinking what to do. If he found out that she had been out all night she would be punished. The thought sickened her, made her stomach churn with pain and fear. She couldn't stay out in the square much longer; the longer she did so, the more chance there was of him discovering that her bed had not been slept in. She made a mental note to invent a story to explain that away to the maid. And she suddenly realised that she felt cold. The sun wasn't fully up yet, and the dawn light offered little warmth. She wished she'd worn her cloak. But she had – she remembered clearly pulling the hood up over her hair. So where was it? What had happened to it? Her mind raced: she'd taken it off, that was it, she'd taken off the cloak because of the blood. The girl had bled so much. She didn't want to wear a bloodstained cloak through the streets. And where was her bag? She certainly didn't want to risk her father, or anyone else for that matter, discovering what she had been doing in Whitechapel – she wasn't even sure herself whether what she was doing was right…

There was nothing else she could do. She walked over to the house and went down the area steps. She stood looking into the big kitchen. It was bright and warm. So different from the bright coldness of the lights coming from the room at the top of the house. She waited, watching the scullery maid poking at the range, coaxing it back into flame, ready for her morning's work. She seemed to take so long.

Celia ducked back as she saw the girl look up from her task. Her hands and apron were covered in black soot, her nose and cheeks streaked with smuts. The maid hauled herself up. 'Coming, Mr Smithson,' she whined begrudgingly.

The moment the girl had disappeared into the butler's parlour, Celia took her chance. She slipped into the back door and dashed through the kitchen up the back stairs to the main hall.

'What're you doing up so early?'

Celia froze.

'Lost your tongue, girl?'

'No, Father.'

'I asked you a question.'

'I couldn't sleep, Father. I felt unwell.'

'You look disgraceful. Get back to your room and straighten yourself. Your hair and clothes are in total disorder.'

Celia bowed her head, trying to control the urge to flee.

'Now get upstairs, before the servants see you.'

'Yes, Father.' Celia moved towards the staircase as quickly as she dared, trying as always to find the balance between following his orders and not displeasing him by carrying them out wrongly.

'And if you really feel ill, I'll be up later.'

She turned, halfway up the stairs, halfway to her escape. 'I'd rather rest, if you are agreeable, Father.'

He snorted and strode towards the dining room.

She hoped it was a snort of agreement. She had to find a way to return to see Ettie, Professor Protsky's medium. She had to sort out her feelings about what she was doing: she needed help, she needed guidance, and she needed a friend.

Chapter 25

Ettie woke to chronic itching on her legs and arms. She gritted her teeth, scratching until she nearly drew blood. She pulled herself up to a sitting position on the hard, rough bed. Her mouth felt like it had been filled with cinders, and her eyeballs stung as though they were filled with hot coals. She experimented with her tongue, seeing if it still worked, licking feebly at her parched lips.

She couldn't be sure because of the other noises that filled her head, but she thought that the low groan she heard must have come from her.

The sound of laughter coming from somewhere nearby made her head pound. As she opened her eyes to see where the torturing row was coming from the summer morning brightness filtering through the skylights almost blinded her.

'State of you!' screamed Florrie, slapping her thighs with a noisy good humour which appalled Ettie.

'Morning, Florrie,' Ettie managed to croak, and let her head sink forward on to her chest.

'I know what you need, girl: a drop of penn'orth and ha'pence,' said Florrie, grabbing Ettie ungraciously by the arm and dragging her to her feet.

'Don't,' moaned Ettie pathetically.

'Listen, I've been sitting here watching yer, twitching and scratching away at yerself. Yer've gone soft, you have, girl. Fancy letting a few bugs get yer down.'

'Gone soft? I feel like I've melted away completely.' Ettie held her hand over her eyes. 'My head, Flo, it feels bloody horrible.'

'Yeah, yeah, we all know. Now come on and pull yerself together. And we ain't got all day, neither. Milly's been gone over an hour already.'

Ettie didn't ask where Milly had gone, but Florrie told her anyway. 'Went down the market, she did. To see if any of the porters fancied spending a few bob out of their last night's earnings. Never one to miss a chance, that Milly.' Florrie laughed happily to herself and steered Ettie along the corridor that led to the front door.

Ettie held down the rising waves of nausea as they stepped out into Thrawl Street. The stench of bread frying in dripping, rising up from the big basement kitchen, was making her almost hysterical with the panic-stricken feeling that she had to get away immediately from the lodging-house and everything in it.

Florrie hooked her arm through Ettie's and, seeing the colour of Ettie's face, she said, 'We'll have to get something down yer to sort yer guts out.' And then she guided her firmly in the direction of the Frying Pan.

The pub was already busy with costers and porters who had finished their work for the day, and just two other women who sat dejectedly drinkless in the comer.

'I don't think this is such a good idea, Flo,' said Ettie gagging at the smell of stale beer and tobacco that hit them as they entered the bar.

'Come on, Ett, be brave,' chuckled Florrie. 'Do yer the world of good.'

Florrie sat Ettie at an empty table and had a quick look round to make sure that Patrick's wife wasn't in the pub. When Florrie was satisfied that the formidable Mrs O'Brien was nowhere to be seen, she leaned across the bar to have a quiet word with the landlord and, in no time at all, had persuaded Patrick to let her have a couple of measures of rum and milk on the slate.

She put one of the glasses down in front of Ettie. 'Go on, yer can still sink a penn'orth and ha'pence, can't yer? Yer ain't changed that much, have yer?'

'Maisie thinks I have,' said Ettie, eyeing the potent mixture self-pityingly.

'Take no notice of her. She's got the hump with yer. Jealous, ain't she? That's all what's the matter with her. Been blabbing her mouth off about how she reckons yer couldn't wait to leave all this behind yer.'

'She's right about that,' said Ettie, cradling her pounding head in her hands. 'I've never pretended otherwise. And wouldn't she if she had the chance?'

'Bloody right,' said Florrie loudly.

'Keep it down, eh Flo?' Ettie pleaded.

'It's all about her precious Billy and all, ain't it? Yer know, she's going round telling everyone how yer've let him down.'

'All right, Flo. Don't rub it in.'

'She's disappointed, see. She always reckoned you two was gonna wind up together. Settling down would've made sure he never got into none of Alfie's ways.' Florrie laughed. 'He's a boy, that Alfie.' She sipped at her drink and smacked her lips appreciatively. 'Yer know how Billy feels about yer, Ett.'

'Are we going to go over all this again?' Ettie took a drop of the rum-and-milk brew and shuddered. 'I like Billy as well, Flo. I always have. More than liked him, to tell you the truth. And who knows what would have happened if things had turned out different. But that's not how it is. I'm the one who's different now. A different person. Not better, or worse—' she looked up at Flo — 'I hope. Just different.'

'Jesus, Mary, Joseph.' Patrick, using the excuse of sprinkling fresh sawdust round their table, had been hoping to listen in to all the gossip about how Ettie was getting on in her new life – Mrs O'Brien would be furious when she got back from the market if her husband didn't have the latest bulletin with all the details. 'Sure, isn't this getting a bit serious for this time of day? How about telling a few stories about yer fine new life, Ettie Wilkins?'

'Give us another couple of glasses, sweetheart, and it might loosen her tongue,' Florrie said, winking suggestively and tweaking his shiny red cheek. 'Go on, me love, and I'll see yer all right later on if yer do. Yer big Irish beauty.'

'Not if the old woman catches yer, yer won't,' he laughed. 'But go on with yers.' He walked over to the bar, followed closely by Florrie, and poured two measures of rum and milk. 'The guvnor's not about, and what she don't see don't hurt her, eh?'

'Good luck to yer, darling,' beamed Florrie, and carried the drinks back to the table where they downed the sickly liquid in silence.

'Dunno about you, Ett, but I'm gonna have to love yer and leave yer. I wanna get me head down for a bit before I start work later on or I'll be fit for nothing.'

'Can't you stay a bit longer?' Ettie asked, her voice unsteady.

'If I didn't know better, Ettie Wilkins, I'd say yer didn't wanna go back to that fancy man of yours.'

'Shut up, Flo, I don't want to start on all that again.' Ettie traced her finger round the sticky mark left by the glass on the table. 'It's not knowing what to do about Mum that's really getting me down.'

Florrie was very fond of Ettie, she'd known her since she was a baby, but she knew that some things just couldn't be changed; some things were meant to be. And the thought of going all through Ettie's guilt and concerns about her drunken mother again was a bit too much for her, and like Patrick said, especially at that time of the morning. So it was with much relief when Florrie saw one of the other local brides, a fine, buxom woman known as Big Bella, come thundering into the pub.

'Blimey, Bella, first time I ever saw yer move so fast. Whatever's the matter?'

'Listen to this, Flo,' she boomed. 'Yer'll never guess what's happened.'

'How can I if yer don't calm down?'

Bella's frantic hollering had attracted the rest of the breakfast-time customers, many of whom were now crowding round the table to hear exactly what it was that could possibly have shocked Big Bella.

'Now,' said Florrie, all authority and calm, Tell us nice and slow, what the bleed'n hell yer talking about?'

'The gel what got done in, all the paper-sellers are calling out about it.'

Disorder degenerated into pandemonium. Voices rose higher as everyone wanted an answer to their questions. Florrie wasn't having such behaviour. She took control. She stood up and brought the flat of her hand down on the table with a dull thwack. Then she pointed at the lad who ran errands for the market workers. 'For gawd's sake run out and fetch us a paper.'

The boy held out his hand and the landlord obliged. 'And don't be forgetting me change,' Patrick shouted after the departing boy.

He was back in a moment, as full of excitement as Bella had been. 'She's right,' he gabbled, holding up the paper. 'They're all talking about it. The newspaper bloke was hollering and hooting. Should have heard him. It's the most horrible murder what ever'r, happened, so they're saying.'

'Give it here before I murder you and all, yer little bugger.' Florrie snatched the paper from the boy's hand and began spreading it out on the ale-stained table. 'Now, let's see whatever it was that the bloke said to yer,' she said, frowning at the boy. It must have been something good: yer ain't even tried to run off with the change.'

'*That's* what he said to him,' Ettie gasped, stabbing her finger at the story in the paper.

Everyone was now crowding round. Ettie ran her finger down the newsprint as she rapidly paraphrased the article for the gawping crowd. 'A woman's been found dead. Here. In Whitechapel. They say there's some kind of maniac on the loose.'

'Go on,' someone urged her. 'Tell us then.'

'Ett?' Florrie shoved her, wanting to hear more. 'Go on. Tell us. What does it say?'

Ettie found her voice. 'It's Polly,' she whispered. 'It was Polly Nichols.' She pushed the newspaper away from her. Half a dozen hands grabbed it, clamouring for the details, hungry for the thrilling particulars of the police report.

Ettie pushed her way past the ghouls, out of the pub, and into the street. She took long gasps of air, but it was too late: she vomited the rum and milk, and most of the night-before's intake with it, into the gutter. She felt like her insides were leaving her.

'Go on, girl,' said Florrie, rubbing her firmly between the shoulder-blades. 'Better out than in.'

'Oh, Flo, it was Polly.' Tears streamed down Ettie's ashen face. 'We could have stopped her.'

'Could we?' said Florrie quietly. 'How d'yer make that out then, Ett? We was skint, remember?'

–

Florrie stopped on the corner where the roadway petered out and was replaced by the warren of lanes and alleys that led to the court where she lodged.

'This is me then, Ett,' she said smiling bravely, trying, not very successfully, to hide her tears.

'Give my love to Ada,' said Ettie solemnly.

Then she and Flo promised each other that they were both all right and that they would see one another again soon.

Ettie waved to her friend until she disappeared into the place that had once been her home. She could hardly drag herself over to the horse-trough to wash the tears and vomit from her face. She could hardly be bothered with anything. She felt hollow inside, empty of everything that had ever filled her life with meaning. She knew there was nothing left for her here in Whitechapel. Polly's death had been the final blow which somehow confirmed the horror of it all. It became clear to her that she had no choice: she had had a taste of a better life, of what she could have instead of filth and violence and abuse. Why should she choose the gutter when she could have clean sheets? But it still didn't make her feel any better about leaving Sarah. She knew she couldn't force her mother to change, she would always be the same. And, deep down, there was a part of her that wished she could say the same about herself – that she still belonged here with her friends, with her old life, and with Billy Bury.

Ettie caught up handfuls of water from the tap that ran continually into the trough, and threw it over her face. It was icy cold. She shook her head like a wet dog dragged from the river, and sat down on the stone steps at the side of the fountain, drying herself on the hem of her now creased and soiled skirts. The sun felt hot on her face.

A voice which must have been hers, for there was no one else around, said, 'For God's sake girl, pull yourself together, you're moping around and you've got things that people round here would murder for.'

She buried her face in her hands. There were so many things that people were prepared to murder for in an area as poor as Whitechapel.

–

'Aren't you pleased to see me?' she asked feebly.

Jacob threw his arms around her. 'Pleased? I've been through hell while you were away.' He gently steered Ettie inside and closed the door behind her. He stared intently at her face, looking for clues about the night they had spent apart. 'Where were you?' He didn't let her answer. 'You do know what happened last night, don't you?'

'Know what happened?' The words came bursting out of her. 'I know the poor bloody bride what copped it.' Ettie was stunned when he made no attempt to correct her language: she had been deliberately provocative, wanting a row, wanting to be angry – with Jacob, with everyone.

'You knew her, Ettie? The woman who was murdered?'

Now she spoke more quietly, more subduedly. 'Course I knew her. I was talking to her last night. Probably one of the last people who saw her alive. It's a small world in there, Jacob.' She backed away from him. 'No, let me go. Don't touch me. I'm running alive with bugs.'

'That doesn't matter.' He folded his arms round her. 'Oh Ettie, you're safe. Thank God.'

The tears began to trickle down her cheeks again. She snuffled as she spoke into his chest. 'She had nothing, Jacob. Not even the price of a night's lodging. They found a bit of poxy soap in her pocket. And a comb, a tattered old handkerchief, and a bit of broken mirror. That's all she had: that and the rags she stood up in.'

He held her closer, so tightly she could hardly breathe. 'Ettie, it could have been you.'

She leaned back to look into his eyes. 'Would you have cared?'

Jacob answered her by covering her mouth with his. He kissed her hard and then said gravely, 'Don't ever go away like that again, Ettie. Don't ever leave me.'

Ettie laughed and pushed him away so she could scratch at whatever was biting at her middle. 'Don't be daft,' she said. 'Where would I go? And who would I go off with?'

'Don't mock me, Ettie.' He ran his hands through his thick, curly black hair. 'I thought you'd gone off with Maisie's brother.'

'Billy? I never even saw him. Well, not for long.'

Jacob took hold of her arms. He tightened his grip until they hurt. 'I love you, Ettie.'

Ettie shook her head. 'Don't mess around, Jacob,' she murmured.

'I'm not,' he said. 'I love you. Haven't you realised that yet?'

She searched his face for the cruel joke that she anticipated, the rejection she had learned to expect from her mother's lodgers after they had used her, the stinging slap across the cheek, the gobbet of phlegm hitting her face. But she could see no rejection there. Perhaps he really meant it.

'I know that I love you, Jacob,' she said eventually. The words surprised her.

He leaned forward to kiss her again but she slipped away. 'I think I'll need a bath first,' she said, trying to smile while she scratched frantically at herself. 'I really am cooty. And you'll catch them off me if you're not careful.'

'Perhaps we both need to cleanse ourselves,' he said, and lifted her in his arms and carried her to the bathroom.

Chapter 26

When Celia woke, her mind was full of nightmares. No matter how hard she shook her head or blinked her eyelids, visions of death, blood and dissection crowded her thoughts. She felt so tired, so completely exhausted, even more now than before she'd crept into bed over eight hours ago. She rubbed her hands over her face and tried keeping her drooping eyes open. The maid must have tidied the room: there was no sign of the clothes she had worn last night. She swung her legs from under the covers and sat on the edge of the bed. She rubbed her hands over her face, tossed her thick fair hair over her shoulder and sighed deeply. Her body ached as though she had been labouring in a scullery. She was worn out, drained both physically and emotionally. And, most alarming of all, she felt as though every barrier that had ever existed to prevent her from doing wrong had simply disappeared – dissolved entirely away. There was nothing left to concern her any more. She had seen and experienced horrors throughout her short life, but now she knew about the real dreads and fears that could exist in a woman's life.

Celia rang for the maid and, when she had bathed and dressed, she went downstairs to speak to her father.

She found him taking tea in the drawing room. The windows were pushed up, open to the top of their sashes, and the curtains fluttered in the warm afternoon breeze. The whole room smelt fresh and the mirrors and ornaments sparkled in the summer sunshine.

'Good afternoon, Father,' she said levelly.

Bartholomew looked up. 'You look rather more presentable. Are you feeling better now?' He didn't pause to allow her to reply.

'I don't expect to see you looking so dishevelled again.' He put a small triangular sandwich in his mouth and fastidiously wiped the crumbs from his lips with a still-folded napkin.

Celia sat in the armchair opposite him, the cake stand, teapot and assorted paraphernalia of an English high tea stood between them, one boundary which still existed.

She was not surprised when an unfamiliar young woman stepped forward to pour her tea. Since childhood, Celia had been accustomed to unexplained changes in the younger members of the female staff.

Celia shook her head when the maid offered her a plate and napkin. 'I would very much like to speak to you alone, Father,' Celia said.

Bartholomew raised his eyebrows and drew in a noisy breath to express his boredom. 'If you must.' He shooed the maid from the room with a limp flick of his hand and settled back in his armchair to suck crumbs loudly from between his teeth whilst preparing himself to listen to the usual tedious prattlings of his daughter.

But Celia did not intend to waste her breath on polite tea-time trivia. She lifted her chin and went immediately to her point. 'Father,' she said, with extraordinary calm. 'I intend to work.'

This time, Bartholomew Tressing's eyebrows were not raised in cynical boredom but in barely suppressed anger. 'You have the temerity to tell me that you intend to take employment?'

'No,' she said, still very calmly. 'Not paid work, no.' She leaned forward, perching on the edge of her chair. 'I might as well tell you everything, I'm sure you'll find out anyway. I have been working with the women of the slums in the East End. Just as I always intended. I am using the skills which you yourself taught me. I have been putting them to good use – offering my services as a...' She lowered her head, considering her words. '... as a nurse. It's what I want to do, you cannot stop me. I have decided. It is to be my life.'

'Your life?' he exploded. 'Your life is here, with me.'

Celia shrank back in her seat, but she was determined to try and hide her fear.

Bartholomew stood up. He strode back and forth across the room. Then, quite unexpectedly he stopped and turned on his heel and loomed over her. He was far too close for her comfort, menacing in both proximity and manner. She could smell the food he had just eaten on his breath, see the little morsels of bread on his lips. She knew that, had he been aware of it, he would have hated it: he was always so scrupulous about his appearance.

'Are you completely mad?' His face, so near to hers, hovering over her, was ugly, screwed up with rage. 'Do you have even the slightest inkling of what really goes on there? You say you are using the skills I taught you.' His eyes bulged, his words came slowly, deliberately. 'But you know nothing. Slicing up the stinking remains of a dead whore in the operating room is no preparation for the real thing.'

Celia grasped the arms of the chair, desperately trying to keep her poise, trying not to allow her fear to show. 'If you were to see the true horrors of childbirth – ill-nourished slum women dying in labour, filthy girls no more than children themselves in their third and fourth pregnancy, then you'd understand that someone has to do something about it.'

'For God's sake, Celia, whatever are you thinking of? You've seen the sorts of messes we deal with in dissection, when they've forced their pathetic potions and rusty knitting needles into one another.' He stood upright and turned his back on her. 'I'll hear no more of it. We're going away for a while, anyway.'

'Going away? Why?'

'That need not concern you,' he said. His voice, even for him, sounded unnaturally agitated. 'All you need know is that we are going away.'

'But I won't go. I don't want to go with you.' Celia sat very still in the armchair. 'I meant what I said, I intend to continue my work in the slums.'

'Continue your work?'

She shrank back as he bent over her again – why hadn't she fled when she had the chance?

'Listen to yourself – "my work".'

His mocking tone was as harsh as any slap across her face could have been.

'And now listen to me and take note of my words: females are not meant to work. This modern obsession with women working. Do you know what happens to the brain of a woman who works? Of course you don't, you know nothing, but you think you know so much.'

Celia flinched as he spat the words at her. He was speaking with that same repulsive, almost deranged glee which took him over when he commented during the dissections.

'The female brain becomes abnormally developed and that, of course, can only happen at the expense of the uterus. That organ becomes starved and withered. It is then that the woman begins to act unnaturally. You do understand what I mean by "unnaturally", don't you, Celia?' His face became inflamed. 'Women developing deviant appetites.' He paused, judging her reaction. 'Women desiring their own sex.'

As Bartholomew's breathing grew more rapid, Celia became more frightened: she recognised all too well the signs she had learnt to fear.

'This perverse fad for ambitious women,' he continued, his voice still almost composed, but his manner growing ever more threatening. 'It can only result in freakishness, sterility, and total degeneration. That is guaranteed for those who choose such a path.'

Celia knew that her only chance was to break the spell he had cast over her. She summoned all her courage and looked at him as steadily and coolly as she could manage, trying to see him as no more than a man with hairs growing from his nostrils and saliva gathering in the corners of his mouth. But in her fear she became almost hypnotised by the drooling lines of spittle; she could hardly take her eyes from it. It took all her reserves of strength to keep her voice even as she spoke, her eyes still fixed on his wet mouth.

'How, Father,' she murmured, 'please tell me, if female labour is such an aberration, do you explain the ability of the female slum-dwellers to work all hours of the night and day? To slave away non-stop, in fact.'

It hardly seemed possible, but the menace in his voice increased. 'You would equate yourself with those strumpets and harridans?' Though full of fury, his words came slowly, ponderously, as he returned to his armchair and began to pick idly at a scone from the cake stand. 'It is as well that we will be going away for a week or so. We will go to the country, to the Brownlows' place in Gloucestershire,' he said, almost brightly. His mood, as always, was totally unpredictable, even for his daughter. 'The rest will give you the opportunity to restore your brain to order, and your manner to obedience.'

'I am not going with you, Father.' The words had left her lips. She waited for him to rise and his hand to strike her and the fist to knock her from the chair to the ground but she had misjudged him: he had chosen another punishment.

'Celia, I need you with me.' His put the barely touched scone back on to his plate. His expression had changed. No longer was it inflamed with fierce anger, now it was contorted into a hellish, ugly parody of pathetic longing. 'I am the only one who can protect you from the real world. You know that. And you know that I have to keep you here with me. I am the one who knows how to save you from other men. I am the one to teach you the true ways of love. Oh, Celia.' His breathing became yet more laboured as his eyes moved slowly over her body, possessing her first with his gaze and then, moving ever closer, with his hands.

'Get away from me. Don't touch me.'

She jerked away from him as he grabbed at the lace at her throat. The delicate material ripped away in his hand and he stumbled backwards against the fireplace. Celia didn't wait to see if he was injured. She fled into the hall, knocking Smithson to one side, and dashed up the stairs to her bedroom.

Bartholomew was a fit, strong man, and he had soon regained his footing and was chasing up the stairs after her. He was close behind, but he was too late: she had locked herself in. She crouched beside her bed, the child again who knew no protection or safety even in her own home. Her father, the man who should have cherished her, was hammering on the door with his fists, not heeding or caring who else in the household was listening to his ranting pleas for his daughter's body.

'I want you, Celia. You belong to me. You will do as I demand. You will go away with me.'

The solid oak door shook as he continued to pummel it with his now bloody knuckles.

'Leave me alone,' she sobbed. 'Leave me alone.'

But Bartholomew Tressing wasn't a man who understood refusal. He always had what he wanted, whenever he chose. And he would have her again, now.

Celia, pale with terror, stood up and walked towards the shuddering door which Bartholomew was now kicking in his demented fury. Her hands were in tight little fists by her side. She tried to speak twice before she could manage to utter a sound, then the words came tumbling out in a terrified rush.

'If you won't leave me alone,' she gasped through her sobs. 'I'll tell the hospital governors about your secret expeditions to the East End.'

The kicking stopped abruptly.

'I'll tell them everything.' Her voice was still quavering, but she felt suddenly braver. 'I'll tell them about the child I saw you knock to the ground and leave to die...'

'Shut up, do you hear me?' His crazed ravings began again. 'Shut up. Shut up now. Now. I command you.' Then the kicking started once more.

'I'll tell them where to find you if you don't leave me alone,' she wailed. 'The police will find you and take you away.'

'Don't waste your breath,' he sneered at her from the other side of the door. 'I shan't be in the country. And you, you can stay here alone. Stay here and rot in hell, damn you. Rot in hell like your damned mother.'

The early autumn evening was growing misty but it was still light enough for Celia to see clearly down on to the square below her bedroom window. She had been locked in the room for hours without food or drink, but she didn't dare to risk ringing for the maid. Celia knew from experience that she could never trust any of the servants. Her tears long since over, she now felt elated – she had actually succeeded in triumphing over what she had come to believe was her father's unassailable will. She passed the time sitting and looking at the world going by, a world where perhaps fathers didn't hurt their daughters, where parents treated their children with love and kindness as hers once had. She watched as a man, who could have been a younger version of her father, threw the delighted, squealing child he was carrying high into the air. Celia sighed, regretting what might have been, thinking how things could have been so different had it not been for her father's madness, which she was sure had been brought on by that terrible disease: her mother would not have taken her life and her baby brother would still be with them. If only he had not gone to find illicit pleasure with those women in the first place.

Celia drew back quickly from the window as two footmen appeared on the front steps, staggering under their load of a large metal-banded travelling trunk. Dodging to the side of the window, she peered down from the safety of the heavy brocade drapes just in time to see her father appear and a carriage – not theirs – pull alongside him at the kerb. The servants, under the direction of Smithson, loaded the big trunk on to the holding rack and then stood back while their master stepped up into the carriage. Smithson moved forward and handed Bartholomew his medical equipment.

She couldn't quite be sure of the words, but Smithson seemed to say, 'See you next week, Mr Tressing, sir.'

With a brief nod to the butler, but without even a glance towards his daughter's bedroom window, Tressing leaned out and tapped the side of the carriage door with his cane, instructing the coachman to move on.

Celia's heart sank. He was travelling alone – Smithson would still be in the house to torment her. But, she thought to herself, if she could deal with her father, then surely she could deal with the likes of Smithson.

She did not stir until the sound of the departing carriage had completely disappeared, then she moved quietly across the room and went to sit at her looking-glass. She did her best to tidy her hair and make herself reasonably presentable. Her face was still a little puffed and blotchy from crying, but there was nothing she could do to change that – she would have to do. She unlocked her door and stepped outside. Smithson was standing there in the corridor. Celia didn't look directly at him – she couldn't bring herself to – but she guessed correctly from experience that he was leering lecherously at her. Neither did she speak. She walked straight past him, directly down the stairs to the library. She waited a few moments to gather her thoughts, then rang for the butler.

Smithson weaselled his way into the once comforting book-lined room.

'My father,' she said, her voice steady. 'He's away for seven days?'

'That's right,' Smithson responded sullenly. 'Why?'

She didn't answer him. 'I want all the servants. *All* of them, in here. Now.' Her voice never wavered.

Smithson opened his mouth to question her, but she held up her hand to still him.

'Now, Smithson.'

'It is unfortunate that you all find the situation so amusing.'

Celia addressed the assembled staff from the far end of the library. They stood in a contemptuously straggling row, their backs to the book-lined wall.

'I understand from Smithson that my father will be away for one week.'

Smithson didn't confirm her words, instead he retained his bored and contemptuous expression. He didn't show it, but he was angry with himself that she'd tricked him into giving her that information.

'As I will not be needing your services, I am instructing you, the whole lot of you, to get out.' She didn't flinch as they shouted their objections.

'But say we ain't got nowhere to go, miss?' complained one of the maids.

'It ain't right. This is our home,' protested one of the footmen.

'You must make your own arrangements,' said Celia coolly.

'You can't do this,' said Smithson, his voice far more calm than the others.

'Can't I?' replied Celia in an equally collected tone. 'You knew, all of you, what was going on. How I was suffering. But not one of you helped me. You showed not a flicker of compassion, so now I'm repaying the favour. Get out, now, every one of you, and don't let me see you anywhere near this house again.'

'What good do you think it'll do getting rid of us?' sneered Smithson.

'Revenge,' she said simply.

'He'll go barmy when he finds out,' he snapped, with far less certainty.

'In my present mood, I really couldn't care less,' she answered, with a steady gaze directed only at Smithson. 'But I think that is for me to deal with, don't you? Now, if you don't leave immediately, I shall summon the constabulary. And I will feel myself compelled, as part of my Christian duty, to tell them all about your stealing. Particularly about your little enterprises Smithson: about the cases of wines you have been selling off from the cellars, and the little services you do for my father: getting his "raw materials", as I believe you call them.'

She walked past the now silent but open-mouthed servants, making her way towards the double doors. When she reached them she took hold of the handles, threw the doors open wide, and then turned to add a few final thoughts.

'I'm sure that the police would be only too happy to help a poor young lady left at the mercy of nasty brutish servants –

they are such snobs.' She lifted her hand at the emergence of a sound like a whimper from one of the footmen. 'Oh no, please don't object, it's so tedious. And, by the way, I shall be telling my father that Smithson accepted an offer from another employer: a rich industrialist, I think he should be. Or a merchant. From the north of England. Yes. That should upset him. And I'll say that Smithson took you all with him, lured away by the prospect of easy riches.' She smiled and held out her hand, directing them out of the room. 'Don't expect to spend another night under this roof. Good evening.'

Chapter 27

'They say John Neil could hardly blow his whistle.' The middle-aged sergeant laughed with the phlegmatic, cynical cackle of an old hand who'd seen it all before. 'Poor sod, his mouth went all dry and horrible with the shock of it.'

The inspector didn't particularly like working with uniformed officers, but the sergeant – despite his over-familiar ways – was known to be a good man, if only he would show a little more respect for his superior.

'I see from the notes,' the inspector said, looking up quizzically from his desk, 'that you thought there might be a link with another case.'

'Seems to me as how it has similarities to that killing done at Easter-time,' said the sergeant, then added as an afterthought: 'sir.'

'Easter-time?' He frowned. 'And which case would that be, sergeant?'

The sergeant didn't conceal his contempt for the inspector: here he was, coming into the station and asking all sorts of time-wasting questions. If he was half the copper he should be, he'd have known all about that case, and any other relevant information, for that matter. 'Easter Monday, it was.'

The inspector leaned back in the hard wooden chair, tipping it against the wall. 'Emma Smith, you mean?' he said, with a barely discernible raising of his eyebrow.

'That's the one,' the sergeant said. Now it was his turn to frown. Perhaps he should show the inspector a bit more attention. 'Emma Smith. Another brass.'

The inspector nodded. 'What do you remember about it, sergeant? Anything special?'

'I remember plenty about that one all right. Face all covered in gore, it was. Ear nearly ripped off her head. And…' He looked down at his boots. The sergeant had seen a lot during his time in the force, but there were still certain things that even he found difficult to say, especially in front of young whipper-snappers like the inspector. 'She'd had something shoved up… Well, you know where, sir.'

'Dead when they found her?'

The sergeant was still studying his boots as though he was about to sit an examination in footwear. 'No. Not dead. She died in the hospital next day. From the, er, wounds like.'

'What were the ideas around at the time?'

'As far as I recall it, sir,' the sergeant ran his finger round the itchy wool of his uniform collar; he was feeling uncomfortably hot, 'it was reckoned as how she probably got worked over by one of the bully gangs – for not bringing home enough at the end of her working day. If yer see what I mean.'

The inspector nodded again and picked up a pile of papers. As he did so, the sergeant flashed him a crafty look – he seemed to know a lot more than the sergeant had given him credit for.

'Well, that's what we all thought, sir. At the time like.'

The sergeant nibbled his lip surprisingly nervously and leaned forward. He went to rest his hands on the inspector's desk, then thought better of it. He straightened up and stared at the wall as he said, 'And there was, what's her name, wasn't there. Taylor? Taber?' The sergeant paused, searching his memory for the name. 'Tabram. That's it, Tabram.'

'*Martha* Tabram?'

'Yes, sir. That's right. Martha Tabram.'

Now the sergeant and the inspector had each other's full attention.

'Another bride, if I recall, sergeant. Murdered at the beginning of August. Correct?'

'Yes, sir.'

'Multiple puncture wounds.'

'Yes.' The sergeant looked the inspector full in the face. 'And you think there might be a connection with her too?'

The inspector nodded at the older man.

'Christ,' said the sergeant. 'What are we dealing with here?

Chapter 28

Bartholomew Tressing instructed the coachman to wait for him outside his club.

As he entered the smoking room he was greeted cheerily by a ruddy-faced man drinking his third after-dinner brandy. 'How's the work going, old man?' he called, raising the big, almost empty balloon glass in salutation.

'Progressing as ever, of course, Garner,' said Tressing arrogantly. 'My techniques are as near as damnit perfected.'

The inebriated Garner raised his glass yet again, and then rang the small handbell to summon one of the stewards. 'You'll be having all those rich ladies that you and Derringer are so fond of arguing over queuing for your services on the operating table, Tressing,' he giggled drunkenly. 'Trying to save their addled bodies for their rich husbands.'

'Never mind them,' Tressing said edgily, bending forward and lowering his voice. 'I hear rumours that someone in the club – you perhaps – has been bragging about the availability of certain young girls.' He straightened up and looked down his nose. 'Or has the brandy been making you fantasise again?'

Garner looked at Tressing as though he were off his head, but before he could answer to that effect, they were interrupted by the attendant answering the bell. Anticipating Garner's orders for more drinks, the elderly servant set down a full decanter of brandy on the side-table, nodded his head in a little bow, and left the room. Tressing opened his mouth to speak, but he was immediately disturbed again, this time by another club member coming into the smoking room.

'Tressing,' he called, the picture of bonhomie, striding across the room with a great, lumbering stride. 'Just the fellow. Need you for dinner. Wife wants a single chap to make up numbers.'

The rosy-faced interloper completely misinterpreted Bartholomew's expression of anger for one of unwillingness to attend a tedious social engagement.

'Bore, I know,' he said, grinning like a fool. 'But the ladies do like to have these little dinners. And one has to keep the wife happy, eh?'

As much as he wanted to shut the man's stupid mouth with his fist, Tressing didn't want to alarm Garner by bringing attention to himself. So Tressing braced himself to be polite.

'So sorry, Jameson,' he said briskly. 'Can't oblige, old man. I'm going away for a while. Down to the country. On my way there now, as a matter of fact.'

'On the run, eh?' Jameson guffawed. It turned his stomach to do so, but Tressing joined in ingratiatingly.

'What's that?' Garner muttered. He'd finished his fourth brandy and was hurriedly pouring another. 'Who's on the run?

'Where've you been, old chap? Everyone's talking about it,' said Jameson. 'The murder. On Tressing's patch, actually, near the London Hospital.' He grinned amiably. 'Expect that's why Lillian wanted you to come to dinner. To give us all the latest gossip.' He shook his head at the thought of displeasing his wife. 'It'll be a pity to disappoint her.' Jameson watched Garner with admiration as he emptied yet another glassful, and then returned his attention to Tressing as he tried to get him at least talking about the murder. 'No mortuary at the London, so I understand.' He stated it as a fact, but he had only heard about it as part of the many rumours circulating about the events in Whitechapel: if he couldn't get Tressing himself to the dinner, at least he'd have to make sure he had plenty of first-hand information for Lillian to show off to her guests. He hated upsetting her, the repercussions were always so very long-lasting. 'So where do you actually put the er... the, you know, the corpses then?'

301

Bartholomew loathed the prissy manners of the non-medical man, but he remained civil in order to impress Garner with his self-control.

'We manage,' he said airily. 'There are sufficient facilities adjoining the workhouse for our purposes.'

Jameson was clearly intrigued and eager for further tidbits with which to tantalise the potentially belligerent Lillian. 'Rum do, this murder,' he said. 'Dissected, in some way, so they say. Could have been a surgeon, so the gossips have it. Fellow like you, perhaps, eh Tressing?' Jameson laughed at his own joke.

Tressing gulped hard, doing his best to keep up the pretence, though his temper was bubbling very close to the surface.

'Confounded fuss over a few whores, if you ask me,' he muttered, flashing Jameson a broad and meaningless smile.

Chapter 29

'I've got it all worked out. I'm going to stay calm, go down there and tell her. She's *got* to let me move her. She can't stay there, not since that business with poor Polly yesterday. Whitechapel's not safe any more. And that's all there is to it.'

'And if she won't move?' Jacob was propped on one elbow, looking down at Ettie lying next to him, the white lace bedspread just covering her nakedness. Gently, he lifted her thick dark hair away from her face, and spread it out around her on the pillow. 'You said she wouldn't leave – Whitechapel or her lodger.'

'Lodger!' Ettie spat the word contemptuously. 'I'll find a way of making her let me get that bastard out of there if it's the last thing I do.' She rolled on to her back and stared up at the ceiling. 'I mean it this time. I'm not scared any more. It's too late for that. I'm determined to get her out.'

'I'll come with you.'

She twisted round till she was facing him. 'You've changed your tune. You said you'd never go back there after all that business at New Year's. You couldn't wait to get away.' She closed her eyes. 'I appreciate it. Thanks. But I'd rather you didn't. And anyway, you being there might make things awkward: you have to be from round there to understand the rules. There's ways of doing things.'

'Whatever you prefer,' Jacob said neutrally.

'I've decided to go there today,' she said, and waited for his reaction. When he didn't answer, Ettie lifted her head and kissed the tip of his nose. 'Don't worry. I'll be back in time to perform for Miss Tressing.' She held her arms up and let out a ghostly wail. 'See? Perfect.'

Jacob dropped back on to the pillow and stretched out his arm for Ettie to rest her head on his chest. She nuzzled into him with an appreciative murmur. He was upset that she didn't want him to go with her, but he didn't question her, didn't even mention it. He didn't want to spoil their new-found closeness. He seemed to be staring up at the ceiling, but although his eyes were fixed on the ornate plaster cornice, he saw nothing. He'd begun to believe that Ettie was growing away from the East End at last – that's what he'd thought and he'd been glad. But now he couldn't help wondering if she planned to go and see Billy Bury, to ask him for the help that she thought he alone could give her. And Jacob knew that Maisie's brother would help her only too gladly. Any man would – and that was another thing which concerned him. He wondered whether he should follow her at a distance, without her knowing, just to keep an eye on her and make sure that no one bothered her – particularly Billy Bury.

–

'Please, Mum, I'm begging you. Let me get you a better place to live.' Ettie could hardly breathe, the summer heat had made the stench in the cramped and filthy room almost unbearable. 'You haven't even got a proper bed any more. Look at you.'

'I'm all right, darling.' Sarah peered up through red-rimmed eyes at her daughter. She was stretched out under a pile of rags on the floor of the hovel that had once been Ettie's home. 'The bed got busted up one night, that's all. When me lodger was a bit upset. We'd had a bit of a row and he got himself into a right two-and-eight.' She licked at her parched lips. 'I know yer mean well, but where would I belong but here with all me old mates?'

Even in the gloom, Ettie could see her mother's condition had deteriorated. She looked even worse than Ettie had dared imagine. Her mother's skin was parchment thin, stretched taut over her cheekbones, yet the rest of her once-strong body was now bloated and sagging.

'Yer musn't worry about yer old mum. There are some good girls round here. They'll see me all right.'

'But you never go out to see no one, Mum. I've asked Flo and Milly – and Ada – to look out for you, but they never see you. And you know they won't come up here, because of him.'

'Don't start on that again. He ain't going.'

'Mum…'

'Nothing'll change me mind, Ett.' Sarah groaned as she shifted under the pile of rags. 'Listen to me – yer've stuck by yer old mum, even if I ain't always treated yer right. I'll never forget that.' She took in a shallow, rasping breath. 'I never meant none of them blokes to hurt yer, yer know. It's how life is, that's all. Yer had to learn about it sooner or later. And look at yer, it ain't done yer no harm, has it?' She made a sound that was halfway between a wheeze and a croaking laugh.

Ettie ignored what she knew was her mother's plea for forgiveness – she would do what she could for her mother, but she didn't think she would ever be able to forgive what she had allowed those men to do to her. She swallowed back the bile rising in her throat. 'That's all in the past. Now, let's get ourselves sorted out. I'm going to get someone round, some blokes, to get shot of that lodger or whatever he calls himself.'

'No, Ett.' Sarah's voice was suddenly urgent. 'Don't do that. Promise me. I don't care what else yer do, but don't do that, girl.'

'Mum, look at me. If you're scared, I can pay to have him got rid of for good, you know. I can get the money.'

'Ettie. I said yer've got to promise me yer'll leave it. Yer don't know what yer messing with with that one. It'd take more than a couple of blokes to get rid of him, and then what'll happen, eh? If he even knew yer was thinking about it, there'd be hell to pay.'

'But, Mum.'

This time it was Sarah who ignored her daughter's pleas. 'It does me right proud to see how lovely yer've turned out. My little girl. Who'd have credited it how yer'd turn out, eh? Just look at yer. Yer like a proper picture.'

'Look at you, you mean, Mum. You're still lovely. And you always will be.' Ettie was ashamed at the repulsion she felt as she took her mother's hand. 'Let me do something for you.'

'Yer can take me down the Frying Pan for a few, if yer like. That old cow came for the rent yesterday morning, and I ain't had a drop since. I ain't got a brass farthing to me name. Not a pot. I ain't even been able to get nothing off the bleed'n lodger – he's been missing for the last couple of days, yer'll be glad to hear. Never been gone this long before.'

Relieved at that piece of news at least, Ettie brightened up. 'Come on then,' she said, and carefully helped her mother to her feet. 'Let's go and have a few.'

As mother and daughter stepped out of the gloomy passage into the court, Sarah shaded her eyes and squinted in the bright sunshine.

'Sod me, I hadn't expected this. I ain't been out for days.'

Ettie looked around the weed-strewn, dusty court and fondly squeezed her mother's bony arm. 'Weather like this reminds me of when I was little, remember, Mum? When you took me out on a picnic that time.'

'Yeah, that's right,' said Sarah, sounding as though she was surprised by the recollection. 'Up the Thames on a boat we went. Blimey, I ain't thought about that for donkey's years.' She turned and looked at her daughter. 'Yeah, some lovely times we had, when you was a nipper. Lovely.' She cackled throatily. 'I wasn't such a bad old mum, was I darling?'

Ettie didn't answer, she was too busy trying to make out who was standing in the shadows of the archway at the far end of the court.

'What's the matter with you? Yer look like yer've been struck,' gasped Sarah, trying to catch her breath after her fit of laughing.

'Nothing, Mum. I thought it was someone I knew, that's all.' Ettie turned back to her mother and took her arm. She was shocked to see that, in daylight, her mother looked even more haggard than she'd realised. The rough linsey cloth covering her mother's waif-like arm felt harsh against Ettie's now softened skin. 'If you won't let me move you, you'll have to let me get some new gear for you, Mum. A frock and some drawers and that. How'd you like that?'

'Handsome,' said Sarah, her face brightening. 'But there's no need to go to no bother. Give us the sponduliks and I'll get something off the barrow meself.'

'I'm not daft, Mum. The only thing you'd buy yourself if I gave you the money is too much gin.'

Sarah chuckled. 'Yer old mum can't fool you, can she, sweetheart?'

'God love us and save us, if it's not Sarah Wilkins.' The landlord of the Frying Pan stood with his hands on his hips and goggled as though he'd seen a ghost. 'I thought you were dead, girl.'

'As yer can see, Patrick, I ain't,' Sarah called over her shoulder, and flicked feebly at her skirts, executing a sad parody of her old saucy walk as she crossed to her once regular table in the corner of the pub.

Ettie responded to the landlord's amazed look with a roll of her eyes and a helpless shrug. 'Two gins, Patrick. Drop of water in mine. I intend getting home tonight.'

'All right, my darling, coming up.'

'Maisie not in yet, Pat?' asked Ettie, nodding and smiling across to the regulars at the bar.

'Not seen her this afternoon.'

'Tell her I was asking after her and Billy,' Ettie said, and took the drinks from him.

The sight of her well-to-do daughter in attendance quickly attracted a group of women, who huddled round Sarah's table, hoping that they might share in her good fortune and get themselves treated to a few. Ettie was pleased to oblige, and bought them several rounds, glad that in that way at least she could make her mother happy.

All the talk was of Polly Nichols and whether the killer had been the same one who had done for two other brides in the area. The women were alternately scared and full of bravado, their theories about the killer's identity growing wilder as the gin glasses were refilled yet again.

'It ain't been bad for business, mind,' said Big Bella, philosophically. 'Plenty of toffs coming down here to get a bit of a thrill, see, Ett. They've read about it in the papers so they wanna see it all for 'emselves.'

'Even the bloody wax theatre up on the Mile End Waste's got in on the act, yer know,' said Ada to Sarah.

But Sarah wasn't listening to her old friend, she was too engrossed in the drink.

'Go on, Ada,' said Ettie, nodding her encouragement. 'I'm listening to yer.'

'They've got models made of the poor girls what's copped it round these parts over the years. That's fetching 'em in, all right.'

Ettie shook her head in distaste.

'Yer, I know, but it's better than all them models they used to have of sailors with the pox,' said Ada indignantly. 'Now that *was* bad for business.'

The women all joined in with Ada's laughter, including Sarah, who by now didn't have a clue where she was, never mind what was supposed to be amusing her.

'You heard this bit?' said Ivy, walking over to the table from the bar. She was younger than the other women, a fresh-faced newcomer to the streets of Whitechapel, up from the Essex marshes from where she'd fled after being exploited by a farmer's wife who'd taken her on as a maid-of-all-work. She had a good brain and a bit of education, and she was keen to use them, to use anything, so that the regulars would accept her. She needed to earn some money, and without their cooperation she knew it would prove very difficult. She pointed to a newspaper she'd scrounged off one of the men standing at the bar. 'They're worried about riots breaking out again, it says. So what's all that about then?'

'We've had 'em all before,' said Bella, waving her hand dismissively. 'Didn't help no one last time they rioted though, did it?

Not one job or home for no one out of that lot. Plenty of broken heads: that's all they got out of that.'

'They say the riots are gonna be against the Jews this time,' said Ivy, frowning as she tried to decipher the words. 'Cor! They reckon it's a Jew what done poor Polly in.'

Ettie startled everyone by snatching the paper viciously from the astonished girl's hands. 'How can you listen to her reading that stuff?' she snapped. 'What's the matter with all of you?'

'You're a bit touchy, ain't yer, Ett?' said Bella, mugging at the others.

'I don't think it's right taking notice of all those stupid stories. All they do is cause more trouble. And, gawd knows, that's something that you don't need round here.'

'So what d'yer want us to do then, Ett? Ignore it? Or wait around crying till it's one of our turns to cop it?' Milly's voice was harsh. 'Three gels been done in. Three. And that's only the ones we know about. It's gotta be a maniac, that's what it is.'

'No one even knows if it's the same man.' Ettie tried to keep calm, to reason with them, but she felt so angry that she couldn't keep the fury from her voice. 'You shouldn't be listening to all these rumours. It's wrong. It's like it said in this book, about how crowds go mad. You're all caught up in wanting to hear about it. It's like the people who all wanted these tulips.'

'Do what?' Bella said. She wasn't the only one looking at Ettie as though she had taken leave of the last of her senses.

'A book I read. Well, no, someone read bits to me. About people going barmy over things.'

'I dunno about the rest of 'em,' said Ada, 'but I ain't got a clue what yer talking about, Ett, honest I ain't.'

'Nor did I once,' said Ettie. 'But I do now.'

'All right, keep yer hair on,' said Milly, stiffly.

'Have another drink, girl, for gawd's sake,' said Bella, trying to restore a bit of order. 'And get her one and all,' she said, pointing to Ivy. 'You've frightened the life out of the poor little mare.'

'The way you're all behaving, anyone'd think you didn't care about the truth of what's happened – that you just want to lap up all the scandal.'

'Don't be so stupid,' said Ada, now as angry as Ettie. 'Course we care, but some of us have to live here, Ettie Wilkins, so we have to make the best of it, don't we? We ain't all had your luck finding ourselves a fancy man.'

Ettie looked round the table at the people who had once been her friends. She felt she hardly knew them any more. And, for the first time, she was aware of the jealous looks at her clothes and clean, styled hair that were being flashed from beneath their lowered lashes.

'So, that's how it is for us, Ett,' said Bella, still trying to prevent an all-out row. 'Make merry tonight, girl, cos tomorrow we might be on the slab. Dead.'

'Better than the bleed'n workhouse, eh Bella?' said Ada, smiling again.

'Too bloody right it is,' said Florrie, strolling over from the bar, having given up on the man she had been trying to entice out into the alley.

The women were now all laughing, except Ettie who sat silently watching, and Sarah who snored loudly, her head on one side, her mouth slack.

'Listen to this bit,' said Ivy, picking up the newspaper again, her confidence in her audience renewed. 'This bit where they reckon it's a Jew. They are looking for an…' She faltered over the word, and held it out to Ada for help.

'No good asking me,' grinned Ada. 'Ettie's the one round here with all the book-learning.'

Ivy looked expectantly at Ettie.

Ettie sighed and took the paper from her. 'They are looking for an "intelligent man, with knowledge of rituals",' she said touchily, then folded the paper in half and handed it back to Ivy.

Ivy grimaced. 'Wonder what sort of horrible things he gets up to?'

Florrie looked steadily at Ettie and smiled gently. 'Take no notice of us mob, Ett. Yer know what we're like round here. Yesterday they was all saying it was a slaughterman.' She raised her glass in salutation. 'Yer well out of it, girl,' she said with a wink. 'Nice and safe with yer fellah over there in Bow.'

A weak smile was all the answer that Ettie could manage. Her eyes were drawn to the newspaper that Ivy was now eagerly showing to Milly. She thought about what Florrie had said to her – was she really better off with Jacob? Was she really safe with him? She drained her glass and looked over to the door. She could hardly admit it, even to herself, but she'd been wishing that Billy would come in, that he'd open the door and walk over to her with that big, shy grin of his.

'Ett?'

She looked round to find Bella tugging on her sleeve.

'I thought yer'd nodded off,' the big, smiling woman said to her.

'Sorry, Bella,' said Ettie. 'I was miles away. What's up?'

Bella tipped her chin towards Sarah. 'Yer mum, she's out for the count. I've gotta be shifting meself soon, so I wondered if yer wanted me to help yer lift her up and get her home before I start work.'

'Ta, Bell,' said Ettie, pushing her chair back and standing up. 'I'd appreciate that. And I'd better be getting off home as well.' Home, she thought to herself as she helped the big, buxom woman get the unconscious Sarah to her feet. Where was that?

Chapter 30

'Have you read what they're saying about the murders, Jacob?' Ettie sat at the table, dressed ready to perform for Celia. She was pretending to study the newspaper, but she was really studying Jacob, watching him from under her lashes as he brushed at his already immaculately clean suit.

'What nonsense are they spreading now?' he asked, checking his sleeves for stray specks of dust. 'More wildly sensational theories, I suppose.'

'There's more talk that it's a Jew who's doing it,' she said in a hushed voice.

Jacob turned and glared at her. 'It hardly astonishes me.'

'Don't look at me like that,' she said uneasily. 'I never meant anything.'

Jacob put his hand to his throat, easing his collar. 'I'd have thought you'd have known better,' he snapped.

'But I was only...'

He slammed his hand down on the table, making Ettie start back in her seat. 'Enough!' he yelled. 'Now, are you ready? Miss Tressing will be here any moment.'

Ettie took a deep breath, determined that she wouldn't let him speak to her like that, and said, 'There's all this stuff they're talking about, rituals and blood and all sorts of horrible things.'

Jacob repeated his words even more firmly. 'I said, are you ready?'

Ettie looked up at him. She opened her mouth as if to speak, then decided against it. Instead, she nodded.

'Good,' he said simply.

'I don't like doing this, you know.' Ettie spoke the words as calmly as she could, not wanting to let him see that his outburst had alarmed her. 'There's something wrong about leading the poor girl on. Being up the duff makes her an easy target. It's not right. The way she rushed off like that the other day. I don't know, she seems like a poor cow. I feel sorry for her.'

Jacob's temper seemed to have calmed. 'Don't get sentimental, Ettie,' he said flatly. 'And she's hardly poor.'

'I'm not talking about money,' she said wearily.

'Well I am, and we stand to earn plenty from the lovely Miss Tressing. And think of all the rich friends she can send to us.'

'Is that all you think of?' Ettie tossed the paper to one side.

'No, of course not,' he said, examining his fingernails for any sign of dirt. 'As you said yourself, your messages are of help to her.'

'Does that mean we have to con her?'

'It's yourself you're conning, as you put it, if you think you can start working for charity. If we don't earn money from the likes of her, would you really be prepared to go back to doing six shows a night in the gaffs for a handful of pennies?'

Ettie shrugged.

'I thought not.' Jacob's face relaxed and he laid a gentle hand on her shoulder. 'Now perhaps you should keep that thought in mind when you're working. And also keep in mind that Miss Tressing needs you. Remember, you're doing the young lady in question a service, a kindness of a very special kind. People only come to you when they are troubled, and your gift is to tell them what they want to hear. She *needs* you, Ettie.'

'I know what the poor cow really needs, and it isn't me. She needs a different sort of help. But I bet she doesn't even know how babies are made, let alone how you get rid of one you don't want to have.'

'Come in, Miss Tressing,' Jacob welcomed her as he ushered her into the hallway. 'It is very good to see you again. I trust you had an easy journey?'

'Yes, thank you,' she said flatly. 'Though I would have travelled much further to see Miss Wilkins.'

Celia kept her eyes averted as she walked along the corridor, but when she entered the sitting room she raised her head and looked imploringly at Ettie who was seated at the table, her hands spread out flat on its shiny surface.

'Miss Wilkins,' said Celia in murmured greeting.

Ettie smiled at her reassuringly and, as she did so, she could not help but admire Celia's apparently effortless elegance. She was dressed far more plainly than usual, in a simple grey silk bodice and skirt, both edged with narrow apricot ribbons, but she looked as lovely as ever. There was something about the manner in which she carried herself, Ettie thought, and her pale, blond colouring – so different from her own, dark-brown curls – which couldn't be imitated no matter how much someone spent on their clothes and grooming. What a shame, Ettie thought: so beautiful, but such a sad, lonely young woman.

'It was very kind of you to agree to see me for a private reading this evening, Miss Wilkins.' It was as though Jacob did not exist. Celia addressed Ettie as if only the two of them were present. 'Particularly after I left so hurriedly last time. I hope I am forgiven.'

'Of course,' said Jacob from behind her.

Celia didn't turn to look at him. She kept her eyes and her attention on Ettie. 'I particularly wanted to ask Miss Wilkins some questions, you see.' She nibbled nervously at her lip as she considered how to frame her thoughts into words. 'I wonder, Professor Protsky,' she said, looking over her shoulder. 'I have had quite a journey across town. I wonder if you might ring for a cup of tea.'

'I'm afraid we don't keep a full-time staff – it disturbs the spirits, you see,' said Jacob. 'But I'm sure that Ettie…'

Celia stopped him. 'I realise I'm overstepping the bounds of politeness, Professor,' she said, lowering her chin. 'But I was hoping for an opportunity to speak privately with Miss Wilkins. I'm afraid that the tea was something of a pretence.'

Jacob widened his eyes and nodded curtly. 'I shall take the opportunity to look over our engagement book,' he said, and then flashed a warning look at Ettie before he swept into the bedroom.

When she was sure that the door was safely closed, Celia smiled poignantly at Ettie. 'It is a pleasure to see you again, Miss Wilkins.'

Ettie returned her smile and indicated that Celia should sit opposite her at the table.

—

'Jacob, would you like to join us?'

As Ettie held open the bedroom door for him, Jacob felt as though he was being summoned into his own sitting room. It was a feeling for which he did not much care.

'I have conducted a most interesting reading with Miss Tressing,' Ettie said to Jacob, her face set in a look of determined challenge. 'But something unexpected has happened.'

Celia fiddled with her lace-trimmed handkerchief and sniffed loudly. 'It was wonderful to begin with,' she snivelled, trying to hold back her tears. 'But then, nothing. The spirits left us. Left us quite alone. Oh, dear, I'm sorry, please excuse me. I always seem to behave so badly when I come here.'

'It's I who am sorry,' said Ettie, apparently addressing Celia, but actually speaking for Jacob's benefit. 'You see, it's my fault. I have developed an affection for you. I would like to say a friendship.'

Celia took the handkerchief away from her face. Her eyes sparkled in anticipation.

'It's because of that, you see, that my attempts to communicate with the beyond won't work any more.' Ettie stood up from the table and glowered at Jacob over Celia's shoulder. 'The spirits refuse to come, our bonding is too strong for them.'

'But we can be friends instead?' asked Celia hopefully.

'Yes, we can be friends,' said Ettie, her voice tender as she looked down at Celia.

Jacob spoke in a harsh whisper. 'If the reading is over, I'll see you to the door, Miss Tressing. We do have other appointments.'

'Please,' said Ettie. 'Let me.' She moved round the table and took Celia by the elbow, helping her to her feet.

Jacob stood there, rooted to the spot and saying nothing, as the two young women brushed past him and walked out of the room.

At the end of the hall, as Celia stood back to let Ettie open the front door for her, she said, 'Miss Wilkins, did you mean what you said about friendship?'

'Yes,' said Ettie, her voice warm. 'Of course.'

'I certainly need a friend,' she said, her voice hoarse from crying.

'We all do,' said Ettie.

'Will you meet me, Miss Wilkins?' Celia bowed her head and added shyly. 'So we can talk again.'

'When would you like to meet?'

Celia's face glowed with anticipation. 'I know you have other appointments this evening…'

'No, I don't,' said Ettie, smiling to cover her irritation with Jacob. 'The Professor was mistaken.'

'Would tonight be too soon?'

'I'd need to go back in first,' said Ettie, looking back along the corridor towards the stairs. 'I might be a little while.'

'I don't mind.'

Celia seemed so full of trust, it made Ettie blush.

'Well…' said Ettie, and looked over her shoulder again.

'I could wait across the road,' Celia said quickly. 'Over there. Near the park gates. Under the lamp-post.'

'But won't someone be expecting you home?'

Celia shook her head.

'Ettie?' Jacob's now obviously impatient voice came from the sitting room.

'Listen,' Ettie whispered. 'Give me a couple of minutes or so. Go on. I'll be as quick as I can.' Then she closed the door, took a deep breath, and turned round. She started back in alarm when she saw that Jacob was walking along the hallway towards her.

'And what exactly was that little performance all about?' Jacob demanded.

He was still walking towards her and she kept backing away until she was pressed tight against the closed front door.

'It wasn't anything.'

'No?'

'Like you said, she needs help.'

'In that case, why did you send her away? Why didn't you help her?'

'She needs *proper* help.' Ettie swallowed hard. 'You didn't hear the things she was saying to me when I was doing the reading.

She was rambling on about babies and revenge and diseases. All sorts of weird things. Even her dead mother.' 'I couldn't make head nor tail of half of it.' She hesitated. 'To be honest, I think all the worry's driving her a bit mad. But what can I do? I'm not a bloody doctor, am I? I'm a fraud, remember? A trickster.'

'You're a fool, you mean, letting such a rich prize get away.'

As Jacob loomed over her, Ettie could feel his hot breath on her cheek.

'You used to be so kind,' she said, searching his face for some remnant of what she once had seen in him. 'Now you're like a stranger. I really don't know you any more.'

'And you know so much about your precious Miss Tressing, do you?'

'I know enough. I know she needs a friend. At least I can be that to her.'

'That's rubbish, and you know it. You know nothing of her – nor she of you. If she knew who you *really* were, where you came from, the life you led, she would have nothing to do with you. Nothing. Do you hear me, Ettie?'

'Don't be so pathetic.' Ettie spat the words at him. 'You're no different from all the others. Tell the truth for once: you're jealous, aren't you? You want to own me, make me into something I'm not.'

'Ettie, don't you realise I'm only trying to protect you? I can see through people like her. People with their phoney society smiles and ever-so polite manners. I can see how she looks at me, just because I'm a Jew.'

'Now you *are* being stupid.' Ettie twisted round and grasped the door handle. 'I'm going out.'

'Ettie, please,' he gripped her wrist, trying to stop her from opening the door.

'Jacob,' she hissed through her gritted teeth. 'Let go of me. You're hurting me.'

'It's getting late, Ettie.' He was pleading with her, but his eyes said more than his words. 'Please, come inside. Please. With me.'

'No, Jacob. I need a walk, to get out in the fresh air.' She shook her head. 'I want to get all this nonsense out of my mind. It's driving me barmy, all this spirits and rituals rubbish.'

'Rituals?' he said coldly. 'Like in the newspaper story, you mean?'

'Don't be deliberately stupid, Jacob. You know I mean what I do in the act. Not everything revolves around you, you know.'

Jacob kept hold of her other arm and stared at her with an intensity that made her squirm.

'I only want to get some air.' Ettie was doing her best to sound reasonable, but his expression was beginning to alarm her, and her wrist ached from his grip.

'If it's only air you want,' he said, expressionlessly, 'then let me go with you.'

'No,' she said. Her mouth was so dry, she could hardly swallow.

'It'll be getting dark soon. It isn't safe for you to go out alone.'

'Is anywhere safe?' she asked, staring steadily back at him.

Quite suddenly, Jacob let her go, turned, and walked back towards the sitting room. Ettie paused for just a split second while she tried to understand what had happened to make him change his mind, then she spun round, grabbed the door handle, and ran down the front steps into the street.

Within moments she was leaning against the park railings panting, trying to regain her breath. 'Sorry I was so long,' she gasped, her chest heaving. 'I thought you'd have gone.'

'No,' said Celia, shyly. 'I would have waited all night.'

Ettie looked along the road back towards the house; Jacob had turned on the gaslights. 'Let's go for a walk, shall we?' she panted.

'If you're sure that being out with me won't get you in trouble,' said Celia, following Ettie's gaze to the house.

'No. I'm all right. How about you?' Ettie flashed another, this time more furtive glance at the house as they moved off.

Celia shook her head in reply.

'Why did you want to see me?' Ettie asked, her breathing coming more easily.

'Because you said you would be my friend,' said Celia plainly. 'And you don't seem to think I'm a fool.'

'Why should I think that? And like I said, we all need friends.'

'Even you?'

'Why not me?' said Ettie.

'I thought that with your gifts you'd have all the answers, Miss Wilkins.'

Ettie hoped that the light cast by the newly illuminated gas-lamp they were approaching would not show her reddening cheeks as she blushed, shame-faced at her deceit. 'Maybe I have, sometimes,' she said, 'but for other people. Not for myself, never for me.'

'You're troubled too?'

'I suppose we all are, in our own way,' said Ettie, stopping in the pool of yellow light. 'But I'm not here to go burdening you with my worries.'

'Please,' Celia pressed her. 'It would be no burden. I'd be honoured.' She bowed her head modestly. 'That, after all, is what a friend should do.'

'Thank you,' said Ettie, touched by her kindness. 'But that can wait for another time. Now, have you thought about seeing a doctor? I could go with you.'

Celia let out a little gasp of surprise and turned so that Ettie could not see her face. 'Would you come and stay with me for a while. I think that might help both of us.'

'I'm the one who's supposed to be able to read thoughts, Miss Tressing,' murmured Ettie.

'Call me Celia, please.'

'Celia. You seem to understand that I wish to… well, not to be here at the moment.'

Celia shuddered. 'The evening has grown quite chilly.'

Ettie took the shawl from her shoulders and draped it around Celia.

'You really are the kindest person I think I've ever met,' said Celia, turning back to face her.

Ettie cringed inside, thinking how she had duped the poor misguided young woman.

'I really would like you to come and stay with me – if you wish.' Celia stared down at the flagstoned pavement. 'I've no intention of meddling in any way, but I couldn't help but notice the atmosphere between you and the Professor this evening.'

'I am going to tell you something, Celia,' Ettie began.

'Oh, forgive me,' said Celia quickly. 'I've gone too far.'

'No. It's not that. It's something I've not really even admitted to myself until now. I'm reluctant to say it, but I have to. I think that I'm…' She closed her eyes and formed the words in her head before she spoke them. '… afraid. Afraid of Jacob.'

'Of Professor Protsky?'

Ettie nodded. 'He's got this secret. He was in some sort of trouble. In a foreign country. And he acts different sometimes, like a stranger.'

Celia replied with a steady, 'I see.'

Ettie interrupted her hurriedly. 'No, sorry. Listen. I shouldn't have said that. Forget it.' She began to fiddle with the locket chain around her neck. 'I'm a bit wild with him, that's all. We had a row and I made all that up.'

Celia shook her head. 'You don't have to worry about me, Ettie. I could see you were afraid of something. You see, I know about fear too. That's why I offered you a place where you can be safe. I promise you: my home will be quite secure for the next week.'

'I don't know what to say,' said Ettie.

'Say you'll think about it.'

'But you don't even know me.'

'Look,' Celia took a small pad and pencil from her reticule. Holding it to the light she scribbled a hasty note. 'This is my address.' She tore the top sheet from the pad and handed it to Ettie. 'My father is not at home at present. He's away on business for seven days. I'm there alone. Think about it.'

'I came down to speak to you because I thought you needed my help, and all I've done is talk about myself and force my way into your life.'

'Please, Miss Wilkins.'

Ettie held up her hand. 'If I'm to call you Celia, then it's Ettie, all right?'

'Ettie.' Celia smiled as she put the pad and pencil away. 'Ettie, you don't understand what it means to me to have your friendship. I won't press you, but please, remember, I can think of nothing I'd like more than to have you as my friend. And I know that we can help each other.'

Ettie looked at the paper Celia had given her and frowned. 'I must say I didn't expect this.'

'But you will think it over?'

'Of course. Thank you.' Ettie put the paper deep into her pocket then gestured back towards the house. 'I'd better be going. I only came out for a moment.'

'I understand,' said Celia. She touched Ettie gently on the arm and then began to walk away. Suddenly she stopped and turned back. 'I'm so sorry,' she said. 'I forgot I had it.' She took the shawl from her shoulders and handed it to Ettie.

Ettie shook her head. 'No. You take it. I'll be back indoors in a minute.'

Celia's face lit up as though she had been given some rich or rare treasure. 'You are so very kind.' Then she smiled and said, 'I can give it back to you next time we meet.'

Ettie nodded. 'Next time.'

She stood under the gaslight and waited until Celia had disappeared from sight. Only then did she reluctantly make her way back across the road. She stood at the bottom of the stone steps and looked up at the middle floor of the house where their rooms were. The lamps were now burning brightly.

She climbed slowly on to the bottom step and stopped, unable to summon the energy to go any further. She didn't know what to do for the best. She knew she'd be grateful for a chance to get away from Jacob all right, just for a while so she could sort out her feelings. She wondered what it was that had made her begin to feel differently about him, uneasy in some way. She certainly couldn't explain it tonight: her head felt as though it was stuffed with old newspapers, with all the stories running through her mind at once. Maybe she was just tired, she reasoned to herself, and what with what had happened in Whitechapel, well, that was enough to upset anyone. And then there was her mum to worry about... Ettie sighed loudly. Why did everything have to be so complicated, she asked herself? Perhaps a few days staying with Celia would be a good idea all round: she could straighten out what she wanted to do – in peace, away from work – and, at the same time, help Celia get herself out of trouble. In fact, that particular mess could be sorted out while Celia's father was still safely away on his business.

Ettie grabbed hold of the iron handrail and dragged herself up the front steps. She could definitely do with a rest; she was exhausted but at least, she told herself, she should cheer up at the thought of being able to do something positive for Celia. She took out her key and fiddled around trying to find the lock. As the door creaked open, Ettie visualised the old woman she planned to introduce to Celia, and wasn't so sure that her advice would be all that welcome once Miss Tressing came face to face with the realities of the trade of the back-street abortionist. Still, she thought, closing the door quietly behind her, Celia was more fortunate than most. At least she could afford to pay the grabbing old girl's prices.

Chapter 31

'I told yer over a week ago, when Polly got done in,' Mad Milly hollered at the top of her voice, 'why didn't yer listen to me then, eh? Tell me that.'

The portly sergeant stood with his back to the bar, arms folded across his wide barrel of a chest, listening patiently as Mad Milly berated him for his stupidity.

'I knew it was that Leather Apron all along,' she went on. 'I knew. That's what I said to all the girls, wasn't it?'

Nods of agreement came from all the brides who almost filled the stiflingly muggy little bar of the Frying Pan – this was too important for them to miss by being out looking for business.

'Now Annie Chapman's been done in and all,' Milly continued, poking her finger a bit too close to the sergeant's face. 'And what did they find by her body?' she asked, twisting round to solicit the support of the other women. 'They found a bit of leather by her body, that's what. So I just hope you're happy.'

'That's right and all, you tell him, Mill,' came the raucous voice of Florrie from one of the tables.

'Ladies,' said the sergeant wearily, 'this "Leather Apron" busi-ness: it's just another daft name the papers have come up with to frighten everyone. Just ignore it.'

'Ignore it?' boomed Milly. 'There's girls getting done in and you're saying ignore it?'

'I mean ignore all these stupid rumours that are doing the rounds,' he responded, trying to calm their excitement. 'One minute it's a slaughterman, then it's a seaman, and now it's a leather worker. It's all speculation. What we need is evidence, not gossip.'

'You wouldn't listen to us if we did have anything to tell yer,' complained Milly, leaning menacingly towards the sergeant.

He held up his hand to quieten the racket which he knew of old could so easily get out of control. 'All right, girls, all right, he shouted above the din. 'Now, if you remember, Milly, a week ago no one would even give me the time of day, let alone talk to me. I popped in here to try and get some information the morning after Sarah Wilkins' girl had been here. Remember?'

'*She'd* gone off to work,' Florrie butted in, pointing at Milly. 'She wasn't even here when Ettie left.'

'Stop poking yer nose in, Flo,' said the sergeant. 'Or at least get yer facts right. Milly was in here when I turned up, right? Ettie Wilkins had gone but you lot was all here getting pissed as puddens, drowning yer sorrows.'

Milly looked away disdainfully. 'Yer wanna talk to Sarah's lodger,' she hissed. 'That one wears a leather apron for work.'

'That's right,' Florrie agreed, nodding. 'I'll give yer that, Mill. He does and all.'

'Daft cows,' said Ada dismissively. 'He ain't been around for ages.'

'Make me out a liar in front of everyone,' shouted Milly.

The sergeant pressed on regardless. 'Now, if I might continue, ladies. This here gentleman is one of the inspectors working on the case. Inspector Grainger.'

The inspector, who had until now been a silent observer, nodded to the women who sat drinking at the tables and beside him at the bar. 'Ladies,' he said, slowly casting his eyes around the over-crowded room. As he did so he wondered what use the women would be as witnesses. His first thoughts on seeing them as he came into the pub had been that they looked for all the world like garishly dressed puppies huddled together for comfort and protection. But he'd soon realised that he'd been wrong. They certainly weren't puppies; more like lionesses from what he'd seen so far. He made a mental note to watch his step. It wasn't his patch, and they all knew it: they could make things easy or very difficult for the inspector.

The sergeant's thoughts were very different. He was a bit alarmed by the inspector's apparent reluctance to speak. From experience he knew that, if you didn't keep on at them, the brides soon lost interest and would all start chatting away amongst themselves or wandering off somewhere. 'I want you ladies to help the inspector all you can,' he bellowed above the increasingly loud murmurings. 'Answer any questions he's got for you.'

'Well, I've got a question for *him*,' yelled Ivy, getting up unsteadily from her seat next to Florrie.

Her boldness found much approval with the other brides: even though she was a new girl in Whitechapel, she was fitting in very nicely.

'Yes?' replied Inspector Grainger levelly.

'Why don't yer get out there and do what yer should be doing?' she challenged him. 'Go out and find the Old Boy and leave us lot alone to earn our living.'

'Don't panic, girl,' said the sergeant coolly. He didn't show it, but he reckoned that if the inspector knew what he was doing, he wouldn't have to be wet-nursing him like this. 'We ain't nicking you, none of you; we just want to ask a few questions, that's all. And get you to hand round a few of these here leaflets.'

Milly took the pile of papers that the sergeant handed her and looked at them suspiciously. She did everything but sniff them before she took one for herself and gave the rest to the other brides, who passed them round between them with much doubtful whispering and questions as to what the leaflets might possibly say.

'What good are these bloody bits of rubbish?' Florrie demanded, waving her sheet of paper at the inspector. Then she crumpled it into a tight ball and tossed it over her shoulder.

'Someone might have seen something,' said Inspector Grainger calmly. 'And that "bit of rubbish" might give us just the lead we're looking for.' It was the first actual sentence he'd spoken since he'd arrived.

'How many yer handing out then?' demanded Milly.

'Eighty thousand,' the inspector said, far too cockily for Milly's liking.

Ada agreed with Milly's opinion of the inspector. 'Pity yer don't spend yer time on the streets looking for him instead of spending money on bits of paper when most of us round here can't read anyway,' she barked, in her gruff, no-nonsense way.

'Yeah. And if yer've got so much money to throw around, how about using some of it to pay for some decent gas lighting round here?' said Ivy. 'That'd be money well spent, that would. So's we can feel safe when we're working. Instead of having to walk about in the pitch dark half the time. And yer can't see a bloody thing once that old fog comes up.'

'Have you finished?' asked the sergeant impatiently.

'You let her have her say,' said Florrie protectively. 'It's a bleed'n good idea she's got there.' She'd taken quite a shine to Ivy. She was a right little chatterbox, but she was bright and still pretty as well. Must be all that country air where she came from, thought Florrie, looking at her admiringly.

'Yeah, a right good idea,' someone near the door called.

'Yeah, gaslights over all the arches,' shouted Ada, getting into the spirit of things. 'That's what we want.'

Then Big Bella stood up ready to add her two pennyworth. But before she could contribute to the already almost unbearable noise level, the inspector turned round and put his hand in his pocket and pulled out a handful of coins. He stepped over to the bar as though he knew all along that this is what he would be doing. 'All right, ladies,' he called over his shoulder, 'so who wants a drink?'

The women looked at each other. Silent signals rapidly moved between them, confirming that maybe they should give the inspector a chance.

'A round of Satins with porter chasers?' Bella asked no one in particular.

The other women nodded or muttered their agreement.

'Right, you heard,' she said to the inspector. 'Get 'em in.'

Patrick shrugged helplessly at the inspector. 'If you're paying, sir,' he said and began to pour what was to amount to three loaded trays full of drinks.

Inspector Grainger shoved a tankard of ale along the bar to the sergeant, and watched as Patrick handed round the drinks to the women. Then he settled himself in a chair close to the bar and took a long pull at his glass of porter. 'So, what have you heard?' he asked, licking the foam from his top lip.

'What they've had in all the papers,' answered Milly stiffly. 'And a bit of gossip. Yer know.'

Bella decided it was time someone started acting in a bit friendlier way to the inspector. 'Is it true what they say about how he done her in?' she asked in, what was for her, a sweetly modulated tone.

The inspector nodded to his companion, indicating that he should speak. 'Sergeant,' he said simply.

The older man didn't sit down, he remained standing at the bar, slightly behind the inspector's chair. He didn't need to consult his notebook: details of events like this latest murder stuck in a man's mind, no matter how long he'd been in the force. 'Annie Chapman, otherwise known as Siffey,' he intoned, 'was found at half-past five in the morning on Saturday 8 September, in the back yard of number Twenty-nine Hanbury Street, Spitalfields.'

'We know *that*,' said Milly, looking at him scornfully. 'We wanna know if the bastard did all them things to her, like what everyone's saying he did.'

'I don't think that either matters or is of any concern to anyone here,' said the sergeant. He was obviously discomforted by her question and kept his eyes firmly on a point somewhere up near the ceiling of the jam-packed bar.

Inspector Grainger said, 'All right, sergeant.' Then he reached into his pocket, took out his pad, and read out a paraphrase of his notes in an even, flat tone: 'Found on her back. Legs bent at knees, wide apart. Clothes, old and dirty, pushed up…'

Florrie held her hand up to silence Ivy who was about to object.

327

'Head almost severed…' He looked up briefly and paused, then went on. '…from the throat being slit. Twice. Knife wounds to the guts.' Inspector Grainger paused, took out his handkerchief and wiped his forehead, taking his time to consider what was fit to be said. He opened his mouth to speak, changed his mind, then finally added: 'Some internal organs were removed.' Then he snapped the notebook shut and put it away.

'Course her clothes was old,' Ivy muttered in a tiny, muted voice.

'I reckon yer could do no better than sorting that George Banner out,' Florrie suddenly declared. 'And there's no need to go looking at me like that, Bella. I know we don't talk about our own round here, but it's different this time. This is serious.'

The inspector turned his head and caught the sergeant's eye. The older man signalled with a brief nod that Banner was a name that was known to him.

'See, Georgie boy likes beating people up,' Florrie persisted, ignoring Bella's disapproval. 'Women especially.'

'Does he now?' The inspector opened his pad again and scribbled himself a note.

Ada had been unusually quiet for once, apart from the odd comment she'd hardly spoken at all, she'd just sat and silently swallowed her gin. 'You wanna find who's responsible for all this?' she snapped, abruptly.

'Don't be stupid. Course we do, yer dozy…'

'Thank you, Sergeant Miller,' said the inspector to his older companion. 'Of course we do, Ada. It is Ada, isn't it?'

She nodded. 'That's right.'

'Well?' he coaxed her.

'Yer need to look no further than that no-good bastard holy Joe from the brewery,' she said, staring round the bar, daring anyone to disagree with her. 'You mark my words.'

'Charrington?' the sergeant asked, sounding and looking surprised.

'That's right,' Ada snorted scornfully. 'Cleaning up the place, he reckons. But who for? That's what I wanna know. Been driving us barmy since last year, he has. Closing down all the case-houses, then buying up all the property. "Development" they call it. The no-good pig.' Her face was contorted with hatred. 'No one ever bothered us round here before, and we never bothered them. Everyone knows what it's like in these parts, what goes on and everything. So if they don't like it they just keep away. But he's stuck his bleed'n nose in and what's happened? I'll tell yer. He's driven us all out on to the streets. That's what he's done. Bloody lovely, innit? Being forced outside to do yer business. Like sitting targets we are, waiting to be knocked off by some maniac.'

'I hardly think...' began the sergeant.

Ada spat on the floor. 'That don't surprise me.'

The inspector filled the embarrassing silence by sending Sergeant Miller to the bar for another round of drinks.

The sergeant wasn't impressed to be running around after whores, but bosses were bosses and he knew better than to argue.

Ivy piped up, 'Is it true what they say, that he hunts the girls down like a savage, sniffing them out? Then, when he catches 'em, he drinks their blood?'

'I know you all have every right to be worried...' the inspector said reassuringly.

'Thanks for nothing,' said Milly, interrupting him.

'But these stories,' he continued, 'they're spreading like wild-fire, and they're doing no one any good. Why don't you all try and keep calm.'

'Keep calm?' an angry voice asked from the doorway.

All eyes turned to see who had just come in.

It was Maisie Bury. 'I know the girls are all worried, they've got every right to be, but there's others what live round here and all,' she said, perching on the table next to where Florrie was sitting. 'Why don't yer come and talk to us as well? Maybe we could tell yer something worthwhile.'

'Keep yer drawers on, girl,' said Bella sarcastically. 'The nice policeman'll talk to you when it's your turn.'

Some of the other brides sniggered, but Florrie said, 'Shut up, you lot. There's enough trouble round here without us arguing amongst ourselves.'

Sergeant Miller slid the final tray of drinks on to the table that was now also occupied by Maisie's wide rear end, then leaned forward and whispered in the inspector's ear, ostensibly to remind him of another appointment, but actually to get him out of the pub before the girls turned nasty. The sergeant knew the warning signs of a row building up to a full-blown punch-up, and that was all he needed: his new governor getting done over by a bunch of brides.

'Inspector Grainger thanked the sergeant for reminding him, and stood up ready to leave. 'Til take you up on that offer, Miss…?'

'Bury,' she said, glaring at Bella. 'Maisie Bury. From Tyvern Court.'

'Thank you, I'll remember, Miss Bury,' he said gallantly.

'Don't matter if yer don't,' scoffed Bella. 'The sergeant here knows where our May lives, don't yer darling? Well, where her brother Alfie lives, anyhow.'

The inspector treated them to a broad, affable smile as though he were taking leave of treasured friends, fixed his hat firmly on his head and then said, 'Be careful, won't you, ladies? Keep safe.'

'Don't worry yerself about us. We're handsome,' jeered Milly. 'I mean, there's only a monster out there on the prowl waiting to cut our throats, ain't there?'

'We do what we can,' growled the sergeant as he opened the door for his governor.

'Aw yeah,' scoffed Ivy. 'Course yer do. Now make sure you coppers get home nice and safe, won't yer? And, like Milly said, don't worry about us, we've got the vigilantes round here now.'

'What, Lusk and his cronies? Don't make me laugh, girl,' sneered Ada. 'They're all a load of bleed'n nutcases. Belong in the loony bin, the lot of 'em. Be a lot safer without them on the loose.'

The women didn't notice that the policemen had left: there was now only one thing that really interested any of them.

'Safe?' said Florrie loudly, shuffling sideways along the bench to make room for Maisie to sit next to her. 'That's a laugh. Them poor girls *could* have been safe if them bastard deputies had trusted 'em for the few pennies for their beds for the night. Then they'd still be alive today. Want a right larruping, the lot of 'em. The no-good arseholes.'

'And a good hiding for Charrington and all,' chipped in Ada.

Ivy, as the brides had come to expect, had a piece of information no else had yet heard. 'D'you hear about what happened in the room where they found her? This girl I met outside the Butcher's Arms told me all about it. Liza, her name was.'

'Who?' Milly piped up, looking towards Florrie. Florrie knew all the brides.

'You know,' Florrie said. 'Liza. From round by Pearl's place.'

'Aw, right. Her. Liza.' Milly nodded, then looked back at Ivy so that she could continue.

'Well.' Ivy widened her eyes dramatically. 'Liza used to share this room with Annie Chapman what was done in.'

'She never did!' Ada pulled her chair closer to the table.

'Truth. And, what do yer think?'

'Come on. What?' Maisie was agog. She wanted to hear more.

Ivy leaned forward and spoke in a loud whisper. 'She woke up to find out that the girl she'd been sharing with had been hacked to bits and left for the dogs in the alley outside.'

There was a collective intake of breath around the bar.

'As God's my witness,' proclaimed Ivy, primly. 'And, what else d'yer think?'

'For gawd's sake, get on with it,' sighed Florrie, wondering if she found Ivy quite as attractive as she'd first thought.

'On the bit of looking-glass they had hung up over the fire-place…' Ivy was enjoying the attention, so dragged out the story for all it was worth.

'Yeah,' they all urged her, collective impatience almost taking over from interest.

'Well, she saw these words, written in blood they was, on the glass: "Lucky yer never woke up and turned on the gaslight," it said, "or it'd have been you and all for the chop!"'

'Bleed'n liar,' yelled Milly. 'Liza can't sodding read.'

'And how could he have got all that on one bit of looking-glass?' Ada wanted to know.

'Yeah, that's right. How?' Bella demanded.

'Leave the kid alone,' said Florrie, reaching out to ruffle Ivy's mop of black hair. 'She was only repeating what Liza told her.'

Ivy flushed red. She felt humiliated. She'd really thought that she was being accepted by the others, and now they were jeering at her.

'Cheer up, darling,' said Florrie kindly. 'Look there's a customer outside.' She pointed towards the fuzzy silhouette of a man against the etched glass of the pub window. 'Now, I think it'd be nice if we let young Ivy take this turn, don't you?'

'Go on then,' said Bella grudgingly.

With all her old bounce completely restored, Ivy stood up and flounced towards the door. 'Ta, ladies,' she said with a cheeky wink.

'And you watch out for Leather Apron,' Milly warned her. 'Wears flannel on his boots, he does, to creep up quiet so yer don't hear him when he's behind yer.' Milly was as irritated by Ivy's prattling as all the other women but, also like the others, she didn't want to see the pretty little thing get hurt, much less get done in by a maniac.

'And don't let him do yer from behind, love,' Florrie called out, much to the amusement of the market porters who were drinking at the bar.

'But it's easier if I throw me frock over me head and bend over,' retorted Ivy, never one to use two words when twenty would do. 'Gets it over and done with and I don't have to look at their ugly mugs neither.'

'But then he can get his hands round yer throat, yer dozy mare,' exploded Ada, smacking the table top and rolling her eyes at the girl's stupidity.

'They're right,' said Milly. 'Make sure yer have him do yer up against the wall. Keep yer eyes on him all the time.'

'I hate looking at 'em,' said Ivy, hovering by the door, but making sure she kept a watchful eye on the prospective customer outside.

'No good being fussy, darling. Yer'll learn that as yer get older,' said Florrie practically. 'And anyway, yer'd hate a knife in yer guts worse than looking at some bloke's buggy eyes, now wouldn't yer?'

Ivy shrugged. 'S'pose so,' she said.

'And don't go in no passages in the buildings,' Ada chipped in. 'Stay where yer can call out for help.'

'Blimey, anything else?' said Ivy. 'It's like having me mum round me. No, worse. It's like having that old cow of a farmer's wife going on at me all the time. Do this, don't do that...'

'Get off with yer,' said Florrie fondly. 'If yer don't move yerself there won't be no one to do yer from behind or anywhere else.'

Ivy stepped out from the pub and on to the street, her hips swinging and her chin up. The warm evening air wasn't like it was in the country, but even in Brick Lane it tasted sweet after the sour atmosphere of the crowded bar. She flashed her eyes at the tall, well-dressed man. 'Hallo, darling,' she said, brazenly. 'Looking for some company, are yer?'

Chapter 32

'So what exactly am I meant to be doing here?' As Jacob spoke he followed the inspector with his eyes, watching him pace up and down the length of the faded, but still luxuriously thick rug which stood in front of his desk.

The inspector glanced briefly over to Sergeant Miller, who was propped up against the wooden filing cabinet in the corner of the office, indicating that he should speak.

'You might have read in the newspapers that we are asking psychics to assist us with our inquiries, sir,' Miller said without the merest hint of the contempt he felt for the primped and groomed man who stood before him.

'I remember something of the kind,' said Jacob cynically, and turned his body towards the inspector. 'If I recall, the article in the *Chronicle* said something along the lines of – now let me see, what was it…? That investigation into the murders gives an unequalled opportunity for psychics and clairvoyants to prove the value of their occult sciences? A chance to prove and make known the sincerity of their art?' He paused for the inspector to nod his confirmation of what he was saying, then continued, 'So, yes. I have read about the challenge.'

'Good. Good.' The inspector sat down in his big leather chair, leaned back and leisurely lit a cigarette. He scratched the side of his neck and exhaled slowly. The blue smoke curled lazily towards the nicotine-stained ceiling. 'You know all about it.'

'But I am not here in response to any such challenge, inspector,' said Jacob firmly. 'I was dragged in here. From my home. Against my will.'

'Dragged?' The inspector looked to the sergeant for verification of such a disparaging suggestion. 'Surely not?'

The sergeant shook his head solemnly. 'As I understood it, sir, the gentleman here came most willingly.'

'Look, I'm a busy man. Just explain what you want from me and I'll be off.'

'Take a seat,' said the inspector with a gracious smile, and picked up a brown cardboard file from his desk which, apart from a heavy crystal ashtray, was now completely empty. 'You might be able to help us, because unlike most of the other psychics who have approached us, I believe you are familiar with the part of the East End where the murders took place.' The inspector stared at Jacob with eyes narrowed against the tobacco smoke. 'You've spent time around Whitechapel.'

Jacob didn't respond in any way to the police officer's assertion; he had no intention of letting the inspector see the discomfort he felt. 'To when are you referring, inspector?' he asked nonchalantly. His voice sounded calm but his mind was racing: how much did they know about him, he wondered? He would have spat if his mouth hadn't gone totally dry; just when he was gaining the reputation he craved, this had to happen. All he needed was for stories about his time playing the penny gaffs to get around and he and Ettie would be laughing-stocks, their career in ruins.

'According to information we've received,' said the sergeant, consulting his notepad, 'you were there on New Year's Eve.' He looked up. 'And on several other occasions since.'

'You look relieved,' said Inspector Grainger, tapping the spent ash from his cigarette.

'Relieved?' repeated Jacob, with a frown. 'What makes you say that?'

Grainger smiled, less affably this time. 'You should understand that we know all about your working the gaffs but, don't alarm yourself, that's of no concern to us.' Grainger turned to the sergeant. 'Well, not for the time being. So, why were you in Whitechapel?'

'I was there with…' Jacob hesitated for a fraction of a second, then carried on speaking almost without missing a beat. 'With a friend. Someone who knows the area well.'

'And who might that be, sir?' said the sergeant, showily licking his pencil in preparation to write the name in his pad.

'I'd rather not say,' said Jacob, folding his arms with what he intended to look like casual ease. 'I was, as you might say, "out slumming" with a friend. It would be most indiscreet of me to mention any names. I'm sure that, as a gentleman and as a man of the world, inspector, you can appreciate the position I'm in.'

'You flatter me,' said the inspector.

The sergeant wrote something down in his pad, tore out the page and handed it to his boss.

The inspector nodded his acknowledgement of the sergeant's assistance and read the note. 'The friend you're so loathe to name, that would be Ettie Wilkins, wouldn't it? The same young lady who shares your rooms and who assists you in your magic act.'

Jacob blinked slowly, holding back his anger.

'There's something I want you to hear,' the inspector continued, then nodded to the sergeant who went to the door and called in a young constable from the outer office.

The junior officer stood in front of the inspector's desk next to Jacob's chair, his hands behind his back and his chin held high, awaiting his orders.

'I have brought in the officer here to inform you about the latest murders,' said the inspector, studying Jacob's face for any signs of a reaction. 'And yes, I did say *murders*. Two women have been killed this time.'

'Why tell me about them?'

'You do have psychic powers, don't you, *Professor* Protsky?'

After only a few minutes of listening to the young officer read out the gruesome details of the most recent victims' deaths, Sergeant Miller was wiping his hands surreptitiously up and down his serge-covered thighs to dry his sweating palms. He was trying to remain cool and retain his dignity. He didn't want to show himself up, either as the lad's superior or in front of his new, albeit temporary boss.

The young officer continued reading out his report in his still not quite adult voice: 'It was at 1 a.m., on Sunday 30 September that we believe the killer was disturbed at the scene of the crime in Berner Street, Whitechapel. It is thought that he heard a pony and cart approaching, sir, and because of that he ran off.' The constable looked up from his notes and stared across at the wall behind the inspector's head. 'But, before doing so, the killer had slit the throat of Elizabeth Stride. A Swedish woman of approximately forty-five years of age – known variously as Long Liz and Epileptic Annie.' He referred to his notes once more, put the back of his hand to his mouth and coughed quietly before adding, 'It would seem that being disturbed like that meant he didn't have time to finish the job off in the way he had before, sir.'

'But he managed to finish off the next job all right, didn't he?' said the inspector, scrutinising Jacob's eyes for any hint of emotion. 'Get on with it, constable.'

'Sir. The night's second victim, Catherine Eddowes, aged forty-three years, was found in Mitre Square, Aldgate. She had been in gaol – drunk in Bishopsgate nick – until 1 a.m. Like the other victims, it appears that she was grabbed by the neck and forced to the ground.' The young officer took a deep breath before going on to read out a detailed description of the mutilations and other atrocities carried out on the woman's body. He did his best not to blanch at the horrors he was listing as he wanted very much to make a good impression on the inspector: he was an ambitious young man, and this was a rare chance to get noticed by someone of importance from outside his own station. By reading his notes as though he were reciting a particularly boring section from one of the legal books he studied after each shift, the youthful constable did a creditable job of keeping control of his emotions, although at one point he only just managed to keep the bile that was rising in his throat from spewing on to the inspector's fancy rug.

The sergeant experienced a similar reaction on hearing the lurid description of Catherine Eddowes' hideously violent death. And although he had seen a lot of terrible things in his time – more than most men could even bear to think about – it still took every ounce of control that he possessed for him not to bring up the fried gammon and bread that Mrs Miller had made for him before he went on duty.

Outwardly, at least, Jacob did not flinch.

When the constable finished relating the macabre catalogue of horror, he replaced his notebook in his tunic pocket and stood to attention. 'That's it, sir.'

'Thank you, constable,' said the inspector. 'Though that hardly seems the correct thing to say in the circumstances. You did well.' He turned to the older man in the corner. 'Sergeant.'

The sergeant directed the young man outside with an encouraging pat on the shoulder and then stood with his back to the closed door, watching as the inspector concentrated his attention on Jacob. 'Now, *Professor*,' he said. 'You are an educated man, and one who makes claim to possessing special abilities, so I wonder whether you might be able to help us with a suggestion or two.'

Jacob looked steadily at the inspector.

'The first puzzle,' he went on, 'is that one of those murders was in Berner Street and the other was right up on the City police's patch – in Mitre Square. But, and this is the tricky bit, they are definitely crimes committed by the same hand, yet they occurred within a very short time of each other. Almost, in fact, at the same time. So how do you think our man could have got from Berner Street to Mitre Square quite so fast?'

'Must have been a bloody magician if you ask me,' said the sergeant from his place by the closed door.

Jacob didn't utter a word; he remained as impassive as a statue as the inspector replied, 'My thoughts exactly, Sergeant Miller. A magician. Or a conjuror. In fact, someone just like the Professor here.'

'Where the hell do you think you've been?' Ettie stood in the doorway with her fists tucked into her waist, barring the way into the hall. 'I got back from buying the paper,' she said, 'and the place was empty. I've been going out of my mind with worry wondering where you'd got to. All bloody day. That's all I need. There's all these murders going on and you do a disappearing act on me.'

'Ettie,' Jacob said through gritted teeth, 'just let me through. It's getting cold out here, I'm tired and I want a drink.'

Ettie clicked her tongue impatiently and stood to one side to let Jacob into the hall. As soon as he was in the sitting room he went straight to the decanter on the sideboard and poured himself a large cognac which he threw back in one gulp. He immediately poured another which he took over to the armchair by the hearth. He sat there, staring into the grate.

'Well?' Ettie demanded, gripping the back of his chair. 'Are you going to explain?'

He sipped at his drink and continued staring. 'You haven't lit the fire yet,' he said absently. 'Why didn't Mrs Hawkins light it before she left?'

'I sent her home early, before it started getting dark. She's scared – like we all are. Now, will you answer me, Jacob? I'm speaking to you.' Ettie knelt down and placed her hand gently on his knee. 'For God's sake, whatever's got into you?'

'The police wanted to talk to me,' he said, twisting the glass round and round in his hands.

'The police? I don't understand. Jacob, what's wrong? Have you been in an accident or something?'

He shook his head.

'So what did they want? Why should they want to talk to you?'

He gestured with his glass towards the paper that lay open on the dining-table. 'The murders,' he said simply and took a long pull on his drink.

'The murders?' Ettie took her hand from his knee, stood up, and walked over to the table where she closed the newspaper. 'But why would they want to talk to you about the murders?'

'Why do you think?' he snapped bitterly. 'Because I'm a foreigner and I'm a Jew, of course.'

'That's stupid,' she said quietly, staring down at the paper, unable to meet his gaze. 'There's hundreds of other foreigners and Jews all over London, especially round Whitechapel. Why should they pick on you?'

'Why do *you* think they picked on me?' he shouted, slamming the glass down on the arm of his chair. 'Because I'm the killer?'

'Don't talk like that,' said Ettie, her voice trembling. 'You're frightening me.'

Jacob finished off his drink and stood up. 'It's time we were getting ready for the performance,' he said icily. 'We have to be there in less than an hour and I don't want these new clients thinking we're unreliable.'

–

Jacob paid the driver and stormed off up the front steps without even bothering to help Ettie down from the cab. He had opened the door and was inside the hall that led to their rooms before she had even stepped on to the pavement.

Ettie mumbled a mortified 'Good night' to the cabman, and warily followed Jacob indoors.

As she entered the sitting room he was standing there waiting for her.

'You made me look a fool tonight, Ettie. A complete and utter fool. And that's something I won't easily forgive. Or forget.' His voice was hard and unrelenting. 'The whole thing was a complete disaster. The so-called messages you gave were useless. Worse, they were embarrassing. That nonsense wouldn't have convinced an idiot.' He moved closer to her. 'Do you know that at one point they were actually yawning? Yawning.' He shook his head contemptuously. 'We were invited there on the Brownlows' recommendation. The Brownlows', Ettie. Just about the most influential family in London. And you did that to me. By tea-time tomorrow it'll be all round Mayfair that the sitting was a bore. How could you do that, Ettie? After all I've done for you: you could hardly be bothered to speak.' He smashed the flat of his hand down on to the table. 'I don't like being made a fool of, Ettie.'

'Nor do I. And I'm the one who's really being a fool,' she said through her tears. 'Not you. I'm the fool for staying here with you.'

Jacob lifted his hand and Ettie recoiled.

'Go on, show me what a clever bloke you are,' she yelled, protecting her face with her arms. 'Show me how you can beat up a woman. Is that what you want to do, eh?' She turned her back on him and, covering her face with her hands, she began to cry softly as she spoke. 'I feel like you've made me into a prisoner. You make me do this, do that. Speak one way, act another. And I can't ever complain, can I? All the time I have to be grateful, grateful that you took me in. But how about me, Jacob? How about what I want?' She sobbed loudly and turned to face him. 'Why can't you just leave me alone?'

Jacob let his hand drop to his side. 'It's this business with the police, isn't it?' he said coldly. 'They've made you doubt me. You're frightened of me, aren't you?'

'I ain't frightened of you,' she said unconvincingly. 'But I'm sick of all this. Being stuck here in these rooms, working night and day. I wanna have some fun for a change. I'm not even bloody twenty years old yet, and I might as well be an old married woman, the life I'm leading.'

Jacob went over to the sideboard where he'd left his cognac glass earlier that evening and poured himself a large drink. 'I don't think you're being entirely honest, Ettie,' he said, putting the stopper back in the decanter. 'But whatever it is that's made you act like this, I don't like it.' He looked over at her as she stood sniffling by the door.

'What you mean is, you don't like me standing up for myself,' she said, lifting her chin. 'Because then you can't control me like some brainless little puppet.'

'No,' he said, walking over to the window and staring down into the dark street below. 'That's not true. I've always admired your spirit.' He paused, and then spoke his words as though he were carefully weighing each one. 'No, what's wrong with me is that I can't cope with the way you've started looking at me. I know there's something on your mind, something that you can't bring yourself to say.'

'It's nothing to do with you,' she said, shivering. 'I'm worried about me mum, all right?'

'Oh, we're back to that now, are we?' he said, turning to face her. His voice dripped with sarcasm. 'The little Whitechapel girl act.'

'One of the girls gave me the whisper that she's on the laudanum as well as the drink now.' Ettie wiped her eyes on the back of her hand and looked at him nervously from under her lashes. 'She'll wind up killing her bloody self at this rate.'

'Even when you're spouting lies, Ettie, can't you at least make the effort to speak properly?' he said wearily. 'Has all I've taught you been a complete waste of time? *Try* and remember your voice.'

'Shove me voice,' she sobbed. 'And shove you, too. I'm going to see my mum.'

She rushed to make a grab for the door-handle but, before she could turn it, Jacob had her hand gripped tightly in his.

'Don't lie to me, Ettie,' he seethed, his face pale with repressed anger. 'We both know what all this is really about, don't we? Go on, admit it. You're fed up with me and you're going to meet Billy, aren't you?'

'No, I ain't going to meet Billy, if you must know,' she hissed through her teeth as she wriggled frenziedly, trying to break free of his grip. 'I'm going to see my mum. But yer right about one thing, I am fed up with you. All you care about is yer bloody clients.'

No matter how hard she struggled, Jacob was too strong for her. He took her roughly by the shoulders and pushed her towards the bedroom door. 'We've both said a lot of things we don't mean, Ettie. We'll go to bed and we can discuss your pathetic excuse for a performance in the morning, when we're both rested. With a bit of luck and a lot of hard work, tonight's debacle will soon be forgotten.'

Knowing that it was useless to struggle further, Ettie allowed Jacob to steer her into the bedroom. She stood quietly by the bed until he had taken off all his top things, then she said apprehensively. 'Jacob. I think I'd rather sleep in the chair in the sitting room tonight.'

'Sleep where you like,' he said. 'It makes no difference to me. There's hardly been any point in us sharing a bed recently anyway.' Then he turned down the gaslight, got into bed, and dragged the covers up over his shoulders.

As she left the bedroom, Ettie went to close the door shut behind her.

'We'll have that open, thank you,' he said without looking at her. 'I can't have you creeping off on any midnight assignations.'

It seemed like she had to wait hours before his breathing became regular and soft, but as soon as she was satisfied that he was asleep, Ettie picked up her bag and shawl – giving silent thanks that she still wasn't tidy enough to have put them away in the bedroom – crept to the door, and let herself out into the hall. She stole along the passage way like a thief in the night. As she slowly turned the catch on the front door, her hand trembled, as though, at any moment, she would be stopped from escaping from the man she had come to feel was imprisoning her and, she finally had to admit, had now started to frighten her as well. As soon as she was safely down the steps and out on to the fog-shrouded street below, she ran as though her life depended on it.

At first, as she made her way closer and closer to Whitechapel, she stayed in the cover of darkness of the side roads, for fear that

Jacob might wake and follow her and take her back. But, as she wove her way down the narrow back streets from Old Ford and on into Bethnal Green, getting ever nearer to her old home, a more powerful dread crept over her. In every murky shadow, and under every dripping arch, she imagined another unknown and unseen horror waiting for her. Each voice she heard coming from the misty depths of the brick alleyways between the tall buildings was a new fright making her start back in terror. Even though she'd been brought up to survive on the streets, the knowledge that a maniac was on the loose in Whitechapel gave her every reason to feel terrified.

Against all her better judgement, Ettie's fear got the better of her; she would have to take the chance of Jacob seeing her if he had woken and followed her. She had to leave the dark, fog-bound passages and side streets and make towards the bigger and brighter roadways where she could at least see if anyone was lurking, waiting for a victim. But as she turned into Three Colts Lane, before she could reach the comforting glow of the gaslit main road ahead, a new horror confronted her. There, through the swirling mists, she saw a huge poster detailing the full, dreadful particulars of the Whitechapel murders. After quickly composing herself she moved on, only to discover similar bills and notices plastered on almost every available wall that she passed.

It all became too much for her, all the running from one fog-dimmed pool of light to the next, hoping above hope that she wouldn't hear footsteps gradually growing louder behind her. She stopped dead in her tracks. She couldn't go on. It was as though her legs were rooted into the ground. She stood panting in the darkness, her mind whirling in confusion. All the reasons she had had for wanting to get away from Whitechapel crowded her mind, as did her memories of the sense of relief she had felt on that first night when Jacob Protsky had given her the long-awaited opportunity to escape the slums and start a new life with him. But now both places – Whitechapel and Bow – held their own special dread for Ettie. Her chest rose and fell in great, gasping sobs as she made up her mind that, wherever else she might go, it wouldn't be to live back in Tyvern Court, nor would it be in Jacob's rooms by Victoria Park.

With sudden, single-minded decisiveness, Ettie sprinted back along the street and stood in the brash, sputtering oil-light of an all-night coffee stall on the corner of Cambridge Heath Road. She held her bag up to the lamp and rooted through it until she found the piece of paper she was looking for then, with a shake of her head at the proprietor who offered her a mug of steaming tea, she rushed determinedly along the main road in the direction of Mile End. And, as soon as she saw what she was looking for – the welcoming lamps of a hansom coming towards her – she leapt wildly out into its path and brought it to a skidding halt.

'Yer bloody silly cow,' hollered the infuriated driver from his high perch on the top of the cab. 'How d'yer expect me to see yer in all this sodding fog. Yer could have killed the both of us. And me horse.'

But the disgruntled cabman forgave Ettie surprisingly easily when, once she was settled in her seat, she reached up through the trap-door in the cab roof and handed him a sizeable tip. In exchange, he willingly gave his solemn promise not to remember the person who had hired him to drive her that night from Bethnal Green to Belgravia. In fact, if he were honest, the whole episode rather amused him – apart from having to stop so suddenly on the wet cobbles: driving an elegant young lady back from a secret assignation in the East End to her fancy address up west.

Following the young lady's request for discretion, the cabman pulled the hansom into the square with the softest jingling of harness and the merest spark of wheels on the cobbles, and set her down where she had instructed him: away from the lamplight and out of sight of the young constable patrolling his beat.

Ettie waited for the cab to disappear into the grimy night air before checking the house number on the piece of paper.

It was a tall, elegant building, with nothing much to distinguish it from all the others in the square, except it was the only one with lights still burning, albeit dimly, on every one of its five floors – from the downstairs basement area to the rooms up in the attics. Yet still she did not approach the front door directly.

Under cover of the gloom of the late hour, Ettie edged along the railings of the adjoining houses, then slipped silently down the area stairs and huddled in the space under the cold iron steps by the entrance door to the big basement kitchen.

Celia had assured Ettie that she was in the house alone, but she was not prepared to take any risks; she would wait until daylight and *then* she would go upstairs and call at the front door. But, for now, the shadowy depths of the area would have to serve as her bed. She pulled her shawl closer about her and curled herself up against the chilly darkness while she waited for the dawn to break. She'd slept in worse places.

It took a moment for Celia to remember that she was in the blissful position of being totally alone in the big, empty house. She yawned slowly, lifting her chin and stretching her neck until she felt the muscles pull tight. She threw back the covers and went over to the window. As she dragged back the curtains she squinted in the bright morning light – such a contrast to the night before. The sun was forcing its way through the last of the autumn dampness, and was drying the dew from the leaves of the potted shrubs and flowers which stood at the foot of the steps of all the houses in the square.

She slipped into her wrap and padded softly downstairs into the big kitchen to boil water for tea.

It was all so wonderful: there was no one – not her father, not Smithson, not even a scullery maid – to bother her. She held her wrap round her and leaned forward to pull the big iron handle beside the range that opened the flue, then she shot some coals from the scuttle into the hopper and set the kettle on the hottest plate to heat up. Celia smiled to herself, remembering fondly how, as a young girl, she had objected so strongly when her mother had insisted that she should know how to look after herself. 'You'll never know when you might need such knowledge,' her wise and caring mother had said to her. She had protested – very loudly

– that she wasn't a scullery maid. But, as with so many other things, and at other times, her mother had proved to be right. Celia sighed. If only she were here with her now…

She made sure that the fire was blazing in the big cast-iron belly of the range, then went over to the basement window to look up at what promised to grow into a brilliant blue sky. But, before she had even glimpsed the narrow patch of heavens above her Celia's mouth dropped open in alarm. There, outside in the area, folded up in a tight bundle, squeezed between the basement window-ledge and the iron stairs which led down from the square above, was what looked like a young woman sleeping.

Celia picked up the poker from the plain, workmanlike companion set which stood next to the range, and silently crept back to the window. When she was sure that the girl was still asleep, she turned the key softly in the lock and threw open the door.

The sound of the squeaking hinge made both young women scream as though they had been set upon, but the sight of one another – Ettie looking up from her makeshift bed on the cold, damp stone and Celia standing over her brandishing the long, blackened poker – was enough to silence them both immediately.

Chapter 33

Jacob rubbed his neck with warily searching fingertips – it ached badly. He felt as though he had slept in a cellar with coal for his pillow rather than in the big, wide bed he shared with Ettie.

Ettie.

The whole, awful ordeal of the night before came flooding back to him. With a slowness that came from cramped, unrested limbs, Jacob heaved himself out of bed and eased himself into his brocade robe and slippers.

'Ettie?' he called softly before entering the sitting room – as much to test her reaction to spending the night propped up in an armchair as to see whether she was awake yet.

There was no reply.

'Ettie?' he tried her name again. And again.

Within minutes of waking, Jacob was dressed, out of the house, and on his way to Whitechapel.

Jacob had no sooner ducked into the dank tunnel of an archway that led into Tyvern Court than Maisie Bury's wide frame was blocking his way forward.

'And what do you want?' she demanded, solidly planting her boots wide apart; there would be no slipping past her, if she had anything to do with it.

'Maisie,' he said – a bit too smoothly for her liking, but she was still taken aback that he'd remembered her name. 'I'm so pleased to see you. I need your help.'

'Aw yeah?' she said suspiciously. 'And why's that then? You in trouble or something?'

'No,' he didn't bother to express anger at her assumption. 'I'm looking for Ettie. I thought that perhaps you...'

'Looking for Ettie? What d'yer mean? She's staying with you, ain't she, at your place over by Vicky Park?'

'Yes, yes,' he said, failing to hide his irritation. 'But, you see, we had a little, what would you say? A tiff. And now I can't find her.' 'And you thought she might be here, eh?' Maisie put her fists firmly on her broad hips.

Jacob stepped towards her.

'All right, moosh,' she said cautiously. 'Keep your distance.' Jacob backed away a couple of paces. 'I was hoping to get out into the fresh air. It's a little musty in here.'

'D'yer think so?'

'Yes. And I am very anxious to get on and find Ettie.'

'Anxious, eh?' said May, infuriatingly slowly.

'Yes. Very,' he replied evenly. 'Now, please, do you have any idea where she might be?'

'Do you?' she asked him in return.

'I thought that she might have come back here.' He hesitated a moment. 'To visit her mother.'

'She wouldn't do that, would she? Not now Sarah's lodger turned up again.'

Jacob scratched the side of his nose and said casually, 'I wondered if she might be looking for your brother.'

'Our Billy, yer mean?'

'Yes. Billy. Where do you think I might find him?'

'You sure, mate?' snorted Maisie scornfully. 'I don't think he's all that keen on you.'

Maisie's eyes flicked away from Jacob and she seemed to be focusing on something in the distance.

The sound of approaching footsteps suddenly broke the silence and echoed though the tunnelled, dripping archway.

Maisie broke into a beaming, brown-toothed grin. 'Looks like yer in luck,' she said, indicating with a lift of her chin that Jacob should look behind him. 'Here's our Billy boy now.'

As Jacob turned around to look, Maisie spoke to her brother. 'Billy,' she said. 'Yer just in time. The Professor here's upset Ettie and she's gone and run off. Now he's out looking for her.'

Jacob didn't even see Billy raise his fist before it hit him directly under the chin and lifted him clean off his feet.

'You'll never guess who's been round the court asking about Ettie,' Maisie screeched as she burst into the Frying Pan. '*And* what our Billy done to him? Yer should have seen it. What a carry-on.'

'Sod your Billy,' protested one of the market porters drinking at the bar. 'Shut that bleed'n door. It's cold enough to freeze yer arse off out there.'

Maisie glowered at the man and then slammed the door, dramatically causing a sharp draught which sent sparks and splutters from the fire dancing into the already smoke-filled room.

'Come and sit yerself down, May,' said Florrie. 'And for gawd's sake, girl, sort yerself out. Calm down and talk a bit sodding slower. I can't make head nor tail of what yer going on about.'

It might have been cold outside in the brisk autumn air, but Maisie was sweating from the exertion of making the short run from Tyvern Court to the pub. She wiped the sweat from her forehead with her sleeve, took a deep breath, and settled herself down at the table.

'Well?' Ivy asked, mugging at Florrie. 'Spit it out then, if yer gonna tell us.'

Florrie giggled at Ivy with a surprising girlishness, then said to May: 'Yeah, go on, Maise. Cough it up, girl.'

Maisie first glared at Ivy, making it clear that she considered her a mouthy little upstart, then she spoke directly to Flo.

'It was only that Professor bloke creeping about. That's all,' she said, with a quick look over her shoulder and with a self-satisfied smugness that suggested only she and her confidantes would have access to the whole fascinating business. 'Protsky.' She lowered her voice, and was now almost silently mouthing the words. 'You know, the posh one she went to live with in Bow. That's who. See what I mean?'

'No,' said Ivy bluntly, shaking her head. 'I don't see. I don't get it at all, in fact. What was he doing round here asking about her, if she lives with him in Bow?'

'Blimey,' said May sadly to Florrie. 'Is she thick, or what?'

'You ain't making yerself all that plain,' Florrie replied, patting Ivy's hand and winking at her affectionately.

Maisie tutted. 'They had what you might call a right old ding-dong, by all accounts. And he, Jacob – the Professor, that is – must've chucked her out. Or she's done a moonlight on him. Cos he was round here, right early, before Billy'd even left for work this morning. See, he'd gone to fetch a screw of tea for a brew-up before he left for Reed's…'

'Blimey, you don't half go on, May. You gonna get on with it or what?' This time Ivy's tone was too cocky even for the indulgent Florrie's liking.

'Go on May,' said Flo gently. 'Tell us.'

May narrowed her eyes scornfully at Ivy and sighed loudly. 'I dunno if I want to tell yer now,' she said sulkily.

'Course yer do,' said Flo placatingly, glaring warningly at Ivy, who didn't seem in the least bit moved by the reprimand.

Maisie took a long, leisurely moment to arrange her skirts, as though she was considering whether to share her story; but she was never one to keep a secret, and was soon back in full, gabbling flow. 'The thing is, he *reckons* he's looking for her.'

'Looking for her?' Ivy shouted the words so loudly that the whole bar fell into silence. 'I bet that's just a cover-up. I bet the bastard's done her in. Moollered her.' She sniggered. 'That'll put paid to all your Billy's big ideas.'

Before Ivy had a chance to duck, the Bury temper let fly and Maisie whacked her full across the chops with the flat of her hand.

Ivy burst into offended and pained tears. 'She really hurt me, Flo,' she grizzled. 'Them great big hands of yours. Yer should work in the bloody slaughterhouse.'

'Aw, shut yer gob, yer wicked little mare,' said May, closer to tears than she wanted anyone to know, and stormed out of the pub, leaving Florrie to comfort the snivelling girl.

'Sometimes I wish I'd never left the farm,' Ivy wailed.

Unusually for her, Florrie spoke quietly with her head bowed. 'Yer think yer'd be better off back down in Essex than here in Whitechapel with me?'

'I might be,' she sobbed, dabbing gingerly at the red, hand-shaped weal on her cheek.

'What with all them swede-bashers?' Florrie wrapped her arm tenderly round Ivy's heaving shoulders.

'Dunno.'

Florrie lifted the edge of her torn and ragged shawl and wiped away the tears from Ivy's cheeks and the long trail of snot which hung from her runny nose. 'Where would you go—not back to that spiteful cow *you* worked for before?'

'I was thinking about it,' said Ivy, looking up at Flo through her tears. 'If she'd take me back. Specially since all these murders.' She sniffed loudly and ran her nose along her sleeve leaving a shiny trail on the dull cloth. 'It's all getting a bit much. And now that rotten bitch's hit me.'

'Don't make too much of it, Ivy love,' said Florrie, her face full of concern. 'It was a little slap, that's all. Yer'd have known it if she'd really meant it. She'd have knocked yer head right off yer bleed'n shoulders if she had.'

Ivy pouted sulkily.

'Yer've gotta see it from May's point of view, darling. She's worried about Ettie. We look out for our own round here. I thought yer'd have learnt that much about us by now.'

'I have, Flo,' said Ivy, and put her hand gently up to Florrie's wrinkled and grimy face. 'And that's why I've stayed here rather than go back to the farm, I suppose.'

'Good girl,' said Florrie, cuddling her close. 'That's what I like to hear.'

'Murders or not,' Ivy added, with a brave attempt at a smile. 'I'd rather take me chance here in Whitechapel with people who care.'

Chapter 34

Celia handed Ettie a steaming cup of hot milk. 'There, drink that,' she said. 'You must be chilled to the marrow.'

Ettie took the drink gratefully, cradling it in both hands to warm her frozen fingers. 'It's getting better out there now the sun's broken through, but it was a bit parky in the night. Really damp and horrible.'

'Wait, before you drink it.' Celia disappeared into the big, double-doored pantry in the far corner of the kitchen and reappeared with a bottle of brandy. She topped up Ettie's drink with a generous measure of the spirit. 'Now try it.'

Ettie sipped at the warming liquid, then looked up at Celia and smiled. 'This'll put the life back into me.'

'You sit and finish your milk and I'll make us some breakfast,' Celia said, her face glowing with delight. She looked for all the world like a child who had just opened her stocking on Christmas morning.

'I didn't expect you to be able to do all this sort of thing,' said Ettie from her place at the long kitchen table. She watched, fascinated, as Celia managed with ease the various pots, pans and dishes on the big, cast-iron range. 'I'm impressed. I thought you'd have a staff like an army in a house this size.'

Celia looked pleased with the compliment as she glanced over her shoulder at Ettie. 'Well, it's nothing very impressive that I'm preparing, I'm afraid.' She put down the wooden spatula she was using, resting it against the edge of a wide iron skillet in which four mutton chops sputtered and sizzled, then she brushed her still undressed mass of fair curls from her forehead with the back

353

of her hand. 'Just a few chops, some kidneys, and a couple of eggs,' she said, returning her attention to the sizzling pans on the range. 'I'm sure I told you, the servants are away with my father. That's why I'm looking after myself for a few days.'

'I remember, but I suppose I was just a bit surprised that they've all gone and left you,' said Ettie pleasantly, looking round at her surroundings. 'All alone to rattle around in this huge place.'

'But I'm not alone now, Ettie,' Celia said without turning to look at her. 'I have you with me.'

Ettie wiped the plate clean with yet another slice of bread and then pushed it away from her with a contented sigh. 'Well, if you ever have to go out to work you could get a job as a cook anywhere. I'd give you a reference.'

'I'm so pleased you enjoyed it,' said Celia, beaming with pleasure. 'Now, let's go upstairs to the drawing room. I'll light the fire and we can drink our tea in comfort.'

Celia put all the tea things on a silver tray and Ettie followed her up the back staff stairs until they came to a green baize-covered door. Celia pushed it open with her shoulder and led Ettie out into a high-ceilinged, circular hall.

'This is beautiful,' murmured Ettie, trying to take it all in. 'That chandelier, I've never seen anything so...'

'Sparkling?' asked Celia with a happy grin.

Ettie nodded and grinned back at her.

'Come on,' said Celia, 'before I drop this lot. I haven't quite got a butler's skills with a tea-tray yet.'

They walked up the curving, thickly carpeted main stairway to the first floor, where Celia nodded towards one of the doors which opened off the landing. 'That's the one. Can you open it for me?' Ettie stepped forward and turned the huge brass doorknob. Her mouth opened as she took her first glimpse of the room. The whole of the wall opposite seemed to be made from tall, elegantly curtained windows which gave such a clear view of the square below that it was almost as though the wall itself did not exist.

'I've never been in anywhere so bright and so…' Ettie paused, searching for the right word. 'So wonderful,' she added feebly, shrugging her shoulders. 'I don't know how else to describe it.'

'I'm glad you like it,' said Celia, brushing past her and setting the tea-tray down on a rosewood side-table. 'This was my mother's favourite room. All the decoration, the pictures, vases, everything, were planned by her. She used to sit here, surrounded by flowers, and read. She always preferred this room to the library. She loved light and fresh air. Sometimes she'd play the piano for me.' Celia sighed softly, went over to the fire and bent down to light the kindling wood which was quickly blazing. Then she flicked her thick fair hair back over her shoulders, lit a taper from the flames, and put it to the spirit warmer under the silver kettle by the hearth.

'You miss your mother, don't you, Celia?' said Ettie gently.

'Did she tell you that?' she asked in a subdued whisper, her eyes fixed on the hissing blue flame.

Ettie frowned, confused for a moment, before she realised that Celia was referring to her supposed psychic powers. 'No, no,' she said hurriedly. 'I could tell from your face, and from the way you spoke of her. It would be obvious to anyone how you feel.'

Celia nodded. 'I see,' she said, straightening up. 'You pour yourself some tea. I won't be a moment.' She left Ettie alone to marvel at the sumptuous room.

'You ought to see this little lot, Jacob Protsky,' Ettie said out loud to herself as she added milk to her cup.

When Celia returned, she was no longer in her night things, but was wearing an elegant lilac day dress. Her hair was pinned up into a smoothly neat roll.

'Shall I pour you a cup?' asked Ettie, eyeing the shawl which Celia carried in her hand.

'Yes, please, and thank you for this,' Celia answered, handing the shawl to Ettie. 'I can't explain how much that simple gesture – your loaning me this shawl – meant to me.'

'It was cold,' said Ettie. 'Anyone would have done the same.'

'No, Ettie, not anyone. But a friend: that's who'd do such a thing.'

Ettie gave Celia her tea, and they both sat staring into the blazing fire which was roaring away up the chimney.

'Do you have a particular friend, Ettie?'

Ettie turned her cup round and round in its saucer. 'I did, but I'm not sure any more. I haven't really seen her for a while.' She glanced over at Celia. 'How about you?'

'The same as you – perhaps that's why we can be friends. Perhaps it was meant to be.'

They sat and drank their tea in introspective silence, each thinking about friendship and what might have been.

Ettie stood up and refilled Celia's cup. 'Thanks for not asking me why I'm here,' she said, sitting down again.

'There's nothing to thank me for,' said Celia emphatically. 'I invited you and you've come.'

'I was going to my mother's, but when I found myself in the streets close to where she lives I was too scared.' Ettie stared into her cup. 'The streets felt so strange. All those terrible murders.'

'Who can blame you for being scared?' Celia comforted her. 'I'm only glad that my house was close by, so that you could come here when you were frightened.'

She didn't notice Ettie blush at the misunderstanding she was allowing to continue.

'I just wish you'd have woken me, so you needn't have spent such an uncomfortable night.'

'I'm very grateful.'

'Nonsense,' said Celia with a wave of her hand. 'It is I who am grateful, for your company.'

'Those murders,' Ettie said, shaking her head slowly, her gaze fixed on the glowing coals in the grate. 'It's as though the whole of London is, I don't know, trembling. There's a terrible atmosphere. It's as though everyone's asking – who'll be next? Ettie rubbed her hand over her eyes. 'The last time I was in Whitechapel, the local girls were all so upset. They even said they were glad of the bully gangs for once.'

'Bully gangs?'

'The protection gangs who take money from the brides,' said Ettie. 'They beat the girls up if they don't bring in enough…' The moment she realised what she was saying, Ettie stopped speaking, as suddenly as if she had been gagged.

'So you know Whitechapel?' asked Celia, clearly surprised.

Ettie nodded and managed a weak smile. 'Oh yes,' she said. 'I know Whitechapel all right.'

'And the girls who *work* there. You know of them?'

'Yes,' Ettie replied flatly.

Celia beamed with pleasure. 'This is wonderful,' she said, clapping her hands. 'We really have so much in common. I just know that we'll be really good friends.' Celia bowed her head coyly. 'When you said earlier, down in the kitchens, that if I ever needed employment, I could be a cook. Remember?'

'Yes,' said Ettie slowly, not really grasping the point Celia was making.

'Well, actually, I already have work. I work in Whitechapel.' Ettie nodded as though she suddenly understood. 'You're part of the anti-vice league. Of course. I remember that friend of yours, the one who came to Bow with you. Sophia, wasn't it?'

'Sophia, that's right.'

'She told Jacob – the Professor – all about it.'

'Oh,' Celia looked crestfallen.

'What exactly do you do?' asked Ettie encouragingly, glad to be on safer ground.

'I wasn't happy with the way the League worked,' began Celia in a small voice. She paused briefly, then lifted her chin and spoke more confidently. 'I do more practical work. Work where I feel I can be of most use; putting my skills and abilities into practice. They are, of course, nothing compared to your skills,' she added hurriedly. 'But I try to make what difference I can in the miserable world of the slums. And can only hope that my small efforts have some effect.'

Ettie frowned. 'What do you do?'

'I realise that it's difficult for people to understand my work. That's why I usually keep it a secret. But you mustn't be alarmed, it's quite safe, charity work, of a sort. I realise that the main concern of the women I come into contact with is how they will find the price of their next bottle of gin but I do what I can. You have to realise that they have been raised in a different way. I suppose what I mean is that they aren't ladies like us.'

Ettie had to swallow hard before she could speak. 'Shall I make some more tea?'

Celia shook her head. 'Never mind that. I've offended you. I'm so sorry. I shouldn't have brought it up. It's obviously not a pleasant subject to discuss over tea. I thought you knew Whitechapel, that's all.'

Ettie put down her empty cup on the side-table next to her chair and took a deep breath. 'I do know Whitechapel. Very well,' she said, looking steadily into the crackling flames. 'And I might as well tell you; I can't see any point in keeping it from you any longer.' She turned her head to face Celia. 'It's not "ladies like us" you should be talking about, it's "ladies like you".'

'What do you mean?' Celia sounded confused.

'I mean that I'm one of them. I'm a Whitechapel girl born and bred.'

'You? But surely you can't…' Celia's cheeks flushed red as she ran out of words.

Ettie saved Celia from further blushes. 'We had different chances in life, Celia, that's all. You started out with everything going for you; but people like me, we have to make our own luck in life.'

'Oh Ettie, when I spoke about those women, I didn't mean you. You're different.'

'No I'm not, I'm just someone who managed to get out of there.'

'But you *are* different – you have special gifts. They mark you out.'

Ettie bit her lip, too ashamed to disclose any more of her secrets. Abruptly she changed the subject. 'What worries me is that my mother's still stuck there. The life we had there was terrible, Celia, I knew I had to get out and find something better, but my mum, she's just as determined to stay put. But with everything that's happened round there lately, I've got to get her out.'

'I see,' said Celia, unable to hide the bewilderment from her voice.

'She's got a terrible man staying with her. And the Lord only knows who she'll take in next.'

Now Celia was startled. 'Your mother has *lodgers*?'

'You could say that,' said Ettie, laughing feebly. 'They certainly pay her.' She stood up, went over to the hearth, and pointed at the padded log bin. 'Shall I?' she asked.

Celia nodded. 'Please.'

Ettie threw a log into the grate and pushed it down into the fire-basket with the long, ornate brass poker, sending sparks dancing up into the soot-lined chimney. 'I told you I was going to my mother's?' She didn't wait for Celia's reply. 'I was going to make her go away with me. I don't know how, and I don't know where to. Just away. But I lost my courage last night and I came here. But I know I won't be able to rest until I've got her away from that place. It'll be easier now I've had a rest and time to think.'

'Surely you're not planning to go there now,' said Celia, her voice full of concern. 'There's been talk of lynch mobs prowling the streets.'

'It's not them I'm worried about,' said Ettie, sitting on the rug and holding out her hands to catch the warmth of the fire. 'It's him.' She hesitated and, despite the fire, shivered as though she were outside in the cold again. 'Jack the Ripper. That terrible name. It makes him, I don't know, real. Like a real person.'

'It's almost,' said Celia, her voice distant, 'as though everyone wants him to exist.'

'You're right,' said Ettie. 'I know exactly what you mean. It's like when I was a little girl and my mum used to say to me, "Don't yer be a bad gel, Ettie Wilkins, or the bogeyman'll have yer arse for yer". It was a way of keeping me down. Making me do what she wanted.'

Ettie turned round from the fire to look at Celia, catching the look of astonishment on Celia's face at the sound of Ettie speaking in her old cockney twang.

'You've got an important lesson to learn about life, Celia,' she said in the voice with which Celia was more familiar, 'Don't believe all you see. And certainly don't believe all you hear.'

'You think I'm gullible?' she asked.

Ettie shook her head, guilt prevented her from answering the question truthfully. Instead, she said: 'It's easy to believe all sorts of things if you listen to gossip or read the newspapers. They're pointing the finger at everyone: foreigners, Jews, slaughtermen, sailors. Even doctors.'

'My father's a doctor,' said Celia. 'A surgeon. But I suppose you knew that without my having to tell you.'

Keen to keep away from the subject of her supposedly super-natural knowledge, Ettie stood up and went over to the piano by the window. 'Do you play?' she asked lightly, running her fingers over the ivory keys, hoping that Celia's attention would be diverted from the spirits. 'I love music. I used to love to hear my mother singing.'

'I'll sing for you,' said Celia happily and began sorting through the piles of sheet music in the mahogany Canterbury which stood by the piano stool.

'These are some of *my* mother's favourites,' Celia said, setting the first manuscript on the stand before her. 'Listen.'

Ettie sat down in the big armchair by the fire and closed her eyes. She let the hauntingly beautiful series of melodies wash over her and the tones of Celia's clear, high voice block out the fears of the outside world from which she at last felt she had escaped.

When Celia eventually finished playing she looked up from the keys and nodded her thanks as Ettie applauded loudly.

'You're very kind,' Celia said modestly, 'but I'm sure that after so many songs even your enthusiasm must be wearing thin.' She held up her hand to still Ettie's objections. 'I think we should organise something for lunch. I know that all that singing has sharpened *my* appetite.'

Ettie and Celia walked down to the basement kitchen side-by-side as if the friendship between them was the most natural thing in the world. As they prepared and ate their food at the big, scrubbed kitchen table, Celia chattered away happily, telling stories of what sounded to Ettie like a magical childhood.

Long after they had finished their meal, Celia was still reminiscing, and Ettie was still captivated by her tales of ponies and picnics and sun-filled days spent by the river.

It was only when Celia happened to glance up at the narrow window set high in the kitchen wall that her expression grew clouded. 'I can't believe it's that late,' she said with a little shiver. 'The nights really are drawing in; it'll be dark again soon. I hate these gloomy November evenings.' She reached out her hand to Ettie. 'Come on, let's go back up, the fire will need seeing to.'

Upstairs, Celia closed the drawing-room doors behind her, and crossed the room to the big, marble fireplace. She threw a log into the grate, then bent down and lit a taper from the sparks. Peering back over her shoulder at Ettie, she said shame-facedly, 'I really had no idea it was this late, I'm so sorry, I was carried away. The day just disappeared.' Shielding the taper with her hand, she stood up and went round the room lighting the gas-lamps.

When she had finished with the lights, Celia went over to the windows and drew shut the heavy brocade curtains. Then, turning to Ettie she said, 'Really, all I seem to have done all day is sing and chatter away about my childhood. You must think me a terrible hostess.'

'The very opposite,' said Ettie gratefully. 'You've been very kind to me. More than kind, in fact. I was just thinking that I shouldn't take advantage. I won't impose on your generosity any longer.'

Celia frowned. 'It wouldn't be imposing,' she replied urgently. 'Please, won't you stay? You know I'm here all by myself. I'd really appreciate your company.'

'What, you mean I can stay here the night?'

'Of course. We're friends aren't we?'

Ettie smiled. 'I don't know what to say.'

'There's nothing to say,' Celia insisted and settled herself back at the piano. 'Come on now, Ettie, it's your turn. We've got the whole evening ahead of us, so let's hear what sort of a voice *you've* got.'

—

Celia knocked on the bedroom door.

'Coming,' called Ettie and let her in.

Celia had the tip of her tongue between her teeth as she concentrated on carrying the jug of hot water over to the bowl on the washstand without spilling it.

'I'm sorry that I couldn't fathom out the workings of the bathroom boiler,' she said. 'But I hope you can manage with this. And I've sorted out a nightgown for you. Although it might be a bit on the short side.'

'You're very kind, Celia,' said Ettie, sincerely, wishing not for the first time that day that she hadn't ever heard of spirit messages and gulling the public.

'I told you before. Your thanks are totally uncalled for. I'm the one who should be grateful.'

'No. I mean it, Celia. I really do appreciate this.' She went over to the washstand and poured the steaming water from the jug into the brightly painted matching china basin. 'I don't think I'll be staying with the Professor for much longer. This has given me the chance to think about what I'm going to do.'

The expression on Celia's face was almost ecstatic. 'I'll train you to work with me,' she said, breathlessly. 'It would be perfect.' She was so excited that she could barely keep still. 'I've some money coming to me soon. From my mother. Not a great deal, but enough for our needs. We could take rooms in one of the ladies' temperance hotels. It could be the base for our work.'

'You're a very generous person, Celia,' said Ettie calmly, although she felt far from composed at this sudden outburst of enthusiasm for working in the slums. 'But I think I've had enough of Whitechapel. For a while anyway. It's too dangerous for the likes of me.'

'I don't know why. We'd be fine if we were together. I know a lot of the women there, Ettie. The brides. Because of my charity work I can move around quite freely. You'd be safe with me.'

'Celia.' Ettie turned from the washstand and spoke gently to her. 'It's not the brides I'm worried about. I'm a Whitechapel girl, remember; I'm from the same streets as them. I'm like them, they're my friends. And, who knows, if I hadn't got away when I did I might have ended up a bride too.'

She waited for Celia to say something, but she just stood there, her face a pale mask.

'I don't think that the Ripper'd be much fussed about whether I worked the streets or not. As far as that maniac's concerned, I reckon I'd be just as much at risk as any other Whitechapel girl. That's why I've decided to go there and get my mum, no matter what she says. I can't stand the thought of her being in danger another single night. I'll drag her out if I have to. Then we can try to start some sort of a new life together.'

'While you get changed for bed,' Celia said vacantly, 'I'll make us both a warm drink.'

The sound of knocking pounded in Ettie's aching head. She tried to turn over, to bury herself under the deep feather pillows, but she could hardly move.

She heard the sound of the bedroom door opening, but she didn't have the energy to open her eyes.

The voice she heard confused her already befuddled brain. She began to think that she was going off her head: the voice Ettie heard was Celia's.

'Not a very nice day I'm afraid,' she heard her say in a cheerful, easy manner. 'Perhaps it'll brighten up this afternoon.'

There was the sound of something being put on the bedside table next to her.

'This will be the second very late breakfast we've shared.' Celia's voice sounded very happy, and very close.

Ettie heard Celia move away from the bed. She concentrated hard on trying to work out what she was doing next. She heard the heavy swish of the curtains being drawn back and then Celia walking back towards her.

She felt the bed shift slightly as Celia sat down next to her.

'What's going on?' Ettie mumbled. Her mouth felt as though it were stuffed full of rags. She opened her eyes wide enough to focus on Celia. 'Where am I?'

'You stayed the night, don't you remember?' Celia said, smiling down at her.

'I remember,' Ettie said and gave a tiny nod. She immediately wished she hadn't. 'Oh God,' she groaned, 'my head.'

Celia's face crumpled in concern. 'Don't worry, Ettie. You'll soon feel better when you've had some breakfast. I promise.' She reached behind Ettie's head and adjusted the pillows, trying to make her more comfortable. 'I did it for your own good, not to hurt you.'

Ettie's chest was rising and falling as though she had been running for her life.

'I put a sleeping draught in the warm drink I fetched you last night.'

'Who d'you think you are?' Ettie yelled, not caring about the pain that seared through her head. 'What gives you the right to do this to me?'

Celia looked imploringly at Ettie. 'I was afraid you'd run off. Go out into the night to your mother. You said you couldn't bear the thought of her being in Whitechapel another night...' Now Celia was crying. 'I wanted you to stay here with me. Maybe it was the wrong thing to do. But I was frightened for you.'

Ettie pulled herself upright and swung her legs out of the bed. She tried to stand but her head was swimming. She fell back on to the pillows and massaged her aching temples.

'I'm sorry.'

'Sorry? Is that all you've got to say? I've run away from one prison and here I am in another.'

'Ettie…'

'Why doesn't everyone leave me alone?' wailed Ettie, the effort of speaking exhausting her, but she was too angry to stop. 'You offered me help, a refuge. Then you did *this* to me.'

Celia turned away from her and, taking the newspaper from the breakfast tray, said softly, 'Ettie, I promise you, I only did it because I wanted you to be safe. And it really was for your own good. Look.' She held the paper so that Ettie could see the headlines. 'Another bride was murdered last night.'

–

The sergeant took his notebook from the breast pocket of his tunic and began to read with a glazed expression: 'Mary Jane Kelly, otherwise known as Marie Jeanette, aged twenty-five years. Found on Friday 9 November. Thirteen Miller's Court, Dorset Street, Spitalfields.' He paused, seeing in his mind's eye how the young constable had slipped on the blood and gore as they'd gone into that vile room. 'Found on bed, almost naked – what there was left of her…'

He carried on reading, reciting the litany of mutilations which, had he not seen them for himself, he would never have believed a human being capable of.

When Sergeant Miller had finished, he put away his notebook and said, 'Her living in Miller's Court, I know it sounds stupid, but that made it worse somehow. And Number Thirteen. Unlucky for her, eh?'

Inspector Grainger nodded and lit a fresh cigarette from the butt of the one he had just finished smoking. 'Yes, sergeant, unlucky. Now, this bloke who identified Kelly – Joseph Barnett – how sure can we be he was right?'

'He knew her well enough. He'd lived with her for almost a year,' said the sergeant, his professional tone recovered. 'If they hadn't had a row, he'd still have been with her.'

'A row?'

'Don't read too much into it, sir. I've seen the state the man's in. But what interested me was when he said he'd been to see her recently, to try and patch things up. I think he was really fond of her, you know.'

'Get on with it, Miller.'

'Yes, sir.' The sergeant straightened his back. 'This might sound daft, but he said that there was a strange woman in the room. Someone he'd never seen before. And you know what it's like in the East End: everyone knows everyone else. Some of 'em even mind everyone else's business for 'em.'

'That can be very useful for us, sergeant,' said the inspector. 'Right, and talking of which, sir, I think there's something might interest you. The officer on desk duty yesterday said he'd had a complaint from one of Protsky's neighbours. Apparently, the night before last, there was an almighty row coming from his rooms, and it wasn't the first. But they said this one was different. They heard a girl's voice, and she wasn't just shouting, she sounded distressed.'

Grainger rubbed his hand over his chin. 'What do you think?'

'Well, they said the young woman who lives with him, Ettie Wilkins, she hasn't been seen since then. And she's a good-looking young thing; striking, if you know what I mean: not the sort to be ignored if she *was* around.'

'Let's have the "Professor" in for another little chat, eh sergeant?'

'Yes, sir.'

'Now, getting back to this woman Barnett said was in Kelly's room. What do we know about her?'

'Well, according to Barnett, she was a bit of a mystery. Nicely dressed, he said. Definitely not like a local woman.'

'Did she say anything to him?'

'No, but he reckoned that she looked very comfortable in the room. Familiar, like. And, there was something else.' The sergeant looked pensive, remembering what Barnett had told him. 'He said that before Mary Kelly said anything, anything at all, she kind of looked at this woman, as if she was checking what she should say. Like this woman had some sort of hold over her. Well, that's what he reckoned.'

'Do you think she was a customer?' asked the inspector, tapping the ash from his cigarette.

'Eh?'

'Do you think she was wearing "queer drawers", as they say round there? From these reports,' Inspector Grainger leafed through a sheaf of papers, 'I see they called her French Marie. Had all sorts of ways to please a customer.'

'I never thought of that, I'm sure, sir,' said the sergeant blushing. 'I just thought maybe…?'

'Yes, sergeant?'

'I just thought, could "Jack" be a woman, sir?'

–

The sight of the uniformed sergeant entering Tyvern Court was nothing surprising to any of its inhabitants, but the appearance of the well-dressed inspector accompanying him soon had most of the court engaged in speculating about what could be going on.

'Keep away from the walls of the buildings, sir,' advised the sergeant, looking cautiously around them.

'Why's that, Miller? Infection?'

'Er… no, sir,' said the sergeant, not quite knowing how to put his point. 'You see, they're not very keen on the police force round these parts, and they're liable to empty their piss-pots – begging your pardon, sir – out of the windows and on to your head.'

'Thank you, Miller,' said the inspector, and joined the sergeant in scanning the upstairs windows for potential missiles.

'Here we are, sir.'

As soon as Ruby saw them go into Number Twelve and start climbing the stairs, she rushed hell-for-leather over to Myrtle Bury's.

'Myrt!' she bellowed along the passage. 'Quick. The law's over at Sarah's!'

Inside Number Twelve, the inspector was trying to get his breath: he had never smelt anything so putrid in all his life.

'For God sake open that window, sergeant,' he gasped through his handkerchief.

While the sergeant struggled with the years of filth and grime cementing the sash cords to the window-frame, the inspector remained near the door – the only source of relatively fresh air. He directed his attention to what he presumed was Mrs Wilkins, although it looked for all the world like a bundle of rags thrown on to the stinking mattress which lay in the corner.

But before he could ask her anything, she started making terrible animal-like noises that came out in wheezing, rasping. It was a moment or two before he realised she was laughing.

'It's that lodger, ain't it?' she hissed. 'He's been put away. I never thought I'd say it, but bloody good job and all.'

'No,' said the inspector, glancing over with a puzzled frown to the sergeant. 'It's not about your lodger.'

'I know who she means,' the sergeant puffed as he battled hopelessly with the window.

'So if it's not him…' Sarah did her best to drag herself into a sitting position. 'What are you two doing here?' Her voice rose with alarm at the possibilities.

'Is your daughter Ettie staying here with you, Mrs Wilkins?'

Sarah's hand flew to her mouth and she began wailing like a banshee.

The inspector held his hand to his ears: he'd have preferred the wild animal noises.

'My Ettie!' she shrieked. 'What d'yer want with my little girl?'

'Ettie? What's the matter with Ettie?' The voice came from behind the inspector, who turned round to see a tall, red-headed man of about twenty standing there, almost filling the doorframe. Behind him was a stout middle-aged woman with faded auburn hair that had probably once been as bright as the hair of the man whom the inspector rightly presumed to be her son.

'Yeah. What d'yer want with her?' asked Myrtle, made bold by the safety of standing behind her son.

'It's all right, Mum,' said Billy over his shoulder. 'I'll sort this out. You go outside and wait with Ruby.'

'That all right with you, Sarah?' said Myrtle, peering round her son into the gloom. Much as she wanted to help, and to know what was going on, she was glad to get out away from the stench.

Sarah didn't answer her, she just continued with her wailing. 'Aw no, my little Ettie. I know what's happened, she's been done in by the Old Boy. It was my little Ettie the paper-boy was hollering about, wasn't it?'

'What!' Billy exploded into the room.

The inspector, preferring to brave the stink than to stand in Billy's way, leapt back to where the sergeant was standing.

'Shit!' hollered the sergeant, making the inspector jump again.

This time he barely missed landing on Sarah. The thought made him gag.

'My sodding hand,' cursed the sergeant, waving his arm about in pain. In his efforts to raise the sash, he'd smashed right through the only pane of glass that wasn't patched with layers of paper and old rags, but he wasn't offered any sympathy.

'Will you tell me what's going on?' Billy hissed menacingly. 'Or have I gotta lose me temper?'

'Mrs Wilkins,' said the inspector, carefully keeping an eye on the big red-haired man. 'It wasn't your daughter who was killed the night before last. It was Mary Kelly.'

'Mary Kelly?' Her wails subsided into pathetic snuffles.

'Marie Jeanette, you might know her as,' said the sergeant, and sucked his teeth as he examined his cut fingers in the gloomy light.

'Aw no,' sniffed Sarah.

The inspector thought that she was threatening to start her wailing again, but she was calmer now.

'The French gel. Pretty little thing she'd been in her time. I don't know,' she said with a loud sigh. 'When will it all stop, eh?'

With her fragile alcoholic's memory, Sarah had forgotten her concern for her daughter and was now becoming philosophical. It was almost more than the inspector could take.

'You know the victim?' he asked bluntly, and nodded for the injured sergeant – who knew better than to argue with his governor – to take notes.

'Yeah. I knew her,' said Sarah, with what might have been a giggle. 'That one shared more than a pipe with some of them girls she used to hang around with down the Chimney Sweep.'

'What do you mean?'

'Lived with a fellah, didn't she? But he was always buggering off to his sister's place. So she found herself some other, more reliable company instead.'

'Who was that then, Mrs Wilkins?' The inspector, sensing he was getting close, ignored his repulsion and bent forward, getting nearer to her, encouraging her to speak.

'You're a new boy round here, ain't yer?' she said patronisingly. 'She wore queer drawers, yer stupid bastard.'

'Thank you, Mrs Wilkins,' said the inspector, raising his eyebrows at the sergeant. 'That's a great help.'

'Aw, just let me know if you need any more information,' said Sarah sarcastically. 'Pop in any time. I'll make sure I've got a drop of something in for yer. Now yer can all piss off out of it. I wanna have a little rest.'

The sergeant stood back, waiting for the inspector to leave first.

'And yer'll do something about that sodding window yer broke and all,' Sarah croaked, as she pulled the filthy covers up over her skinny shoulders. 'Dirty bastard coppers.'

Billy stepped forward, positioned himself by the doorway and stared while the two police officers filed out of the room.

'And you, son,' the sergeant said, 'had better watch yerself, or we'll have to find something to drag that Alfie of yours in for again, won't we? And that young Tommy of yours. Following in his big brother's footsteps, so I've heard from the local beat constable.' The sergeant pointed down the stairs and said to Billy. 'Now, let's leave the lady in peace, shall we, and go outside and have a little chat?'

Billy followed the now intrigued inspector down the wooden stairway and out into the court, where Myrtle, Ruby and the other women stood waiting, surrounded by their various broods of snotty-nosed, ragged children.

The inspector watched silently as the big red-haired man spoke to the sergeant.

Billy lifted his chin and stared down at the uniformed officer. 'So what was you talking to Sarah about Mary Kelly for?'

'That's not why we came here. We came because we've been having discussions, you might say, down at the station with the man Sarah's girl's got herself hiked up with.'

'Ettie?' Billy suddenly didn't look so cocky.

'Yeah, that's right, Bury; but you know what it's like trying to get sense out of Sarah: might as well...'

'Ne'mind Sarah,' Billy interrupted. 'Why've yer taken Protsky in?'

'We've been talking to him about the murders, son,' the sergeant said, gauging Billy's reaction to the information. He didn't need to be an expert to see how he felt.

'Protsky!' Billy's face flared scarlet with rage. 'I never trusted that bastard.' He gripped his hands into tight fists. 'I *told* her he was no good. I *told* her. I should have made her come back.'

'When was Ettie round here last?' the sergeant asked, flashing a look back to the inspector.

'The night when Polly Nichols copped it, she was here then.' Billy's voice was so quiet, the sergeant had to strain to hear him. 'And then about a week later, I think it was, she turned up in the Frying Pan with Sarah. She asked about me, Patrick said, but I missed her. I was still at work, see…' Billy's voice trailed away as he stared blankly into the distance.

'Billy?' Myrtle pushed past the inspector and stood between her son and Sergeant Miller. 'I ain't standing back no more. Tell me, what's going on here?'

It was as though his mother's voice woke him from a dream. 'That geezer Ettie went off with, Mum,' said Billy, rubbing his hands over his pale, horrified face. 'They've only got him down the nick. About the murders.'

'Jesus!' Myrtle ran with surprising speed for a woman of her size and was up the stairs of Number Twelve before anyone could stop her.

'Go and sort her out, Ruby, for gawd's sake,' said the sergeant wearily, scratching his head so that his helmet wobbled from side to side. 'Sarah don't know yet that we're even worried about the girl.'

Ruby bobbed her head in agreement and made to follow Myrtle. But it was too late – Sarah's screams could be heard loud and clear from the room above.

'Sod me,' groaned the sergeant, and turned to his boss for orders.

With a look of surrender on his face, the inspector shook his head at the sergeant. 'Don't ask me, Miller,' he said. 'You're the one whose patch this is.'

Chapter 35

'Is this yours?' the inspector asked Jacob as he walked over to the filing cabinet.

'Is what mine?' lisped Jacob through cut and swollen lips.

'This.' Inspector Grainger picked up a brown paper parcel from on top of the cabinet and carried it back to his desk. Remaining standing, he unfolded the packet and took out a black cloak which he shook out in front of him.

'No,' said Protsky abruptly.

'How can you be so sure?'

'I was wearing mine, wasn't I?' he replied scornfully. 'When you dragged me in again at some God-forsaken time this morning.'

'What,' chimed in the sergeant, 'a fine gentleman like yourself with, if you don't mind me saying, a bit of the dandy about you, and only one cloak?'

'Where is she, Protsky?' demanded the inspector, stepping round the desk to Jacob. 'You might as well tell us.'

'I told you, she's gone to her mother's.' He said the words slowly, deliberately, through gritted teeth. 'Now, can I go home, or are you going to keep me here for another pointless round of questions?'

'You should be grateful we've brought you in this time, Protsky, as much for your own protection as anything else.' Grainger sat himself down at his desk.

'My own protection?' Jacob sneered, gingerly touching his wounded mouth with his fingertips. 'I'd be safer down the docks at closing time.'

'Are you suggesting that these injuries happened whilst you've been at the station, sir?' The sergeant smiled derisively.

'Ask those young constables of yours,' snapped Jacob, wincing at the pain of opening his mouth too widely.

'Do you wish to bring a complaint against one of the officers?' asked the sergeant coldly.

'What do you think?' answered Jacob cynically.

'Very similar names, aren't they?' the inspector said, lighting, as had become his habit, a cigarette from the butt of the one he had just finished. 'Jacob. Jack.' He inhaled deeply on the fresh cigarette while he ground the other out in the already overflowing ashtray. 'Do you know anything about sending letters from hell, Professor Protsky?'

Jacob let out a strangled laugh. 'What?'

'Or how about the "Old Boss"? Does that mean anything to you?'

'Foreigner, aren't you?' said the sergeant.

'I'm as English as you are.'

'I'm Irish,' said the sergeant raising his eyebrows.

'Exactly,' said Jacob.

'Just what sort of a name is Protsky?' snapped the sergeant less evenly.

Jacob shook his head contemptuously.

'We were in Whitechapel earlier this afternoon, Protsky. Mind you, you probably knew that, what with your special powers.' Grainger stared at him through the cigarette smoke. 'There's a lot of talk going round about you and Miss Wilkins. All sorts of gossip. Shame we can't get her side of it. You see, she still hasn't been traced.'

Jacob swallowed hard and shifted uncomfortably in the hard, upright chair.

'We have a new method of detection, you know, Professor. One that I'm quite keen to try out if we can find the right person to do it for us.' The inspector spoke slowly, easily. 'Perhaps you have heard of the procedure, an educated man like yourself. A photographic image of the killer is taken from the retina – the eye – of the dead woman.' He took a long drag on his cigarette.

'Remarkable isn't it, science?'

'It sounds more like trickery to me,' sneered Jacob.

'And you'd know all about that, Protsky, wouldn't you?' replied the inspector scornfully.

Chapter 36

'Ettie?'

Ettie opened her eyes slowly.

'Thank goodness you're awake.' Celia's concerned frown softened into a relieved smile. 'I thought you were going to sleep forever. You went back to sleep yesterday morning and you've been out cold ever since.'

Now it was Ettie who was frowning. 'Out cold? What day is it? What time?'

'It's Sunday morning.' She dipped her head apologetically. 'Yes, I know, I'm sorry, I misjudged the dosage of the drug.'

Ettie levered herself up on her elbow. 'I don't believe you. You drug me, keep me here against my will, and now you're smiling.'

'Would you like some breakfast?' Celia asked briskly, getting up and fiddling with a food-laden tray which stood on the bedside table.

'No,' Ettie said bluntly, shaking her head. She wished she hadn't moved, her brain still felt as if it were rattling loose inside her skull. She lowered herself gently back on to the pillows.

'I don't know why you're so upset,' said Celia, in a small, hurt voice. 'I explained why I had to do it. It really was for the best.'

'What do you know about what's for the best for the likes of me?' As Ettie again pulled herself up in the bed, the pain pulsed through her head. Her throat was so dry. 'You're all the same,' she croaked. 'You go into the slums, you wallow in all the horror you see, but it's not real for you, is it? You've got all the refinements and comforts of your oh-so-civilised life to run home to.'

'That isn't true, Ettie.' Celia sat down on the edge of the bed.

'Isn't it? What makes you so different from any of the others?'

'The work I do. It's important. I can make a difference. There are more than enough mouths to feed in those terrible places as it is. So that a few less is a genuine blessing.'

Ettie frowned. She tried to blink away the thickness in her head, she could hardly think straight, couldn't make out what Celia meant.

'The work I do is valuable, Ettie,' Celia added with a very dignified tilt of her chin.

'How noble,' said Ettie, her bitterness not dulled by the drug. 'After your night's slumming you go home to a roof over your head and a decent meal. The likes of you don't have to worry about being beaten up or raped.'

'Don't I?'

Celia's sharpness startled Ettie.

'I have a roof, certainly. And all the food I can eat. But I also know fear, Ettie.'

'I'm sure.'

'If anything, it's harder for someone like me. Lower-class women are naturally more... Well, sensual.'

'What?'

'That's why so many of them choose to become unfortunates.'

'Whores, you mean?'

'If you insist.' Celia poured a cup of tea and handed it to Ettie, whose resolve to refuse anything Celia offered crumbled before her terrible thirst.

'I don't know why you, or the other Whitechapel girls, are so unkind to me. Why you aren't more grateful.'

Ettie nearly choked on the tea. 'Look, Celia, you reckon you know about the brides' way of life. Well, let me tell you, you know nothing. If they could choose, don't you think that all the Whitechapel girls would choose a decent place to sleep? Have warm clothes without bugs to wear? Enough money for the rent without going out whoring? Hot food in their bellies?' Ettie slammed the empty cup on to the tray. 'And, you believe me, dirt, starvation, dying kids and drunks hardly make you feel "sensual", as you put it so nicely. Having a bit of the other is the last thing on their minds. The girls are earning a crust, not having a lark.'

'I understand all that, but…' Celia objected weakly.

'Oh yeah, it's easy enough to "understand" when you've got food in your belly. But you imagine *living* like that, having to either watch *your* kid waste away cos you haven't got the half-penny for the soup kitchen or going with someone for a couple of bob. Which would you choose, eh?'

'But I don't have a child.'

'No, course not,' said Ettie caustically, and stared pointedly at Celia's stomach. 'Little miss perfect virgin, aren't you?'

'No,' said Celia bowing her head. 'I'm no virgin, Ettie. Children are always warned to be wary of certain men who might bother us, but…'

'No one warned me,' Ettie interrupted her harshly. 'My mother used to encourage men to *bother* me. It meant they left her alone. The men who were living in our house – that's the ones who bothered me.'

'Do you know,' said Celia, her words blurred by tears. 'We could almost swap our lives, our families and their bullying men.'

'Bullying men? Don't make me laugh.'

'And,' snapped Celia, turning away to busy herself with refilling the tea-cups, 'don't mock me, Ettie.'

Again Ettie was surprised by the harshness of Celia's tone. She looked at the pretty fair-haired young woman bending over the silver tray, and tried to understand her. She had the cheek to complain about Ettie's attitude towards her, when it was Ettie who should be shouting the house down about being drugged, of all things. And, puzzled Ettie, it was odd that she no longer showed *any* remorse about it at all. The only explanation Ettie could come up with was that Celia was ill in some way – she had already said to Jacob, maybe not entirely seriously, that she thought that the strain was telling on the girl's sanity. Perhaps she'd been right, and she should be sympathetic, not angry, and humour her. She had to remember that Celia was, after all, capable of drugging her. So what else might she do?

'I'm sorry,' said Ettie softly.

'And I'm serious,' Celia replied firmly, handing Ettie her fresh cup. 'Are our lives so very different? I'm not talking about things I have, about comfort. I mean the way we're treated, the way we're abused. How we've suffered.'

'Aw, Celia, do me a favour.' Ettie resolved to try and curb her impatience. She gulped the tea down and put her empty cup back on the tray, then she swung her legs out from under the covers and sat on the side of the bed. She patted the cover next to her for Celia to sit down.

'Look,' she went on. 'I know you're in trouble, Celia, but there's things can be done about that. Just don't get it out of proportion, that's all. It's not that bad, honestly.'

'Oh no?'

'No, it's not. Take my life. My youngest brother was burnt to death when I was six years old.' She held up her hand. 'Let me finish. Please. Mum left me looking after him while she went down the pub, looking for customers, to earn a few shillings to keep body and soul together. My brother and I were starving. It was so freezing cold and we hadn't had anything to eat for nearly two days. I hated to hear him crying, it was pitiful, so I went out scavenging on the streets to see what I could find – rotten fruit and vegetables from under the market stalls, that sort of thing. Maybe even some stale bread if I was lucky.' Ettie hesitated. 'When I came back the room was burnt out. I blame myself still. It was the perishing cold night you see. I'd broken up the old chair we had and made up the fire with it to keep the poor little bugger warm.'

'That's terrible,' murmured Celia, the tears flowing down her cheeks.

'But not unusual enough where I come from to cause much of a business.'

'Was there no one else there? No one who could have saved him?'

'There was my older brother. He used to help out, but that was before he was sent for disposal.'

'Disposal?' The very sound of the word was horrific to Celia.

'To Canada. Group emigration they called it. He looked strong, he was even taller than me. Capable of working hard for his new so-called family where they sent him. Mum wasn't stupid, she knew they were sending all the kids out there to be servants – slaves, more like. But what choices did she have? Great big hulk like him to feed?' Ettie took hold of the side-table to steady herself and wobbled to her feet. 'Mum did the best she could.'

With a great deal of effort, Ettie made her way slowly over to the washstand, splashed water over her face, and then looked over her shoulder at Celia who was still sitting on the side of the bed. 'Now, they're the sort of problems that can't be solved. The ones that cause real suffering.'

Celia stood up and hesitantly crossed the room to stand beside her. She paused, reached out to Ettie but, before she actually touched her, she drew back her hand. 'I'm sorry,' she whispered. 'I had no idea.'

Ettie shrugged. 'Well, it's not something I find very easy to talk about – to anyone.' She stared into the washbasin. 'I don't know why I even mentioned it to you.'

'Oh, but I'm so glad you did, Ettie,' Celia reassured her. 'Friends shouldn't have secrets from one another.' She nodded to herself then, with her voice reduced to a croaking whisper, she said: 'There's something that I find it difficult to speak about.' She paused again. 'When your mother was...' She swallowed hard. 'You know, on the streets. Was she scared of disease? Diseases like syphilis?'

'Not only when she was on the streets,' said Ettie. She didn't turn to face Celia, but busied herself with rubbing her face dry on the towel that she took from the peg on the washstand. There were mum's lodgers for her to worry about as well. They worried me too. Most of them didn't look too healthy, I can tell you. But, like all the other women and girls from round there, worrying about disease wasn't that high on the list. What with hoping they wouldn't get bashed up by someone who didn't feel like paying, not having the money for the rent, having another baby they didn't want and couldn't feed…' She laughed ironically. 'No, disease wasn't such a worry, I don't suppose.'

'It can cause insanity, you know?' breathed Celia. 'Syphilis.'

'Yes,' said Ettie cautiously, as she returned the towel to its hook. 'I know.'

For a moment neither of them spoke, then Celia began more brightly, 'Ettie, I realise that the authorities can't help the women…'

'You're not wrong there,' Ettie chipped in with a smile, then, looking round the big, richly decorated room, she said with sudden urgency, 'What have you done with my clothes, Celia?'

Celia went to the big, double-fronted wardrobe, took out Ettie's things and laid them lovingly on the bed.

Relieved, Ettie pulled the nightgown off over her head and began dressing. 'You're definitely right about the authorities being no help,' she said, poking her head through her underslip. 'They're all the same: not one of them'd give the brides the drippings off their nose – if they were honest.'

'You're wrong, Ettie,' said Celia, handing her her overthings. 'What I'm doing *does* help. I really *am* doing some good.'

'Oh yeah?' said Ettie, stepping into the skirt.

'I'd like to share a confidence with you,' Celia said quietly. 'More of a confession really.'

Ettie didn't say anything, she just went and stood in front of the cheval glass and started buttoning her bodice.

'I know you're cross with me about the drug, Ettie, but I hope you're still my friend.'

'Friend or not,' said Ettie, looking at her in the glass. 'I already know your little secret.'

Celia's mouth fell open.

'Look,' said Ettie turning round from the mirror to face her. 'I'm lucky, it's never happened to me, the life I've been forced to lead at times. But you, with your old man a doctor and everything, I don't know how you got yourself pregnant.'

Celia laughed with relief. 'You think I'm having a child?'

'You mean you're not?' Ettie's mind raced. This would well and truly expose her as a sham, then who knew what Celia might do if she really was insane.

'You must have misunderstood the spirit messages,' said Celia happily.

'Yeah. I must have,' said Ettie, hurriedly twisting back to the glass so that her expression wouldn't give her away.

Celia began pacing the room as she spoke. 'Everyone is talking about "Jack", the murderer, as a man,' she said, forming the words with difficulty. 'What would people do, Ettie, do you suppose, if they realised that the female of the species – girls, just like you and me – were capable of murder?'

Ettie gulped for air, she felt dizzy, but it wasn't from the aftereffects of the drug.

'What if it was revealed,' Celia went on, her tears flowing again, 'that we could kill? Those who find such thrills in reading the details in those scandal sheets, they don't understand, they think that killing is free of pain. They see the ghastly illustrations and haunt the streets in their wicked desire to get near the scenes of the crimes. They have no idea what murder really involves. But I do, Ettie. Yes, me. I'm talking about me. I have committed the greatest of all sins. I have taken life.' Celia threw herself on to the bed, her shoulders heaving with great racking sobs as she cried as though she would never stop.

Ettie stared at Celia's reflection in the glass, watching her as she lay across the bed, wailing like a wounded animal. She had been so angry with Celia for keeping her captive that she had felt like slapping her pretty face for her, and now she knew that if she had even tried such a thing she might now be lying dead. Ettie couldn't take it all in. Celia was a monster. A maniac who had brutally murdered the Lord alone knew how many women. A monster who could kill. She had to get away. She ran to the door and grabbed the handle.

Celia's imploring words came from behind her. 'Don't you understand, Ettie? When I saw that world in which they had to live, I thought it really was better that life be denied them.'

Ettie spun round to face her, ready to protect herself from attack. But, in that moment, she saw not a monster but a wretched creature begging for help. She had been right all along, the pathetic young woman was all-too-clearly insane. She had to help her, not hate or fear her. Taking a deep breath, Ettie stepped towards the bed, struggling to bury her concern for her safety beneath compassion.

'Celia,' she said softly, taking her arm and helping her to her feet. 'I'm your friend, aren't I?'

Celia nodded, looking for all the world like a lost child who someone had promised to reunite with its mother.

'Good,' said Ettie, hoping that Celia wouldn't notice her quavering voice and trembling hands. 'Now, listen to me. We're going to the police station and you're going to tell them all about it.'

A look of panic crossed Celia's tearstained face as she tried to pull away from Ettie.

'It's okay, they'll understand. I'll tell them it's not your fault, Celia. I'll tell them that you're ill.'

'Oh Ettie,' she said. 'You really do understand everything.' Then, smiling with relief, she sat back down on the bed and began to talk.

Ettie sat on a straight-backed chair close to the door and listened in appalled silence as Celia told stories of her relationship with her father that were horrifyingly at odds with the sun-filled memories she had taken such pleasure in before.

Chapter 37

'Are you ready yet?' Ettie asked from the hallway outside the bathroom. Her voice was cajoling, gentle. 'Have you washed your face?' She pushed open the bathroom door and stepped inside.

Celia looked exhausted. She had talked all the previous day and most of the evening, eventually crying herself to sleep. Now it was Monday morning and she was standing there, staring into the looking-glass over the washbasin. Her eyes were fixed vacantly on the reflection of herself, a pretty, if red-eyed, fairhaired girl, with the image of Ettie, a darkly beautiful young woman, standing behind her.

'Come on,' Ettie coaxed her, reaching out to take her arm, but she gasped and started back when she saw that, in her hand, Celia gripped her father's cut-throat razor.

'He had syphilis, you know, my father,' she said flatly, her face as expressionless as her voice. 'Probably still does. There isn't really a satisfactory cure, you see. I've read all the books, hoping that I might find one.' She paused. 'I was afraid, you see, afraid that I too was losing my reason.' Celia smiled vacantly. 'He was kind once – my father – before the madness took him over: I used to think he was the kindest man in the world. Did I tell you about that?' She frowned, not quite remembering whether she had spoken to Ettie about her father.

Ettie tried to smile. 'Yes,' she said softly, 'you told me all about your father last night.'

Celia continued as though Ettie hadn't uttered a word. 'My mother had a little boy after she had me. I was only given a glimpse or two of him. He was kept with mother while I was banished to the nursery, but I can remember him so clearly. He was a pathetic little thing, like a wizened old man. He died, of course. And my mother died soon afterwards.'

She brushed a loose, blond curl away from her face and, as she moved her hand over her hair, the cut-throat blade of the razor caught the rays of the late morning light which slanted in through the window set high in the bathroom wall.

'I think she knew, you see, that she carried the disease and had passed it on to the baby. She didn't want to spiral down into madness and become cruel like my father. I'm sure that's why she killed herself. She wouldn't have left me otherwise, would she? Maybe it was for the best. I would have hated to have seen her suffer. I loved her so much.'

Ettie touched Celia gently on the shoulder.

Celia didn't respond she just continued speaking, her face a blank, impenetrable mask. 'I often remember, when I was awake at night, how things used to be, how happy we all once were. And how things might still have been.'

'Celia, please, give that to me.'

Celia looked into the mirror at Ettie's reflection. It was as though she were seeing Ettie for the first time since she had begun speaking, as though she had been addressing herself all along. She looked down at the razor. Then half turned and handed it to Ettie. She bowed her head and tears started to flow uncontrollably down her cheeks.

'It's all right, Celia, I'm here.' Ettie cradled Celia in her arms and let her cry.

Then she said in a soothing, tender voice like a mother encouraging a distressed and reluctant child: 'Come on now, Celia, we'll have to be going.'

-

'I would like to speak to someone about what has been happening in Whitechapel.' Ettie leaned close to the waist-high counter, speaking to the young constable in hushed tones so that Celia would not hear her words.

'One moment, miss,' said the constable, and disappeared through a door behind him into the duty-sergeant's office.

'There's another one out there, sarge,' said the constable, jerking his head towards the door. 'One of them posh tarts. Reckons she wants to talk about *Jack the Ripper*!' He pulled a face of mock horror as he said the name.

The sergeant shook his head. 'Haven't they got anything better to do with their time? I can't see what sort of a thrill they get from it, I really can't. Send her down the East End to Miller. Let him sort her out.'

'Righto, sarge.'

No matter how strongly Ettie objected, nor how persistently she demanded to be seen by the young man's superior, the constable merely smiled – pleasantly enough – while he instructed Ettie how to get to Whitechapel. He wasn't silly; he was experienced enough to know not to be too difficult with ladies like her: they could be related to all sorts of important people who would kick up a fuss at the merest hint of rudeness.

As he gave Ettie the quite unnecessary directions to the East End, she drummed her fingers impatiently on the counter. Then, when he had finished, she put her arm round Celia's shoulders and guided her towards the big front doors which opened on to the street.

The constable called after them in a friendly, helpful voice, 'Don't forget, it's Sergeant Miller you want.'

Then, when the doors had closed behind them, he added cheerfully, 'And bloody good luck to him, and all.'

–

Ettie went back to the bench where Celia sat waiting quietly.

'They're finding someone to talk to us,' Ettie said to her, but Celia didn't seem to register her words. She looked as though she were in a waking dream, her eyes open but focused on nothing.

Ettie took Celia's hand gently in hers, ignoring the duty-constable who was looking them over admiringly.

'You wanted to see me?' Sergeant Miller lifted the wooden flap and stepped from behind the counter.

'Sergeant Miller?' asked Ettie hesitantly in her acquired accent. She'd been out of the East End for a while, but the old apprehension about talking to the law was still there. The fact that she was a 'lady' still didn't help her confidence much.

'That's me, miss,' said the sergeant in an even, neutral tone. 'What can I do for you?'

Ettie turned to Celia. 'I won't be long. You wait here.'

Celia nodded wordlessly.

Ettie looked at her anxiously. 'You will be all right?'

She nodded again.

'Would you mind if we spoke privately?' Ettie asked the sergeant.

The sergeant led Ettie to the corner of the room.

'This *has* to be discussed in confidence,' she insisted.

'I'm a very busy man, I'm afraid, miss...' Miller began.

'But you don't understand,' Ettie interrupted. 'No, please, don't walk away, I'm not being intentionally rude.'

She moved closer to the sergeant, making him feel most uncomfortable. He backed off warily, he was never sure what young ladies might do nowadays.

'Sergeant Miller,' Ettie said determinedly through her teeth. 'You must listen to me. That young woman, over there. Celia Tressing. Is...' She bit her lip as she fought back the tears which threatened to roll down her cheeks. 'That young woman is Jack the Ripper.'

The sergeant whispered something hurriedly to the constable and then said to Ettie, 'You go with the officer here. I'll be with you shortly.'

The constable took Ettie and Celia into a small, shabby room, bare except for two chairs and a rickety, unpolished table. He closed the door and stood by it, as though he were posted on guard duty, which in fact he had been, by Sergeant Miller.

In his spacious office, the inspector paced back and forth, wearing a track in the deep pile of the rug which stood in front of his broad partner's desk. Each time he went in there, the sergeant was still amazed at the transformation the inspector had worked on the room. Police officers in his day had never bothered about rugs and fancy desks. But it was a modern world, and he supposed he would have to get used to it.

But there were some things the sergeant would never be able to get used to, and one of them was how the inspector could even begin to think that a young lady like Miss Tressing could have anything to do with the murders. He had to admit that he had been the one to bring up the idea of the killer being a woman in the first place, but he hadn't meant someone like Miss Tressing: that was just ridiculous.

'It would be more understandable if it was her father, sir,' said Miller. 'I understand several of his colleagues have been implicated in that buying bodies for experiments business.'

The inspector didn't answer, he just kept pacing.

'That could make someone an obvious suspect,' Miller went on, trying in his own way to make sense of these ridiculous developments. 'Perhaps getting fed up with paying, he organises his own supply. Who knows, maybe the girl found out, and now she's covering up for her old man.'

Again no response. The inspector was too busy thinking about whether it really was such an illogical idea that it could be a woman who committed the crimes? Being very keen on logic, the inspector liked to spend time working through his ideas.

'Why shouldn't it be her?' he said at last.

That certainly wasn't what the sergeant had wanted to hear. 'How *could* it be her?' Miller protested. 'It's got to be some sort of beast. A monster. Some creature who can't get, well, pleasure, if you take my meaning, from a woman in the normal way.' The sergeant was trying desperately to create some sort of order out of his confusion. 'Or a secretive maniac,' he said. 'Someone who nobody would ever suspect.'

'Like a Jekyll and Hyde?' asked the inspector, pausing just long enough to look inquiringly at the sergeant.

'Jekyll and who?' As soon as the words had left his lips, the sergeant wished he hadn't asked; the inspector either said very little or went into a full-scale lecture full of fancy ideas that he could neither follow, nor much wished to. This might well turn out to be one of the long answers.

'The play in the West End that everyone's talking about.'

Abruptly, the inspector stopped pacing and sat at his desk. He flicked through a sheaf of papers. 'I have to agree with you, Sergeant Miller. It couldn't be this young woman.' He looked at the growing piles of paper which now covered every surface of the tooled leather desk-top. 'What shall we do with them, Miller?'

'Shall I go out and send 'em away with a flea in their ear?' suggested the sergeant. 'We've got more than enough on our plate as it is. There's that young girl from Tyvern Court, Ettie Wilkins, still not been traced, for a start. Who knows, the way things are going, she might well be the next horrible surprise for some poor devil to come across in a foggy alley.'

The inspector took a cigarette from his case and tapped the end thoughtfully on the back of his hand. 'No.' He put the cigarette in the corner of his mouth and spoke through half-open lips. 'I'll tell you what. Send in that friend of hers. What's her name?'

'Says it's Miss Smith,' said the sergeant, rolling his eyes. 'Doesn't want us to know her identity, I'd say,' he added with an obviousness that set the inspector's teeth on edge.

'I'll have a quick word with her.'

Sergeant Miller looked out into the hall and told a passing constable to bring Miss Smith into the inspector's office.

The constable and Ettie stood framed in the doorway.

Inspector Grainger told them to come in, pointed to a seat for Ettie, and carried on talking to the sergeant. Apparently interested only in his cigarette, his notes, and the sergeant's opinions, the inspector was actually concentrating closely on Ettie's every reaction to the discussion.

'So, we're agreed on one thing then, Sergeant Miller,' said Grainger, releasing a plume of blue smoke with his words. 'It isn't feasible that a young lady could be responsible for atrocities such as those committed on the dead women.'

The sergeant thought his governor had taken leave of his senses. He had only just become accustomed to discussing the case with the inspector, another man; he certainly wasn't used to speaking in front of members of the public, particularly female ones. Maybe the inspector had cracked under the strain of the investigation. Red-faced, the sergeant pointed out Ettie's presence with a sideways gesture of his head. But the inspector indicated that the older man should carry on and answer him. Before Miller could think of an inoffensive enough reply to utter in front of a young woman, the young constable who had fetched Ettie surprised everyone present by coughing loudly and asking for permission to speak.

'You have a view on this matter, constable?' asked Inspector Grainger.

'It could be a woman, sir, begging your pardon. I was thinking about it only the other day. About the handywomen. You know about them?'

The sergeant squirmed uncomfortably. He ran his fingers round the stiff serge of his uniform collar. This was not going the way he would have liked.

'The abortionists?' asked the inspector, very interested now in the constable's opinion.

Sergeant Miller was less impressed. His embarrassment was becoming acute. He dealt every day with all sorts of things, but it still didn't feel right to speak about such issues out loud, especially in front of a young woman like Miss Smith, or whatever her name was.

'They're more than that, sir – if you don't mind me saying. They do all sorts of things. Help women have their babies. Lay out the dead. Even take in washing, some of them. Oh yeah, they've got all sorts of knowledge, the handywomen. So why shouldn't it be one of them?' asked the constable. He was obviously warming to his subject. 'You see, it makes sense. They're well known to all the locals, so they can move around freely, but they're also wary of the whores. They have to be. The brides are all very friendly to them when they want them to shove one of their rusty knitting needles up them, but they'd grass them as soon as look at them for a couple of glasses of Satin.' He nodded in what would, in other less gruesome circumstances, have seemed a farcical imitation of a man many years older and wiser than he. 'It could easily make one of the handywomen the killer, and the tarts are an obvious target if some of them were getting a bit mouthy.'

'An interesting point of view,' said the inspector. 'Constable...?'

'Jennings, sir. PC Jennings.'

Sergeant Miller saw that the inspector was noting something down. He was probably taking the young man's name for future reference. He tutted despondently to himself; they had it so easy, the young officers of today. All they had to do was stick their heads into a few books and they thought they knew it all.

'But are you convinced that a woman could make those cuts?' The inspector pressed the young officer. 'There were some really deep wounds.' He saw Ettie pale. 'My apologies, Miss Smith.' He reconsidered his words. 'Could a woman manage that?'

Sergeant Miller liked the way the inspector was letting the constable take over the discussion even less than he liked such talk in front of the young lady. He swallowed hard and interrupted: he felt obliged to. 'A woman who worked as a slaughterhouse cleaner would be strong enough, governor,' he said. 'Or someone with a bit of medical training and the right tools. But a lady like her? Never. She wouldn't know where to start.'

The young constable looked put out.

'Well, that precludes Miss Tressing from our investigations then,' said the inspector, happy to have a closure to at least one loose end in the whole sorry mess.

This time it was Ettie who felt she had to interrupt. Her words came in a soft, barely discernible whisper. 'Celia–' she corrected herself – 'Miss Tressing, has midwifery skills. She told me. She is also fully trained in the dissection of bodies.'

'How do you know this?' asked Inspector Grainger, addressing her directly for the first time since the constable had brought her into the office.

'We had a long talk,' she said, studying her lap. 'She told me all about it.'

'And how long have you been friends with the lady in question?'

'I'm not her friend exactly,' said Ettie. 'Not really. Actually I've only just met her.'

'And where was that, Miss Smith?'

Ettie thought quickly: the last thing she wanted was for the inspector to arrest her on a fortune-telling charge. 'At a meeting,' she invented as she went along. 'A religious discussion about life on the Other Side. A meeting at…'

'Never mind all that.' The inspector was growing impatient now that he seemed to be getting somewhere. 'Sergeant, bring the girl in and set Jennings here on tracing her father.'

'I don't think…' Ettie began.

'I'm not much interested in what you think, Miss Smith.

'Sergeant Miller, show the young lady out when you go to fetch Miss Tressing.'

'I'm sorry for all that talk back there, miss,' said Sergeant Miller to Ettie, holding open the wide double doors which led out to the street.

Ettie smiled. 'You're very kind, thank you.'

'I'll get one of the constables to escort you to your carriage. Or did you come by hansom?'

'I'm fine, really sergeant. In fact, I'd like to walk.'

'But it's late, must be gone ten o'clock, miss,' he persisted. 'And these streets aren't exactly safe for a young lady like yourself at any time of the night, or day for that matter. Specially with this fog coming up.'

'I'm really absolutely fine. And I do want to walk for a while.' But the sergeant wouldn't hear of it; he seemed very interested in her welfare. He stood between her and the street, preventing her from leaving. 'Are you sure?'

'Yes. And thank you again. You've been very kind.'

'The streets round here can be very dodgy.'

Ettie was growing tired of his persistence. 'I assure you, I'm fine. I even have friends in the area.' She noticed the look that flashed momentarily across his face. 'From my charitable work,' she added hurriedly.

At that the sergeant stood back to let her pass. He was more than pleased with himself. He'd known she wasn't the lady the others in there had believed her to be – call themselves investigating officers! A fancy accent couldn't fool him. There was Whitechapel in that young woman's blood, as sure as there was champagne in the veins of the Prince of Wales.

As she stepped out into the cool night air, Ettie was glad to see the back of Sergeant Miller and the whole of the rotten cop shop with him. As much as Celia's confession had horrified her, her instinctive slum-dweller's fear of the police got the better of her and she hated the thought of leaving the poor, deranged creature with them. But it was all out of her hands now. She'd come back to see her in the morning. Bring her some decent food and a piece of soap. Even she deserved that. Ettie stretched her aching limbs and took in a deep, welcome breath. Even with the stench of the sewers, horse muck and factory smoke filling her nostrils, she still felt like she was breathing in the freshest of country air – not that she'd ever been to the country – but after the smell of fear and despair which hung as thick as a curtain in the police station, she could just imagine what it must be like.

Back inside the inspector's office, Celia was sitting opposite his desk in the seat that Ettie had recently vacated.

'Miss Tressing,' said the constable, pencil at the ready. 'We need to check your address.'

'We intend to send for your father,' said the sergeant, not wanting to be left out.

'He's not at home,' said Celia vaguely. 'He went away. For a week, Smithson said.'

The inspector leaned back in his chair and pressed his fingertips together across his chest. 'So where is he then, Miss Tressing? We intend to speak to him, with or without your cooperation.'

'He'll be back tomorrow. Or is it the day after?' It sounded as though each word she uttered took the most painful effort. She paused and stared about her.

'And he left you all alone?' asked the inspector sceptically.

'Oh yes,' said Celia, her eyes hollow with exhaustion. 'Quite alone.'

Chapter 38

Ettie stood outside the police station in Leman Street, leaning against the rough brick wall. She was surprised at just *how* reluctant she was, despite all she now knew about her, to leave Celia alone in there. But, if nothing else, Ettie had always been practical, and she knew she couldn't do any more for her tonight. And she also knew that she didn't fancy going back to Bow. She had decided several hours ago, when it finally dawned on her that what Celia was telling her made Jacob an innocent victim of others' – including her own – suspicions, that she couldn't face him yet. She knew she needed a clear head and the broad light of day to be able to pluck up enough courage to make her peace with him. She felt ashamed that she'd ever suspected him of such terrible things, and cringed when she thought about the way she'd treated him lately, especially compared to the compassion she felt for Celia. And even if he did have his funny ways, didn't all men, she reasoned to herself. And he'd been so good to her: he'd got her out of that hell-hole in Tyvern Court and away from that lodger; and this was how she had repaid him.

Tyvern Court – it was less than a quarter of a mile away from the police station; she would go there first to see her mum, then go back to Bow and make her peace with Jacob, show him she was sorry. Ettie sighed loudly and pushed herself away from the wall. Now that Celia was locked away in the cells, the East End streets were a much safer place to be: at least she could walk without fear of the Ripper's knife.

Ettie crossed the busy junction at the end of Leman Street and made her way along Commercial Street and on towards Brick

Lane. She yawned loudly. Her head ached from tiredness, from the after-effects of the sleeping draught and, worst of all, from the madness of the last few days. The last thing she needed or expected was a child's shrill voice yelling her name.

'Ett! Over here! It's me, Tommy!'

She looked across the street and there, in the queue outside the fried-fish shop on the corner of Flower and Dean Street, stood young Tommy Bury, waving his arms at her like a sailor signalling his distress on a sinking ship.

'Hello, Tom,' she said, going over to him, pleased, despite her exhaustion, to see his familiar, freckled face. 'I bet Myrtle don't know you're out this late.'

'Yer wanna worry about yerself,' said Tommy, imitating the bravura of his older brothers. 'Yer must have heard about all the murders what's been happening round here.' He hooked his thumbs under his braces and pulled himself up to his full four feet ten. 'Us blokes are all right, it's you girls what wanna worry.'

Ettie pinched his cheek affectionately. 'Don't worry about me, love,' she said.

Tommy's face coloured blood-red – a family trait of the redheaded Burys – and he looked round hurriedly to check that Ettie's petting him hadn't been noticed by any of his mates who might be passing by.

'I'm just waiting for 'em to do another pan of chips,' he said, keen to change the subject. 'I'm fetching some fish and taters for two reporter geezers in the Frying Pan.'

'Reporters? What, from the newspapers?'

He nodded. 'Yeah, from the *Globe* they are. They've been hanging round for a couple of weeks, getting stories from all the old whores about the Old Boy and the horrible murders.'

'Don't you be so saucy,' she said, swiping him round the back of the head.

Tommy grinned up at her and shuffled forward expertly, making sure he left no gap in the queue of which interlopers might take advantage.

'Do you know if my mum's lodger's around, Tom?' she asked as she rummaged through her bag. As she spoke, she held up what she had been looking for: a shiny silver threepenny bit.

'I ain't sure,' said Tom, eyeing the prize that would be his if he said the right thing. 'Gives me the real willies that one. Yer see him creeping about down by the meat market. Great big bugger. There was talk that he might have something to do with the murders, yer know?'

'There's been too much talk about who the murderer might be if you ask me,' Ettie replied sternly.

Tommy smiled up at her, the blameless smile of a cherub and asked sweetly, as though it had just occurred to him: 'Anyway, what d'yer wanna know about him for?'

'I want to go to Tyvern Court to see me mum, if you must know, nose ointment. If it's all right with you, of course. And I don't fancy running into him. Specially this time of night.'

'I don't blame yer,' said Tommy, puffing out his cheeks. 'I tell yer what, Ettie,' he added, craftily getting to what he'd intended to say all along. 'If I fetch our Billy, he could go with yer to make sure yer all right. How would that be?'

Ettie deliberately made a show of considering the proposition for a moment or two. 'That'd be fine, Tom,' she said eventually. 'But you know how early he has to get up for work. He'll have been in his bed ages.'

'No he won't,' said Tommy confidently. 'I know where he'll be. Trouble is though,' he said with an exaggerated sigh, 'I'll have to go and fetch him. It'll take me a couple of minutes.' He gazed sadly at the queue. 'The reporter fellahs usually give me a shilling for running errands for 'em. And they are me regular customers. I'd hate to lose me place and let 'em down. It wouldn't look good. I might miss out another time.'

Ettie narrowed her eyes at him. 'You're just like your Alfie,' she said. 'Go on, I'll give you sixpence and I'll keep your place in the queue, how'd that be?'

Within five minutes Billy was sprinting along towards Ettie with his little brother trailing behind him calling out for him to wait.

'Ettie,' Billy panted. 'Am I pleased to see you.' He bent forward, grasping his thighs as he tried to steady his breathing. 'Yer don't know how worried we've all been.' He lifted his head to look at her. 'We've been trying to find yer for days. We thought, with all this going on, that, well, that yer might have…'

Ettie reached out and touched him tenderly on his muscled, working-man's arm. 'I'm glad you care, Bill. Thanks.'

'And our Maisie's been going spare,' he said, straightening up. 'Turned out she even went over to Bow looking for yer. And yer know what a lazy mare she is.'

'I really am sorry. I never realised I was worrying everyone.' She lifted her chin and kissed him briefly on the lips. 'Sorry, Bill.'

'Oi oi,' mocked the old man standing behind Ettie in the queue. 'What's all this then, the entertainment?'

Billy turned round and glared at him, but Tommy interrupted the potential row by racing up to Ettie, coughing loudly, and holding out his hand. 'I said I'd bring him,' he reminded her, his hand still outstretched.

'Here you are, sweetheart,' she said, and gave him his reward.

Billy flashed his little brother a warning look.

'It's all right, Bill. I never asked her for nothing, honest.'

'Yer better hadn't have,' said Billy. 'Now I'm just gonna have a little stroll and a bit of a chat with Ettie.'

'That what they call it now?' mumbled the elderly man sourly, just to show he wasn't scared of any jumped-up youngsters.

Billy chose to ignore him. 'You make sure yer don't wake Mum up when yer get in, Tom,' he warned his little brother. 'Or they'll be hell to pay for all of us.'

Billy took Ettie by the arm and lead her away from the busy pavement outside the fried-fish shop and into Brick Lane. He guided her along until they neared the high, gloomy walls of the brewery. It was darker there and free from prying eyes and ears;

there weren't many people in those parts who chose to walk in the shadows.

'Ettie,' he said, taking her gently by the shoulders. 'I've got something to tell you.'

'Come on then,' she urged him. 'Spit it out.' She wasn't scared of the shadows, but she hated the stink of the brewery; all those years of living so close to it, and yet she'd never got used to the smell.

'Ettie,' he said again, and paused. 'It's yer mum.'

'Mum?'

'Ettie, I'm sorry.' He wrapped his arms tightly round her.

She pulled away and looked up into his face. 'You mean she's dead, don't you?'

Billy nodded. Then he bowed his head and said, 'We tried to find you.'

Ettie's words came out in an expressionless whisper. 'What happened?'

'Mum and Ruby went over to see her the day before yesterday. She'd got herself in a state over the rumours that yer'd been, you know, done in, and they found her. She had this clutched in her hand.' He dug into his trouser pocket and handed Ettie a sheet of paper folded into a small square. 'Mum guessed it was for you. She didn't show it to no one. Not even Ruby. She thought it might be private like. So I've been holding on to it for yer. Maisie said she should look after it, but I wanted to.'

'Where is she?' said Ettie, looking at the little square of paper.

'I'm sorry, Ett,' he said again. 'They took her away.' He hesitated. 'They put her in a pauper's grave, Ett. I'm so sorry. It was too late for us to do anything.'

Ettie held up her hand to stop him. 'It's not your fault, Bill. I know that.'

She unfolded the paper with trembling hands. It was a note from her mother – rough, ill-formed letters scratched on the tatty piece of paper. It read:

*My little Ettie I don't know if you are dead or alive but I
know I am not long for this world. Before I go I want you
to know that I let him stay here because he said he would
kill you if I threw him out. Please believe that I did it for
you.*

You are all I've got.

Ettie carefully refolded the note and held it tight in her hand.
'What happened to him, Bill?' Her voice was shaking.

'Who?'

'The lodger. That bastard slaughterman who was living with
her.'

'Him?' Billy kicked a stone across the street. 'He's still there,' he
said through clenched teeth. 'Moved a young girl and her couple
of kids in yesterday.'

'What? In my mum's room?' Her voice rose in anger and she
clenched her hands into tight fists. 'But why? Why is he still there?
What does he want?'

'Because he's a bully, that's why. Because he can do what he
likes to someone weaker than him. But he won't be there for
much longer. Aw no. You mark my words, Ett. Now he can't
hurt Sarah no more, and now everyone's seen the callous bastard
for what he is, that he wasn't just another one of the no-goods
what Sarah took up with...' His words stopped. 'Aw, Ett, I didn't
mean to say that.'

'That's all right, Bill,' she said, shaking her head sorrowfully. 'I
know exactly what you mean.'

'I asked her loads of times, yer know, if she'd let me get rid of
him for her.'

'Did yer, Bill? I'm pleased. I bet she liked that, knowing she
had you caring about her. She always was fond of you.'

'But she wouldn't let me do nothing though, would she? I
never understood why.'

Ettie stared at the note as she turned it over in her hands. 'She
had her reasons,' she whispered, and handed it to him.

'I can't read, can I?' he said, shrugging. 'None of us can, 'cept Tommy.'

Ettie took the note back, closed her eyes for a moment, and then read it to him.

Billy turned round and slammed his hand against the soot-covered bricks of the brewery wall. 'The *bastard*!' Then he grabbed Ettie to him and clung on to her.

'I know I should be crying, Bill,' she whispered into his shoulder. 'But I can't. I feel like I've got a great big heavy stone wedged in my chest and it's weighing me down.'

'You ain't gotta worry about nothing,' he said, his voice set with fury. 'Do you hear me?'

Ettie nodded.

'He'd better watch his back. I'm gonna get Alfie and a mob of the boys from down the market, and I'm gonna make it more than clear that the time's come for him to sling his hook. I just wish I'd have done it before, that's all.'

'No, don't blame yourself, Bill. You did what she wanted. And it was something she could do for me, as me mum, because she loved me.' Her shoulders shook as she began to weep, softly at first, then in great gulping sobs. 'She really did love me, yer know. No matter what she did to me at times, I always knew she loved me.'

'I love yer and all, Ett,' he said, pulling her closer to him.

'I don't half miss it round here, Bill,' she said, shuddering with her sobs.

'I know,' he soothed her.

'Sometimes I don't know why I ever left.'

'Don't make it sound too cosy, girl,' he said, stroking her hair. He bent his head to look down at her as she rested against his chest. 'You take my word for it, Ett, most of 'em would get out if they could.'

'And sod all their old mates, like I did, eh Bill?' she sniffled.

'Not you, Ett. That's not what you did. And don't let no soppy ideas make yer feel guilty about getting on in life. I know it's what I intend doing.'

Billy took her hand in his great rough paw and led her to the nearest street-light. He wrapped his handkerchief round his fingers, held it out for her to lick, then held her face gently in his other hand while he wiped away the stains of her tears.

'I was three years old when I first saw someone dead from hunger,' he said. 'Down Goulston Street, it was. He was in the gutter like a pile of old rubbish that'd fell off a cart. Me and the other kids all crowded round to have a look. One of the boys – Lukey Wright, you remember him – started kicking at the body. Body? More like a bag of bones it was so thin. But we all laughed. We laughed all right. Laughed till we nearly pissed ourselves. It took me a couple of years to know you only laugh like that when yer scared out of yer wits.' He breathed deeply. 'No, Ett, yer don't wanna be ashamed of getting away from being poor.'

'You're a good man, Billy Bury,' she said. 'A really good man. If only things had turned out different.' Ettie felt her eyes brimming with tears again. 'Look,' she said, 'I'll have to be getting off.'

'I'll go with yer. Yer can't walk the streets, it ain't safe.'

'I'll be all right.'

'No, Ett, yer not. Yer don't know who or where he might strike next. I ain't letting yer go wandering off in the dark, and that's final.'

'Yer can walk me till I find a cab. How about that?'

'A cab, eh?' he said wistfully. 'Yer really are doing all right for yerself then, helping that Professor geezer.'

The last thing Ettie wanted was to start discussing Jacob, she had enough on her mind, thinking about her poor mum *and* about Celia. Worrying about Jacob would have to wait its turn.

'Bill,' she said through her tears. 'I'd appreciate yer walking with me. I really would. But I'll have to go now. I've got some things I've got to sort out.'

'And I've some few things I wanna sort out before I get to me bed and all.' He studied his hands. 'I'd like to tell yer about 'em. Will yer be coming back some time?'

'Try and stop me,' she said, wiping her nose on the back of her hand. Then she pulled out the locket he'd given her from inside her blouse.

He grinned with pleasure as she gave him a gentle shove, 'Come on then, let's go and find a cab for me. Now, which way are you going?'

'I've gotta go Shoreditch way,' he said. 'But I can go whatever way yer like.'

'That'll be fine,' she said. 'I'll be able to get a cab coming down from Bethnal Green.'

–

Billy put two fingers in his mouth and let out a piercing shriek of a whistle. The hansom driver twisted round on his perch to get a look at his would-be customer, then, satisfied that it was a couple and not some black-caped killer, he shook the reins to signal for his horse to turn round. He shrugged down into his greatcoat. What were things coming to, eh, he said to himself, when an honest man had to check who he took in his cab for fear of being murdered.

Billy helped Ettie into her seat and then called up to the driver. 'Bow, please, cabby, and make sure yer see the lady safely into her front door before yer drive off.'

'Very sensible, guv,' he said, touching his hand to his cap. 'Glad to be of service.'

Billy hesitantly reached into the cab and touched Ettie's cheek. 'Look after yerself, Ett,' he said, and without another word he sprinted off in the direction of Shoreditch.

'Wait until he's out of sight,' Ettie called up to the driver.

The driver waited.

As Billy reached the corner of Montclare Street, he stopped, turned, and waved to her.

'See yer soon?' he called hopefully.

'Get on with you,' Ettie called back, shooing him on his way with a smile.

'He wants to get a move on,' said the driver. 'That's no place to hang about. Not by the Old Nichol. Even for a great big bloke like him.'

Ettie squinted in the dark, watching for him to be on his way, then, content that he had indeed done as she'd hoped, she said, 'You can go now, but not to Bow. I'd like you to take me to Leman Street police station, please driver.'

Ettie stepped through the now familiar double doors of the police station. There was a different young constable at the desk. 'Can I help you, miss?' he said, eyeing her appreciatively. 'Don't often get ladies like you in here. Specially not this time of night.'

'Ladies like me, eh darling?'

His mouth fell open in astonishment as the elegantly costumed Ettie slipped into her old cockney twang.

'Well there yer wrong, ain't yer, darling? I'm from the courts of Whitechapel me – proud of it and all. And I can tell you, compared to what I've seen and heard these last few days, I reckon them courts and the people in 'em was bleed'n paradise.' She sat herself down on the hard, wooden bench. 'Now, if yer don't mind, I'm gonna close me eyes and wait till the morning, when I plan to see one of yer guests yer've got in the cells.'

Ettie wriggled into the corner and made herself as comfortable as the bench would allow. 'Good night,' she said, and shut her eyes, although she knew she wouldn't sleep – she had a lot of thinking to do, so much on her mind and, until she had the energy to make her peace with Jacob, she had nowhere else to go.

'Oh no you don't,' he protested, lifting the flap and coming round from the other side of the counter. This isn't some common lodging-house. You want to get yourself down Brick Lane.' He stood over her. 'I'll call the sergeant if you won't move yourself.' She opened her eyes. 'Please yourself, constable,' she said in the clipped, ladylike tones she'd learned so well from Jacob. 'But I'm sure that neither Sergeant Miller nor Inspector Grainger would mind me waiting. You can ask them if you like.' She closed her eyes again. 'Now shut yer gob up, constable, or yer'll swallow a bleed'n fly.'

Ettie dozed fitfully on the bench under the watchful eye of Police-Constable Walker. He'd been warned not to disturb Inspector Grainger except in the event of a serious emergency and, summoning all his rather limited experience, he decided that a crazy woman sleeping on a bench did not constitute an emergency. So Walker left Ettie where she was and got on with reading the latest chapter of his serial about the savage natives of the Wild West of America.

Behind where Walker sat crouched over his book was the door which led to Inspector Grainger's office. In the office sat the inspector himself, Sergeant Miller and young Police-Constable Jennings. All three listened with varying degrees of interest, horror and speculation as a surgeon, specially summoned from the London Hospital in Whitechapel Road, quizzed Celia Tressing on matters of medical and surgical procedure.

Much to the sergeant's very evident distaste, Celia was able to answer accurately and coherently on everything from the sight and the sound of the cutting and lifting of flaps of skin, to the sundry probings and scrapings on various parts of the human anatomy. But it wasn't until Celia outlined the stages involved in terminating a pregnancy that the sergeant went extremely pale and was forced to leave the office in an extreme hurry, headed in the direction of the lavatory.

'I think you can take Miss Tressing back to the cells now, constable,' said Grainger, running his hand through his hair. 'I want to have a word with Doctor Jackson here.' He took out yet another cigarette from his case. 'And I think you might sit in on the discussion,' he added. 'So move yourself, Jennings.'

Doctor Jackson said nothing but raised a surprised eyebrow – junior staff in discussions certainly wasn't how *he* thought a department ought to be run, but then, he reminded himself, the inspector was hardly a gentleman.

As Jennings led the expressionless Celia to the door, he almost collided with Sergeant Miller returning from his ablutions.

'I trust that you are quite well now, sergeant,' said Celia, her face a picture of concern. 'You did look so very pale.'

The sergeant nodded mechanically as he stepped back for her to pass. 'Quite well, thank you, Miss Tressing,' he said, wondering as he spoke what Mrs Miller would make of it all.

'Doctor Jackson,' said the inspector, lighting his cigarette and then tossing his match box on to his crowded desk. 'In your opinion, and considering the scientific categorisation of facial types, do you believe that a young lady of such fair countenance – an angel to look at, some might say – would really have it in her to carry out such atrocities?'

Jackson smirked with the confidence of one with superior knowledge. 'A very dated concept, if I might say so, inspector,' he said smugly.

Grainger inclined his head in apparent acceptance of the doctor's wisdom and noted something down on his pad. 'In that case, let us ask a different question.'

Jennings slipped quietly back into the room and stood in the corner.

'In your own, honest opinion, Doctor Jackson,' the inspector continued. 'Based on your interviewing of Miss Tressing, could she actually have carried out the killings and mutilations?'

'I would like to answer you in the following way,' said the doctor, picking up his attache case and rising to his feet. 'Her father, Bartholomew Tressing, has for many years been a colleague of mine. I would have been most reluctant to have come along had I realised the young lady's identity beforehand. Now, if you will excuse me, Mrs Jackson was expecting me home over five hours ago. I bid you good night, gentlemen.'

'Good night, sir,' Grainger replied with hardly a glimmer of the surprise he felt. Then, just as the doctor opened the door, he added, 'Please don't concern yourself, but we might need to speak to you further.'

Jackson didn't answer; he just closed the door behind him.

'Interesting,' said Grainger, and drew hard on his cigarette.

'Very,' said Jennings, trying to ingratiate himself.

'Why?' said Miller.

Grainger peered at the sergeant through a haze of smoke. 'It's been a tough time, Miller,' he said. 'Particularly these last couple of days. You must be very tired. Why don't you get yourself off home for a few hours' sleep?'

Miller stood up very straight. 'I'm fine, guv. Thank you very much,' he added, and pulled at the hem of his tunic.

Grainger nodded briefly, then stubbed out his cigarette and said very slowly and deliberately, 'If the doctor hadn't suspected that Miss Tressing might possibly be... responsible, then he wouldn't have been quite so contained, now would he? He'd be demanding to see all sorts of people and protesting at my outrageous suggestions. Are you with me?'

'Yes,' said Miller equally slowly. 'But if he *did* think she might be...' He paused as realisation dawned. 'Oh, I see.'

'Good,' said Grainger. 'Now, Jennings, organise some tea.' Jennings looked disgruntled and Miller looked pleased.

The inspector might be impatient with the older man's lack of speed in deduction, but he knew the importance of keeping the hierarchy intact in the force, *and* the officers on their toes.

The constable returned with a tray carrying a brown earthenware teapot, a sugar basin, a milk jug and three tin mugs.

'Shall I be mother?' he asked, with a risky tinge of sarcasm. 'No,' said Miller, taking the tray from him and balancing it on the top of the filing cabinet. 'I'll be father.'

Grainger stirred his tea with the end of his letter knife then sucked the drips off the bone handle. 'Take a seat, gentlemen,' he said, blinking his eyes in an effort to retain some semblance of being alert. 'There are a few things I want to go over. Number one.' He pursed his lips and blew on the scalding tea before sipping gingerly at the steaming mug. 'We're all agreed, are we, that she's the sort of person who could move around Whitechapel at night without arousing the suspicion of others?'

Jennings dived straight in with an opinion. 'Definitely. And she would have little trouble being let into the girls' company because of all the charity work she reckons she's been involved in. And she's certainly familiar with the area.'

Miller decided it was time for him to chip in with his twopenny-worth. 'And, according to the so-called Miss Smith, the girl has no mother, and her father frequents his club more than his dining room, so she's got no one to miss her when she's not at home, guv.' Grainger nodded thoughtfully. 'Number two: how about the bloodstains?'

'Easy,' said Jennings. 'If anyone found her, she'd have an alibi – she'd been attending a birth. And that would explain her bag of instruments.'

'Good point, Jennings.'

'She could always cover her bloodied clothes with her cloak,' said the sergeant. 'I know you two aren't married,' he added wisely. 'But a lady's cloak can be a voluminous garment, you take it from me.'

'Or she could turn her things inside out,' said the constable, heady from the inspector's recognition of his ability, and not wanting to be outdone by a sergeant whom he considered to hold hopelessly out-dated ideas. 'Even dump her bloodstained skirts and be stark naked under her cape,' he speculated wildly. 'It would be a doddle down those dark alleys and passageways.'

The sergeant looked aghast at the suggestion that Miss Tressing might shed her clothes in public. Murder was one thing, but a young lady without her necessaries – particularly in a public place – was too terrible a thought. 'No,' he said, eyeing the constable sternly. 'She wouldn't need to do that. Nobody would even think to suspect a young woman. And even if she was seen leaving the house in Miller's Court, she could quite easily be taken for the victim herself going out to do a bit of business. Especially in the dark. It would certainly keep any suspicion away until the body was found.'

'Good,' said the inspector, making sure that this time he praised the sergeant. He was delighted that he was provoking the two men into constructive thinking. 'Now, number three: why would she do it?' He took another sip of tea. 'Why?'

'She was sickened by the way of life she saw in the slums, that's why,' said Sergeant Miller conclusively. 'She's a well-brought-up young lady; should have stayed with her own.' He pursed his lips in disgust. 'Enough to turn anyone, all those carryings-on, let alone someone with her sheltered upbringing.'

'I'm not so sure about the sheltered upbringing,' said the constable, chancing a knowing smirk at the inspector. 'Not with air the abortions she reckons she's done. Nor when you think about the things she says her old man's done to her.'

The inspector didn't share the constable's amusement at the older man's preference for delicacy and euphemism. 'Interesting point, sergeant,' he said, much to Jennings' annoyance. 'And apart from Kelly, none of them was expecting. Not even young enough to be that way, some of them.'

Constable Jennings wasn't, however, put off from airing his theories. 'She could be covering up for something else.'

Grainger looked interested, so Jennings carried on.

'There might be a first killing we don't even know about. More of an accident really. You see, she could have done an abortion that went wrong – illegal, but still an accident. Then she got the taste for it, killing whores.'

'So how would that explain the missing bits of body?' asked Grainger. 'And the mutilations?'

'How d'you explain madness?' said the constable in a flash of inspiration.

The inspector rubbed his hand over his face. His chin was harsh with stubble from want of a shave. It had been another very long night.

'Sergeant,' the inspector said, stifling a yawn. 'It'll be light soon. Send a couple of men round to see if Miss Tressing's father is back at his home address yet.' He drained his tea-cup, then leant back exhausted in his chair. 'And make sure you send a pair who know how to behave. We're dealing with an eminent surgeon here, not a market trader.'

'Right away, sir,' said Miller. 'Jennings can go with Walker.' Jennings jumped to his feet, unsure whether the sergeant was being sarcastic or not.

'Oh, and sergeant,' said the inspector, gingerly lifting his aching legs and balancing his heels on the only empty bit of his desk.

'Yes, sir?'

'I think we can let Protsky go.'

—

'Walker,' said the sergeant to the young man behind the front desk. 'I'll take over here till the next shift comes on.'

'Ta, sarge,' said the constable with a wide grin.

'No need to look so pleased with yourself,' said Miller. 'You and the future Chief-Constable Jennings here are going to run a little errand to Belgravia for me – if you can tear yourself away from your cowboy book, that is.'

'Yes, sarge,' said the chastened Walker, shoving the thin paper book uncomfortably up the sleeve of his tunic. 'Right, sarge.' And he lifted the flap of the counter.

'Hold hard, Walker lad,' growled the sergeant. 'Who is it that you've let doss down in the corner? Not a lady friend of yours, I do hope?'

'Bloody cheek,' said Ettie, opening her eyes sleepily. 'What do you take me for? A copper's tart?' She stretched her arms high above her head. 'I'll just nip out for a bit of breakfast,' she said to the now puce-faced sergeant, 'then perhaps you'd be so kind as to organise for me to see Miss Tressing.'

Chapter 39

As Ettie breakfasted on cold toast scraped with dripping, and stewed, dark-brown tea at a coffee stall in Alie Street, thinking with a heavy heart about her mother and Celia, little did she realise that Jacob was at that moment being released from the very same police station where she had just spent such a tormented and uncomfortable night.

'Right,' barked the burly police-constable responsible for Jacob's bruised and aching ribs, his cut eye and bloody nose. 'Gawd and Inspector Grainger alone know why, but they're letting you go again.'

The officer pushed his face up close to the bars.

'Now, if it was up to me, I know what I'd do to you, you murdering, foreign bastard. I'd chop your whatsits off and stuff 'em down your throat. What do you think of that? Or are you too busy thinking about butchering the next poor cow?'

Jacob glared contemptuously at the man. He certainly didn't feel like giving him the distinction of an answer, so he merely stood up, collected his cape from the hard, wooden platform on which he had lain awake all night, and walked over to the barred cell door.

'Haven't you got nothing to say for yourself?' sneered the officer as he turned the jangling bunch of keys over and over in his hand.

'And have you no explanation for why you kept me here and why you maltreated me?' asked Jacob, with his head held high.

'Get out of my sight!' spat the officer, swinging the door back on its hinges. He was hardly able to contain himself as Jacob stepped past him. 'Go on. Before I do something you might regret.'

All the while, as Jacob walked as calmly as he could along the corridors and up the stairs which would lead him back up to the almost normal atmosphere of the public part of the police station, the police-constable continued to provoke him.

'You reckon you get in touch with the spirits, don't you?' he jeered. 'Funny how they never warned you that you were going to have that little accident in the night, when you bashed your face up against the cell wall.'

Jacob kept walking. He knew better than to antagonise a man with a heavy bunch of keys in his hand.

When they reached the big double doors which opened on to Leman Street, the officer folded his arms and stood belligerently, half blocking the exit, waiting for Jacob to have to push past him.

Sergeant Miller looked up briefly and said, 'Everything all right, Parsons?'

Parsons nodded. 'Sir,' he said in his deep, booming voice.

'Good man,' said Miller, begrudgingly getting on with the endless round of paperwork that the inspector insisted on for everything they did: everything from listing every single maniac who came in claiming to be the Ripper, to ordering more bloody paper to do the writing on in the first place.

Jacob took a deep breath and with a curt, 'Excuse me,' he stepped round the constable and grasped the brass door-handles with both hands, his final barrier to freedom.

One of Parsons' rough, pudgy hands closed around Jacob's pale, slender fingers. He gripped hard, but Jacob didn't dare show any sign of weakness by complaining.

'Do everyone a favour, yourself included,' Parsons warned him in a low, deep rumble. 'Tell all them posh old girls who flock round you that you're a con merchant. Oh, yeah, and piss off out of it back to where you come from.'

Jacob turned round and looked long and hard at the man who had beaten him repeatedly throughout the night. 'They wouldn't believe me if I did,' he said, without any trace of emotion. 'People need to have hope of a better life when they live in this Hell.'

Then he summoned all his strength and flung open the doors and stumbled humiliatingly down the steps into the cold, predawn light of Leman Street.

Jacob was aware that no cab would stop for a man in his condition: he looked too much like the drunks who were always to be found staggering around there on their way back to their ships. So, ignoring his aching chest and the pains in his limbs, he set off walking swiftly in the direction of Bow.

The door creaked loudly as he tried to slip quietly into the hallway. He didn't want to alarm Ettie by waking her before he'd had a chance to clean himself up a bit. He knew exactly what he'd say to her when she did wake up. He'd spent the whole, agonising walk from Whitechapel working it out. If he'd got it right, then she'd be sure to forgive him and they would go off and start afresh – he certainly had plenty of experience of that. And this time it would be so much easier with Ettie by his side.

When he was satisfied that his face looked as presentable as he could make it, he made a pot of strong tea and carried it carefully into the bedroom. He set it on the side-table and went over and drew back the curtains.

At first he couldn't take in what he was seeing – the room was exactly as he'd left it when the police had come and taken him away three days ago: the bed was still unmade, his nightshirt flung across the chair, his book open where he'd left it on the bedside rug.

He closed his eyes, trying to block out what he knew had happened: Ettie hadn't been back since she'd run off in the night. She'd threatened it enough times lately, but this time she really had left him.

Mechanically, Jacob pulled a leather overnight bag from the top of the wardrobe and threw in a couple of shirts, some under-clothes, and a pair of trousers. Then he went into the sitting room, took down a book from the top shelf, and opened it.

The book was a sham, a hollowed out cover in which he kept a sheaf of bankers' orders and a bag of gold sovereigns – he had fled before and knew always to have money where he might readily lay his hands on it.

Jacob next sat at his desk and wrote a letter which he sealed in an envelope addressed to Ettie. Then he stood up and propped the letter on the mantelpiece against an alabaster carving of a cat, where, if she ever did come back, she would be sure to see it. Finally he sorted through his papers, selecting a few of the files which he packed in his bag, and stuffed the rest into the grate and put a match to them.

As he poked at the charred remains, he glanced over towards the window. So much had happened to him, and yet the day still hadn't fully dawned. Satisfied that he had done everything that needed to be done, Jacob picked up his bag and left the rooms overlooking Victoria Park for the last time.

Under cover of the fog-bound, early morning streets, Jacob Protsky made his way back in the direction of Leman Street. But this time he had no intention of going to the police station; this time he was heading for the docks.

Chapter 40

Sergeant Miller nodded Ettie through into the shabby little side room with the two chairs and the rickety unpolished table, where she and Celia had first waited to see Inspector Grainger.

Celia was sitting sideways on to the table, staring down, ashen-faced, at her hands which rested in her lap. Only when the sergeant left the room, closing the door shut behind him, did she look up.

'Ettie,' she said, her voice raw from weeping. 'I'm so glad you've come.' She returned her gaze to her lap. 'I was hoping you'd do something for me.'

'Of course,' said Ettie, sitting down and taking Celia's hand in hers. 'That's why I'm here. I'll do whatever I can.'

She let go of Celia's hand and placed a small brown paper packet on the table between them.

'It's only a cold bacon sandwich,' she said. 'It's all I could get. But you've got to eat something.'

Celia looked down blankly at the grease-stained packet. 'You've been very kind to me, Ettie. I don't know how I would have got through all this without you.'

'Don't thank me too soon,' said Ettie, swallowing back her tears and trying to arrange a smile on her face. 'You haven't tried the sandwich yet.'

'What I want,' said Celia, suddenly looking directly into Ettie's eyes, 'is for you to go to the house for me. I need you to fetch some of my things.'

'All right,' said Ettie cautiously, wondering if Celia's father was still safely out of the way.

'You seem worried,' she said anxiously. 'It won't take very long.'

'I didn't really want to bump into your father.'

Celia hesitated. 'I can't lie to you, Ettie, he *is* due back today, but he'll go straight to the hospital, I promise. He's a creature of habit.'

Ettie nibbled her lip. 'Are you sure?'

'I truly wouldn't ask you unless I was,' Celia replied anxiously.

'Well, if you say so.'

Celia managed a smile.

'It's fine, of course I'll go.'

'Oh Ettie, thank you.'

'Don't worry about that. Now, what is it you want? I know you could do with some soap, but I've already thought of that.' Ettie dug into her pocket and produced a thin slice of soap that she'd bought from a passing bride whom she'd delighted by giving her a half-crown for the almost transparent fraction of the original, once rectangular cake.

Celia picked up the soap and examined it as though it were a precious jewel. 'Thank you. Again. But what I was really hoping was that you would fetch me a phial from my father's pharmacology cabinets.'

Ettie looked alarmed.

'Even though I'm exhausted, I'm finding it impossible to sleep in here. This tincture would help me.' She handed Ettie a scrap of paper. 'The cabinets are kept in his operating room,' she explained, 'up in the attics.'

'I can't make head nor tail of this,' said Ettie, frowning at the strange words.

'It's in Latin. But it's all right, his pharmacy is organised in a very simple way. You'll be able to go straight to what I want.' Celia was beginning to sound desperate, her voice betraying her concern that Ettie might be reconsidering whether she would help her. 'My father is obsessively tidy with his things. Everything is kept in strict alphabetical order.' She paused. 'Oh, is that a difficulty?'

'It's all right,' Ettie assured her. 'I do know my alphabet.'

'Of course, it was very rude of me to think otherwise.'

'I think we've got beyond all this apologising, Celia,' Ettie said softly, then added more briskly: 'I'll sort it out.' She tucked the paper safely into her bag. 'Now, what else was it you wanted?'

'A packet.' She looked at the now grease-soaked covering of the sandwich. 'Not unlike the one you were kind enough to bring me. You'll find it in the drawer of the writing desk in my bedroom.' Celia handed her a tiny, golden key. 'Thank you, Ettie. Thank you.'

Neither Ettie nor Celia knew that, on the other side of the stout brick wall, only a matter of feet from where they were sitting, Bartholomew Tressing was being invited to take a seat by Inspector Grainger.

'I'm sorry to have brought you here at such an early hour, Mr Tressing,' said Grainger.

'I should think so,' fumed Tressing. 'I return to the hospital after a week's leave of absence doing research and you immediately come in and disturb me, prevent me from getting on with my work. I'm a busy man, Inspector Grainger, extremely busy.'

'Yes, sir,' the inspector said flatly, 'we all are. But I'm afraid it was unavoidable. You see, your daughter is being held in custody.'

'She's what?' exploded Tressing, looking round at Jennings and Miller who were posted by the door. 'I thought your men said it was to do with a hospital matter.'

'Well, in some ways it is,' said Grainger, searching around for the right words.

'Look, inspector, I don't have the time to play these ridiculous games. I'm in the middle of a very complicated piece of work which has to be finished before I go to America in the New Year. Do you understand me?'

Grainger decided that he had better come straight out and say what he had to say. 'Mr Tressing, your daughter has been making some extraordinary claims and, not to put too fine a point on it, we are quite concerned for her mental state.'

'What sort of claims, man?' demanded Tressing.

'It has to be said, sir, that your daughter, Miss Celia Tressing, has been making all kinds of accusations about you.'

'Accusations about me? What do you mean, accusations?'

'That you, well, *knew* her. In the carnal sense.'

'What?' he yelled. 'Has the damned girl taken complete leave of her senses?'

'That's exactly what we are concerned about, Mr Tressing.' The inspector wiped the sweat from his palms on his handkerchief. 'She is also claiming,' he continued, 'to be responsible for the murders in Whitechapel, sir. The murders that are being associated with the person known as Jack the Ripper.'

Tressing's face was crimson. He levered himself unsteadily to his feet and paced over to the window.

'We were wondering about your using your powers to certify patients as insane, sir,' said Grainger in an appeasing, controlled voice, as if he were trying to subdue a crazed bear.

'Under the '43 rules?' asked Tressing, staring down at the now busy street below.

'I don't think that would be necessary, Mr Tressing,' Grainger said as evenly as he could manage. 'We could, if you wish, keep this a private matter. It would prevent any scandal. Keep it out of the papers. That sort of thing.'

'That would seem to be satisfactory,' said Tressing.

'It has been suggested, by a colleague of yours, in fact, that arrangements might be made in this establishment,' said Grainger, holding up a sheet of headed writing paper.

'A colleague of mine,' thundered Tressing. 'You mean...'
'Please, don't alarm yourself, sir. Dr Jackson's advice...'

'Dr Jackson?'

'His advice,' Grainger persisted, 'had already been sought regarding Miss Tressing, when it transpired that he knew you. We thought that the fewer people who were involved in all this, the better it would be for all concerned.'

Seeing that Tressing was almost bursting with rage, Grainger hurriedly carried on speaking.

'All you would need to do,' he continued, 'is sign your agreement to pay the fees as her parent and guardian. And, of course, to certify her, in your capacity as a man of medicine.' Tressing strode over to the inspector's desk, snatched a pen without asking from the ink-stand, and signed the paper with a, but without so much as a glance at the contents of the letter.

'I knew she'd finally lose her grasp on reality,' he sneered, shoving the signed document towards the inspector. 'Same as her mother before her.' He leaned across the desk. 'Quite insane, you see, Grainger. Exactly like her mother.'

Grainger said, 'I see.'

Tressing looked over his shoulder at Jennings and Miller, then turned back to the inspector and said in a low, conspiratorial voice. 'She actually claimed that she saw someone...' He hesitated for a brief moment. 'A colleague of mine, kill a slum child.'

'I see,' Inspector Grainger said again.

Then Tressing straightened himself up, pulled on his gloves and walked, almost casually, over to the door. As he waited for Jennings to open it for him, he added, 'Organise any other paperwork and send it over to me either at my house or my club.'

He handed Jennings a card without bothering to look at him.

'I'll be going home later this morning, staying until about noon, and will return late tonight after dining at my club.'

Jennings stood to attention as Tressing brushed past, then he followed him, closing the door behind them.

'Hard man, that,' said Grainger, 'visiting his club for dinner.'

'Shock maybe?' said Sergeant Miller.

'Maybe,' said Grainger.

Ettie hurried along the corridor that only hours earlier Jacob himself had strode along with the same intention – to leave the police station as quickly as possible.

As Ettie came to the wide central office, she heard the unmistakable voice of a man loudly addressing someone whom he considered to be his inferior.

'Take your hand from my sleeve, constable, I am quite able to leave the office without your assistance.'

'My apologies, Mr Tressing, sir,' said the hapless Jennings as he stepped aside to let him through.

Tressing... Ettie shrank back at the name, ducking behind a green painted pillar from where she watched the man who had driven his own daughter insane by his violation and abuse of her.

'I'll be expecting to receive *personally* any news regarding my daughter's committal,' he said insistently. 'You are absolutely clear where to find me?'

'Yes, sir,' said Jennings.

'And I don't expect to read a single word about it in any of the newspapers. That is also quite clear, is it, constable?'

'Yes, sir,' said Jennings timidly. Then, in an effort to ingratiate himself he added, 'And don't worry yourself, sir, Miss Tressing will be quite safe here with us.'

Tressing looked at the constable as though he were also in need of certifying. 'Do you think I care?' he said scornfully, and strode through the wide doors and out on to the street.

Ettie rushed up to the young constable and simpered in her most elegant voice. 'Constable, wasn't that Miss Tressing's father?'

'Yes, Miss Smith,' he said, with what he felt and hoped was an irresistible smile − it wasn't often that he came across good-looking, elegant young ladies like her in the Leman Street nick.

'Is he going home, do you know?' she asked shyly. 'I should very much like to speak to him about Celia. To see if I might be of some assistance.'

'As I recall,' said the constable, flamboyantly producing his notebook. 'Ah yes. He said he'd be going home for a bit later on this morning, then he's off to his club this evening. For a spot of supper. If that's of any help.'

'Thank you, constable,' whispered Ettie, touching his arm with her gloved fingertips. 'I'm very grateful to you.'

Little did he realise how grateful; even though her mind was racing with other problems and sadness − about her mother's death, about making up with Jacob, about her life in general and what she was going to do with herself – at least the information had given her the peace of mind of knowing when it would be safe to go to the house.

Chapter 41

'Ivy!' wailed Flo. 'Come on, girl, It's bloody freezing out here.' She held up her bag and shook it, making it jingle as a few loose coppers rattled around inside. 'Look, I've got more than enough for the two of us. Come on. Let's go down the Butcher's and have a few for our breakfast.'

Ivy was hanging around at the far end of Fournier Street looking for trade, but Florrie's powerful bellow of a voice easily carried from where she was standing hollering at the other end by the corner of Brick Lane.

'No,' Ivy shouted back emphatically, her fists tucked into her slender waist. 'I told yer, I wanna get that little blue bonnet I saw in the pawn shop window. I only need another couple of bob and I've got enough. And put that bloody bag away before you go and get yourself coshed.'

'But Ivy...'

'Listen, Flo,' she shouted back, pausing only to stare down the nosy cow who'd stopped to listen to their row. 'I reckon yer've still got a skinful from last night. You poured more than enough down yer gullet to get the both of us pissed.' Ivy's tone softened. 'So why don't you get off home? Go on, and I'll fetch yer a couple of pig's trotters later on. With loads of vinegar on 'em.'

Florrie pouted. 'I want you to come home with me.'

'Florrie, I said no.'

'Is that person bothering you?'

At the unmistakable sound of a gentleman speaking, Ivy turned round and placed a pert smile on her face: this could well be her pretty blue bonnet standing there. 'You talking to me, darling?'

she said, her head cocked cheekily on one side. She had him weighed up in a flash: he was out slumming, always a good bet for paying over the odds.

'Are you working?' he asked haughtily.

'Looks like I might be,' she replied saucily.

'Have you a room we can go to?' he said, consulting his watch.

'How about the railway arches?' she asked, swinging her shoulders flirtatiously.

'And how about you coming home with me?' demanded Florrie.

'What do *you* want?' snapped Ivy, her smile disappearing when she turned round to find Florrie standing right behind her.

'I told yer, I want yer to come home with me,' said Florrie. She sounded unusually serious.

'Get on your way before I lose my temper, you run-down old hag,' snarled Tressing.

'Oi,' said Ivy. 'Who d'yer think yer talking to?'

'Your grandmother?' he asked maliciously.

'You bleed'n…' Florrie raised her hand, but before she could bring it stinging round his smugly sneering face, Tressing had grabbed her wrist.

'If you won't go,' he said evenly, 'then I'm going to have to make you.'

Tressing jerked Florrie by the arm as though she had no more substance than a rag doll, and sent her reeling into the narrow roadway. She lost her balance and, trying to save herself from going under the wheels of a passing wagon, she lurched sideways and fell into a steaming heap of freshly deposited horse droppings.

'Flo!' screeched Ivy, running to her friend's rescue, all thoughts of the new bonnet completely forgotten.

'I'm all right,' said Florrie, impatiently scrambling to her feet. 'Blimey,' she said, turning her nose up at the realisation of what she'd been sitting in. 'Where's that bastard? Let me get me hands on him. I'll have him, all right.'

They looked around, but Tressing had disappeared.

'I'm sorry about yer bonnet,' said Florrie, in a surprisingly deflated voice, as she brushed half-heartedly at her skirts. 'I didn't mean to spoil everything for yer.'

'S'all right,' said Ivy shrugging. 'Plenty more punters where he come from. Anyway, I didn't really like the look of him.'

'I'm glad yer said that,' said Florrie. 'He seemed monkey to me and all. Did you see that bag he was carrying?' She pulled a face. 'I've never liked doctors. They give me the creeps.'

She shivered violently.

'What's the matter?' asked Ivy. 'You all right, Flo?'

'Aw, I hate that,' said Florrie, hugging herself. 'Someone just walked over me grave.'

'Come on,' Ivy said. 'Let's get down the Butcher's for our breakfast.' Then she burst out laughing. 'If they let you in, that is. You don't half stink, Flo.'

Chapter 42

Ettie stood across the square, staring up at the dark windows of the Tressings' house. The cloudy winter sky had faded into night over an hour ago, and still no lights had been lit, but Ettie wasn't taking any chances. She waited for another ten minutes to satisfy herself that the elegant town-house was truly empty before crossing the road and walking up the flight of ornately railed stone steps then letting herself in through the heavy wooden front door.

Following Celia's instruction and remembering her earlier, equally strange visit to the house, she felt her way along the pitch-dark hall until she came to the broad staircase. Grasping the banister rail, she went carefully up to the first floor, then made her way up to the second landing where she crept to the end of the corridor; there she took the narrow back stairs intended for the staff, and finally found herself at the very top of the house in the attics.

Ettie's heartbeat drummed in her ears as she went through the fourth door on the right of the corridor which led into the operating room, the room where Celia had told her she would find the pharmacy. She had to be quick – she knew Tressing would be returning from his club after he had dined – but she didn't want to be too hasty: she couldn't risk making a noise. Even though the house was empty, she could almost feel a presence, as though she were being watched.

Her eyes were becoming accustomed to the gloom, but she still couldn't see clearly enough to find what she was looking for, so, with shaking hands, she rummaged in her bag and took out the matches and the candle she had brought with her.

The match flared and the wick of the candle burst into a yellow and blue flame. What Ettie saw in the shadowy candlelight made her gasp with horror. Her hands flew up to cover her face and she threw herself back against the wall, sending her bag and everything in it scattering across the scrubbed wooden floor. There, on the other side of the room, was a glass sided coffin. No, she was wrong, it was worse, there were three of them. Each contained a dark-haired woman stretched out as though she was sleeping.

Ettie's mind was racing almost as fast as her heart was beating. Surely Celia wouldn't have left such blatant evidence of her crimes, she thought wildly. This would mean the hangman's noose for sure. It was as though she wanted to be punished.

She had to gather her thoughts, think what to do.

Desperately trying to keep her mounting panic under control, Ettie first set the candle down safely on one of the bizarrely hinged wooden tables, and then scrabbled around the floor collecting all her things – she wanted no trace of her visit left in this terrible place.

Next, taking the candle in her trembling hand, and with a cold sweat breaking on her forehead, she walked directly over to the dreadful caskets.

Had she not been so terrified of being discovered, she would have laughed out loud with relief. Inside the coffins were not three dead women, but wax models with peculiar, apparently removable lids to their torsos. She was not surprised that she had been mistaken in the flickering candlelight: the figures were far more realistic than any she had ever seen in the penny gaffs or even in the travelling shows.

Her chest rose and fell more slowly as her breathing calmed, and the welcome relief of her discovery that they were only effigies let her go about her task more easily.

She found the cabinets lined with jars and bottles of strange-coloured substances, exactly as Celia had described. And, checking the label against the paper on which Celia had written the Latin words, Ettie took out the glass phial with the matching label. Then she closed the cabinet and hurried down to Celia's room on the second floor – the room in which only a few days ago she had been drugged and held prisoner. It all seemed such a long time ago.

She went to the writing desk, turned the tiny golden key, and took out the oblong packet from the long, central drawer. Apart from its surprising heaviness, it might have been a wrapped slab of cheese from the corner shop. Ettie put the parcel in her bag, which she tucked under her arm – she couldn't trust the handle not to break under such a weight – then made her way back down the stairs and into the front hall.

She blew out the candle before opening the front door just a crack and, peering out into the square, checked that her exit was clear. Then she slipped out into the square and ran as though she were fleeing for her life.

As soon as she was satisfied that she wasn't being followed, Ettie slowed down and, instead of running, she now wandered slowly through the streets back towards the East End. Although she had the packet in her bag and the phial in her pocket, she was in no hurry to get to Leman Street. And even though she took almost two hours to get there, she still felt that she had arrived all too soon. No matter what Celia had done, the thought of seeing her sitting there in her madness, pale-faced and hollow-eyed, was almost more than Ettie could bear; but she had promised to help her.

'I'm sorry it's so late,' she said simply to the young constable behind the desk. 'But I've come to see Miss Tressing.'

'They're planning to take me away in the morning,' Celia said through her tears as Ettie sat down. 'To an asylum. Oh Ettie, even though I'm sure now that I'm ill, that I contracted that terrible disease from my father, I still don't think I'll be able to survive in a place like that.' She wiped her nose on her already soaking-wet handkerchief.

Ettie took out her own handkerchief from her sleeve and handed it to Celia.

Celia took it with a brief nod of thanks and continued speaking. 'My own father has certified me insane.'

'Oh Celia,' Ettie reached out to her across the table.

'It's all right,' Celia sniffed. 'In a way it's easier for everyone. At least they don't have to believe that I'm a monster, a barbarous, unnatural beast.'

Ettie looked down at her bag which she had propped on her lap. She couldn't face this girl who had called her her only friend. She couldn't stand seeing her in so much pain.

'Is it really any wonder that you're unwell?' Ettie said, her voice cracking with the strain of holding back her own tears. 'What he did to you, what that man forced you to do. That would drive anyone from reason.'

'But you have to see, Ettie, especially you, that I'm not completely mad.'

'Please, Celia, don't upset yourself.'

It was as though Celia didn't hear her. 'They just need to believe I am. It's the only explanation they can find for what I did. Why can't they see that I did what I honestly thought was for the best?' She took in a long, slow breath. 'I wish you hadn't persuaded me to put the razor down, Ettie, then you needn't have become involved with this whole sorry business.'

'Don't say that, please Celia. I feel guilty enough as it is, convincing you to give yourself up, and now they're sending you to that place.'

'I'm sorry, Ettie, I didn't mean to make you feel responsible in any way. You've been a good friend to me.'

Ettie rubbed her hands over her face. For a moment she was distracted by how soft her hands had become. But the moment passed and she began to speak, slowly finding the words to try and explain to Celia her own confusion, and how other people would feel about her terrible crimes.

'You have to understand something, Celia,' she said. 'Everyone realises that it's only the toughest who survive where I come from. You have to be hard, vicious, just to get by from day to day. Even the police know that, and treat us almost with kindness at times. But you Celia, what you did, and coming from where you do; for them, in their eyes, it makes you more savage than anyone. All they see is a pretty fair-haired girl dressed in fashionable silks and ribbons. And when they think of what you did…'

Celia bowed her head. 'I was helping those women, Ettie, I promise you. No matter what anyone thinks.'

Ettie drew in a sharp breath. 'You don't have to explain yourself to me, Celia. I know what you went through and that you think what you did was right.'

'My father has arranged for me to go into a very nice private asylum.' Celia giggled for a brief, hysterical moment. 'But I can't go to that place. You know that, don't you, Ettie?'

'I know.' Ettie's voice was a barely discernible whisper.

'Did you bring what I asked?'

Silently, Ettie took the thin brown bottle from her pocket and handed it across the scarred and rickety table. Their eyes met and their fingertips touched as Celia took it from her.

'Thank you,' said Celia, and slipped it into her bodice. 'At last I'll be able to rest.'

Then Ettie lifted the weighty, paper-wrapped parcel from her bag and thudded it down on the table between them.

Celia shook her head. 'That's for you,' she said, pushing the packet back towards Ettie. 'And this.'

She took a letter from under her shawl and gave it to Ettie.

'The sergeant was kind enough to fetch me some writing things.'

Ettie started to unseal the letter.

'No. Put it away. And the packet. Look at them later.' She gazed around the dingy room with its single gas jet. 'I think you should go now,' she said.

Celia stood up and walked round the table to Ettie. She placed her hands on Ettie's shoulders, raised herself on tiptoes and kissed her tenderly on the forehead.

'Thank you, Ettie,' she said. 'You have been a true and dear friend.'

Then she went over to the door, paused briefly, then knocked on it firmly with her knuckles.

Two police officers entered the room.

'I'm ready to return to the cells now,' said Celia with quiet dignity. 'And my visitor is leaving. Please see that she has a hansom to see her safely home.'

Ettie mouthed a hasty, 'Goodbye, Celia. God bless,' and let the police constable lead her by the arm out of the mean little room.

Less than eighteen months ago, Ettie would have jerked away at a policeman's touch; she would have acted the bold little madam with the constable just to show him that she wasn't scared of him, no matter who he was, although inside she'd have been trembling. But now she was a 'lady' and she knew who was really in control, and it wasn't some trumped up little rozzer. Now she was a lady, she couldn't give a damn about him. All she could think about was Celia being buried away in an asylum; even though she knew Celia had done those terrible things, it was still a dreadful fate to be locked away in one of those places. But that was the lot of the insane.

When she reached the big upstairs office, Ettie paused and looked back along the corridor where she'd last seen Celia. She thought she would probably never see her again, the thought made her unspeakably sad; and yet, she had to admit, she was relieved that the whole terrible episode was over.

'This way, miss,' said the constable solicitously, urging her along. 'Nasty old business, seeing someone in the nick.'

Ettie nodded wordlessly.

'You're looking a bit peaky, if you don't mind me saying. Would you like me to fetch you a drink of water or something?'

Ettie looked at him and wondered to herself if he'd have been so nice to her when she was the old Ettie Wilkins. Some hope, she thought. But what did it matter?

'I would like some water,' she said, 'thanks,' and dropped down exhausted on the hard, wooden bench which, the previous night, had been her bed.

The constable returned with her drink. 'Sorry it's only a tin mug,' he apologised, 'we don't run to fancy china here.'

Ettie smiled weakly and sipped at the metallic-tasting water.

'You sit there a minute,' he said kindly. 'Give yourself a chance to recover.'

Ettie thanked him again, then leaned back against the wall. With her eyes closed, she remembered the times she'd been in that very same police station, trying to get her mother released from charges of drunkenness or assault or common prostitution or the endless other charges they'd brought against her at different times. Remembered how she and her mother had been abused and mocked by the officers.

She couldn't sit there in that place for a moment longer. She put the mug down on the bench beside her, gathered her things and stood up to leave.

But she hadn't even finished fastening her cape round her shoulders before she was running back down the corridor towards the sound of a woman's terrible screams and of excited male voices shouting for help, followed by the echoing sound of heavy boots pounding along the stone floors.

A police officer, not quite as tall as Ettie, barred her way. 'No, miss, you can't go though there,' he said, holding up his hands. He looked over his shoulder to see what was happening. 'Now, go back upstairs. Please, miss. Do as you're told.'

Ettie tried to push past him, but he wouldn't budge.

She could hear the loud voices, more and more agitated, coming from just along the passage way.

'It's Tressing,' shouted one. 'She's swallowed this whole bottle of something or other.'

'Give it here.'

There was a pause.

'Aw, Christ! Sniff that.'

'What? What is it?'

'Prussic Acid. Can't you smell the bitter almonds?'

'Shall I go for the doc?'

'No, leave her. There's no helping her now, the poor cow. What a way to go.'

'God rest her soul.'

'You're joking. Straight to Hell that one.'

'What?'

The loud male voice dropped to a whisper. 'Didn't you know? She's the Ripper.'

'Her? Are you saying Whitechapel Jack's a woman?'

'Well done,' said the other officer sarcastically. 'You should join the detectives, mate.'

Outside in the street, Ettie took great gulping breaths that formed moist clouds in the late night air. She hadn't slept properly since she couldn't remember when, but she didn't want to hail a cab. She wanted to walk; she needed to clear her head of the stink of the police station far more than she needed sleep. And where would she tell the driver to take her anyway? She didn't even have a bed to go to. Not until she could be sure how Jacob would take her apologies for doubting him.

But eventually exhaustion overtook her and she came gratefully to the churchyard of St Jude's. She knew she would have to share the cold and damp place with the homeless and wayward inhabitants for whom it provided their only shelter at night, but she had seen far worse than a few tramps slumped together in a drunken haze. There wasn't much left that could still hold fear for Ettie Wilkins.

She found herself a damp stone seat in the deep shadows of the church wall, wrapped her cloak around her and soon, in her exhausted distress, fell into a disturbed, dream-troubled sleep.

The next thing Ettie knew about was the sight of bright winter sunshine slanting across the moss-covered headstones and monuments marking the graves.

She shivered and pulled her cape more closely round her. She stretched her aching limbs slowly, trying to relieve the cold stiffness. As she rubbed at her calves and ankles, Ettie looked across at the memorials. They seemed so beautiful to her in the clear winter light: solemnly grand last resting-places of loved ones who had been buried properly, with a dignity which had been denied her own mother.

Ettie stood up and was surprised at the heaviness of her bag. Then she remembered the letter and packet. She sat down again on the damp stone seat to see what it was that Celia Tressing had wanted her to have.

First she opened the packet. In it was a soft leather pouch, and when Ettie loosened the drawstring to look inside she could hardly believe what she was seeing. Never before had she seen so many gold sovereigns together.

Hurriedly Ettie gathered up the packet and shoved it deep into her bag, which she slipped under her cloak. She might have been tired, shocked, and even confused by what had happened but she wasn't stupid: she knew better than to flash money about. She had changed a lot, but she hadn't forgotten the lessons she'd learned in the gutter.

Next she tore open the letter to try and find some explanation as to why Celia had given it to her.

The words were so deftly penned and the paper was so smooth, it couldn't have been more unlike the scruffy note that was all she had left of her mother.

She brushed a dark, stray curl away from her eyes and started to read:

> *My only true friend* [it began]
>
> *I need you to know that I never intended anything other than good when I performed those abortions. Some might believe it to be murder, but I think they are wrong. If I hadn't offered my help to those desperate women, what would have become of them? Burdened with yet another mouth to feed, they would have been forced back out on to the streets to find money, and so the whole sorry process would begin again.*

I admit that at first I did blame the women for the lives they lead, but I trust that I have come to understand them better and the necessities which drive them to their life of shame and sin. Maybe I was mistaken to think it was the right thing to do, to help them, but it might have been better had I used my time speaking out for them at public meetings. Maybe the madness I fear is creeping upon me would have prevented such work. I do not know the answer to that. I only know that, even though it was a crime and I must pay for it, doing the abortions was what the women themselves wanted me to do.

I hope that I will be forgiven now you understand why I did what I had to do. I also like to think that you have forgiven me for keeping you against your will that night. I didn't want you to go out in the night and become another victim of that fearful creature who stalks the night.

You, Ettie, have given me so much, but most important of all you have given me the strength to escape. By showing me that there is a world beyond the veil, I know now that I have no need to fear death.

The packet contains money that was to finance my escape in this world rather than the next. That was not to be. So I hope that it is of use for whatever escape you feel that you might need to make.

I thank you, my dear friend, from the bottom of my heart.

Celia

Ettie screwed the letter up and flung it from her as hard as she could.

'What have I done?' she moaned to herself, burying her face in her hands, sickened at the thought of Celia's pale, haunted face staring at her. She had thought her such a privileged, silly girl at one time. Now she was dead, her lovely body poisoned with acid and the disease that had driven her to madness, and Ettie had completely misjudged her.

434

She let her head drop back against the cold stone of the church wall, but almost immediately she sat up straight again. A look of horror crept over her face as it slowly dawned on her: if Celia really hadn't done the murders, then – while she was lying dead on a cold marble slab in a mortuary – the killer was still roaming free.

Ettie jumped to her feet and began hurrying towards the gate. She had to get away from the graveyard, from that place of death and decay.

As she rushed along the gravel-covered path, an old woman, bent almost double with age, came shambling towards her, a mean little posy of wax flowers grasped in her hand.

'Don't be in such a hurry, dear,' the old woman said kindly as she shuffled past her. 'No matter how fast yer run, yer can't escape the reaper man, yer know.'

Ettie turned and watched her.

With enormous effort she lowered herself on to her knees beside an ill-carved, ivy-covered angel. When she eventually settled herself on the damp, dew-covered grass, she let out a loud gasp of relief and placed her little bouquet at the base of the memorial.

She put her hands together and mumbled a few indistinct words and then lifted her eyes to Ettie. Tears were finding their way through the wrinkled crepe of her skin.

'Visiting one of yer family were yer, sweetheart? Yer never forget them yer love, do yer?'

She rose painfully to her feet, gladly taking Ettie's offered hand to steady herself.

'Do you want to sit down for a bit?' asked Ettie.

'I could do with a sit-down,' she said. 'But them old stone benches they've got here don't do yer rheumatics no good, do they? They chill yer right through to yer bones.'

She brushed some flakes of mud from her threadbare coat.

'Dead nearly three years, my Georgie,' she said. 'And d'yer know what? What I'm really sorry about is that I never treated him decent when he was still around to appreciate it. It's a terrible thing to be left alone with no one. If only we thought a bit more about what we do eh? Then perhaps we wouldn't make such a pig's ear out of things. There's so much I wished I'd have told him.' She shook her head. 'And things I wished I'd asked him.'

Ettie folded her arms round the woman and wept. Clinging on to her, she sobbed like a little child.

'That's all right, sweetheart,' the woman said, patting Ettie's back. 'You cry. You let it all out.'

Ettie wiped her nose on the back of her hand and smiled down at the woman through her tears. 'It makes a lot of sense what you said. There's a lot of things I should do before it's too late. I'm going to sort my life out.'

'Good for you, girl,' said the old woman, and smiled back at her.

Ettie bowed her head and said to the woman, 'I blamed someone for something she didn't do. I was stupid and vain. I thought I knew everything. What I should have been doing was listening to what she was *really* telling me. I don't intend making the same mistake again. There's someone I mean to make my peace with.'

'Well,' said the woman, 'I'm glad to hear it. Regrets are a terrible thing. They eat you away. But they don't have to. You've got a chance. If you make up your mind you can do something about it, you can try to put things right. Make amends. Still, nice as it is to have a chat,' she said, 'this won't buy the baby a new bonnet, will it? I'll have to be off now. I've got me cleaning jobs to do. Can't afford to upset your boss nowadays, can yer, sweetheart? Not with work the way it is.'

Ettie said her goodbyes and stood and watched as the elderly woman made her way painfully towards the gate.

'Wait,' she called out, and ran to stop the woman before she left the churchyard. Ettie pressed five of the golden sovereigns into her hand. 'Get yourself a nice warm coat,' she said. 'This weather's bitter.'

The woman looked at the money. 'Yer very kind, love, but I don't need no charity.'

'It's not charity,' Ettie said firmly. 'It's payment. For good advice.'

As she made her way along Old Ford Road, Ettie saw Mrs Hawkins walking along ahead of her, just about to cross the bridge. Ettie caught up with her and tapped her on the back.

Mrs Hawkins turned round. She looked satisfied at seeing her, but not very pleased.

'Mrs H.,' she said. 'I was hoping you'd be calling in this morning.'

'Aw yeah,' said Mrs Hawkins coldly.

'Yes.' Ettie tried to sound light-hearted. 'The Professor and I had a bit of a disagreement a couple of days ago. Well, last week, really. And I've been staying with a friend. I wanted a bit of moral support when I went back in.'

Mrs Hawkins stood there, tight-lipped.

'I'm sure you noticed I've not been around.'

'Can't say as I have, actually,' said Mrs Hawkins, eyeing her knowingly. 'I've not been around for a few days myself, yer see.'

'Oh?'

'No,' she said primly. 'I've been speaking to Mr H. and we've decided, the two of us, like. That what with all the–' she looked over her shoulder and then mouthed – '*trouble* going on… Well.' She folded her arms across her chest. 'We decided I should terminate my employment with the Professor. That's why I'm on my way there now, to tell him. Mr H. wanted to come with me, but I said, don't you worry yourself about me, I said. Let him lay one finger on me and I'll have that bread knife to his throat.' She fiddled with her hat pin and said, without much conviction: 'Nothing against you, dearie, of course. It's just, what with the gentleman being so foreign and everything, Mr H. don't like it. There's talk about the Ripper being of a foreign persuasion, *yer.*'

Ettie said quietly, 'So I've heard.'

They made the last part of their journey in silence.

Ettie unlocked the front door and called along the passageway, 'Jacob. Jacob, it's me. Ettie. I've got Mrs Hawkins here with me.'

Loathe as she was to admit it – even to herself – Ettie was more than glad to have Mrs Hawkins with her, and not only because she would help break what would otherwise be a difficult atmosphere between Jacob and her.

As they walked into the sitting room, Mrs Hawkins peered round Ettie's shoulder.

'No sign of him,' she said, stating what was obvious to both of them. 'Must be out.'

Ettie went into the bedroom, then the kitchen, and then the bathroom.

'Not like him to be out this time of the morning,' said Mrs Hawkins wisely. 'Don't look like he's been home all night, if you ask me. In fact I wonder if he's...' The words stopped as she spotted the letter on the mantelpiece. 'Here look,' she said, taking down the envelope. 'It's a letter. What does it say?'

Ettie took the letter from her with trembling hands. 'It's addressed to me,' she said. She, who had never had so much as a note before now, had had three in such a short time: the one from her mother, then the one from Celia, and now this. She dreaded what bad news this one would contain.

'Here, I bet he's gone and done a moonlight.' Mrs Hawkins' face lit up at the possibility of a scandal which she could spread around the neighbourhood.

'I don't think so,' said Ettie briskly.

'Here, if he has buggered off, how about my back wages then?' Mrs Hawkins' face was now sour with hostility.

'I'll settle that,' said Ettie. 'Don't worry. If you could wait in the kitchen a moment, please.'

With a loud sniff, Mrs Hawkins went into the other room as she was told.

As Ettie took down the imitation book in which Jacob kept the money, she could hear Mrs Hawkins mumbling away in the kitchen about the state of the dirty plates and cups that had been left in the sink.

In the moment it took Ettie to see that all the money was gone and the book was empty, she knew that Mrs Hawkins was right: Jacob had run away.

Ettie took three sovereigns from the packet Celia had given her, and then called Mrs Hawkins back into the sitting room.

At the sight of the gold coins, Mrs H. smiled winningly. 'That's ever so good of yer, dear,' she said in a very friendly way. Then added sullenly, 'It'll make up for all the worry I've had these last few weeks.'

'Good,' said Ettie, guiding her towards the passage.

As she went to close the front door, Ettie heard her mutter. 'I wonder how she got hold of this sort of money to throw around? As if everyone don't know.'

Ettie didn't bother to answer her, she just slammed the door hard and went back to the sitting room to find out what bad news this latest letter held for her.

She sat on the edge of one of the armchairs by the lifeless, empty hearth and read what Jacob had to say:

> Ettie, my dear, sweet, Ettie,
>
> I want to explain to you why I left Paris, as it has become an increasing barrier between us, making you suspicious of many things that I say.
>
> I had been the darling of the salons in that elegant city, the object of many fashionable women's desire. I am not being conceited, what I am telling you is simply a matter of fact. Bored rich women rarely have enough to fill their days, and I had many offers from those ladies who wanted to tempt me into helping them pass their time. And, be assured, they had no interest in my communicating with the spirits on their behalf, they were concerned with far more worldly pleasures. But I resisted them all.
>
> I was not being saintly, Ettie, I did so mainly for the reason that I did not want to upset any of them. They were a wonderful source of wealth for me and, also, I admit it, I had a mistress already. She was an artist's model who had

as much pleasure from the relationship as I. There was no restraint on either of us. We enjoyed each other's company in my big feather bed. We were both independent. It was fun. You would have liked her. Do not be shocked, it ended quite amicably, months before I left. And remember I never pretended I was anything I was not – not to you, Ettie.

My life was going too well, I should have been suspicious: fate usually has something to throw at us when we are being at our most complacent. And so it happened. One of the high ladies who attended my circles found herself embarrassingly with child. No matter how she conjured with the dates, her husband could not have been the father. The brave Monsieur X, let us call him, was busy in Africa claiming vast tracts of that continent for France.

Madame X chose to point the finger of blame at me. It saved her lover from her brother's pistol, but made life in Paris impossible for me. I was marked out as the Jew seducer. I thought – foolishly – that by my not speaking of it, it would be wiped away but now I know I should have told you that I was forced to flee Paris because of the sins of others – not because of anything I had done but because of the hatred of Jews which had touched me so often before, including the terrifying time when I was a child and that hatred resulted in the death of my beloved mother at our home in Russia.

Now that hatred threatened to kill me also. And so I had to get away. I did not wait for the bank to open the next morning, I took what little money was in my rooms and disappeared into the night. At least that was one lesson I learned. This time, when I was forced to flee from yet another false accusation, I had all the money I needed at hand. I left you without any money – that was wrong of me. But that is all I have done. I am not the savage slayer of those wretched women, Ettie, whatever people might say. I need you to believe me that those accusations are false.

By the time you read this, I will have sailed for New York. I intend to make a new life in America. And, Ettie, I want you to be with me. We could create a new show and take it into the wild Western states. The pioneer men there will love you and you will know exactly how to deal with them.

You will be a sensation. Or, if you prefer, we could stay on the East coast and delight the polite parlours of Boston.

Who knows what we will do – the world is ours for the taking.

I want you to sell everything from the rooms, get whatever price you can for it. I need none of it now that I have you. You must join me, Ettie, please. If I ever meant anything to you, join me. And believe me when I say that in my own way, Ettie, I love you. Come to me. We can have such a wonderful life together.

I'll write again when I arrive. I will send the letter care of Patrick at the Frying Pan because I know you well enough to understand that that is a place to where you will always return, my beautiful Whitechapel girl.

I pray that you will come to me, but I have a feeling, a fear, that your beloved East End is where you will choose to stay.

Ettie stood up and watched blankly as the letter fluttered from her hand and down into the empty grate.

A terrible heaviness filled her heart. She had misjudged Celia and she had misjudged Jacob, not once but many times, and all because she had allowed the suspicions of others to cloud her judgement.

She threw back her head and closed her eyes, thinking about what the old woman had said to her: what else, Ettie wondered, had she done that she would always regret?

Suddenly, a look of determination came over Ettie's face and, very firmly, she said out loud to herself, 'Well, moping around won't help no one, Ettie girl. You wanna pull yourself together.'

Then she turned on her heel, walked from the sitting room, along the passageway and out of the front door.

Ettie hurried along the streets towards Whitechapel. It was midmorning so, if she was lucky, all the girls would be in the Frying Pan having their breakfast before they started looking for business – although some of them might already be touting round at the market hoping to separate the costers from some of their hard-won earnings.

All she wanted was to see some familiar faces, to talk to all her old friends – Maisie especially. And maybe even, with a bit more luck, to see Billy.

As she turned from the Bethnal Green Road into Brick Lane, Ettie took a long, deep breath and sniffed the air like a young pony that had been let into a field after being kept in a dark stable. After the gloom of the terrible night before, the fog had cleared completely, and it was a bright, brisk winter's day. Cold as it was, the sky was blue and everything had a fresh, hopeful look to it. Even the fruit and vegetables on the stalls shone as though they'd been polished.

A stall holder picked out a big, rosy apple which he rubbed to a shine on his tatty sleeve and held it out to Ettie as she passed by.

'Here y'are, darling,' he chirped, 'how about getting your lips round this, then?'

But Ettie was too preoccupied with her thoughts as she rushed along the busy street even to realise that his cheeky suggestion had been aimed at her.

'Your loss, sweetheart,' he called after her, and looked round for another likely catch.

Within moments, Ettie had reached her goal, and was standing in the doorway of the Frying Pan, pulling back the thick plush curtain that kept out the winter cold from the fug of the smoke-filled bar.

'Hello, Ett!' hollered Ada from her usual place at the table in the corner. 'Good to see yer, girl. Come over here and sit with us.'

Ettie waved. 'Hang on, Ada,' she said, and dipped into her bag. Discreetly she produced one of the gold sovereigns which she gave to Patrick.

'Good to see yer, Ettie love,' he said in his soft Irish brogue. 'We were all glad to hear you'd been found safe and sound.'

'Ta, Pat,' she smiled back at him. 'Set up another round of whatever they're having, and a glass of milk stout for me, please.'

'Right you are, darling,' said the landlord, pocketing the shiny coin. 'You go and sit yourself down and I'll bring them over to you.'

'Hello, May,' she said, sliding along the bench until she was sitting up close to her. 'I'm glad you're here, I wanted to ask you a favour.'

'Aw yeah,' said May, frostily. 'We don't see yer from one week to the next and now yer asking favours?'

'I was wondering where I could get some decent lodgings round here, that's all. I'm a bit out of touch with who's living where these days.'

'So how about your place over at Bow with the Professor?' Maisie asked, her eyes narrowed.

'It's time for me to get out of Bow, May,' said Ettie quietly. 'There's nothing there for me any more. Jacob's left the country. He's gone to America.'

'America, eh?' said Ada, thoughtfully. 'Fancy that. That's a long way that is. In fact, didn't that sailor who was in here the other day say that...'

Maisie wasn't listening to Ada's geography lesson, she was too busy beaming at Ettie with a face that had lit up as though the sun had just come out. 'I tell yer what,' she gabbled excitedly, 'I'm sure me mum'd be only too pleased to have yer stay with us.' She paused. 'Till yer get settled like,' she added more calmly.

'That's a good idea,' said Ada, nodding wisely. 'Yer'll be better off staying with them what yer know, till they catch the Ripper.'

'Ada's right,' said May. 'Yer'll be safe with us. And it'll be a right lark and all.' She shoved Ettie in the ribs. 'Here, yer can share with me.'

'Thanks, May,' Ettie said gratefully. 'I'd like that. I really would.'

'And yer know what this means,' said Ada. 'You'll be home with us lot for Christmas. We'll be able to have a right old knees up.'

'I wish I wasn't so bleed'n hefty,' said May, eyeing Ettie's dress and cape wistfully. 'Then I could borrow some of them posh clothes of yours.'

Patrick came over and put a tray of drinks down on the table in front of Ettie and handed her her change. 'From Miss Wilkins,' he said with an extravagant, joking bow. 'A little treat.'

'Ta, Pat,' Ettie said with a grin, and handed him back a sixpence. 'Have one for yourself.'

Patrick winked his thanks and returned to his place behind the bar.

'I might have one or two bits that might suit you just right, you know, May,' mused Ettie, and took a deep swallow of her stout.

'What, a bonnet and a handbag, yer mean?' chipped in Bella. 'Me and you Maise: built to last, we are girl.'

Maisie tutted self-pityingly. 'Don't I know it.'

'You be proud of yer body,' said Bella, heaving her huge bosoms upwards with the back of her great plate-sized hands. 'These are me fortune, these are.'

'We was all sorry to hear about yer mum,' said Ada, suddenly serious. She raised her glass and said, 'God rest her soul.'

'Yer right,' said Bella. 'It don't seem possible she ain't going to stick her head round that door and give us a little dance just like she used to. We all miss her.' She wiped her mouth with the back of her hand and raised her glass. 'Here's to Sarah.'

'Sarah,' they chorused.

'Ta,' said Ettie. 'Here's to you, Mum.'

For a moment nobody spoke, each alone with their own memory of Sarah Wilkins. Then Ettie set down her glass and asked: 'Tell me, what do you think of this? I've thought about having a wooden seat, a nice bench, put in the churchyard at St Jude's. And having Mum's name put on it on a little brass plate, as a memorial to her.'

'What a lovely idea,' said Ada, trying to work out how much that little lot was going to cost.

'Aw, yeah, smashing. Yer mum would have liked that,' said May. 'There in the churchyard with all the flowers and trees and everything. Like being out in the country. Really thoughtful, that is, Ett. Here, and I know what, yer can ask our Billy to make it for you. How about that?' She stood up excitedly and barged past Ettie before anyone could stop her. 'I'll send our Tommy to go and fetch him right now; he'll be having his break soon.'

—

'Hello, Ett,' said Billy, taking off his cap and wringing it round in his hands. 'Tommy said you wanted to see me, urgent like. Everything all right, is it?'

Maisie grinned and jabbed Ettie in the ribs. 'Say something,' she urged her.

'It wasn't urgent, Bill. I didn't mean to drag you away from work or nothing.'

'That's all right,' he said. 'I'm pleased to see yer. And I'm on me dinner now, anyway.'

Bella looked across at May and raised her eyebrows knowingly.

'It's about having a wooden bench made, sort of in memory of Mum. May said you might be able to do it for me.'

'Sure,' Billy nodded. 'Sure. Tell yer what, come with me now and I'll show yer some of me wood.'

Ada burst out in unseemly gales of laughter. 'Yeah go on, Ett, go and look at his planks.'

'Ignore her, Ett,' said May, scowling at Ada. 'You go with Billy and I'll wait here for you.' She paused, then looked up at her brother and added, 'Then we can go and see me mum and ask her about you coming to lodge with us.'

Billy broke into a broad, delighted smile. 'You coming to lodge with us?'

'That's right,' said Ettie, smiling back at him.

Billy nodded his head again. 'Coming to lodge with us, eh? Right.'

'Watch it,' Ada said. 'Yer'll nod yer flaming head right off your shoulders if yer carry on like that. Go on, Ett, for Christ's sake take him out of here and go and look at his wood.'

The moment Billy held open the door for Ettie to step out of the pub into the cold winter air, the whispers started.

'Looks like she's come home for good to me,' said Bella.

'And it looks like they're settled back together and all,' said Ada. 'I like to see things back to how they should be. It's only right somehow.'

Maisie didn't say anything. She just grinned and looked totally chuffed with it all.

'Mind you,' said Ada. 'Ettie wants to be a bit lively if she is interested. That young Ivy's had her eye on your Billy lately.'

'She wouldn't stand a chance,' said Maisie confidently.

–

'This isn't the way to Reed's,' said Ettie, as Billy led her down a narrow, almost hidden cut-through between two of the tall, blank-walled warehouses in Hanbury Street.

'I know.' Billy turned to her and smiled and held up a key. 'Wait till you see in here,' he said, and stopped beside a peeling wooden door set in a soot-covered brick wall.

He pushed the door open and ushered her into a big open space lit from three tall windows which lined one whole side of the room. At the other side stood a series of shelves stacked with wood of different lengths and colours. In pride of place, in the middle of the room, stood a large workbench. On the workbench was a beautifully carved and crafted chair.

'I could make the rest of the set if yer like,' Billy said, lifting it down for Ettie to sit on. 'And a table as well. Round, square, whatever yer fancy.'

She looked at him, puzzled. 'What do you mean? I wanted a seat for the churchyard, not a dining-room set.'

446

'I know, I'll make a lovely seat for yer mum, you wait and see. And I'll carve it all and everything.'

'So what's this for?' She ran her hands up and down the smooth polished arms of the carver chair.

'For our new home,' he said, and began fiddling around with one of the planes that stood in a graduated line on the workbench.

'Our what?'

Billy went over to the wall and took down a piece of paper that was speared on a nail.

'Look at this,' he said, walking back to her, his head bowed shyly. 'Mr Reed sorted it all out for me.'

Ettie studied the crumpled sheet of paper. 'It's a receipt for the down deposit on the lease of a workshop,' she said, looking up at him. 'And the rooms above it.'

'This workshop,' he said proudly. 'I'm setting up on me own. Me very own business.'

Ettie didn't say anything; she just stared at the paper as though it was about to speak to her.

'Don't be angry, Ett, I never meant to presume nothing.'

'I'm not angry, Bill,' she said slowly. 'You surprised me, that's all.'

'I only put down the deposit. I don't have to take the whole lot. Mr Reed explained it to me. I can just rent the workshop if I like. But I jumped at the chance when it came up a couple of weeks back. I've always hoped you'd come home to Whitechapel. And now you have and you're looking for lodgings and everything. I thought I might as well...' He levered himself up on to the workbench and said flatly. 'I've messed this up, ain't I?'

Ettie stood up from the chair, went over to him, and gently touched his face. 'You're daft, you are,' she said fondly.

'Yeah, and I got some daft idea that you loved me,' he said abruptly. 'But yer did used to care for me,' he said. 'Yer did, didn't you, Ett?'

'Yes, Bill. And I still do care for you. *More* than care for you.' She smiled gently at him. 'I've always loved you, Billy Bury,' she said. 'Ever since we were a pair of snotty-nosed kids playing out in the court together.' She dropped her chin and stared at the floor. 'I just forgot for a while, that's all.'

'Do yer really love me?' he asked, his voice full of hope.

'Of course I do, Bill.'

'But, by the sound of yer voice, not as much as yer do that Professor geezer, eh?' He sighed loudly, folded his arms, and stared over his shoulder towards the tall windows.

'Don't start acting daft again, Bill.'

'I know I'm not like him, Ett.'

'No,' she said softly, 'you're not. And I'm glad. It wouldn't do for everyone to be the same. You're a straightforward, honest, decent bloke. That's what I love about you.'

Billy swallowed hard. 'And I love you and all, Ett. Yer know that.'

'I know, Bill.'

He jumped down from the workbench and looked at her expectantly. 'So, what d'yer think then? D'yer think yer could live here with me?'

Ettie turned away from him. 'Don't get carried away by what I've said, Bill, yer'll have to let me think about it. I'm sorry, but I need a bit of time. So much has happened to me lately, I don't want to make any more decisions without really sorting out what I should do.' She walked over to the shelves and looked at the neatly stacked piles of timber.

'But yer really *will* think about it, won't yer?' Billy said, going over to her. 'You ain't just saying that to shut me up, are you, Ett?'

'No, Bill, I promise. I really will think about it. And don't get me wrong, I'm really pleased, happy as anything, that you've asked me. But I don't want to say I'll do something then regret it, that's all.'

'I don't understand. You say you love me, so what's there to regret?' Billy stood behind her and took her by the arm, trying to make her turn to face him.

She pulled her arm free and said quietly: 'I've been given the chance to get away from here, Bill. Right away. To really make a new start this time.'

'What d'yer mean?'

At last she turned to face him. 'Billy. I've got the chance to go to America.'

PART FOUR

The New Year 1889

'I didn't think you two was coming,' Maisie said, linking arms with Ettie. 'Mum's been making me come out here and look for yer every couple of minutes. Like a cat on hot coals, she is. What yer been up to – kissing and cuddling in that workshop of yours, Bill?'

'Maisie,' he warned her, 'I thought I'd told yer about that big gob of yours.'

'Come on, Bill, cheer up. And get a move on while yer at it,' she said, shoving open the door to the Frying Pan. 'Yer know how busy the pub gets on Old Year's night. Mum'll do her crust if we have to share a table with too many others. She'll get the right hump and spoil everything.'

'Aw yeah,' Billy taunted her as he nodded towards his mother. 'Just look at her. She's well unhappy having to sit with all the girls. I don't think.'

Myrtle Bury was sitting at the corner table surrounded by Ruby, Ada, Big Bella, Mad Milly, Flo and Ivy. They were all laughing like they were fit to burst.

'Aw, stop moaning, Bill, and go up and get us some drinks.' May shoved her brother hard in the ribs, propelling him towards the bar. 'And see if Patrick's seen that no-good Alfie of ours yet.'

Billy rolled his eyes in reply.

'Aw yeah, and see if yer can find our Tommy and have a word with him and all later on,' she continued. 'I'll bet he's out there in the street, hanging around, and getting up to gawd-alone-knows what sort of mischief.'

'Blimey, sis,' said Billy shaking his head. 'Don't your tongue ache?'

'No, but me eyeballs do, having to stare at your ugly mug all day.'

Ettie stood smiling happily to herself, watching them bicker. She'd been lodging with the Burys for nearly five weeks, and had grown to love the way they good-naturedly and constantly teased one another. They were a noisy, rowdy lot at times, arguing and shouting with the best of them, but they had a fierce loyalty that everyone in the court knew about and respected. But it was only since she'd actually lived with them that Ettie had seen just how intense, and impressive, their love for their family really was. Circumstances had meant that she had never known what it was like to have a proper family, not one like the Burys, anyway, and she'd come to cherish the closeness and affection they shared: it gave them the sort of strength she envied.

'Squeeze up,' she said to Bella, her gaze following Billy as he made his way through the crowd to the bar 'Let's get on the bench.'

Bella moved over without stopping speaking for even a split second. She was telling Myrtle and the rest of them a long, complicated joke which had become even more convoluted when the punchline had completely escaped her. But it didn't matter: her audience still found her performance hilarious, and wept with laughter as she screwed up her big, broad face trying to remember what happened next to the vicar and his teapot.

As her friends hugged their aching sides, Ettie looked around at all the other people in the jam-packed bar. The faces she saw were optimistic, bright with hope that the New Year might just be better than the last one. And, as they had so often lately, her thoughts turned to the old woman she had met in the churchyard of St Jude's. The more she had thought about what the woman had said about the poisonous effect of letting regrets gnaw away at you, the more it had made sense to Ettie. Over the weeks she had come to admit to herself that she did still have some regrets but, as they were mostly to do with events that had long-since passed, she couldn't do anything about them, no matter how hard she wished otherwise. And, tough as it was, Ettie knew that, for her, the only sensible thing to do was to put them behind her and face to the future, not to the past.

'Oi! Dreamer.' Milly leaned across the table and poked Ettie on the shoulder. 'Wake up. Billy's brought us some drinks over.'

'Ta, Bill,' Ettie said, smiling up at him and taking her glass from the tray he held out to her.

'How's that fancy fellah you used to knock about with getting on, Ett?' asked Milly, wiping the foam from the stout off her lips. 'You heard anything from him?'

Just as Milly spoke, Billy was taking a swig of beer and nearly choked himself. His sister and mum turned on Milly and flashed warnings with their eyes.

'Shut up, Milly!' Florrie hissed at her under her breath.

'No, it's all right, Flo. Leave her alone,' Ettie said, glancing up at Billy who was standing, red-faced, next to her. 'There's no secret about it, Mill. You know he's gone to live in America, don't you? In New York?'

'Yeah, I know that,' Milly answered primly, pulling a face at Florrie.

'Well, I've sold up everything from the place in Bow. And now I'm waiting to get a letter from him, with his address, so that I can get the money to him.'

'What? All of it?' asked Milly incredulously.

'All of it.'

The company sitting round the table, Maisie and Myrtle included, mumbled their surprise at such profligacy.

Billy stood there, silently.

'It's his money,' said Ettie firmly.

'And you don't need it. Not now you've got that job,' piped up the usually tight-lipped Ruby. 'Didn't ever think that no one from Tyvern Court would ever get a job like that, and that's the truth.'

'Yeah,' said May admiringly. 'Fancy a friend of mine working in an office, eh? Yer should be well chuffed with yerself, Ettie Wilkins.'

'And happy to stay where you are. More than happy,' added Myrtle firmly.

'I know yer old mum would have been well pleased to see yer doing so good for yerself,' Ruby added, raising her glass to Ettie.

'And seeing what a good girl she been to me and all,' said Myrtle. 'It's like having another daughter about the place, it is.'

'And a sister,' said May, patting Ettie's hand.

'I don't know how he could stand to leave yer behind, someone as perfect as you,' simpered Ivy, flapping her eyelashes at Billy. Then she said slyly: 'Or has he asked yer to go out to America to be with him, Ett?'

Ivy's crafty expression soon changed when Billy snapped at her: 'Why don't yer mind yer own business?'

He swallowed the last of his beer, slammed down his glass on the table and went over to stand with the crowd at the bar.

'Well?' persisted Ivy, bluntly, 'has he asked yer?'

'Yes, he has if yer must know. And yes, before you ask, I *have* thought about it,' Ettie said levelly, staring at her.

'How d'yer mean, you've thought about it?' Ivy exclaimed. 'Yer must be mad. I know if I had the chance to go to America I'd be off like a shot.'

'Bleed'n good job that'd be and all, if yer ask me,' mumbled May. Ivy ignored her. 'They've got gold mines out there, and all yer have to do is pick the nuggets up right off the ground.' She snapped her fingers. 'Easy as that and yer a millionaire.'

'Yeah, I've heard those stories,' said Ettie, looking across to where Billy was hunched over against the bar.

'Well, are yer going or ain't yer?' demanded Ivy impatiently. 'Like I said, I've thought about it. Like I've thought about going to a lot of different places in my time.' Ettie turned to look Ivy full in the face. 'It's easy going away, believe me.'

'I do know,' sniped Ivy, petulantly. 'I did come here all the way from Essex. Remember?'

'Well then, you should know as well as anyone, it's easy going away but it's not always so easy going back.'

'What's she going on about?' sneered Ivy, mugging at Flo.

'Why don't you belt up, Ivy?' hissed Myrtle. She had just been thinking how nicely things had been going between Ettie and her Billy during the past few weeks – just the way she wanted, in fact – and now this little madam was poking her nose in.

'I was only asking,' pouted Ivy. 'What's so special about her that she can't even answer a straight question?'

'Well, if you must know,' Ettie began, 'I've decided to...'

But before she could finish what she saying, Ettie was interrupted by young Tommy Bury who came bursting into the bar waving a newspaper.

'You,' said Myrtle, jerking her thumb towards the door before he had the chance to open his mouth. 'Out. Or I'll call our Billy over to yer.'

'No, Mum, listen. Please,' he appealed to her excitedly. 'Listen to this.' He shoved in between Florrie and Ivy and spread the paper out on the table, balancing it precariously on top of all the glasses.

'It's about the Old Boy,' he said, stabbing his finger at the headlines.

'Aw no, not Jack the Ripper,' wailed Ada, squinting at the words she couldn't read. 'I thought we'd heard the last of that bastard.'

'We have,' gasped Tommy. 'This time he's up to his old tricks in New York. Did this girl in just the same way as he did in all the brides round here.'

Even though the room was stiflingly hot, Ettie shuddered. 'Show me that, Tom,' she said, taking the newspaper and folding it back on itself so that just the one story was visible. Quickly she scanned the dense fines of black print.

'Looks like Tommy's right,' she said quietly. 'The killings might have come to an end here in Whitechapel, but America had better prepare itself.'

Tommy took the paper back from her and spread it out on the table again.

'Fancy old Jack doing his dirty deeds in New York,' said Ivy, running her fingers along the words, then looking up under her lashes at Ettie. 'Makes yer go all cold, don't it?' She put her hand to her mouth and said sarcastically, 'Here, didn't you say that that was where your fancy man's taken himself off to? He's a Jew, ain't he? A foreigner.'

Ettie stared at her disbelievingly. 'What's wrong with people like you, Ivy? Can't you just mind your own business?'

The table fell into an uncomfortable silence, but they were soon back talking amongst themselves when Big Bella took some of the money from the kitty and dragged Ivy over to the bar with her to fetch another round of drinks.

Ettie, however, didn't join in their chatter. She sat quietly with her thoughts, telling herself that she wouldn't let the likes of Ivy upset her or ever again make her think the foolish, prejudiced things that had once made her misjudge people and cause such pain. She'd learnt from seeing the tragic results of suspicion and doubt, and had become a wiser and, she hoped, a better person because of it. And she knew that, no matter what others thought, Jacob could not be a killer. He was a man with flaws, certainly, but a man who had been wronged. She had been disloyal to him once, betrayed him by doubting his word, but she would never do that to him again.

Through her relationship with Jacob, she had found the wisdom to know that she could make a new life for herself, a good life; and where she had once thought that the only way to escape was to run away, she knew now that you could never escape from what was in your heart – she would always be grateful to him for that.

'Are you all right, Ettie love?'

Ettie looked up to see Myrtle frowning at her.

'Yeah,' Ettie said. 'Just thinking, Myrt, that's all.'

'Right.' Myrtle nodded, then stood up and hollered across to her son. 'Billy, it's nearly midnight, son. Get all us girls a little drop of something to see in the New Year. And get that paper out of the way, Tommy.'

As Billy set the tray on the table next to Ettie, she reached up to him, threw her arms round his neck, and kissed him full on the lips.

'Blimey,' said Billy, his face scarlet. 'What was that all about?' Ettie got up and stood in front of him. She nibbled at her lip, and fiddled anxiously with the chain of her locket, then, taking a deep breath, she said solemnly: 'I've come to a decision, Bill.'

Billy gulped, his eyes fixed on hers. 'Yeah?'

Everyone at the table listened intently, hanging on to their every word.

'I know I've not been fair to you, keeping you waiting around like this while I sorted out what I should do.' Her face relaxed into a smile. 'And I know how hard it is for you Burys to be patient.'

Billy didn't return her smile. 'Look, Ett,' he said, rubbing his hand nervously over his jaw. 'I ain't rushing yer. Take all the time yer need. I don't want yer saying anything sudden-like. Anything yer'd regret.' He swallowed hard then added, 'Or that I'd regret.'

'No, Bill, I don't think I'll regret what I've got to say to you. I've decided it's time to start a new life.'

He nodded, just once, and said, 'All right then, Ett, if yer've really made up yer mind and yer sure that's what yer want. I'm happy for yer.'

Then he turned away from her, pulled his cap out of his pocket, jammed it hard on his head and started to push his way through the crowd to the door.

Myrtle let out a gasp of despair, closed her eyes, and clutched on to Maisie's hand.

'Billy!' Ettie called after him. 'Please, listen to me.'

He turned back to face her. 'What more is there to say?'

'A lot.' She walked towards him.

'Yeah?' he said flatly.

'Like about renting those rooms over the workshop. What I'd decided, if you'd let me finish, was to ask you if you thought we should get ourselves a few bits and pieces to put in them. I've got some money put by that we can use for a bed and that. And now I've got regular wages from the office...'

'Yer mean?'

'Yes, Bill.'

Billy threw his cap into the air, picked Ettie up, and swung her round.

Myrtle grinned with pleasure and jabbed Maisie hard in the ribs. 'Aw bless 'em,' she sighed, and started to cry.

Florrie stood up, dragging Ada and the sullen-faced Ivy with her.

'Get yerself on that piano, Ada,' she shouted. 'We're gonna have ourselves a right old party, and not just to see in the New Year neither!'

Postscript

In London, on the 6th July 1889, after receiving another award for outstanding services to the advancement of surgical techniques to add to the one he had received in December in New York, Bartholomew Tressing celebrated in the way he liked best – he went slumming with the brides of Whitechapel.

At one o'clock on the morning of the 7th of July, the body of Alice Mackenzie – 'Clay-Pipe Alice' – a known prostitute, was found by Police-Constable Andrews in Castle Alley, Whitechapel. She had been savagely stabbed to death.

According to some, she was the last-known victim of the Whitechapel murderer who had come to be known as Jack the Ripper.